THE FLIGHT OF THE WREN

Orla McAlinden

RED STAG

MENTOR

Published in 2018 by:

RED STAG

(a Mentor Books imprint)

Mentor Books Ltd

43 Furze Road

Sandyford Industrial Estate

Dublin 18

Republic of Ireland

Tel: +353 1 295 2112 / 3

Fax: +353 1 295 2114

Email: admin@mentorbooks.ie

Website: www.mentorbooks.ie

The author thanks Kildare County Council Arts Service
for part-funding the research of this novel.

Comhairle Contae Chill Dara
Kildare County Council

ISBN 978-1-912514-26-7

Cover Design: Anú Design

Edited by: Fiona Biggs

Visit our websites: www.mentorbooks.ie

    www.redstag.ie

Early Praise for *The Flight of the Wren*

'Fascinating... graphic... I was appalled and horrified yet compelled to continue reading... Challenging. Impassioned.' *Mairead Hearne, reviewer at SwirlandThread. com*

'Feminist with a capital F. ...This harrowing, honest and deeply beautiful piece of writing.' *Shane Dunphy, author*

'...very emotional... this amazing rollercoaster of what seems the longest boat journey ever...an addictive read.' *Margaret Madden, reviewer at Bleach House Library*

'Historical fiction at its best... one to keep on the shelf and read again and again' *Tara Maria Lovett, playwright*

'Gritty realism... well researched... a wide readership is fully deserved... an important part of Irish history.' *Lorna Sixsmith, author*

Praise for *The Accidental Wife* by Orla McAlinden

'A superb collection of stories with a sting in the tail. Confident and stylish.' *Beginner's Pluck, The Irish Examiner*

'This author has a sure touch, and a real understanding for the characters she portrays. McAlinden is a writer of great originality and promise.' *Sue Leonard, Books Ireland*

'McAlinden's stories are threaded with uncompromising everyday feminism, sharply, unswervingly observed, yet compassionate and told with directness and pathos. Leavened with wry wit and great humanity.' *Alex Reece Abbott at theshortstory.co.uk*

'*The Accidental Wife* is written with passion, truth and honesty... Orla McAlinden is a new name in Irish literature.' *Mairead Hearne at SwirlandThread.com*

'...a raw and inspirational read... This is an author with a sharp, concise and engaging literary edge. McAlinden is sure to impress with her debut and is definitely one to watch out for. Highly recommended.' *Margaret Madden at Bleach House Library*

'Orla writes so powerfully and with such a vivid sense of the environment her characters inhabit... like being plunged into a pool of water... earthy, sometimes harsh, deeply and darkly humorous. A powerful and strident voice...' *Shane Dunphy, author of The Boy they tried to Hide*

'Orla McAlinden has a rare talent. Each and every story is a complete delight to be read, savoured and re-read and she deserves her place among Ireland's great talents...' *Margaret Scott, author of The Fallout*

Full of Grace, the companion volume to *The Accidental Wife* will be published by Red Stag in January 2019

This book is dedicated to the memory of the Irishwomen who inhabit its pages: Mary Regan, Mary Saunders, Anne Daly, Eliza Guilfoyle, Ellen Doyle, Elizabeth Curry and Catherine Colligan; to Surgeon Alex Kilroy who battled to keep them alive; and to the tens of thousands of Irishmen and women who were sent across the oceans at the behest of the British Crown.

Chapter One

Hobart, Tasmania, October 1919, Sally

My granddaughter is on her knees again, pleading with the big bogey-man in the sky. Praying is a harmless enough habit she picked up from the nuns during her mother's failed attempts to have her educated alongside the other daughters of Hobart. I told her mother all those years ago that she was wasting her time and her money. I would tell my granddaughter now that she is wasting her time and her breath, but my own breath catches in my throat and racks my battered lungs with coughing until I feel my ribs will break and end me.

Saoirse's knees crack like two rifles as she struggles upright and comes over to aid me. She is not even forty-five years old and has never known a day's physical hardship in her life, yet this time last month I was a younger woman than she is.

She does what she can to ease me, salves my cracked and bleeding lips with grease, dabs my beaded brow with lemon water. 'Throw open the casement,' I say. 'I want to die in the fresh air.' Those were the last words my father said to me: *Don't let them take me to the big house ... let me die in the fresh air.* Although I was only a child at the time, I had nodded and agreed to his request, but Saoirse rears back as though I have struck her.

'Don't be saying things like that, Nanna.'

'The dying are allowed to speak the truth, Saoirse, it's the only freedom we have left to us.'

She dips a red flannel cloth into a basin and lets a few drops of water trickle into my mouth. From the stale, oily taste I recognise that it is holy water, blessed with the oil of chrism and mixed with the ashes of last Palm Sunday.

'I think I could manage to sip from my cup,' I tell her. There will be no deathbed conversions in this house. I will tolerate her belief if she can pretend to ignore my lack. Sighing, she draws a draught of fresh, clean water from the jug and pats my throat dry as a little water trickles down over my chin hairs, before I start to cough again.

The looking-glass over the dresser reflects the dusky hue of the crêpey skin of my face and throat, so different from the fine pale skin of healthy old age, or the apple-ruddy face I remember from my childhood. I am drowning slowly, drowning blackly in my own dark fluids. *The Hobart Critic* calls this malady the Spanish Influenza, but the soldiers' newspaper, *The Tassie Digger,* has a simpler name for it, the Black Death.

Saoirse pulls my shift over my head and sponges me down. I am lying in a pool of sweat, and although cool spring air is washing through the chamber now, she will have to close the window soon and set a shovel containing a few grains of sulphur on the heat of the embers in the fireplace. Sulphur fumes are the only way to combat the flu, and Doctor Jenkinson will stop coming if he learns I am ignoring his advice, that I will not bear the acrid and filthy smoke in my sealed chamber. God knows he is busy enough, now that this modern plague has finally arrived on our shores, without making daily visits to a woman in her ninth decade, and long since ready for death. I'd tell him to leave me be, but Saoirse's conscience will not stand for it.

'Mistress,' there is a tap and a whisper at the door, one of the serving girls, afraid to leave the corridor and enter the sickroom. 'Mistress, Mrs Hendron has sent up some broth, and some for the old mistress too.' The girl sets the tray on the polished boards of the floor and flees.

'I wish they wouldn't do that,' Saoirse snaps, 'when they know I am not mistress of this house.'

'You can't blame them,' I laugh. 'Life goes on. Deirdre, Joanna and Honora know that.'

Since Saoirse's mother, Margaret, died last year, the three girls call Saoirse 'mistress', and defer to her for answers and instructions, although Mrs Hendron in the kitchen still defers to me. Josie Hendron wiped Saoirse's arse when she was a baby, held her hands as she took her first faltering steps across the flags of the kitchen floor, and hugged me and Margaret with joy when both measles and scarlatina passed Saoirse by, unscathed but for a few scars. When Josie Hendron starts to call Saoirse 'mistress', then I'll know I've crossed the invisible line.

Josie has sent me a bowl of chicken broth, in defiance of the doctor's gloomy pronouncement that death is imminent. My stomach rebels at the thought of food.

'Saoirse, drink up your good broth. Drink them both. Wilful waste makes woeful want. My mother used to say that. And a lot more, besides. When I was a child, there were so many sins, but now I think there are only two, and waste of food is nearly the worst of them.'

'And what's the other?'

I shake my head. I have never told her the other. Not even the bones of the tale.

'Wilful waste makes woeful want,' she mutters, glancing to me for permission or approval, and she drains the second bowl, my bowl. I watch her, but I don't grudge her. I have known hunger far beyond any hunger that a few days' illness could bring upon me.

She clatters the two bowls back into the hallway and once again draws her rosary from her pocket. She tells her beads in silence, now that she knows I am awake and watching. I have never tried to prise her from her faith, but since the illness came upon me, she will not afford me the same courtesy.

I will have the doctor, at her insistence, for all the good it will do, but while I have breath to resist it, I will not have the priest. Who, in her right mind, could believe in God in the year nineteen hundred and nineteen? For almost a year now, young men have been streaming back into Hobart from the war in Europe. In some you can clearly see the damage; blind, crippled, the halt and the lame. The men who appear to be intact are often the worst of all; jumping at shadows, their screams echoing through the night as they spend their first few days back home, temporarily billeted here in the Australasia, the finest – or at least not the worst – of Hobart's boarding houses. At breakfast the next day, some retain a fierce dignity, pretending they slept peacefully, but others whisper into my open ears, pouring out the poison they will keep trapped within when they are reunited with parents, wives and children. They tell me there are no atheists in a trench or in no man's land. They tell me there are no atheists in a ship during a storm. But I know from bitter experience that they are wrong.

A footstep in the hallway. Joanna will have slipped cotton gloves over her hands before she came to collect the tray. The girls are right to be afraid, for this disease is unlike others – along with the infants and the ancients like me, it is sweeping away the youngest and the strongest as well. Those boys and men young enough, or lucky enough, to have escaped or survived the trenches are being blasted into early graves nonetheless. At the port, a strict quarantine of seven days for each ship, enforced by a ring of steel and by mounted officers with guns, has failed at last to protect us.

Since August, the flu has swept through Hobart, a full year after the outbreak was first confirmed in Boston. America seemed so distant then. How could a disease thousands of miles away cast a shadow as far as Tasmania? We thanked our lucky stars for our island status, and welcomed our paying guests into the warm, clean chambers of the Australasia, only after they had served out their quarantine.

Doctor Jenkinson finds Saoirse sitting over the stinking sulphurous ashes in the fireplace weeping, while I feign sleep. I am too weak to comfort her, and surely it is her job to comfort me, in any case. Laying a practised hand on my brow, the doctor tuts and frowns.

'The fever is gone and her breathing is quiet. That's not right. That's not the correct course of the malady. Not for the flu.'

'She doesn't have the flu? Mrs Hendron in the kitchen always maintained she didn't have the flu.'

'And which school of medicine did Mrs Hendron attend?'

'I'm so sorry, Doctor, forgive me.'

If I weren't pretending to sleep, I'd use my last ounce of strength to get up and slap Saoirse's face for her subservience.

'Nonetheless, the abrupt improvement in Mrs Gordon's health is unusual in the extreme. I may perhaps have been hasty in my diagnosis.'

The doctor sighs and I can feel the bombast drain from him. He is not a young man either, and the flu has swept away many of his colleagues. He is working every hour of the day and half the night and can ill afford to waste his time here with me.

'She's not dying?'

'Not yet.'

'She will live?'

He laughs, but not unkindly, and stifles it as fast as he can manage. 'Oh dear me, no, Miss Gordon, she cannot live, but with God's help, I think she might pass on in command of her faculties at least. The fever is gone, but the heart and lungs are too damaged and too old for survival. A priest might be in order.'

He collects his fee and departs.

A coal shifts in the grate and Saoirse hurries over to quench the stinking sulphur and flings open the window once more. The sounds of the nearby port wash over me – whistles, shouts, the banging of swarming dockers and gangers as they unload the wares from a recently arrived ship. A ship whose healthy, quarantine-certified passengers have been sent elsewhere, to find a lodging that is not polluted with the so-called Spanish illness. I have money in the bank, down on Main Street, but Saoirse cannot afford to keep the Australasia closed forever. I'd better hurry up and die.

And I don't want to die as Sally Gordon. Sally Gordon cannot die, for she never lived. If I'm to spend all eternity in hell, as I know Saoirse believes I must if I will not repent, I want to do it under my own name. Like every other Sally in Ireland, I was christened Sarah. And the Gordon came later, in a flurry of lies. On my headstone I want my real name. My name is, and always has been, Sarah Mahon.

Chapter Two

Parish of Clonsast, King's County, 14 November 1848

The heavy dew of early winter sparkled in the low-hanging dawn, casting a glitter like diamonds over the grass and stones of the paupers' boneyard, and over the small, still form of Sally Mahon. Her barely breathing body might have been mistaken for a pile of discarded rags tossed on the lightly tamped grave in which both her parents lay. She sprawled upon the furthest extremity of the long trench, which was rapidly filling with the corpses of the Reverend Henry Joly's indigent tenantry.

Any child of fourteen years would have been hard pressed to bear the bone-chilling, teeth-chattering cold of a night on the bare soil, even wrapped in the warmest of garments, with a well-stoked blazing fire. Sally had neither kindling nor tinderbox, and her thin ragged dress offered so little protection that one night soon she was going to slip away and join the corpses under the soil. Up until this morning, she hadn't cared, would have welcomed the kind hand of death, but now a final valiant spark of humanity drove her up from the soil and she noticed at last the red-hot ripple of starvation in her gut.

She dragged herself to her knees and slowly upright, beating her thin arms against her body, stamping her feet. Gradually, as slowly as a wizened granny in the inglenook, she straightened her spine and surveyed what the late dawn revealed – on the soft mound of her parents' grave, the long imprint of her light body, the evidence of three days spent almost senseless with grief and fearful of the future. The two emotions fought for ascendance. Grief will not wait, but neither will hunger.

Beneath the rough wall which bounded the boneyard she searched for a lump of limestone or a discarded slab of slate, careful as any mason, weighing up and rejecting stone after stone until she found a white-grey, table-smooth slab, as large as her own head and so heavy that she could not lift it. She dragged the slab, her sinews straining and her breath hanging in a widening cloud in the cold damp air, over to the heap of clay containing all that she knew — every memory, every joyful laugh, every pain of past childhood and of the adulthood now so prematurely thrust upon her.

The stone flopped onto the soft, recently turned earth and sank a little before settling. Here and there other stones could be seen. Some bore, painted with whitewash or lime, the names of the departed. In this, the more recently and hastily opened stretch of the field, the long trenches were unmarked.

She wished she could mark their names, Malachy and Nuala Mahon, dead as dreams, blackened and bloated, waiting beneath the stone for their next neighbour to come along to be buried at the expense of the Parish of Clonsast in King's County. They would not be waiting long.

Keep that man out of the house, her father had roared at the first sight of the stranger. *We've nothing to share, let him go on his way.* But her mother had insisted on sharing the only thing she had, a few smoky flames from a bog-damp, peat-sullen fire in the middle of the cabin. The stranger had barely spoken, wheezing and panting away the short autumn day in the silky ashes, before sidling out at dusk to slip round the barricades thrown up by Reverend Henry Joly's men to protect the village from road fever. He paused on the threshold to leave the Mahons his blessing. And typhus. Sally's parents were dead within days of each other. And she was still alive. Alive and hungry.

At the boundary hedge of a field close-by she gathered some late blackberries. The berries were almost finished for this year, half the fruits had a fat, glistening maggot hidden within them, and the birds had had their share too. She washed down the few good berries with a fistful of water from a fast-flowing stream, shaking her head at her reflection — she was filthy, wasted and wan, with tear tracks running through the dirt plastered to her cheeks. There was no way the people of the village would let her back among them while she looked as though death lurked just over her shoulder. She would have to smarten up. She splashed her face, gasping at the icy chill of the water, and rubbed some colour back into her skin.

My parents are five days dead and three days dead by now, she thought, as she checked her body and her reflection for signs of typhus. *I'm not going to die this time, and lying on the ground weeping won't feed me.*

Her freezing feet stung and burned as she passed, wraith-light, over the hoar-rimmed ridges of the field, and slipped into the still-sleeping village of Clonbullogue.

'Thomas,' she called, half hidden behind the wall of the baker's yard — even at six paces distance she could feel the heat radiating out from the oven and she stretched the length of her body close along the warm bricks of the wall, soaking every ounce of heat into her limbs and belly. 'Thomas Crampton, it's me, Sally Mahon. Could you spare me a farl, or a heel, for the love of God?'

The Crampton brothers, Samuel, Henry and Thomas, owned half the businesses in the village — bakery, forge, wheelwright and store. Her father had always said they were descended on the distaff side from the Crampton gentry, but for all that, they were neither particularly cruel nor dishonest. Sally's father had often done a day's labour drawing kindling, turf and coal for the forge. *Them bastards of Cramptons*, Malachy would say, *they give me the labour because they know I'll do it for half nothing.* Her mother would sigh when he said that. *Aren't you bloody lucky to get it, and you with only one child, when there's men with half a dozen would bite the Cramptons' hands off for the few hours' work.* If the Cramptons would support Sally in public, the rest of the village would, however grudgingly, follow.

Thomas Crampton glanced up from the door of the huge oven and caught her gaze for a moment before dropping his to the hard-packed earth of the yard. With an audible hiss of indrawn breath, he quickly made the sign of the cross and followed it with a sign to ward off the evil eye. He hacked the heel off a loaf in silence, then glanced once more in Sally's direction.

'In the name of God, get away from my door, girl,' he growled. 'What fool will buy my bread if they see the child of the bloody typhus house standing by the oven?'

'Thomas Crampton, sir, for the memory of my blessed father, won't you help me? Look at me, you know as much about the road fever as I do, or more. Can't you see there's not a thing wrong with me, sir? I would be dead long since, if that was God's will.'

He raised his right arm and she shrank back, expecting a slap. Instead, he threw, as hard as he could, and the precious bread sailed past her, landing on the ground five feet away.

'Get away now, girl, get away. Come back tomorrow, but come in the dark of the morning. And tell no one I spoke to you. Don't salute me in the street, don't even look at me.'

'May God be good to you, Tom Crampton, sir,' she called back. 'God bless you.' She brushed the dirt of the road off the heel of bread, stuffed it down the front of her dress and ran.

★ ★ ★

When she had eaten the bread, she cleaned herself a little more in the stream. She held out less hope now of being accepted back into the village, not unless Thomas had a change of heart and acknowledged her, but she needed to look as decent as was possible. The soil of the graveyard ran in brown rivulets and mingled with the green juice of a handful of dock leaves as she scrubbed at her legs and arms, neck and face. She watched the water as it carried away the graveyard clay and she resolved to waste no more time lying stretched upon the bones of her parents.

The icy water punched the blood around her body and gave her the semblance of a healthy glow as she walked, with weary legs, the half mile to her mother's cabin on the edge of the Bog of Allen, half-expecting her home of fourteen years to be gone. The word had come out, weeks since, from Joly's agent, that typhus cabins were to be knocked down and burned, over the bodies of the dead, destroying the pestilential vapours and the poisoned breath of the victims, halting the new scourge of the road-fever.

For the same reason, barricades had been thrown up on all sides of the village to keep the starving, filthy wanderers away, even though some slipped through, like the man who had killed Sally's parents.

Three days ago, the men of the burial crew had arrived — men once friends and neighbours, transformed by terror of contagion into anonymous, angry, frightened eyes flashing above mouths and noses well wrapped in vinegar-soaked scarfs. They had not come within the walls of the cabin, but had ordered Sally to drag out, first her father, then her mother, and heave them up, stiff and brittle as kindling, onto a cart. There had been no talk of tumbling the roof, nor of setting flame to the thatch as Joly had ordered.

And the cabin stood still, unscathed, the half door open at the top as always — the wrecking crew had turned a blind eye. It sat in a tiny patch of a third of an acre. The turf pile was almost emptied down to the ground, for Malachy Mahon had been too weak, too weary after his starveling days of labour on Joly's meadows, to foot and win the turf he was entitled to, from a carefully measured row on the Bog of Allen. Sally and her mother had saved what turf they could, but it was little enough. *If the typhus didn't take my parents, the winds of winter would have finished them off anyway,* thought Sally.

At the other end of the gable wall, the lazy bed where the potatoes should be growing was bare and untilled. *Never eat the seed potatoes,* her father had always said, year after year, regardless of temporary hardships, *never, it's the laziest act of the laziest fool.* And yet, in this bitter blighted spring just past they had eaten their few seed potatoes long before the planting time of Saint Patrick's Day had come. *What's the point of planting them?* her mother had asked, knife hovering over the pot on the ashes, as she begged her husband's forgiveness and his permission. *What's the point of planting what we know will rot in the ground come harvest time, when we might eat them and be full today, maybe for the last time?* Sally's father had shrugged and the potatoes had gone into the pot.

Half of their neighbours had done the same and Joly's man had cursed them all to hell and back for their stupidity, eating the seed Reverend Joly had seen fit to provide for his destitute tenants. Others had planted, and all year long her father had watched and waited, jealously inspecting the green leaves of the white-flowered potato plants in his neighbours' lazy beds for the dreaded tell-tale black spots that marked the advent of the blight below the ground.

And the blight had not come. As the realisation sank into Malachy Mahon's heart that in this year Clonsast's potatoes were to be spared, he became more silent, more wretched, and the cabin itself, neglected and unloved, seemed to sink further and further into the soft soil of King's County.

Even so, it was still, in the main, a good cabin, nearly watertight, with real thatch under the moss and sods of grass in places, and Joly's estate man had broken the rules and given it to a new family. *They must have had a few coins set aside to square him, either that or they have some hold over him.*

Through the half-door, Sally could see a woman and a man inside. Two children sprawled in the ash of the hearth, too young for field work, and the woman's belly was swelling large under her apron.

'God be with you,' Sally called quietly.

The woman looked up, 'God and Mary be with you,' before swallowing suddenly and turning to tug her husband's sleeve.

'Jesus, get away from the door.' His face was hard and gaunt, there wasn't much more flesh on him than on Sally herself. *Where the hell did he get the money from, he must have stolen it.* 'Get away, you're not welcome here,' he shouted, 'spreading disease among decent people.'

'I'm fine, I swear it to God and his mother. There's not a hint of sickness on me. I'm probably healthier than you. Just the hunger, is all.' Sally turned to the woman. 'For the love of God, this was my only home my whole life past, I just came for a few things.'

The woman grabbed a broom of twigs bound to a long ash-plant as a handle, and waved it at the door as Sally reached out to touch the latch. 'There's nothing left of your people here. I burned the lot of it. Why would I keep the oul' rags and dirt of the typhus house? Sure, it's a miracle the house itself is still standing.'

'But the knife, maybe? My mother had a knife, for cutting the seed potatoes into quarters. It was wooden-handled and sharpened over the years into the shape of the crescent moon. You wouldn't burn a knife.'

'It's gone.' But she slipped her hand into her apron pocket, and Sally knew she was lying.

'And the three-legged pot? If you just let me have it, I might get a shilling for it, somewhere.'

The woman moved over and stood in front of the fire, where the pot hung on a chain above the smoke and heat. The bubbling steam carried a familiar scent to Sally's nose; nettles, grass and weeds mixed with the smallest amount of Indian meal.

'That's my own pot, I brought it here with me,' the woman said. She stared directly into Sally's eyes, a hard, furious glare, until Sally could take it no more and looked away. 'There was no pot here when we came, if ever there was one. Someone must have taken it, if you had one at all.'

'May God forgive you, you lying bitch.'

The man of the house came closer to the door. 'Get away out of it, or I'll stick my boot up yer hole. There's nothing left for you here. Stay away from my wife and stay away from my children. Joly's man gave us this cabin, fair and square. Take it up with him, if you dare.'

The man's angry, shame-filled eyes followed Sally as she walked slowly away. It was the blessing of God that he had, a week ago, found Joly's agent, with his hand clamped across the mouth of one of the youngest serving girls, up in the kitchen garden of Hollywood House, while she writhed and kicked and scratched beneath him. The gift of Malachy Mahon's cabin had bought his silence. A man with a wife and his third child on the way couldn't afford to throw away God's gift of a good cabin, and the rights to a line of turf on the bog, to help a penniless orphan whose remaining months on this earth could surely be counted on the fingers of one hand. *People talk*, he thought, *of charity, of alms, of tithes to the Church, and of how poor James must be made to help poorer John.* He sighed and spat a gob of green-stained grassy phlegm into the hearth. *Those pious bastards who talk of charity have always had more than they need. Who will share with a stranger when his own child's belly is swollen with air and his wife's breast has no milk for the baby?*

Sally Mahon walked away from the home of her childhood, where there had been good years before the bad, where her parents had smiled and sometimes laughed, where the screel of a visiting fiddler had brought neighbours to the yard and the dancing had continued late under the warm stars of summer days long since.

Without the support of the Cramptons, without the shelter of the cabin walls, Sally would have to prove herself to the village of Clonbullogue. In a week or two, in continued good health with no sign of the fever, the village people might let her back in. But in a week or two, she would have starved to death. The squirrels had been hard at work, the trees were stripped bare by animal and child alike, and the hedgehogs had all but vanished. Great pointed skeins of duck and geese no longer flew overhead, honking a farewell to Ireland. Winter was coming.

Soon it would be the village Pattern Day, the third day of December; time to walk with the people of Clonsast to the ancient well of their patron, Saint Brochan, and pray for salvation. But Sally could not wait that long, not for Brochan, nor for anyone else to save her. She could starve, or she could find work, or she could hand herself over to the Orphans and Foundlings Committee, where Mr Ridgeway would suck his luxurious moustache and have her sent to the workhouse. Only Protestant orphans of good family were ever permitted to be fostered out.

★ ★ ★

Nowhere in the village could Sally find a woman who needed a girl. God knows they had enough children of their own and next to nothing to put in their mouths at night. She was strong enough when fed, but lately she was mostly fasting, or hedge-fed. Now she was whippy as a willow wand, and there was neither strength nor staying power in her frail frame. She had no particular skill – her father had been a good scythe-man and a hard labourer, before hunger, guilt and remorse had fashioned a shadow of the man she remembered – but that was of no help to her now. Joly had all the workers he needed, at starvation rates, and the other men were off doing pointless famine-relief works, building walls around nothing and roads to nowhere. This year's grain harvest was long since cut and stacked in the barns. The swede harvest would not begin until after the first heavy frost, and Joly would give that work to his favourites.

She could help with the threshing of the grain in the long, dark winter evenings, whacking each bundle of stalks with a long flail until all the grain was separated from the straw, then scooping up the gleanings of the precious wheat into sacks for the miller. There was no skill in that task. But although the boneyard was filling up fast, the village was still well-provided with toothless old men, for whom threshing was their last occupation, the only job keeping them out of their own shrouds. They would not take her on, and their families would drive her from the threshing shed with curses and blows, accuse her of stealing the food from the mouths of the elderly.

Last month, she had watched a swoop of twittering swallows rise up as one, a dancing, swaying cloud, and then fly off, deserting the huge bogs around Clonsast, as she had watched them every year of her life. If she wanted to survive the winter, she would have to follow them.

Sally's destination was clear in her mind and it seemed to her to be attainable, barely twenty-five miles away, the new town at the new bridge, in County Kildare. The winter would be harsh and hungry there also, but no one there knew her, nor knew about the typhus. There would be churches too, where a homeless girl might shelter during the day, shivering but dry.

Sally's life had never taken her further than the outskirts of her own village, or as far into the bog as was required to stack and stook the sods of turf on her father's ridge. Twenty-five miles, she thought, didn't seem too great a demand to place upon her wasted body, her legs with the big knee bones clearly visible. It was walk and starve, or stay and starve. Her choice was made.

She knew she would find work in the thriving garrison town, home to twelve hundred of Her Majesty's soldiers, and nearly as many horses. Newbridge sucked up and gobbled all the surplus produce of King's County, Queen's County and Kildare. *Why do you think that bastard Joly lives such a fine life,* her father had asked, *and him with only one and a half thousand statute acres, and a quarter of it just bog?*

Joly's father had been granted all the land of the parish of Clonsast by his master – FitzGerald, Duke of Leinster. *Oh, a fine reward for laundering a man's shirts and dusting his wig.* Old Jean Jasper Joly may have been *just a valet,* but he had rushed twice into the roaring flames during the burning of the House of Lords in Dublin, and had rescued two fine tapestries showing the Battle of the Boyne and the 'Prentice boys of Derry. FitzGerald had been generous to his loyal servant, and Sally's father couldn't have hated Joly more. *A fine reward for a Frenchman who turned his coat, abandoning the faith of his fathers and coming over here to press the drawers of a Protestant.*

Sally thought it was a fine reward indeed. *What will you get, Daddy,* she had laughed, *for ploughing Joly's soil and scattering his seed and reaping it? You're as much a servant as oul' Frenchie Joly ever was.*

And although the land of the parish of Clonsast where the Reverend Joly now lived was poor enough, and a mere pleasure garden when compared with FitzGerald's tens of thousands of acres, the garrison at Newbridge had made him rich beyond any normal expectation.

At the village of Clonbullogue, the angle where three counties touch, and where Joly's estate bounded those of Lord Downshire and of the duke himself, Sally had seen the drovers, the carters, the loads of corn, and the fat, axe-ready cattle making their final journey towards the dining-plates of the garrison town. She set her mind towards Newbridge and towards salvation.

★ ★ ★

Four years previously, when the potatoes still flourished, and the land smelt of bog flowers and blossom instead of death and starvation, she had gone to the market in Clonbullogue with her father. His small business done, Malachy Mahon had sat despairing, head on hands, at a table outside the inn, jingling some coins in his pocket, sipping slowly on a well-watered mug of black porter, and his daughter had squatted in the dust beside him, a small girl, unnoticed, with her mouth closed and her ears open.

'Newbridge,' said a drover, a fat, greasy man who, it seemed to Sally, might eat more at that table than her family would in a week. 'Newbridge, that's the place. When I am too old and too rich… ' He chuckled a big-bellied laugh and belched in Malachy's silent, down-turned face. 'When I am too rich to walk any longer behind the cattle on the way to Newbridge's meat markets, I'm going to find me a good, fat serving girl, marry her and set up a tavern.'

'That's the worst idea you've ever had,' laughed his companion. 'You wouldn't be long ruining yourself if you owned a tavern. Sure you'd be your own best customer; like throwing water into a barrel of sawdust.'

'Nonsense, man, nonsense.'

The drover pushed back his stool from the board and gazed around. On the market square a few asses and jennets stood, awaiting their owners, and some laggards were haggling still over the spoiled remnants of the day's produce. The rest were crammed into, and spilling out of, public houses and taverns, or strapping their empty creels back onto the pack saddles. The drover waved his hand, encompassing all the life before him, the biggest crowd of people Sally had ever seen. His eyes were glazed from liquor. He was drinking good stout, and it had not been watered. He slammed his fist on the table, and the reek of fresh cow dung rose from his clothing as he adjusted himself and scratched idly at his crotch.

'The man who can't make a fortune in Newbridge is no man at all. Even a fool can make his way in that town. With the right tavern, and the right woman, I'll soon be a rich man taking shillings and pennies from travellers.'

'The right woman isn't so easy to find,' laughed his friend.

'Don't you worry about that side of it.'

'And you'll settle in the town?'

'I will. All roads round here lead to Newbridge town.'

Sally's father raised his head shyly, catching the stranger's eye for the first time, made bold by his cup of beer.

'Is that true, sir?' he asked. 'A man might make his way in the world?'

'It's true enough. I'll tell you this. The streets of Newbridge is paved with horse shit and with gold. Paved with gold for the taking, for any man strong enough, and bold enough, to take his chance.'

'And for a girl? Would there be a living for a hard-working lass? The girl has no brother, and the rights to lease the patch of land can hardly be expected to go to a girl, in the fullness of time.'

Her father bent forward respectfully for the answer, but snapped his head back, ears ringing, as the two drinkers burst into roars and whoops, slapping and punching each other on the shoulder.

'Work for a girl, in Newbridge? My God, man, there's work in Newbridge surely, for any woman, and plenty of it, morning, noon and night.'

'That's good to hear.' Malachy nodded his head wisely and pulled with satisfaction on his near-empty mug.

The drover raised his hand and his voice and called for a jug of stout. 'Give me that piss-water,' he laughed, wrestling Malachy's cup from his hand and pouring the dregs onto the dust of the road. The drover and his friend poured cup after cup of stout, and as Malachy grew ever less steady, they laughed louder and faster. Malachy sang and the drover joined in, his rich, well-lubricated voice stumbling over the words like a riddle.

Occasionally, the drover would drop his hand down onto Sally's shoulder and give it a friendly squeeze. His lips grew slack and his red tongue flickered over them from time to time. He smiled at her and she smiled back, although she was hungry and thirsty and bored with the drunken talk. He pinched her cheek and slipped his hand back down onto her thin shoulder.

At last, she had risen from the ground and half-pulled, half-carried her father home, over fields and ditch, pushing his bockety handcart before her, her muscles burning as the wooden wheels groaned and creaked over every rut in the path.

Next morning Malachy had lain among the ashes of the fire, groaning and clutching his head while his wife swept and clattered and banged with an unusual ferocity.

'How much of the rent money did you give to that oul' bitch Mary O'Connor last night?'

'Not more than a ha'penny, I told you already. Another man paid for the drink.'

'Am I as green as God's good grass?' Nuala snapped. 'Where the hell is the rest of the money? You had three bushels of potatoes in that handcart and now you have neither potatoes nor money. So where is it?'

Silence reigned in the cabin. Malachy raised his head and supported it gingerly on the crook of his elbow, as a bead of sweat trickled from under his hair and dropped the few inches to the floor.

'Look at you! The porter is dripping out of you. What did I ever do to deserve such a drunken sot of a husband? How much did you spend, and in the name of God, where is the remainder?'

'There is no money, Mammy,' said Sally at last. 'There was no market for the potatoes. Every man in the townland was there, with as many potatoes as ourselves, or more.'

'What?'

'It's true, Nuala, love. Never has such a harvest been seen. Haven't we ourselves more than twice what we expected? You couldn't give them away. What can you do with a glut of potatoes? They can't be stored longer than a few months, you know they can't.'

'But where are they?'

Malachy was silent.

'Where are they?'

'They are in the ditch, Mammy.'

'Jesus Christ of almighty. In the ditch?'

'Yes, Mammy, and every man did the same.'

Nuala blessed herself and reached for the rosary of acorns and twine that hung from her waist. 'In the ditch.' She started to tell the beads, rubbing each smooth, shiny nut between her forefinger and thumb. 'In the ditch, may God almighty forgive you. Wilful waste makes woeful want, as the old people say.'

'The old people never before saw a year where every lazy bed and every potato pasture in the country has yielded three or four times its due. What should I have done? There were men there with asses and even with carts, who have been to Edenderry and every market in the county, and away to Rathangan and to Queen's County too. You cannot give them away, even the pig-keepers have more than they need.'

'And the money for the rent?'

'Joly will have to wait, Nuala. He has waited before. He won't turn us out, for every tenant in the parish is in the same boat. If it was a surplus of grain, it could be stored, but potatoes?'

'We were never late before.'

'That's right. There's plenty others on his farm have been late, or short, year after year. The agent will curse and shake his fist in my face on rent day, but what can he do? We'll make it up next year.' Malachy sighed and belched, a huge, stinking waft of porter and acid. 'One thing is for certain, there'll never be a potato harvest like this one again in my lifetime.'

★ ★ ★

He was right about that one thing, thought Sally. *There's been no harvest at all.* She set her foot on the path. The streets of Newbridge were paved with gold, and she would dig up some of that gold, or die trying. She had no fear of missing the way, for didn't all roads lead to Newbridge?

Chapter Three

Hobart, October 1919, Sally

In Hobart, I used to think, all roads lead to the port. Propped on my pillow, I can see, if I turn my head laboriously to the left, the rigging of the old sailing ships in the harbour. I can hear the chimney blasts and the chugging of the newer steam liners. Lines of screaming gulls and kittiwakes perch on the masts of the anchored vessels, swooping off to plummet out of my eye line into the waters below, returning to fight over a scrap of offal or a small fish plucked from the water. The birds are now my only companions when Saoirse is not with me.

She will return soon and then I will begin my story. For me now, all remaining roads lead, not to the port, but to the boneyard, where most of those I love already lie. I am ready to face the next stage, whether it be endless silent oblivion, or Saoirse's gory hell of taunting devils. But I will clear my conscience before I go. She may not thank me for it.

She closes the door gently behind her, pokes the fire with one or two gestures. Everything she does is controlled, measured. I think I have never seen her take a risk, never seen her less than perfectly attired, decent, sober, respectable. How did Margaret, Patsy and I create between us a woman so trammelled, so hemmed in by her own overweening drive for respectability above all? So unquestioning of the suffocation of Hobart society and of her role within it? The story I have to tell will not be to her liking.

'How are you this morning, Nanna?'

'Alive, Saoirse, and that is better than the alternative, for the time being.'

She reaches out to smooth my pillow but I take her hand in mine. Hers is cool and dry, mine still somewhat hot and damp, but with nothing like the heat that radiated off me in the days and nights when I thrashed helplessly in and out of mindless delirium, and came to fear that I would take my secret to my grave. My mind turns inevitably and repeatedly to my grave, and to its marker stone.

'Do you love me, Saoirse?'

'You know I do.'

'I know.'

I smile then and send her to the bureau for paper and pen. She always had a fine hand, can write like a schoolma'am, but I never saw her write a letter. She says she has no one to write to. As for me, I have written enough letters to last a lifetime.

'Write this down, Saoirse. "Sarah Mahon born 1834, died 1919". That's what I want on my stone. I want to go to hell …' she winces and blesses herself, so I add ' … or to heaven, under my own name.'

'Mahon? What on earth do you mean? You mean O'Hanlon? Your maiden name?'

'I mean Mahon, my only name.' But she is not listening, she is looking at the dates.

'Did you mean 1824, perhaps Nanna? 1834 is too young.' She does the sums in her head. 'You came to Van Diemen's Land in 1849. 1834 is too young, Nanna.'

'I was born in 1834.' My voice trembles and I know that, before my story is over, I will have broken her heart. 'If you don't believe me, you can look for the birth of Sarah Mahon in the parish records of Clonsast, King's County. You'll find her.'

She looks down at the paper in her hands.

'Write it down, Saoirse, please. It is my dying wish, you won't deny me.'

Saoirse looks at me with doubt in her eyes. She thinks I am doting. Thinks I am slipping once more into the half–lucid dreams of my recent illness.

'Nanna.' She pauses, but after a deep breath finds the courage to continue. 'Nanna, while you were sick, you were shouting, and calling out in the night.'

I nod. My mind is still full of the nightmare visions I had thought were so far buried that nothing could uncover them. I was wrong.

'Names, Nanna. Lots of names. Names I never heard before. Davey, Molly, Grainne. And Nellie. Always Nellie, over and over again.'

'Nellie Gordon.' How long is it since that name passed my lips?

'Gordon?' she says. 'The same as your own name. The sister of your husband? Or his mother maybe?'

'To the Devil with Nellie Gordon, and all the Gordons on earth, bar you. I've lived my life under her cursed name long enough.' Saoirse's eyes slam open and for the first time I realise how hard this is going to be, how slowly I must proceed. I want to free her, not smash her. 'I'm not Sally Gordon. Never was, never will be. Don't carve that name on my stone, or I'll rest uneasy in my grave.'

'You're doting, Nanna,' she says. 'You're Sally Gordon, mother of Margaret Gordon and grandmother to myself. Will you take a drop of water?'

I sip from the cup, to buy some time and steel myself for the next part.

'Do you know where you are, Nanna Gordon? You're in the Australasia, the boarding house in Hobart. You owned it with your sister, Patsy O'Hanlon, and later with my mother, Margaret Gordon, your daughter.'

'Names are important, Saoirse. Names will tell you everything you need to know about a person. The Australasia. Do you know that was the name of the ship which brought me here? The ship *Australasia* ... that's where I did it. The worst sin.' I grasp the coverlet and draw it up to my throat, as though huddling under the light fabric will protect me from the confusion and anger she is bound to feel. 'That's where *we* did it, Patsy and me. Before I was Gordon.'

'You have lost the thread of time, Nanna, don't distress yourself.' She is regretting this conversation now, wishes she had let the matter rest, but I will not let it rest.

'You were Gordon before you boarded any ship, Nanna, for your husband, Jack Gordon, died back in Ireland.' She smooths the eiderdown. 'It is not surprising that you're rambling a little, after such a close brush with …' She pauses and finally says weakly, ' … illness.'

'You still haven't written it down. Sarah Mahon.'

'You mean O'Hanlon, Nanna? Your maiden name?'

'I mean Mahon, my only name.'

She is determined to disagree further. Who knows what she will engrave on my headstone? I will still be dead, and she will still be alone here in the Australasia, unmarried and past child-bearing, too afraid of the disapproval of the town to live her life in any way outside the ordinary. If she knew what we have done, what we have endured, Patsy, Margaret and I, to bring her to a world where she could do and be anything. Where a woman may own her own rooming-house and vote for her own parliament, a life of which the women of Ireland can as yet only dream. And this, Saoirse's chosen life of wizened spinster, is not yet carved in stone. Her true story may free her. Or kill her. She will have to make that choice.

'I'll put Sarah Gordon, née O'Hanlon? Would that do? The maiden name along with the married name?'

'Put "Sarah Mahon née Mahon, lived a lie as Sally Gordon", if you can afford to pay the stonemason for all the extra words.' My elbow slips a little and I fall back onto the pillow in a heap. She should reach out to settle me more safely on the mattress, but she doesn't.

'You're Sarah Gordon. Widow of Jack Gordon. Sister of Patsy O'Hanlon, mother of Margaret Gordon, and my own grandmother.'

She looks at me. I have been sick and been raving but now I look at her with eyes clear and calm. My voice is steady.

'I'm none of those people.'

'Who are you then, Nanna?' she breathes. 'Who have you been all these years?'

'Sally Mahon. Daughter of Malachy and Nuala.'

She is silent and I sink deeper into the embrace of the lumpy, unsmoothed pillow. The fierce barking of a mongrel cur echoes from the port, along with the shouts of the sailors and dockers who have disturbed him. His barking follows me down into the oblivion of sleep and the mists of time.

Chapter Four

Clonsast, Wednesday, 22 November 1848

A few dogs stirred and barked lazily in the lanes and byways of Clonbullogue as Sally left the parish of Clonsast, but no human saw her leave, for why would you rise before the sun in winter? In the village, life might run to the chiming of the clock on the church tower, a testament to a Protestant man who had died and left the church a whole boot filled to the brim with gold coins, back in the long ago, when these things did happen. The busy and prosperous Cramptons might rise with the clock, the priest and the teacher too, but in the countryside, where Sally had hidden, the people rose late. Only a man with a candle gets up in the dark, and the cottiers had no candles left, no breakfast to rise for, no animals left alive to tend. In the winter, the tenantry rose late, and by the time they stirred, she was gone.

She had no bundle, no pack. She had the rags she stood up in and three heels of bread from Tom Crampton. Crampton would not go so far even as to discuss her case with his brothers, to bring the weight of respectable opinion down upon the scales weighing Sally's survival, but at the same time, he had not let her starve. Each morning, under cover of the late, late sunrise, he had selected the most misshapen, the lumpiest or the most burnt loaf and tossed her the heel or the dole. The bread was tucked into the bodice of her dress and by midday would attain a salty, pungent flavour which stoked her appetite as she measured the bites; one every five hundred steps.

Her breath hung and sparkled on the frosty air and at first she walked more by feel than by sight, the hard-packed earth of the roadway firm under her bare, calloused feet. The long grass of the verge was easier on the soles, but the perishing cold of the dew-soaked grass drove her back into the ruts of the roadway. The rising sun cut harshly into her lowered eyes and she dashed the tears away.

At the Figile River, just outside the village, she ducked her face into the ice-cold stream, gasping and spluttering. All along the banks, the trees stood leafless and gaunt, tall and straight, as they had always done in this part of the world. Before the Battle of Clontarf Brian Boru had cut a thousand trees from Fidh Gabhaile, on the banks of the Figile River, to build a fleet to defy the Norsemen. *How well for us,* her father used to say, *that the parish of Clonsast grows the straightest trees and the bentest, most twisted men in the whole of Ireland.*

Sally gulped water from the river until her stomach bulged, for she was at the limits of her knowledge now. She had never passed further along the road in this direction, nor did she know when next she might drink. She had no bottle or jar to carry water, but she knew enough to avoid the brackish, still ponds and puddles, and to drink only from the fresh running waters of streams and rivulets. Her mother had known that dirty water was a cause of sickness, although Nuala had curtseyed and nodded politely when Father Peter Dunne explained that she was wrong, and that illness, and especially the potato blight, was a warning, a call to repentance, and a punishment from God for the sins of his creation.

Sally's father had laughed, quietly, and in the safety of their own cabin. *A punishment for our sins, eh! For his sins, maybe, but the rest of us, we don't have time to sin.* Her mother blessed herself against his blasphemy and hushed him. *For the love of God, Malachy, don't be contradicting the holy priest, sure what would you know about the plans of the Almighty?*

When she could drink no more, Sally placed her hand in the small of her back and tried to straighten. She had been sleeping outdoors for over a week, covered as best she could in the ferny stalks of the ditches and hedgerows, and each morning found her stiff as a stick.

As she inched her spine upwards towards a semblance of straightness, a sound froze the marrow in her bones. *What did you stop for, you fool? What will you see when you turn your head?*

A slinking yellow cur inched towards her, hackles standing like a collar round his throat, from which came a low, insistent growl. His teeth, when the curled lips drew back, were shiny and white in his dark gums. A trickle of piss was splattering on the soil beneath Sally and she could do nothing to stop it. The dog inched forward, flat against the ground.

Sally knew exactly what she must do. *Never run from a cur,* her father had told her a hundred times. *Swing yer foot into his ribs as hard as ye can, and if he comes back for more, swing for the jaw next time.* She had nodded and agreed, a hundred times, never once mentioning the difference between her father's strong brown leather boots, and her own bare feet. She had never yet needed to kick a dog for, apart from those belonging to the gentry, most dogs had disappeared, years since, and everyone knew they had, silently and in secret, been butchered and boiled for stew.

The strange dog inched forward again then settled in the long grass of the bank, and he never took his eyes off her, like Joly's well trained collies, who could bring a hundred sheep off the land near the bog, with just a whistle to guide them. She looked for a smooth hard rock to throw, but found only pebbles and grit.

Stick yer boot in him, and she thought of how her father's feet had trailed across the packed earthen floor of the cabin as she dragged him out to the burial crew. The good brown boots, with years left in them and barely patched at all, had long since been sold, and the ridged and blackened nails of his toes seemed to have grown a quarter inch in the hours since the breath left him. She looked at the dog again, looked down at her bare feet, heard her father's voice clear in her ears. *Daddy, can you see me, are you looking down and protecting me?*

Slowly she stood and loosed herself ready to kick. The yellow cur snaked upright in one smooth movement, lips drawn back. Sally turned and ran, screaming – the sight of the banshee herself could not have lent her greater speed. Three, four, five hundred yards, the blood pulsing in her ears, blocking every sound of pursuit, every hint of whether the dog followed her or not. A swingeing pain in her left side finally stopped her flight and she bent over a stump by the wayside, feeling, for the first time, the soughing suck of the breath that does not fill the lungs, and makes the stabbing stitch more painful yet. The dog was nowhere to be seen.

She leaned her forehead on the stump and wept. *You're gone, Daddy, you're gone and you're never coming back.*

In time the ache in her side grew dull and the ache in her heart grew larger and sharper. She knew that she must go forward. Whatever she met on the road ahead, she could never face the yellow dog again, never face Clonbullogue cemetery again, never again face the vision of her father's toes poking out, the last things to disappear under the carelessly tossed shovelfuls of soil as the burial crew hastened to escape, as quickly as possible, the poisoned air of the boneyard.

★ ★ ★

Mid-afternoon. The sun already sending rays towards the western horizon. The rooks gathering in the branches of the roadside trees. Sally struggling to place one foot in front of the other. Behind her on the road, the heavy, regular thud of horses' hooves.

She had met almost no traffic on the journey; villagers and tenants walked the meadows and cowpaths, while the roads served mainly wealthy men on longer journeys, and they were few. The small number of carriages that had passed her had swept by at a canter or dazzling trot, while she panted and scrambled onto the steep bank at the side of the roadway, to avoid the flashing hooves. The drivers had not looked her way nor paid her any heed, bar one, a bearded, sallow fellow who had flicked the tip of his long whip in her direction, for the fun of seeing her leap and tumble backwards, sprawling among the tree roots.

Now, from behind approached, not a brightly coloured carriage, but a sturdy farm wagon pulled by two enormous chestnut horses. Their manes and the huge tufts of feathers on their heels fluttered in step as they thrust their massive shoulders against the shining shafts of the wagon. Even Reverend Joly didn't own such magnificent animals. She stopped to stare at the fine animals, who pushed all their weight into their strong, leather collars, making the load of straw behind them seem a trifle. She didn't need to scramble out of their way, they were moving almost as slowly as she.

At a word from the driver, the horses pulled up to a halt and stood, snatching mouthfuls of tough grasses from the overgrown banks on either side. Their bits jingled and rang as the horses shook their heads and chewed. The driver stared down at Sally, grinding a straw between his back teeth, putting her in mind of one of his own horses, and then spat thoughtfully on the ground close by.

'The blessings of God on the work, sir.'

He gazed her straight in the eye, spat again and cleared his throat.

'Don't *sir* me, child,' he growled. 'There is no sir on this path that I can see.'

Sally's cheeks flared red and she held her peace, waiting for him to spit, or strike, or depart.

'What are you doing here, child, alone in the middle of nowhere? I haven't passed a house or homestead this five miles past. Are you not afraid of robbers and the wild men?'

Sally laughed aloud, and suddenly it seemed she might never stop. The whooping laughs tore from her, more easily than the tears she had shed earlier and with less reason, until she realised that she was, in fact, crying, and had been for some time. The man sat impassive on the bench of the cart, chewing; chewing and silent. She had not laughed aloud since her parents died, and she'd had little enough to laugh at before then.

'Robbers?' she choked. 'Good luck to any robber who meets me, he will end up poorer than he was before our paths crossed. I haven't a coin, nor a pocket to put one in. I haven't even a crust of bread left, sir. I mean … .' She tailed off, for she could think of no other way to address a man with a large belly, riding behind two fine horses.

'You could call me Mr O'Loughlin, I suppose,' he said at length, his bushy eyebrows nearly meeting above his hooked and greasy nose. 'Or you could call me Patrick, which is what I would prefer, seeing as how that's my name. You can call me go-to-the-Devil, but don't call me sir.'

'Patrick,' she said. 'Good man, Patrick, that you are, would you ever have a cut of bread, or a cold potato you could spare me? I can't remember when I last held a hot potato in my fingers.'

'Is that so? And the parents both dead, I suppose?'

He sucked on his lips, till it seemed that his wiry brown beard would disappear into his mouth. Sally waited in silence. She might as well wait all day. *What difference does it make, me begging on the road from a stranger and putting my mother to shame? Won't I have to beg a few days in Newbridge till I find work? He can give me something, or he can laugh in my face and drive off, and I'll be none the worse, and my mother will still be dead.*

A minute passed, and then another. Sally refused to look away, or walk off. He sighed.

'Houl' on till I have a look.'

He fumbled around inside a cloth bag that lay beside him on the driver's bench and at length pulled a whole farl of soda bread out and tossed it to her. She ripped into the floury crust with her teeth and had gnawed off three huge chews before she thought once more of her mother gazing down from heaven, and her shame at her daughter's behaviour. Carefully, she broke off the bread surrounding the chewed margin and offered the rest, about half the farl, back to the man.

'A hundred thousand thanks to you.' She choked out the words around the crumbs and clots of dry bread that her parched mouth could scarcely moisten.

Bread wasn't really Sally's dish in those days. Her mother had rarely had the luxury of the flour or the salt to make a flat bread, and the buttermilk to make a raised loaf was as out of her reach as the stars at night, or a guinea fowl from Reverend Joly's table. Bread was eaten when nothing else could be found and every penny handed over for flour was weighed and debated and begrudged.

Like the rest of Ireland's tenants and labourers, the Mahons had lived well enough, just well enough to keep a narrow layer of fat under the skin that held their bones together, until the bad times came. And they had lived, like everyone else, on the coarse, heavy-yielding Irish Lumper potato, steamed over a pot of boiling water until the coarse, grey-brown skins exploded open and called out to them. Then, when they had cooled enough to hold, Sally, Malachy and Nuala had eaten the Lumpers straight from the pan, dipped in a small bowl of salt-water, when salt was to be had, and washed down with fresh water from the river near the cabin.

'Thank you,' she said again. 'Hunger is a good sauce.' She held out the remaining half of the farl to Patrick, and tried to keep the longing out of her voice and her eyes.

'Keep it. Keep it, for God's sake,' he muttered, a half smile playing on his lips, 'unless you're not hungry, or it's not fancy enough for you.'

She had done what decency required, she had offered to share, but she would not be so stupid as to offer again. She fell upon the loaf like the starving children of Israel in the desert that Father Peter was never done recalling to the parishioners of Clonsast since the potato troubles started.

But no bread had fallen from the skies in response to their prayer, and her father had said that even Joly, Lord Downshire, or Lord Rosse, were more likely to help than *the man above,* and her mother had blessed herself against his blasphemy, and Sally had gone back to rooting around in the bottom of the potato clamp outside the cabin, desperate to find a few Lumpers that had not yet decayed to a stinking black mush.

Chapter Five

Hobart, October 1919, Sally

Saoirse brings me bread soaked in warm milk and spoons it into my mouth. I would like a drop of whiskey in it, the way Patsy always took it when her life was drawing towards a close, but there is no point in my asking Saoirse for liquor.

Patsy and I shared this bed for over fifty years, from the opening of the Australasia during Hobart's gold rush, until her death a decade ago. When Saoirse was a child nothing pleased her more than to climb in between her grandmother and her great-aunt, in the warm fug of our bodies, and sing. We preferred her bright and cheerful childish songs of Tasmania to the woeful sorrows of the songs the homesick Irishmen sang in the parlour down below, waving their tankards and splashing whiskey onto the heavily-waxed tabletops.

Since Saoirse took over the running of the place, the men must go to a tavern if they want anything stronger than tea. A room-keeper should be a little flexible, a little malleable in her thinking, but the child who chirped like a wren in the cocoon of blankets between Patsy and me has grown up to be as rigid as the whalebone stays in her corset.

She hasn't said a word to me about yesterday's conversation. Curiosity and fear are battling within her. Yesterday she asked me who I am, but I was too weak to answer. The bread and milk will give me strength, but she must find her own strength too. She must find the strength to ask again. But if she doesn't yet know who I am, it's time to inform her of what I am.

'Saoirse, what does Josie Hendron say in the kitchen?'

'She says you will be on your feet by summer, and you will bury us all.'

'And what do you think?'

'I think it's time to make your peace with God and man.' She turns away and fusses with the window hangings.

'Thank you.'

'For what?'

'For the truth of your answer. I feel I have a few days left. Not much more. I have no God to make peace with, but as for the people I love … ' I gesture towards the bureau and she opens it. 'In the third drawer down.' She reaches in and pulls out a bank deposit book. 'It's my own money. It's separate from the Australasia's money; Patsy and I had always our own books too.'

She looks to me for permission and I nod. She flips it open and gasps. 'Nanna, there's four hundred pounds here. What are you doing with four hundred pounds?'

'Look to the account-holders and read the names to me.'

'Sarah Gordon and Saoirse Gordon. Half of this money is mine?'

'No, Saoirse, none of that money is yours, but soon it will be and you will be free to use it as you wish.'

'The last withdrawal is for fifty pounds. All the deposits are a few pounds here, ten shillings there, but all the withdrawals are for fifty pounds.'

'Can you see the dates?'

'Yes. But they don't mean anything to me.'

'They are marriages. Fifty pounds to every serving girl who ever worked here, smaller sums of course in the years gone by, when money was worth something. In fact, some of the withdrawals weren't marriages. Some of the girls left for other reasons, but very few.'

'Hardly surprising, nowhere treats its girls like the Australasia.'

'That's right, and don't forget that when I'm gone.'

'Are you serious? Our girls get well paid, and aren't overworked. Fifty pounds for a wedding gift is a fortune.'

'Who said they were wedding gifts?'

'You did.'

'I said the withdrawals were dated around the time of the marriages. But the money wasn't a wedding gift.'

'What, then?'

'An open door, an escape, running-away money. A choice.'

'You're mad.'

'Most girls took the money, thanked us and walked up to the altar, happy and rich. We were glad for them. That was their choice. But a few fell to the floor to thank us, took their money and were never seen again.' I smile. 'We gave them that choice, and we were even more glad for those ones. No one runs, a few days before their marriage, unless they really need to.'

'I can't believe it.' She stares at me and I can see that her forty-five years on earth have taught her very little about the cold, hard calculations of desperation. We made her life too soft and she has repaid us by becoming a woman of certitude and iron rectitude.

'You can't let anyone be happy? Is that what it is? My mother didn't marry my father, or couldn't, or wouldn't, so you wanted to try to make sure every woman was in the same boat?'

'That's not how it was, at all. We wanted them to have a choice, that's all.'

'The same choice I had? I had no choice. Everyone knows what I am. And you encouraged other women to do the same to their babies … to make more little …' She struggles and I wait to see will she say the word, but she doesn't. I know where the shame comes from, but it never came from us. She has paid too much heed to the whispering of the world, a whispering which might have died away if she had held her head up. Perhaps we asked too much of her, asked her to shine in a cruel world, and instead she took to the shadows, to the drabbest of blacks and browns and greys, to the tightest of stays, to the most careful of conformities.

'There is a hundred pounds set aside for Josie. She's not likely to marry at her age, and she might well want to stay in the Australasia for ever. If I know

Josie she'll drop dead at the stove one day without a word of complaint. But I want her to have the money as soon as I'm buried, as soon as it's too late to try to thank me. I want her to have a choice, to stay or to leave, as she sees fit.'

'A choice? That word again. Interference is what it is.'

'Saoirse, do you know why the Australasia has always treated its girls so well?'

'Because you were decent people?'

I laugh at her innocence. 'It's exactly the opposite. It's because we weren't decent people, not me, nor Patsy, nor your mother. You would have crossed the street to avoid us, when we were young. And when we were old and grey and settled we treated our girls well because we knew what it's like to have no choice.'

A fit of coughing seizes me, and when it passes, I fall back on to the pillow and feel my eyes closing, against my will, while Saoirse stands, mouth open, questions formed but as yet unspoken.

Chapter Six

King's County, Wednesday, 22 November 1848

Patrick O'Loughlin's cart rocked and dipped from side to side as the wheels fell into and out of the deep ruts on the dirt road leading ever further from Sally's home, but she made herself as comfortable on the bench beside him as she could.

The sun was falling now, and, at this time of the year, daylight would fade hours earlier than the Angelus bell.

'Where are you headed for, Sally? I dare say you're striking out to meet an aunt or sister?' He looked at her bare, mud-streaked feet. 'Headed for Dublin, I suppose? And do they know yet that your parents are under the soil?'

'No, sir ... Patrick.' She crinkled up her eyes against the blinding rays of the sinking sun, and blinked away the sudden tears that rose unbidden and threatened to spill over her lashes. 'I have no one left in the world. Our neighbour Brigid always told my mother how lucky she was, with just the one child to worry after, and Brigid with a clatter of them hanging out of her morning, noon and night. But for all Brigid envied my mother, being an only child leaves me in a sorry state.'

Patrick pulled the sodden, mangled straw out of his mouth and pointed it at her, waggling it like an admonishing finger.

'Sally, yer on yer way to stay with your Auntie Caitlín, d'you hear me? She knows yer coming and she's expecting you any day. What's more, you've a rake of older brothers coming along behind you, they walk fast and they'll catch you up soon on the road.'

He sighed and clamped the straw between his grinders again. 'Tell no one that you are alone in the world. The least bad thing that will happen is that you'll end up in the workhouse, and them as goes into the big house these days soon comes out again – in a shroud. And trust me, lass, there's even worse things in the world than that, for a girl with no brothers.'

He looked at her, full in the face, and saw that despite her smile and nod, she had no idea what his words meant. Patrick had no inclination to explain the ways of the world to a motherless child. They proceeded in silence.

The horses plodded on, hoof after feathered hoof, the cart lurching and rolling, shaking Sally to her core. Patrick was securely braced against the floor of the wagon, but Sally's feet dangled an inch from the boards. A massive lurch to the left sent her sprawling against Patrick's shoulder and he reached out and grasped her by the upper arm, firm but gentle. She was weary to her bones and her eyelids were closing, grating viciously across the dried-out sand of her eyeballs.

'You're like an oul' toothless granny on a stool in the ingle-corner,' laughed Patrick. 'Did you ever see an oul' doll with her pipe clutched between her gums, head drooping lower and lower, until you fear she will fall arse-over-tit into the fire itself, set herself and the whole cabin alight?'

Sally thought of the long-ago wakes and marriages, the drinking and dancing deep into the hours of night, and the memory of some kind-hearted woman shooing the drowsy old crones away from the danger of the glowing embers and into whatever piles of rags served them for a bed.

'Patrick, I'm thinking about all the neighbours I seen buried. It's a long day since I seen an old woman like that – the hunger carried off the oldest and the youngest first.'

He set his right hand upon her and rubbed her shoulder gently. The last time a man touched her like that was the drover outside the inn, and he had filled her with a nameless, unspeakable dread. Patrick's touch felt like home.

'Make a bed in the straw back yonder,' he said. 'Climb up into the body of the cart. When you wake in the morning we'll be only a half hour's journey to go. I don't pay for lodging when I don't need to.'

Sally hesitated, daunted by the ordeal of clambering over the back board of the bench and onto the load, while the cart pitched and rocked beneath her.

'Go on,' he said, 'there's no need to stay awake on my account.' He looked at her, a rare, straightforward glance. 'You know yer safe with me, don't you? I'm many things, but I'm not *that*.'

Sally shrugged carelessly and nodded and didn't ask for explanation. Her belly was full, and she was about to bed down in a fine, warm pile of dry wheat straw; by recent reckoning, she had nothing to fear. She sank down into the straw and it enveloped her like a caress. The stalks prickled and scratched through her thin dress, but her eyes drooped and the weariness of a week of sleeping on the ground with one eye open, and a week before that spent barely sleeping, guarding the frail lives and then the swelling corpses of her parents, overwhelmed her. She felt nothing more as the steady beat of eight giant hooves blended with her own pulse and lulled her to sleep.

When she woke, it was dark, a bitterly cold, star-filled dark. Although the cart had stopped it was not the ceasing of the rocking and swaying that had woken her, but a fierce, burning twisting in her guts.

'Oh Mother of God, I'm poisoned. Oh, for the love of God, get me off this wagon.'

Patrick was snoring, just a few feet away at the back of the load, wrapped in his greatcoat, his boots in a sack under his head. A long thread of drool snaked from his open lips to the collar below his chin, pulsing and stretching with each gentle snore and pop as he puffed a lacework of breath out into the night sky. The horses, spancilled hind to fore with soft súgán ropes, snatched quiet mouthfuls of grass by the verge, and Patrick had unharnessed, fed and settled them so quietly that Sally would have slept through till morning, but for the knives stabbing in her bowels.

Shaking, coated in a light film of sweat, she heaved herself over the side of the wagon, cracking her shin against the top rail in her hurry, then stumbled into the ferns and bracken at the side of the road. The cramping pains were so great that she managed to put only a few feet between herself and the cart before, with a giant steaming and a gush of pain, the rich, heavy soda bread flowed out of her, and she fell over and rolled in the grass, arms wrapped so tightly round her middle that she thought her hands might meet behind her.

'Oh God,' she whimpered, 'oh merciful God almighty.' Her mother's voice echoed through her memory, as plain as day. *And that, my girl, is God's punishment for gluttony.*

★ ★ ★

God's punishment had been a constant theme of the Mahon's lives at home. *Oh Lord, oh Lord, what did I do to deserve this?* Nuala would cry at intervals, at one time frequent, but less so in recent years. *What did I do that you should punish me so?* She would lie on the straw-stuffed tick, all the household rags and clothes piled upon her in a heap to warm her, face white as the clouds on a summer's day. Fists clenched, eyes popping, groaning and straining, she would send Sally to the hearth for a warm, flat stone and, having wrapped it in a rag, she would cuddle it to her belly and weep.

In time she would ask Sally to bring a bucket, and to scald it with clean, hot water. *Now get out.* Sally never looked twice behind her but followed her mother's instruction and her pointed finger out the door. *And don't come back till your father is home from the fields, let him come in first. And bring a few potatoes round to Brigid.*

Brigid Deegan would already be at the door of her hut, leaning out over the closed bottom half, shut against the dirt, while the open top half allowed in some light and air. Even at this distance, across Brigid's half-acre plot, Nuala Mahon's voice could be clearly discerned over the winds of the Bog of Allen. Prayers and incantations mingled with cries and roars of pain.

'Get in and scrub that handful of praties, lass, and add them to our pot. There'll be no food cooked in your house the night.'

Then Sally and Brigid's eldest daughter, Molly, kept a watch on the tumbling, laughing Deegan brothers and sisters as they fell in and out of the trees and ditches. And Sally kept a watch on Brigid likewise, striding across to her mother's house and, some time later, emerging, carrying the tin bucket, carefully covered with a blood-red cloth, and a spade in the other hand. Sally wondered where the special red cloths came from, for she never saw a red cloth in her house on an ordinary work-a-day.

'What do you think does be in that bucket, Molly?'

'Sure how would I know?' her friend answered, 'D'you think I have the second sight? But there's none of that carry-on in this house. That screaming and roaring and taking to the bed never happens here.'

In the distance the girls could see Brigid, now at the very edge of the bog, flat on the horizon, far from the midden and far from the potato bed, digging, digging and then tipping up the bucket into the shallow hole.

'It must be something important, though Molly, look at the careful way she fills in the hole. Would you never ask her for me?'

'Would you never ask your own mother?'

'Sure, I'm sick asking mine, and the last time she showed me the back of her hand. Nearly knocked me out of my standing. All she said after, was that it was a mystery and in the hands of God, that I would be an only child all my life, and what had she ever done to deserve it? Sure, I was none the wiser.'

★ ★ ★

Tears and weeping and slaps and mystery. Secrets wrenched with pain and screaming from the bodies of women and buried quietly in the bog. That was how the ever-loving almighty God dealt with you, apparently.

Sally lay, almost naked, on the ground, a few inches from her own steaming shit, in the company of a man she didn't know, and still none the wiser. The only thing she was sure of was the ever-present probability of God's punishment, and of the fact that her mother would never again have to decide whether to answer her or to knock her down. She turned her face into the ground and wept.

In the morning she was grey and exhausted and stank to high heaven, but Patrick said nothing as she climbed up beside him on the bench. He shook the reins and chirruped and the horses set off, haunches swelling and swaying as the cart slowly started to move.

They had walked the horses at first light to a nearby stream, and there they had drunk their fill, snuffling and snorting and shaking the icy drops off their long whiskers.

Sally had slipped her feet and legs into the stream, gasping and wincing against the icy rush, and had splashed and rubbed what bits of herself she decently could. If Patrick had left her for a minute, she would have taken off her clothes and entered the stream, freezing though it was, but he had stood by the bank, cooing and crooning to the horses, like a man who might say that he loved them. Sally had often heard the priests say that animals are soulless creatures, not made in the image of God. She had looked at Patrick as he rubbed the velvet muzzles and whispered in the tufts of chestnut ear-hair. Watching him now, guiding them with the gentlest of touches on the reins, she felt that Patrick might prefer hell to heaven, if he could take his horses with him.

He must have read her thoughts, for he gently, almost with affection, drew the knout of his long whip across the huge croup of one of the horses, which flickered its skin and shrugged off the knotted leather as though it were no more than a cleg, seeking a soft spot to bite. Patrick spoke without prompting.

'Them's my own horses, Sally. Mother and son they are, never been separated, which is the right way. And when Bessie is too old to draw the heavy load, her daughter will step into the traces beside this fella and draw it for me, with the help of God.'

'And your master? Does he pay you for the use of the horses?'

Patrick pulled himself up, like a bantam cock swelling and puffing at a stray dog that has dared enter the hens' garden.

'Master.' He sniffed loudly then shot a huge wad of phlegm over the side of the cart. 'I have no master and I don't miss him. I'm a free man, Sally, and I tell you, there will be more like me soon enough. The times is changing. Did you see much hunger, in the parish of Clonsast?'

'Sure you know we did, Patrick, what kind of a question is that? There is hunger every place throughout the land. These three years past, a potato that looks prime in your hand may be just a shell like an egg, full of mush and stink when you cut into it. And I haven't even seen a potato, good, bad or indifferent at all this year.'

'Listen to me, Sally, you haven't known hunger, at all. Not like I've seen and heard. I drive the lanes and byways of four counties and I talk to the travelling men. To the tinker-men and the drovers and the landless rascals too.'

It wasn't Sally's place to go correcting the notions of fat, ruddy-faced men who owned their own brace of fine horses, but she couldn't let it pass.

'Not seen hunger? Patrick, what're you on about? Sure, there's hardly an old woman left on the whole of Joly's land, so they say. Babies dead by the score too, from want of mother's milk. Mickey Dooley died of the want, and his rent unpaid, and Joly had the family put out of the cabin and the roof tumbled.'

She paused for a moment, until she was strong enough to continue. 'And aren't my own parents under the soil? Typhus carried them off, but, I tell you, I've seen terrible ailments on the both of them before, and they stood up again afterwards. Too weak this time, Patrick, too weak, too cold. My father too hungry even to cut a bank of turf for us this year, and we burning the few scraps left over from before.'

Sally's voice tailed off into silence. She had known for weeks before her death that Nuala Mahon was taking far less than her fair share of the few tiny meals she could salvage. Sally had known, but hadn't cared. Her own belly had been shrieking and hollow and she thought it only right that her mother would sneak extra onto Sally's side of the pot, and spend longer eating her own few mouthfuls, to take the bad look off the thing.

Patrick plucked himself a new straw from the load, as he pretended not to notice her tears and the gulping in her throat, and chewed it for a few moments. He was not a man for easy talking – yesterday they had said little to each other.

'Girl, there's villages, whole parishes, in this country that has neither man, woman nor child left, save for the landlord's agent and his house servants. Not in King's County, nor in Kildare neither, but in the faraway places. In Connacht, where Cromwell said there wasn't food enough to feed a man, nor wood enough to make a gallows to hang him.'

They both blessed themselves instinctively, and spat, at the mention of the English monster. *The curse of Cromwell on ya* the men would shout in the fields, when the scythe slipped in their hand and gashed them, or a rock fell upon a poorly shod foot during the building of a dry-stone wall.

'Oh the Irish ate meat, like the rest of the world, and counted our riches in fine hides of beef, before that English bastard came over and swept through the land like a plague.'

Patrick was roaring now, but it was old news to Sally. Every child knew that the woes of the Irish had started in earnest when Cromwell bid them get to hell, or to Connacht.

Sally didn't know much about men, but she knew enough not to interrupt Patrick, or try to halt his angry flow of words – next he would be singing ballads of despair and conquest, of the brave pikemen of '98, mown down by the English guns, or brought to Dublin to be murdered on the Croppy Acre.

Patrick neither sang nor wept, but kept his mouth in a firm scowl, though his eyes twinkled. 'Oh, I'm telling you, there's a change coming, Sally. Who's going to work the land? The little homes are tumbled to the ground, the wreckers have put the still-living out onto the long acre and told them walk to perdition. The coffin ships are loaded past their bearing with the stick-thin people heading to America, and many of them make their graves in the water before ever seeing the New World.'

His voice shook and climbed in pitch, spittle flew from his lips, landing on Sally's face, but she controlled herself with an effort and did not reach up to wipe it away.

'The unplanted lazy beds are being grazed by sheep now and the landlords are rubbing their hands in glee to be rid of the bloody nuisance of the Irish people off their lands. But, mark my words,' he clapped his hands and looked to heaven for confirmation, 'as God is my witness, land can't be worked by sheep. There are places, I've heard tell, where there are so few Irish left, that the landlords' agents are paying women in coin for their labour for the first time since I was a boy. *Women.*'

Sally thought about that. The idea of holding a coin of her own.

'Maybe I should go there, Patrick, go to the far places? I could work the land, maybe?'

He laughed without humour. 'No, lass. For a start it would kill you to get there. These places are hundreds of miles away. And they wouldn't take you, anyway, a stranger, when they have buried their own daughters, or left them to rot in the ditches.'

She blessed herself and shivered.

'You're just trying to frighten me. Who ever heard of such a thing, Patrick? Sure wouldn't the parish bury them? In Black '47 we found poor Kate Lawlor dead in the ditch beside Captain Nelson's garden, and two men dead on the road at Timmy's Cross, but they were picked up and buried at the expense of the parish vestry, the same way they buried my own parents.'

She dashed two sudden, burning tears from her eyes and Patrick answered, in a gentler tone.

'Lass, there's no-one left to bury them. And, oftentimes, they do fall by the roadside, as they walk from Billy to Jack, to see will one or other take pity on them. But Billy sends them away empty, and Jack cannot be disturbed from his dinner, for he has the doctor and the parson dining with him, so he bids his butler draw the curtains and he shouts to the keeper to unleash the dogs. And the corpses lie where they fall on the trail of tears.'

A long silence followed. The creaking leather harness punctuated the clip-clop of the heavy hooves and the jangle of metal from the horses' mouths. Patrick held the reins, but it was through force of habit – he was no more directing the animals than Sally was. The narrow road snaked into the distance, with neither left nor right turn as far as the eye could see. The horses plodded on relentlessly, carrying Sally further and further from Clonsast where at least, surely to God, someone would have laid her in the ground, if the need arose, beside her parents.

'So, Sally,' Patrick finally spoke again, 'what will you do in Dublin? Where will you go? You must know someone there, I take it, to be heading such a big distance alone.'

'But I'm not going to Dublin. What would take me to Dublin? Isn't the town of Newbridge close around here somewhere, and that's where I'm going. I thought you were going there too, with your big load of straw?'

'Newbridge? Yes, I'm bound for Newbridge and it won't take half an hour more to get there. But I have a good reason to go to Newbridge – eight hundred army horses, shittin' and pissin' all day long, that's a lot of straw needed. And I'll carry away in my cart the black gold from the army's steaming dung heaps to richen up my small perches of land at home. What in the name of God is *your* reason for going to Newbridge?'

Patrick's face darkened with a deep red flush and his brows knit closer and closer as Sally explained about the friendly drovers, the pints of porter and the endless work for a woman in Newbridge. Morning, noon and night. Plenty of work for a lass, *if she's strong enough to take it*, they had said. Patrick shook his head and whistled through tightly clenched teeth.

'Girl, it's the workhouse for you, I think. When we get to Newbridge, I'll fill your belly for you and set you on the road to Nás Na Ríogh. There's a workhouse there. That's a better notion than staying in Newbridge.'

She started from the bench in horror, but the height of the cart made her think twice about jumping down.

'I'll never go to the workhouse, Patrick. In the workhouse in Parsonstown a hundred and one people died of typhus in the space of seven days, so Father Peter read in the newspaper. And in Edenderry there's two thousand crammed into the space intended for six hundred. My father always said he'd rather die than go to the workhouse.'

Patrick looked away from her and sighed, and there was sorrow and yet anger in his voice. 'Seems to me that your father didn't know much about the world, Sally, and that any little your mother did know about it, she didn't pass on. Sure, you must have known those men were making a sow's tit of your father? It's rare for strangers to buy drink and laugh with a fool they never met before, without some malice in their hearts.'

'Is there no work, Patrick? Is there no need for women in Newbridge at all? What am I going to do? I can't travel the whole road to Dublin alone. And I would be as friendless in Dublin as in Newbridge, only more tired and more worn out.'

'What the women are needed for in Newbridge is not what yer mother would want you to work at. Now, don't ask me again.'

Silence fell over the pair as the cart wended its way through the brightening day towards the town.

Patrick pulled another lump of wheaten bread from his leather bag, but this time he moistened it by rubbing it on a greasy white lump before handing it over.

'Pig fat,' he said.

It was the strongest taste Sally had ever known. The bread blossomed into a feast in her mouth and juice squirted out of her gums like when she'd bite into a sour apple too early in the season. Every autumn her father had spent a day at Hollywood House with other men, to help in the slaughter of Joly's pigs, and the stories he'd told afterwards had sickened her. *Then you hould the bowl right tight under his jollers and the pig-sticker comes, fast as you like, and slits him … ear to ear … and he screams, like a newborn baby, just one time.*

Her mother had slammed out of the house into the yard and Sally had clamped her hands over her own ears and vowed never to eat the meat of a murdered pig.

She turned the greasy bread from side to side, held it up to her mouth and sniffed it. She licked it, then took another smaller nibble, the memory of last night's agony, and the shit running out of her, counselling caution.

'Delicious, Patrick. It's good stuff, right enough. No wonder the gentry is so keen on pigs.' She took another tiny morsel. 'My mother used to say that when she was a girl, the Irish had pigs of their own, one per family, or even more, raised up to sell at the autumn fair, to pay the rent on the landlord's cabin.'

'That's right. My mother had pigs too, and hens. The pigs grew fat on slugs and worms, acorns, peelings and leftovers.'

'What are leftovers?'

Patrick sniffed and wiped his eye, where Sally supposed the wind must have blown some dust in.

She tried to put her mother and father out of her mind and gnawed the bread, slowly savouring it, nodding and smiling politely as Patrick gave her directions to the workhouse in Nás Na Ríogh, the Place of the Kings, just six or seven miles from the new bridge.

Chapter Seven

Hobart, October 1919, Sally

From my prone position on the pillow I can no more see the Church of St John down in the New Town than I can see the church in Clonbullogue, ten thousand nautical miles away. But I do not need to see them. They are both imprinted upon my eyelids.

On Murray Street, a few miles from where I lie, the square tower and arched windows of the Anglican church stretch to the sky, bisecting the vast bulk of snow-capped Wellington Mountain behind.

And nestled on either side of St John's on Murray Street are the long, low twin buildings, girls on the right, boys on the left, of Queen's orphan asylum.

No one who ever saw a workhouse could stand in front of Queen's orphanage and mistake it for anything other than a newer, bigger, brighter workhouse. Nowadays the city has crept up around it and the old stone buildings blend into the homes, businesses and industries of a thriving modern port. In the years around Saoirse's birth, it stood aloof at the end of a long stretch of farmland, huddled under the mountain, maintaining its distance from the decent citizens of Hobart. Even after the gold rush, when the island was flooded with freemen, and the people left, right and centre were shedding off their old selves – convict, prisoner, gaoler, soldier's wife – even in those halcyon days when a woman might set up a boarding house and reap a fortune from the shiploads of gold-crazed prospectors, even then, some shames could not be borne … Even then, and for years after, the doors of the orphanage swung open to reveal another newborn infant in a basket on the doorstep, or a woman in the first stages of labour, begging for admission until the child was born and signed over.

I never could find it in my heart to blame the women who made that choice, who handed over the fruits of their forbidden love, or their innocent misunderstandings of the ways of men, or the child foisted upon them with violence as they shrieked under the heavy bodies of their employers. I never blamed them. But there was no way on this wide earth that Margaret, Patsy and I could have approached those doors. We never even discussed it, when Margaret told us the child was on its way. Workhouse or orphan asylum, call it what you will, we had all had our workhouse fears. The child would stay with us, though that decision cast a shadow over the respectability and, more importantly, the profitability of the Australasia for many years to come.

I wrench my heavy eyelids open, a greater task each time I awake, and gesture to Saoirse to sit with me. I pull air into my lungs for what may be one of my last conversations with her. My heart is beating weaker in my chest than ever I have felt it before, but my mind is clear and my conscience urges me to try to help her winnow some joy from the chaff of her remaining years. At last, she has asked some of the questions I have been waiting for. Of course, I might not tell her absolutely everything …

'Nanna,' she begins at last, still kneading and rubbing her rosary without conscious thought, 'I don't know why you started this. But I want an end to it. You say you're not the woman I have known. All my life I have lived among women. All my life I have known I was … different.'

I nod. I'll save her the effort. I have never heard her say the word and I doubt she will say it now. At the middle school, Sister Agatha took great pleasure in telling Saoirse that a girl does not share a surname with her mother's mother. Not unless something *odd* has happened. Not unless the girl is *a little bastard*. Not unless the girl belongs in the Queen's asylum, not swanning around Hobart's best school, dressed to the nines, among the daughters of decent people.

'I have no father.'

That is the closest I have ever heard Saoirse come to speaking of it, since the day I led her by the hand out of Sister Agatha's classroom, never to return.

'I have no father. No sister, brother, cousin.' She counts off her woes on her fingers. 'And until yesterday I knew some things for facts. That my grand-mother Sarah Gordon née O'Hanlon lay in her deathbed, that my mother Margaret Gordon lay in the grave in which you will soon join her, and that my grandfather Jack Gordon lay buried and unheeded in a cemetery ten thousand miles away in Ireland, under the North Star.'

I nod, for there are so many lies and half-truths, I'm not sure which one to start with, which thread to pull to start unravelling this tangled knot of well-intentioned deceit.

'Nanna, I'm begging you. You said yesterday that you came to Hobart "before you were Gordon". If you didn't meet Jack Gordon until you came here, where is he? Is there a chance to find a family for me? Is there a cousin? A cousin-in-law? Even a grave to visit?'

I lie silent for an extra moment and refuse to meet her eye. So many hopes are about to be dashed.

'Nanna, don't leave me alone in the world, if there is a chance, however slim, that I have kin of my grandfather.' She swallows and asks the question, the most natural question in the world, that she has never asked before. 'Or my father?'

'Try to find love,' I answer. It is a hoarse whisper, she has to bring her ear almost to my lips to catch the words. She laughs.

'Look at me, Nanna, and ask, what have I now to attract a husband, that I didn't have when I was a fresh-faced young … fatherless … girl of twenty?'

'I told you to find love. I never said a word about a husband.'

She frowns.

'The deeds to a boarding house will help.' I cackle, surprising even myself with the harsh sound in the quiet room. 'You might be surprised how many men fall arse-over-tit in love with a woman past childbearing who owns a ten-bedroom boarding house.'

'Nanna, for heaven's sake. You shouldn't say such things.'

'They need to be said. I'm older than most in Hobart and I remember the way things were. I will be under the ground before long. I come from a time and a place where death was accompanied by keening and drinking, music and stories all night long. After the life I have lived, I don't fear to speak of death. The deeds to the Australasia are in the top drawer of the bureau, and my testament also. It's yours, of course, everything, as you deserve.'

She laughs in shock and for a moment the child I remember shines through, the one who laughed when I spat on the floor of Sister Agatha's classroom, and brought Saoirse home, pencils, slate, copybook and all, never to return.

Chapter Eight

Newbridge, County Kildare, Thursday, 23 November 1848

The noise of Newbridge rose in a roar and assaulted Sally's ears almost as a physical blow. So many people gathered in one place, ten times the number of a fair in Clonbullogue. Hand-clapping dealers shouted in the market, spitting on their palms to seal the deal in a manly handshake. Young, terrified horses, fresh out of the meadows, galloped up and down the main thoroughfare, wiry boys clinging to their manes and necks while the officers looked on, judging their paces and their wildness.

'Ah, you want a wild, brave type of a horse to train up as an officer's charger,' Patrick said. 'But the thing is, if he's *too* wild, will he be more trouble to break than he's worth? The army has plenty of strong, young Irish horse-wranglers, sons of the wandering tinkers a lot of them are, but the army don't like to see them horse-gifted tinker boys dying of a broken neck here in Ireland.' He sniffed and hawked out a huge gob, near but not dangerously near, the feet of an officer's gleaming thigh boots. 'Don't want them dying here in Ireland, when there's plenty of need for them to go to the wars out foreign, and die abroad.'

Out of the way of the charging young-stock stood dejected jennets and asses, with pairs of wicker creels strapped on their backs, while the women in charge of them spread eggs, bread, cloth and other goods on their shawls, laid down over the muck of the street. Every class of ware was to be had; green vegetables, long, pointy, muddy things called carrots, and brown papery balls called onions. Pails of milk. Pens of last spring's fat lambs ready for slaughter. Women drove long, hollow corers deep into barrels to show that the good, creamy butter was sound the whole way from top to bottom. But nowhere could Sally see a stall selling potatoes.

★ ★ ★

Since the year of '45, the potato crop had been dwindling and decaying. Now, nearly three years since news of the blight first reached Clonsast, Sally still remembered every detail of that first day. Panting, sweat dripping, her father had appeared over the rise and tumbled down the small boreen towards the cabin. He'd been labouring in a distant part of the estate, building a wall with dressed stone carted in from a distance, for the boggy land of Clonsast yielded little in the way of good masonry.

'Nuala, for the love of God, come with me, and help me check the potatoes.' His wife and daughter had followed, mystified, as he raced to the small lazy beds behind the house, where the potatoes had been grown for all of his life, the beds getting higher and higher each month as he raised the sods against the rising stalks, until, come October or November, he flattened them and rooted out the fine, floury Lumpers.

Malachy doubled up, wheezing and gasping. Nuala placed a careful hand on his shoulder, cautious, in case he hit her a thump. 'What is it at all, Malachy? For the love of God, what's the matter? Are you struck?' But when he raised his head, they could see that his face was not fallen, and his mouth was not slack. He hadn't had a stroke, but seemed to be in some kind of fit, nonetheless.

'Father Peter has been reading the newspaper in the village square. The word is all over Clon, and will soon be all over the country.' The breath died in his throat and he wheezed in another sobbing gulp of air. 'The potatoes are dying. A sickness has come upon them, the first sign is a brown spot on the leaves. Every potato in the ground will rot. Help me, woman, in the name of God.'

He seized the closest plant and turned over the fresh green leaves. For upward of an hour, all three searched carefully, turning over every leaf, examining every stalk and stem. Father Peter said each cankered plant must be ripped from the ground and burnt. But they had none. And although they heard of fearsome suffering in other places, and although they inspected their plants daily for the remainder of the season, their third of an acre of King's County had escaped.

In all of King's County the potatoes had been saved, sold and clamped, as had always happened before, and the pace of life maintained its pattern of births and wakes and marriages and betrayals.

The following years, though, the blight had not spared Clonsast. Upon the advice of Father Peter's newspaper, the people had harvested the early potatoes in June '46 for fear of leaving them in the ground for their proper spell, and though they were small, they were sound. A great gathering of the people had come together to sing and dance in joyful thanks, to the music of a flute played by Paddy Campion.

'Dance with me, Nuala,' Malachy said, and she laughed and called him an eejit and went back to dancing with the rest of the married women. 'Dance with me, Sally.' And she had whirled and flown in her father's strong arms.

But in September, the winds had brought the dirty smoke of Dublin blowing their way, and other foul and pestilential changes in the air, and the half-grown main-crop potatoes were harvested in a rush, as they wilted and decayed faster than they could be pulled unready from the soil. After that, things had gone hard with the Mahons and with their friends and neighbours.

★ ★ ★

Now, while hawkers shrieked their wares into the chaos of Newbridge town, Sally could see that though there was food in abundance to be sold, there was not a potato to be seen.

The town stretched into the distance, a wide street, bounded its full length on one side by the high, dark stone wall of the barracks, and the other side boasting stone and brick buildings of two storeys each; here an inn, there a victualler, a maker of horse blankets, and a shop with a fully dressed man standing in the window while a smaller, bow-legged man took the measure of his shoulders, his arms, then ran his hand down the full length of his breeches, while his customer paid him as little heed as Sally might pay to a bog-cotton seed settling in her hair.

'Why wouldn't the street be wide?' Patrick said. 'Why wouldn't the army build fine and wide, when they are building on someone else's land? Not one stone stood on top of another here, less than forty year ago. There was nothing here at all, save for the new bridge, put up when the last one swept away, a few miles east,' he pointed vaguely into the distance, 'and they built the new one here, straightening the road between Nás na Ríogh and Kildare town.'

'That can't be right. This big, bustling town, brand new?'

'Younger than me,' Patrick laughed. 'I remember when this was all pasture and hedgerow. I tell you, you've got Boney, rattling his sabre over in France, to thank for this. The English were certain sure that the Frog army would attack England through Ireland, and, God knows, they couldn't trust *us* to hinder any enemies of His English Majesty.'

These last words he muttered so softly, Sally had to bend her head closer to make them out. In her mind she pictured bony skeletons wielding swords, rushing through the land, and an army of hopping, croaking frogs. She nodded and smiled in respectful silence. Patrick was a much-travelled man, who knew things, and hadn't Father Peter spoken of the army of locusts, and of the plague of frogs, and didn't these strange things happen sometimes in the faraway and olden times? Who was Sally to question it?

The heavily laden wagon creaked and crept its way down the thronged Main Street, Patrick cursing and shaking his fist at those who impeded its progress, until at length they reached a vast, long building, roughly made, but larger than any Sally had seen before.

'Quartermaster's storehouse,' said Patrick. 'The boyo who will pay me for the straw and send a man to direct me to unload. Keep your own trap shut and let me do the talking.'

A fat, whiskery man bustled out of the stout wooden door and sauntered across to the wagon. The low-hung winter sun shone fiercely off his shining buttons and buckles so that Sally winced and screwed her eyes up against the glare. The quartermaster carried a fine leather crop which he slapped insolently against his gleaming black boots, punctuating his discourse with the sound.

'O'Loughlin!'

'Good day to you, sir.' Sally glanced at Patrick in surprise, but how a man behaves in front of a friendless child may differ from how he speaks to a man in uniform, with a bagful of coin in his pocket and a pistol in his belt.

'Wheat straw, is it?' The quartermaster pulled a few stalks from the load, sniffing deeply and breathing in. He gave a selected straw a good chew, then grabbed a handful and shook it harshly. 'Dusty as hell, my man. Bad enough to choke a horse. Wouldn't touch the stuff.'

Sally gasped and sneaked a look at Patrick from the corner of her left eye, expecting him to raise his huge fist and shake it to heaven, but he smiled gently, leaped down from the bench onto the ground where he stood, towering over the other man, and thrust his hand deep into the load of straw.

'You see, sir, that's just the dust of the journey on the outer stalks, sir. The bulk of the load is grand and clean.' He smiled shyly, and held out his handful gently. It seemed as though another man's soul was wearing Patrick's body; Sally would not have dreamed his voice could be so soft and coaxing. 'Indeed, sir, with the rain that came upon the country this summer, 'tis a wonder there's any straw at all, of any condition. You know me well, sir. Honest Paddy, that's me.'

'Honest Paddy, there's a fine contradiction.' The quartermaster sniffed and turned abruptly away from them. 'I never met an honest Paddy in three long years in this bloody hellhole.'

Just before he disappeared through the door, he swung on the heel of his finely polished boot, marched back and rammed his hand deep into the load of straw, considering, smelling and tasting as before. 'I'll take it, and be damned to you. Get away to the back of the stores and have it weighed and unloaded, before I change my mind.'

As Patrick swung up onto the bench beside Sally he tipped a large wink and whispered in his own natural voice, 'One day, Sally, I'm going to meet Mr Quartermaster-Sir in a nice dark alley, all on his ownsome. And when I do … '

His huge fist slammed onto the bench beside her, making her jump and almost tumble to the ground. 'There'll be no more Honest Paddy, when that time comes. That bastard's not even a soldier, just a servant to the battalion, swanning around in his boots and revolver. Maggot!'

At the unloading bay at the back of the huge store Patrick drove the wagon carefully onto a metal plate laid in the ground. 'It's a weighbridge, Sally, they'll pay me for the difference between the loaded weight and the empty weight, and I'd say it's the crookedest weighbridge in the land.'

'Ah, quit your moaning, Patrick,' laughed a young soldier standing beside the weighbridge, plainly Irish and speaking in the soft, flat tone of the boglands. 'You can take it, or you can leave it, but the 'master here is not special crooked; I've seen a lot worse in other places.'

Patrick jumped down and jerked his thumb at Sally and she scrambled down to join him while the wagon was weighed.

'Didn't know you were a married man?' laughed the soldier, and Patrick laughed with him.

'Christ, and I'm not. Never put my head in that noose, nor never will. It's the sister's child I have with me.'

The soldier slapped his hands together and winked. 'Right, right. It's amazing how many men have *nieces* these days, that never had none before.'

'She's ten years old, for the love of God. Shut your trap, or I'll shut it for you.'

Sally was fourteen, and Patrick knew it, but she held her tongue and did not contradict him, and the two men went about their work, silent now, reckoning, unloading, reckoning again until Patrick was given a slip of inked paper and he returned to the quartermaster for a short, quiet argument. After much wheedling, pleading and banging of tabletops, a final agreement was reached and a pile of coins was counted, twice, into Patrick's rough palm.

★ ★ ★

'Do you want my money, or will I take it elsewhere?' Patrick slammed his open hand on the counter of the inn. Sally stared at the floor of the parlour in shame, the floor that was flagged, as fancy as the floor of the church in Clonbullogue.

'She's filthy,' the serving woman flapped her hand in front of her face and curled her lip, 'and she stinks to the high heavens. Is that the best you could find? You're easy pleased.'

Patrick turned on his heel, dragging Sally by the elbow towards the door of the inn, until the woman's voice called out anxiously, 'Ah, come on now, Patrick, can you not take a wee joke, go you on out to the back hall, and I'll bring you something there.'

Patrick had a cup of ale and a giant platter of meat stew. The serving woman brought Sally a brimming bowl of broth, yellow and green with a fine layer of grease floating on top. Sally burnt her lips as she lifted the bowl to her mouth for the first time.

'Bring the child a spoon, for the love of God.'

'I better get that back,' the woman said as she slammed a wooden spoon down onto the board, 'and the bowl too.' Sally's cheeks flared red, and hot, shaming tears rose up behind her lashes, but she managed to hold them back.

Sally's mother had had the knife, gone now to the new family, along with the cabin, and the loy and sleán her father had for planting the seed potatoes and for harvesting his bank of turf. The blade of her mother's knife was a thin lash of a thing, and she had used it to cut the bad bits off the Lumpers and winkle out the sprouting eyes, back in the days when she was fussy about that kind of thing. But Sally had never held a spoon before and she was clumsy, spilling nearly as much as she drank. Nuala Mahon had stirred her pot with a sturdy twig, peeled clean, in the last months of her life, when the potatoes were totally gone and she had had to cook a thin gruel made with grass and nettles and precious handfuls of Indian meal, doled out once or twice a month to some of those who could prove they had need of it.

Sally set the spoon down and sighed. She would leave the broth to cool a little and then she would suck it from the wooden bowl rather than risk further humiliation with the broad flat spoon.

Patrick belched and waved his knife at her. 'In the fine houses round here, and up in Ryston, where the officers do dine, they eat their dinners off of delph so thin you can damn-near see through it, and they sup their soup with silver spoons. Would you believe that?'

Sally shrugged. 'I don't care what the gentry do with their spoons, what odds is that to me? And I've seen delph before, it's no big matter; Brigid had one from her mother, blue and white pictures on a big, round platter.'

Like the rest of Brigid Deegan's dowry, that platter was long gone now, taken from Brigid by the Poor Relief, in exchange for Indian meal. She had gone to the relief store, as it was called, that Reverend Joly and Father Peter had set up in the village of Clonbullogue, the Protestant and the Catholic clergyman both equally hard to please, and had begged them to see her as *deserving*. In exchange for the delph they had given her a chit for a monthly sack of Sir Robert Peel's brimstone, low quality Indian meal, purchased by the shipload from England's colonies at a fraction of the cost Joly got for his own fine grains from the merchants of Newbridge and of Liverpool.

Peel's brimstone was unsieved and raw, full of tiny, sharp stones that would break a tooth, or gouge the gullet of anyone unlucky enough to swallow one. With seven children in the Deegan household, that carefully guarded monthly sack of meal had lasted only two weeks. Molly and Sally had been set to whin the stones from the grains, and oftentimes they were so hungry they had slipped a few hard, raw grains into their mouths and chewed them until they were nothing but pulp.

Patrick finished his meal, wiping up the rich juices with another slice of soda bread from his pouch, then thrust out his legs and starting tamping down his pipe.

'Use that spoon, girl, for God's sake, don't be slurping like a heathen. You're not a dog lapping at his bowl.'

Sally sighed, but she picked up the spoon again and, scraping down to the bottom of the bowl, she found something soft and heavy, a lump of fibrous stringy stuff.

'What's this?'

'I told her to dig down to the bottom of the broth for you, not to be skimming the water off the surface.' He smiled like a lord out hunting and surveying his lands. 'Good woman that she is, there's a fine lump of mutton for you.'

Almost afraid to taste it, remembering the hot, stinking mess she had made in the ditch just the night before, Sally gently tipped the lump of meat from the bowl of the spoon into her mouth and chewed on it. It was firm and, at the same time, soft. It was greasy and slippery and yet it stuck to her teeth and between them. The flavour, earthy and rank, poured into her mouth and her brain, filling it up, delicious, and strange.

'That's the first time I ever tasted meat, I think, Patrick,' she confessed. 'And it's right good. Better than potatoes, even.'

He shook his head. 'There's plenty more asides you in King's County that have never tasted mutton afore, and plenty that never will.'

She scraped deep into the cloudy broth, searching for another piece of meat, but there was none.

The bowl of Patrick's pipe glowed as he took a final puff, then died with a waft of sweet-smelling smoke.

'Make sure you leave that oul' bitch her spoon,' he laughed. 'For all her sharp tongue, she keeps a good kitchen and a clean bed, and I'll be back here again, even if you're not.'

He stood up and Sally followed him to the door. He turned her around on the street and pointed ahead of her, over the bridge, at the meadows beyond.

'I've done what little I can for you now, Sally.' She opened her mouth but he spoke right over her. 'There's no thanks needed or wanted, but I have a heavy, dirty job ahead of me now, loading up the dung onto the wagon, and I want to see you right on the road to Nás Na Ríogh betimes.'

They crossed the three-arched stone bridge together. The highway stretched wide and straight ahead, so wide that two carts could travel in opposite directions at once, and neither have to make way for the other to pass.

'It's seven, maybe eight miles to Nás Na Ríogh, then you go straight to the church and tell the good father that you are bound for the workhouse, and can you have a ticket to get you in faster.' He put his hand on her shoulder and looked deep into her eyes. 'Don't dawdle on the road, gawping around you, it'll be dark soon. Walk fast. You can't stay alone in Newbridge, and for God's sake, when night falls, you need to be safely in Nás already. If the doors of the workhouse are closed, hide, and let no sinner see you till the sun is high in the morning.'

Into her unresisting hands, he pressed the remnants of his two-day-old wheaten loaf and, turning abruptly on his heel, strode off, never once looking back.

Sally put the bread inside her dress and walked on for a scant quarter of a mile before breaking out into the fields to find a sheltered and half-dry spot. No point walking any further on tired feet when, as soon as tomorrow's dawn had fully broken, and she could be sure that Patrick O'Loughlin's cart was creaking its way back home, she was heading straight back to Newbridge. She lay down in the lee of a blackthorn hedgerow and spread a few crumbs in the palm of her hand for a robin which strutted and preened on a branch above her. The bird looked at the crumbs, head cocked, eyes bright, but did not venture down.

'I'll dig up some of Newbridge's gold,' she told the robin, 'or I swear to God as my witness, I will starve in the street.'

But even if she starved, she would not enter through the door of the workhouse. That much she owed to her father. Whatever else Malachy Mahon had not told her, he had told her to stay away from the workhouse.

Chapter Nine

Hobart, October 1919, Sally

Saoirse bangs the door of my chamber with unaccustomed vigour, and I start and shudder in the bed. In the looking-glass, as I raise my eyes towards her, I see that the white wisps of my hair are awry, sticking out from under my cap. Ordinarily, she would take a moment to smooth the wisps away, tidy me up and moisten my lips, but not now. Her bewilderment and confusion surge across the room and I see a flicker of fear in her eyes. How long have I been asleep? Is it today still or tomorrow? And what has happened to Saoirse, to the mouse of a woman I have known? She seems taller and her shoulders hold her head a little higher.

'Do you know where I have been, Nanna?'

I shake my head and turn to stare at the wall. It seems as though the stream of talk yesterday has further hollowed me out. I am an empty husk. I could not have imagined how the process I set in train would exhaust my frail reserves of strength. For hours on end and late into the night Saoirse sat by my bed and I wheezed, sentence by sentence, the story of my parents' deaths, the flight from Clonsast. I wept to speak of Nuala and Malachy, her *great-grandparents*, while she had remained dry-eyed and hard, as though hearing the story of a stranger woman, or the plot of one of Mr Dickens's novels.

'Guess where I have been.'

She moves to the other side of the bed and stands where I cannot avoid looking at her. 'I have been to the port registrar, asking about the *Australasia*. And most helpful he was too. In one hour, he is going to show me the manifest.'

She expects a response, a remonstration; that I will beg her to desist. I have steeled myself to resist her pleas for privacy, for letting sleeping dogs lie. But she is a different woman now.

'I want to know the full story, Nanna. Don't you dare die before the story is finished. You are the one who kicked the devil's cage, sending him screaming and whirling round as he does at the zoo when the keepers taunt him and poke him with a sharp pole. I have always hated the sound of the Tasmanian devil, and now you have unleashed his crazed chattering in my mind. While you slept the sleep of the soon-to-be-dead, I lay awake all night long and wondered if I am not, in fact, alone in this world.'

I stare at her, for I do not know what is coming next and I don't recognise this hard, angry woman.

'Do you understand me, Nanna? I'm going to see the manifest with my own eyes. You cannot have it both ways, Nanna. You cannot ask me to believe that in 1848, orphan Sally Mahon left the parish of Clonsast at the age of fourteen years, and in 1849 widowed Sally Gordon stepped off the *Australasia*. Courted, married, widowed, birthed and emigrated in the space of a twelvemonth? You must have met Jack Gordon here, in Tasmania. I know it. I want to know everything you can tell me about Jack Gordon. I want to find the rest of my family.'

She steps closer, grips my wrist loosely and attempts to shake an answer out of me. I have all the strength of an injured fairy-wren. She could crush me with one hand. Instead, she slips her right hand under me and settles me in a sitting position. Under the weight of the bright white eiderdown which she has returned to the bed since my fever broke, I am tiny.

'I have told you,' I say. 'Forget about Jack Gordon. I won't go to my grave carrying the Gordon name.'

I am frightened now, frightened of what I have already done to Saoirse and of what remains to be done. I have always been the colossus of the house, the axis around which they all orbit. As she probes deeper into my lies and half-truths, do I risk uncoupling her from the secure Southern Cross of her life, the constant and loving constellation which has guided her for forty-five years?

'Nanna, you can go to meet your maker under whichever name you choose, but for the love of God, do not leave me this way. I'm going right now to see the manifest. If Sally Mahon stepped off the *Australasia* a single child, not a widowed woman, and my mother had not yet been born, I want to know the truth about your husband. How did you meet Jack Gordon and where is he buried? Had he brothers or sisters? Were there nieces and nephews? And what about my great-aunt Patsy? How does an orphaned only child acquire a sister? I want to know what I can about myself and there is no one left to ask but you. Either you are lying to me on your deathbed, or you have been lying to me all my life. Which is it, Nanna?'

Chapter Ten

Newbridge, Friday, 24 November, 1848

Despite the gurgling and pains in her belly from the mutton, and her hard bed in the ditch, Sally managed to toss and turn and sleep until early light. As the feeble winter sun struggled to rise over the hedgerows, she turned her back on Nás Na Ríogh, the Place of the Kings.

'The only royalty left these days is them bastards in England, the young queen as it now is,' she muttered. 'I'd look well throwing myself on the mercy of the gentry of Nás Na Ríogh.'

The old laws and customs, the old language itself, had all but died in this part of the country, so close to Dublin. In all of Joly's lands she had known only a few wrinkled crones who spoke Irish. The language lived on only in the place names and the family names, the Os and the Macs. She knew that the priest of Nás Na Ríogh would be cut from the same cloth as Father Peter Dunne. He would have Sally cast herself on her knees and pray for the forgiveness of the sins that had killed the potato harvest, then he would push her through the dark oak doors of the workhouse and go home to his breakfast of milk and wheaten bread. Her mind was clear, she would stay and take her chances here.

A dozen head of fat, glossy cattle rose up slowly out of the thick morning mist that clung to the damp meadows in this low-lying plain, hoisting their arses awkwardly to the rising sun before lunging forward with their necks and bodies to struggle to their feet. She followed them to the slippery, mud-churned bank of a slow-trickling sheugh at the far end of the meadow, but was too afraid to join them or to hoosh them away, and had to stand aside, the tongue stuck to the roof of her mouth, her eyeballs dry and gritty, until each of the great beasts had had his fill and stepped away to tear at the short grass with giant, head-shaking gulps.

She plunged her face right into the stream, the shock and the chill leaving her gasping and weak. Hateful though the task was, she must clean herself properly, rid herself of the cloying stink, if she was to find the work that Newbridge promised. She slipped out of her dress and shook her head to see the state of it. Her mother had always washed the Mahon's clothes regularly, twice each year, once before the feast of Easter, when the long winter was finally passed, and again at Samhain, gathering all the garments she could find, and layering them up in preparation for the snow and wind. Now Sally's dress was fit only for a scarecrow, and filthy.

She couldn't wash the dress for, at this late time of the year, it would take a full day, or even two, to dry, spread out on a hedge, and would attract attention. The most she could do was immerse herself in the freezing trickle of water, scrubbing with a handful of dock leaves, washing away every trace of the diarrhoea and the graveyard. Her toenails were black and she took a long thorn from the blackthorn tree and pared out the worst of the rim of filth. She rebound her hair with its rag. She could do no more.

Right, Sally, let's go.

The road was well-kept and flat, with no big ruts, and a wide grass verge for foot traffic. Already, women and girls from the farms around were returning from the early morning deliveries, their egg baskets and milk pails swinging empty in the crooks of their elbows.

'God be with you,' Sally said to a friendly looking girl of her own age. 'Where would a body find work around the town?' The girl drew her shawl close round her, curled her lips and looked away, before hurrying on.

One girl, older than the others, old enough even to be a wife, perhaps, tossed her white-scarfed head, made the sign against the evil eye at Sally and crossed the highway to the verge on the other side. Sally tried hard to catch her eye, then dropped her head as the girl shouted, 'Fly away home, little wren, and don't be out here, fouling up the paths for decent women.'

Sally trudged on. It was only a short stroll back to the town from her hiding place, and the grass was pleasant and cool to the foot. When she reached the busy streets of the town, it was a different matter – the cold, or steaming, shit of horses, dogs and children, lay on the pavements and roadway, and she picked her steps carefully, hoping to present herself as clean as possible to the women of the town.

No one spoke as she walked along the wide footpath, although a man winked and a fine lady gathered her skirt close about her as she swept past with a rustle. All the length of the eye's distance, on Sally's left-hand side, the high, grey stones of the barrack's outer wall stretched, featureless except here and there where a distant chimney protruded above. The stones oozed damp in the shadow they cast, and the faint low sun did not reach her to warm away her shivers. When she reached the gates of the barracks, she was shaking as though palsied.

'Where d'you think you're going, then?' A soldier boy, barely old enough to shave, snapped his heels together and then sauntered out from behind the barrier laid in the path. 'No doxies in the daytime, and don't be caught in the night, neither, 'less you want Father Francis to take the skin off your back with a blackthorn stick.'

'Oh no, sir, the blessings of God on you, sir.' She bobbed a little drop-curtsey as her mother used to do when Mistress Martha Joly's carriage passed by on the roads and lanes around Clonbullogue. The soldier stifled a laugh and tried to look fierce. 'I'm looking for work. Is there any chance of a start?' She stood as tall as she could manage and lifted her chin until she had to slit her eyes to see his grinning face.

'I am a fine strong girl, fourteen years of age, and in need of work.'

'A fine strong girl? And I'm Lord Cardigan, come to gather up the hussars from training and take them back to England!'

He spat thoughtfully on the ground and sighed before answering.

'Listen, there's more 'n a thousand men here behind this wall. What do you think we do all day?' His shoulders slumped. 'It's not all square-bashing and prize fights, you know. We bake our own bread, brew our own beer, wash our own duds and the officers each has a batman to care for him. There's no need for women here, for the British soldier is as good as a woman with a packet of starch and a smoothing iron.'

'Oi! Stand to attention, Private!'

The young soldier's ears and cheeks flamed as an officer strode towards them, his buttons and boots flashing, gold braid on his shoulders.

'What the bally hell are you doing, Private? Back to your post.' The officer's voice fell to a vicious hiss. 'Get away out of it, girl, we've no need for your likes on this side of the road. Get away back to the she-barracks where you came from.'

His wide-flung arm gestured to the other side of the broad street where inns and eating houses lined the way, and when he stepped closer to Sally, she spun as quickly as she could and raced across the street.

She started at the far end of town, and worked her way back towards the bridge, rapping upon every door, bar the one inn she had so nearly been turned away from the day before. The women in the kitchens of the eating houses and inns reeled back from the sight of her, if she even made it through the doorways into the kitchens. They laughed at her lack of skill. *Tell me your receipt for a fine wheaten bread.* She shrugged hopelessly. *Can you bleach a stained sheet? Can you darn a hole in a pillowcase?* 'What's a pillowcase?' she asked, just before the lady of the house closed the door in her face.

She crossed over to where a shaft of weak sunlight barely warmed the stone step outside an important-looking building, sat down and gathered a list of her abilities in her head. She could sweep a hut with a bunch of twigs and bracken. She could dig in soft ground and bed up growing potatoes in a lazy bed, if ever a potato was to grow in the land again. She could mind Brigid's children, laugh with them, scramble over the sweet-scented flowering summer bog with them and pull them out of the ditch when they tumbled in.

She could comb her father's hair with her fingers, and always took great care to crush any lice that she found, grinding them between the nails of her thumb and first finger, so he would be comfortable.

She thought of him under the ground, beside her mother, two of the only people in Clonsast parish ever she knew to be buried without a proper wake. There had been no wake, not only from the lack of even as much money as would pay for just a half barrel of porter, but more so for the fear their neighbours had of the fever.

No one had come. She'd kept vigil alone, eyes drooping, wall-falling with hunger and exhaustion. The words of the Rosary had died on her lips for tiredness and lack of water. She couldn't be sure, even still, that she had never dropped her guard fully during those two long, lonesome nights. Perhaps she had closed her eyes momentarily, just long enough for the fairies — the banshee and the pooka — to sneak into the house and suck the souls clean out from the unguarded corpses. Even Brigid and Molly, a shout away across the field and ditch, had kept clear.

During this long year past, Nuala Mahon and Sally had walked with Brigid to the boneyard, wailing and keening, supporting her under both oxters. Three times they had walked with her as, month after hungry month, her three youngest children had withered away, for lack of potatoes and mother's milk.

The need for coffins was so severe in King's County, and the timber for them so short in supply in the flat bogland, that Brian, Mary and baby Seanie Deegan had each been piled in their turn into the newly designed trick-coffin. *Back her up, left a bit, left, steady. Stop!* The undertaker's man had called out to his helper, who tugged and dragged at the horse's head until the coffin cart was in position.

Pull the handle, for the love of God, cried the undertaker, *the smell would kill a body stone dead*.

The false bottom of the coffin slid away, tumbling the small, stiff bodies down into the big children's pit, full of lime and corpses. Brigid sank to her knees and howled like a dog with distemper. Nuala and Sally had hauled her to her feet and half-dragged her home, Molly trailing behind with the remaining little ones.

But Sally's parents had died not of hunger, but of the shameful, catching fever, and not even Brigid had been brave enough to walk with her to the paupers' plot.

Until Sally tasted the salt tang of snot in her mouth, she didn't know she was weeping.

Chapter Eleven

Hobart, October 1919, Sally

Crying again. It seems I will spend my last few days on earth crying, for all that I have been content for the bulk of my life. I cried enough in my childhood to last a lifetime, but here in the Australasia I sang and smiled and laughed.

The tears are leaking out of the corners of my eyes, running across my cheeks and pooling inside my ears, a strange and uncomfortable sensation. With an effort I wipe my cheeks with my right hand. If Saoirse were here, she would dry my face and raise me up.

But she is not here, she has gone to the registrar seeking answers and she will gain only questions.

The time has come to tell the tale in earnest.

What she will do with it, I can only guess. Why did we not tell her the truth from the start?

Chapter Twelve

Newbridge, Friday, 24 November 1848

'Get away out of it,' a thin, pock-marked woman screamed in Sally's face. 'What are you thinking, bringing her to darken our door, Grainne? Don't bring that road-rat into the cabin – bringing the fever into the place.'

Behind the woman, two small children rolled on the filth of the floor. The hut had clearly not been swept out or cleaned recently, the hum that leaked out through the door made Sally gag, and tears started from her eyes with the ammonia reek.

'Shush, now, shush, Mother, and listen to me.' The other, younger woman gripping Sally's upper arm pushed her forward towards the doorway. 'Can't you see she's fresh? Can't you see?'

'In the name of God and his holy mother, it's true,' said Sally, 'I'm not sick. There's no hint of the fever upon me. I know what road fever looks like, for a starving, stray vagabond brought it to my own village and it carried off both my parents.'

She blessed herself, but the two women didn't, and she should have known enough from that to take to her heels and run. 'But that was more than a week ago and I'm clean, I swear it.'

Grainne loosened her grip slightly, leaving red angry fingerprints on the paleness of Sally's flesh. 'I found her sitting weeping on the doorstep of the officers' chapel, and isn't she lucky it was me found her, and not a constable? Or that bastard Father Byrne.' She glanced at the remnants of Sally's filthy dress and whispered.

'She's straight in from the country and not been on the town before, I'd stake my oath on it. Worth a good few shillings, fresh, for her first, if she was cleaned up a bit.'

Martha stood aside and allowed her daughter to half push, half drag Sally into the enveloping gloom. Sally had found her way into the she-barracks.

Just behind the bustling, wide street of Newbridge, just beyond the yards and cesspools of the fine, respectable inns and the purveyors of clothing to the War Department, pulsed a whole ragged, broken world belonging to women. Huts and hovels, curtained alcoves, darkened alleys, all teemed with women and children, each dirtier than the other. The cries of the infants shattered the peace of the day and the wailing of their mothers threatened to wake the dead during the night. There was never a potato to be seen, nor a fresh lump of bread, but porter and whiskey abounded. The whiskey came in jugs, the porter came by the bucketful. And it came in the dark hours, swinging, in the hands of uniformed men.

★ ★ ★

'Not one drop now, Grainne,' Martha counselled her daughter every evening as dusk fell. 'Not one drop of drink is to pass your lips before the coin is handed over. The whiskey is well enough, and what is to happen will happen easier and less painful, maybe, with a few sups in the belly. But never before the payment.'

Grainne sighed and looked out into the November drizzle.

'I know,' she whispered, sullen, her black hair hanging lank as she dropped her gaze to the stinking floor. 'I know, never raise the glass nor the skirt before the money is in me hand, or I'll end up on the Curragh, with the wrens.'

Sally pricked up her ears. This was not the first time Grainne had mentioned the wrens, a class of wild woman, who lived close by on the broad expanse of the Curragh plain. They lived in groups and they sheltered under the roofs of the broad-growing furze bushes, like the little birds from whom they took their name. Grainne was frightened of the wrens, but Sally could see that she admired them too.

For three days, Sally was kept busy. She minded Martha's small children, Davey and Peggy, and found that they knew nothing; neither letters, nor prayer, nor curse. She trembled to think of the children, without even a Hail Mary to stand between them and the gates of hell. She taught them the holy words, and some of the simpler curses. It was all she had to give them.

She had other jobs too. Each day she walked to the tanners' yard, carrying a slopping porcelain pot carefully in one hand, the other arm extended like a bird's wing, holding her barely upright against the weight. There was no class of muck that could not find a use in the tanners' trade. Newbridge housed a thousand soldiers and eight hundred horses, and had no shortage of chamber pots. Even so, the tanners would sometimes give Sally a penny, and then Martha and Grainne jeered at their neighbours and lorded it over some of the other women of the she-barracks, who were too poor even to have a pot to piss in.

Sally was no longer a girl. Her name was Sam and she wore a pair of ragged trousers and what little hair she had was piled up under a cap. Martha said the world was a dangerous place, and more so for young girls of Sally's age. In truth, she was safe enough, for during daylight hours the soldiers were mainly confined to barracks, the sound of hundreds of marching feet echoing through the town while the men tramped round and round the vast expanse of the drill-ground, and the *Left, left, left-right-left* of the sergeants major roaring like Satan himself. And by night Sally was hidden and well protected, shivering in a large wooden box at the back of the hut, with the two sleeping little ones, Davey and Peggy, pressed close against her breast for warmth and for the comfort of a human touch.

The noises in the cabin at night bewildered and terrified Sally in equal measure. Martha warned her, 'Keep yer nose from sniffin' out what doesn't concern you, and above all keep yer beak shut, and stay hidden in the night.'

Martha's eye was freshly swollen and there was a red pattern of angry welts round her throat – they had not been there when Peggy, Davey and Sally had hidden away the night before.

'When our gentlemen guests come of an evening, they mustn't find you,

Sam, for I can't answer as to what might happen to a nice, fresh girl like you. And I haven't money to waste – you'll have to bring your price fresh, as soon as I can find the loan of a decent dress for you, and that'll not be easy round here.'

Martha hawked painfully, bent double, hand clutching at the damaged tissues of her throat, and spat into the miserable, smoky collection of damp twigs that burned in the centre of the room. Sally backed away and nodded, clutching the stinking pisspot close in front, like a charm or hex to ward off evil.

Martha needn't have feared, Sally would sooner have plunged her arm into that sad excuse for a fire, than make her presence felt when the soldiers came at night.

The first two days, no more than three or four men had come during the whole evening, to sit by the fire and drink, but last night, while she had hidden out of sight, it seemed a multitude, some voices coming, some going, some constant throughout the hours. The men had been singing old songs, 'Johnny is Gone For a Soldier', a few verses of 'The Recruiting Sergeant'. The words got coarser, the voices louder, and slurring, as the hours wore on. And then the fighting started.

Sally's panicked breath whooped and gasped, echoing in the big wooden box where she crouched with her hands over the children's ears.

'One at a time, one at a time!' Grainne was shrieking. 'Christ, stop dragging at me, there's time enough for all.'

The sound of a sharp slap rang through the darkness, and then the soft, pounding, meaty noises that Sally had heard before, but shot through, this night, with curses, shrieks, roars and blows.

Martha was wheedling, cajoling, 'For the love of God, gentlemen, isn't there the two of us here? Sure, come on over in the corner, and I'll give you ease while you wait.'

But her words were wasted, for now Sally could clearly hear the sounds of men fighting, the few bits of stools and the table falling to the ground as they leapt to their feet. And above all, a thin keening whine from Grainne, punctuated by gasps and groans. Sally nuzzled her head into Peggy's thin, barely covered shoulder and slipped her hand over Davey's mouth.

'No, no!' shrieked Grainne. 'Wait. Stop. No. No. Stop. No!'

'Gentlemen, please, for the love of God,' cried her mother.

A crash as a bottle fell to the ground and smashed. A grunt and a choking sound as a man slammed his fist into the whiskey-full belly of his erstwhile friend, sending the other man to the floor.

'No!' screamed Grainne. 'No! No!'

Sally prayed and sent up entreaties to Saint Brochan, Saint Patrick, Saint Brigid and every other saint she had heard of, until she heard the merciful sound of the curfew bell, a few minutes to midnight. Any man of Her Majesty's army found wandering the streets of Newbridge after midnight by the military police, with their sticks and polished boots, would live to regret it. All arguments forgotten, half-carrying, half-dragging each other, the men staggered out into the pitch-dark, shit-fouled laneway, weaved their way back to the respectability of Main Street, and in through the barrier at the gate of the barracks.

And Sally's prayer followed them – that an evil fate might befall them and all belonging to them; that they might depart from this place quickly, to fight and to bleed on a foreign field. And that they might die roaring.

Martha, to her credit, had bent over Grainne's cot for the most part of the next day, sponging and wiping, and stroking her face. She'd made an effort to straighten the worst tangles from her daughter's hair with an old bone comb, but each time she teased the teeth of the comb through, another clump of hair fell out, some matted with blood, some with scraps of scalp attached.

Now she stood up straight and glared at Sally, still standing motionless, trying to make sense of last night's brawl.

'Stop standing there gawking like a gom. Take that pot to the tanners' yard,' Martha called to Sally, 'and beg them for a penny, or two pennies on trust, they must know your face by now. And keep that cap pulled well down.'

Sally hefted the porcelain pot, which had somehow survived the melee of the night. Elsewhere in the cabin the evidence of the brawl was clear to see. The leg of one stool was charred through from falling in the fire at some stage, and another had a leg ripped clean off, when one of the men, in his madness, had thrashed all round him, landing blows on friend and foe alike.

'Will I take the children with me? Give you a few moments' peace?'

'Do that, and hurry back with the penny, for Christ's sake, for one of those bad bastards must have made off with all the coins that were paid over last night, before the rí-rá of it all.'

Sally pushed the two small children out through the waxed canvas door covering, setting it carefully ajar to allow some of the smoke to escape from the cabin, then smiled brightly at Peggy and Davey.

'Now, we're going for a walk.'

Peggy held Davey's hand, he held Sally's, and she balanced the full pot in her free hand as they set off down the long, filthy stretch of the back street. Women leaned over the half-doors of their hovels, or twitched aside the canvas which served in place of a door, and called to their children or puffed on their pipes. The gutter ran with the waste of women and children and splashed up onto Sally's legs. Wrapped round her waist, under the itching, chafing trousers was the ragged, old dress in which she had left Clonsast, less than a week earlier, and a lifetime ago. And in the folds of the dress – each one carefully separated, held in a twist or fold, to stop a clink or chink betraying her – was every coin Martha possessed. Crouched last night in the safety of the wooden box, Sally had heard the crash of the wooden bowl against the wall and the rain of copper falling down onto the floor of the cabin as the table was sent spinning across the room. For ten heart-pounding minutes at first light this morning she had crawled through the stinking rushes on her belly, her probing, seeking fingers sifting through the rotting detritus to recover the scattered coins, while Martha and Grainne slept the pitiful, tortured sleep of those rocked to slumber by the combination of whiskey, exhaustion and violence.

Sally had no clear picture of what exactly she was escaping, but she wanted no part of it. Stealing Martha's money was a sin, she knew that for certain, but God would forgive her, when he tallied it up against the two innocent souls Sally was determined to save for him. She had thought for a moment of leaving Davey with his mother – surely any woman would keep a boy child from harm, for the sake of the work he might find and the coin he might provide in years to come, but Martha had made no effort to save Grainne, and her other daughter would surely grow up to be equally at risk. Sally was escaping, Peggy was coming with her, and Sally knew Peggy wouldn't come without Davey.

A mother who didn't teach her own children their prayers, sure they're better off without her. They don't even know how to curse, or ward off the evil eye. Better off with me.

And if she said it often enough, it would become true.

She carried the heavy pot away with her also, because it was true that the tanners *might* give her a penny, and one more wouldn't hurt. A twinge of guilt tried to make its way into her consciousness, and fear too, of course – a girl could end up in prison for a lesser crime than the stealing of a valuable pot, but she would give it to Peggy, when the time came, a keepsake from her real mother, whose memory, Sally was sure, would fade with time.

The tanners refused to give Sally a penny, and she had to slop the potful of piss over the wall into the fast-flowing waters of the River Liffey, but one of the men threw her a hard rind of cheese he was chewing which, despite the stink, was better than nothing.

'Oh Sally, we can't eat that. The hum off it would make a body sick,' said Davey.

'Watch me,' said Sally, nibbling a few specks of cheese from the rind. 'You've not been hungry enough if you can't eat this.'

'But the smell!'

'There's a reason tanners only marry tanners' daughters – it's a stench a body would have to spend a lifetime getting used to.' Sally offered the rind to Peggy who scraped off the last remaining shreds with her tiny, sharp milk teeth.

Sally took a small, sticky hand in each of hers and, skirting right behind the narrow strip of town, they walked across the meadows, muck and slime squelching up between their freezing toes, and headed towards the high, distant mountains, already white-capped and glittering, for, just a few miles in that direction, lay the wide open plains of the Curragh.

Davey and Peggy screamed and whooped, bending to touch the squishing, slippery muck and laughing when Sally showed them how to fling a dried pat of cow clap so that it flew in a low, long arc and shattered upon hitting the ground. They gathered all the dried clap they could find, cramming it into the pot.

'My mother told me once that people in other parts, lacking the good turf of King's County, would burn dried cow shit in their hearths,' Sally said. 'How I laughed. I never before thought it might be true, or that anyone might be so poor that they didn't have their own row of turf. We'll find out soon enough if it will burn.'

'When are we going home, Sally?'

'Oh, soon, soon. Don't you remember that Grainne is sick? We'll just go a little further, stay away one night, as your mother asked me.'

'And we'll go back tomorrow?'

'Of course. It's just an adventure.'

Behind them lay the rich farmlands and the bustling town of Newbridge. A wide, flat, desolate expanse of tight-cropped grassland stretched far into the distance on every side. Even the flat land of Sally's home on the boglands in King's County had not prepared her for the limitless sweep of the Curragh of Kildare. Sheep moved across the landscape, grazing the grass down almost to the soil, and small boys with willow wands guarded them. Furze bushes dotted the plains, the last of their yellow blooms illuminating the early dusk. Dozens of miles away to their left, the wind rose on the snow-capped peaks of the Dublin mountains, and swept, unimpeded, down the tree-studded mountainsides, across the wide plain, meeting no obstacle until it slammed straight into the three small figures, standing, holding hands, nearly naked in the November twilight.

'I'm cold, Sally.'

Sally picked Peggy up and wrapped her frail arms around her, rubbing her cheek upon the child's cheek.

'Hush, pet. Don't call me Sally, I'm your big brother Sam now, and that's what you must tell anyone who asks.'

Sally knelt down awkwardly with her load – although Peggy was as light as an empty tick in her arms she was contrary, and she struggled and twisted against Sally's grip. Sally looked Davey close in the eye. 'Did you hear me, Davey? You heard your mother tell me I'm to call myself Sam. And from now on I am Sam, even when we're alone together. The more people think I'm your brother, the better off we'll all be. They'll be looking for a girl and two children. If they're looking at all.'

'Who? Who'll be looking for us?' His bright brown eyes pricked her conscience and she grew angry and full of shame. 'Who'll be looking? When are we going home to Mammy?'

She took him by the tiny thinness of his wrist and dragged him away from the roadway, prying eyes and curious ears. The three walked towards the furze bushes to find the homes of the wrens of the Curragh of whom Sally had heard Grainne speak.

As they walked, the weak rays of the low winter sun glinted off a shimmering tent city in the foreground. Rank upon rank of white and grey canvas tents stretched into the distance. The guy ropes thrummed and sang in the bitter howling gusts, keening a strange high-pitched song over the sound of a steam train disappearing into the distance to their right, on its journey to King's County and beyond, or to Dublin, for all Sally knew. She thought for a moment of the pennies and halfpennies wrapped around her waist.

If I send the children home, put them in the right direction, I might get a ticket on the next engine, and end up back more or less where I started, near the graves of my own people, where I could lie down and die in peace.

'What's them things, Sal...Sam?' Peggy pointed to the tents, which stretched for half a mile and covered dozens of acres. Her filthy, snub-nosed face was close to Sally's and her trusting gaze swept over the older girl, who felt the cold bleakness of the orphan drop suddenly off her narrow shoulders. Her heart filled with the need for warmth, the longing for company, for joy and childish prattle. Kneeling once again, she gathered both children into an embrace.

'Them's the soldiers' tents, Peggy. That's where they live now, the ones there's no space for in the barracks in Newbridge. They plant theirselves out here in the Curragh, and if it's good enough for them, it'll be good enough for us.'

'You're crushing the life out of me,' Davey said, wriggling and squirming in her arms.

Sally had never held anything tighter, or more dear. Those two wriggling, stinking children, with their sores and their scabs, were now the most precious people on earth. She shrugged away the memory of the whistling locomotive, the siren call of the lands of home. Her parents were dead. At last she could believe it. Her parents were dead. The weight of realisation bowed her face to the grass, the smell of sheep shit fresh and close. A gaping void opened in her breast and she filled it with the two innocent lives she held in her care.

★ ★ ★

Sally needed to find a wren, and she needed to find her fast. For all Grainne's scorn of the wrens and their wretched, outdoor life on the Curragh, there'd been a hint of admiration barely hidden in her voice. *Oh, hardy women, the wrens. Oh, there'd be no messin' with the wrens, sure they'd pull a man's arm off and beat him to death with it. No, they wouldn't take kindly to the sorts of treatment we do sometimes take here in the town. And every damn one of them carries a blade.*

Sally must find a wren, and offer themselves to her, buying their safety and a hiding place with all the stolen money. She had fourteen pence and the pot.

It was impossible to go back to Newbridge; the risk of meeting Martha was too high if she entered the she-barracks, and the risk of the constabulary was too high on the main streets. On their first morning, as the children tossed and dreamed fretfully in the shade of a dense furze bush, Sally had walked to a small market outside the soldiers' camp. Her first purchase was a box of Lucifers — long, sulphurous matches — and nearly the entire box was spent before the meagre pile of moss, tinder and twig they had gathered deep inside a prickly furze bush finally sputtered to sullen, smoky life. For the next few days, feeding the fire became the primary goal of each day, and it was a bitter tyrant, constantly threatening either to consume the wretched shelter or to die entirely.

Sally cooked a bitter soup of nettles each day in the chamber pot suspended above the flames, and she taught Davey how fine a line existed between a heat great enough to stir the green, slimy liquid to a gentle bubble, and the heat that would crack the thick porcelain, leaving them shiftless.

'I hate it here,' he whispered, just loud enough for her to hear. 'I wish Mammy was still alive, and we had bread, and could sleep warm and safe in the wooden box.'

'I wish that too, Davey.' Sally looked him straight in his pinched, six-year old face and the lies came tripping out, as if she didn't even know she had an immortal soul to lose. 'I told you, your mother's cabin burnt down, I heard it while you were sleeping and I was at the market, buying the matches. Isn't it just the grace of God that I had you with me, on our adventure? Or you'd be dead too, like your mother and sister, instead of here, with your fill of good soup.'

Peggy and Sally gleaned the nettles from the plains and Peggy wept and sighed all the while. 'It hurts me, Sally.' She held her hands outwards, red, angry weals raised up across her palms and the balls of her fingers. 'It hurts me a lot and the soup tastes bad. I want bread.'

'Well, there's no point in wanting. *Wanting* stuck a feather in the ground and thought it would grow a chicken.'

The child sighed and the trembling of the small chin made Sally want to die, or to take back the harshness of the words that hung on the still air. She rubbed a dock leaf on the poor swollen hands, for all the good that did, and returned to her own plucking. 'There's precious few nettles left anyway, with all these hungry sheep, so be a good girl and pick as many as you can.' Peggy raised her face again and tried to smile, her short fat fingers reaching out for a half-chewed stalk.

How Sally longed for a twist of salt. *Half a loaf is better than no bread,* she had heard the old people say, and now she said it too, as they sat outside their nest, drinking the soup, straight from the pot once it had cooled enough to hold. 'Eat up the nice soup, it's good for you, and will make you strong like the sheep.'

'I could take a big stone,' Davey said, idly watching the sheep and their guardians in the distance. 'I could whack a sheep on the head, I think. I could find a small, weak one.'

'And then what would we do? For we've no knife. Would we rip it apart with our teeth and have it raw?' Sally hated the sound of the angry words as they spilled from her mouth, but they vomited out in a fast, angry flow and she seemed powerless to halt them. 'And most important of all, the warden would come and take us all to prison. It's one thing to leave half the people in the country starve to death, but it's something else indeed to steal the landlord's sheep.'

Tears started to the boy's eyes and were trembling on the feathery tips of the black lashes when she grabbed his arm and shook gently. 'Quiet, Davey. Peggy, for the love of God, be quiet.' The skin of her scalp crawled and itched and she knew beyond doubt that they were no longer alone. 'There's someone coming. It's a man.'

She started to her feet and saw, hundreds of yards away still, but without question approaching them, a figure, well wrapped against the winter's chill. 'It's a soldier.' She put her finger to her lips and the terror on her face spread a quick contagion to the two children. Their cheeks drained to a ghastly grey, the colour of a winter rain cloud.

They scrambled back inside to the fire, spilling some of the soup out of the pot as they pushed their way through the fierce thorns into the hollow dome of the bush. The sharp prickles of the furze bush tore long scratches down their arms and legs on the way. Peggy whimpered like a thrashed pup, at the sound of a stick whacking at the furze bush, the leaves shivering and some falling to the ground, bare and nearly dry under the thick encircling roof of branches. Sally gently put her hand over Peggy's mouth, but it was a pointless gesture — they could not hide their presence, for a thin curl of smoke was percolating its way through the furzy roof, and the acrid smell of charring wood was unmistakeable.

At last, the whacking and prodding stopped and voice rang out. 'Come away out of that, and let the fox see the rabbit.'

'Merciful God, it's a woman,' whispered Davey.

'Maybe we'll stay put where we are, missus?' Sally said, her voice trembling like the bleat of an hour-old lamb.

'Well, you can maybe do that. Maybe you can please yourself.' There was a silence and a hesitation. 'Yer none of mine kith or kin, and you can do as you please. But, would it interest you to know that the ranger is out, with a brigade, raiding nests and burning them to the ground?' The voice sniffed and added, 'But ye'll know yer own minds, of course.'

'Maybe we'll just stay here and take our chances?'

'You're more than welcome. Stay and burn, or end up in the workhouse, it's no skin off my nose. I do have a rabbit stew on the boil in my own nest, but if you're not hungry ... '

Davey made a bolt for the small tunnel they used as an entrance, and wriggled his way through to the outside. Cursing under her breath, Sally took Peggy's arm and followed him.

'Jesus, look at the cut of you,' the woman said, 'three wild savages.'

Their nest didn't even have a piece of cloth to drape over the roof, like the others they had seen from a distance, so they'd been wet through more than once since setting up camp. The wood smoke had blackened their skin.

'You look more like animals than children, and you smell worse.'

The woman was well wrapped in a black woollen shawl and as she held her skirts up out of the mud she revealed a pair of real leather boots with many shining buttons and small blocky heels which gave her an extra inch or two. Sally shivered as she stared at the well-dressed stranger.

'So here you are, the new nest of childer that has every wren on the Curragh wondering.' She turned to Sally, then jabbed her in the chest with a forefinger, so lightning quick and unexpected that the girl ended up arse-over-tit, sprawled in the short grass.

'What brings you here? Only little boys are welcome on the Curragh. Boys your age soon grow up to be men. And men is one thing the wrens is not short of. Men and trouble.'

In her left hand the woman held a stout ash stick, with which she had been beating the branches of the furze bush. It would have made a powerful weapon. Yet she had not raised it, but instead had jabbed Sally with her finger. On this one act of kindness, Sally weighed and judged her next step; should it be the truth, or to continue the pretence?

'And what is to happen to me, missus, if no boys my age are allowed on the Curragh? Would you tell me where you think I might go, and what to do with the children?'

The woman reached down a hand, as brown, calloused and short-nailed as Sally's own, and hauled her to her feet. 'In the name of God, I couldn't care less. Take yerself to hell, if ye've a mind to. Just clear on out of this.'

She gestured to the wide horizon out of which rose thick plumes of grey smoke, dotted here and there across the wide expanse of the Curragh, in places Sally had never seen smoke before, too thick and dense to be campfires.

'He's doing it? The ranger's burning the wrens' nests?'

'Well, he'll not burn mine.' She laughed and smoothed her dress-front. She looked warm. Sally couldn't remember the last time she had been properly warm.

'Oh, no, he'll not burn mine, for I have paid my *tax* to him, both in the coin and in the flesh. But he'll be along here soon enough, and I take it you have no coin.' She smiled strangely. 'And although there's plenty around here who would get up on a boy, he's not one of them. So you've absolutely nothing to give.'

And that was the crux. Remain as a boy and be driven from the Curragh by the wrens. Remain as a girl and be driven out by the warden. Sally had spent a week growing accustomed to the itchy woollen trousers, to the extra bit of warmth and to the comfort and ease of striding easily, without a skirt to catch upon the weeds, or to trap underfoot. Now this plump, warmly dressed woman was telling her it was not a man's world after all.

Sally pulled off her cap and dropped a curtsey, swishing her wisps of long, dirty hair, although she knew this was not the kind of woman Nuala Mahon would have bent the knee to.

'Sally is my name, if you please, missus, and this is my brother Davey, and the little one is Peggy.'

Hands on her well-covered hips, the woman walked a full circle around Sally, looking her up and down. At the speed of the wind, she reached out from behind and pinched the girl's chest hard, twisting each nipple till she shrieked. Sally gasped and flinched, but the woman looked more curious than vicious.

'Age?'

'Fourteen years, missus.'

'Fourteen years, and as flat as a lathe. Not a hint of a bud on you. Are you in your flowers, yet, girl? I'd warrant you're not.'

'In my flowers?'

'Your flowers, the bleeding? The monthly bleeding?' She stopped and rubbed her hands together, the image of a hard-dealing market-man fixing a price.

'You don't even know what I'm on about. As green as God's good grass. Oh, you'll do very nicely, I've been waiting for the likes of you.' She held out her hand to take Sally's, which was limp and unresisting, and then Sally looked at the little ones.

'Not alone, missus, wherever I go, the children goes too.'

A struggle played out on the woman's face, one grimace followed by another.

'Oh, come on to hell, the whole boiling lot of you. Sure, the babies can come too.'

Chapter Thirteen

Hobart, October 1919, Saoirse

'Well, we certainly don't have a Sarah Mahon listed.'

'I knew it. She was already married when she came over. How could she suddenly have become Mahon, after all these years?'

Mr Milligan, the registrar, says nothing, but I can see the look of bored resignation in his eyes. He thinks I will be here all day, wasting his time on my fool's errand. He thinks I am a silly woman. Mortified, I fall silent.

'Now, let's try Sarah Gordon,' he says.

I smile and try to look calm again. 'It's rather complicated, you see, I'm not quite sure which name she would have been using at that time.'

'Gordon … Gordon … let's see. Flanaghan … Furey … Gandon … Gordon.' Mr Milligan smiles and taps his beautifully manicured index finger happily on the page marked out in rows and columns. 'There you are, my dear. Your grandmother. Sarah Gordon. Embarked 26 June 1849, Kingstown, County Dublin.'

'Is her date of birth listed?

'21 June 1834.'

'That's what she said, but that's too young. Is she a married woman?'

'Married? My dear, she was just a child. Not married, and in the company of her sister, Eleanor McMurrough, known as Gordon. Eleanor was a once-married woman, a widow, perhaps that's where the confusion arises?'

'Not Eleanor. No. Her sister's name was Patsy. Patsy O'Hanlon.' I can hardly hear my words emerge. The sound of the blood surging in my head drowns out Mr Milligan's refined, educated voice, and the pounding of my heart in my throat makes me want to vomit right down onto the pages of the manifest of the ship *Australasia*. The *prison* ship, *Australasia*.

'Patsy? Patricia, I daresay?' He looks and looks again. 'There are several young women of that name listed in the manifest, a common enough name among Irish women of that time, being the patron saint, of course. There she is; Patricia O'Hanlon. But certainly not a sister to anyone on board.'

He pauses and sucks his upper lip inwards, stroking his thin, light brown moustache. 'Of course, my dear lady, it is not uncommon at all for these old family stories to be somewhat lacking in detail, somewhat confused, of course. It was a long time ago, seven full decades since the transit of the *Australasia*, and, of course … a rather distressing period in the country's history. One upon which it is perhaps wisest not to dwell.'

'Of course,' I echo. 'Of course.'

'I say, are you quite all right?'

★ ★ ★

When I return to my senses, five or six people have come to my assistance. Mr Milligan is in the background, horrified, chewing his moustache distractedly. I have placed him in a very indelicate position, of course, to be found alone with a prostrate woman on the floor of his office. Naturally, he is also concerned about contagion – the death toll from the flu rises every day, despite all the patent formulas in the chemist shops. Poor Mr Milligan, I almost feel sorry for him.

A stout, respectably dressed lady has a phial of smelling salts under my nose. I didn't know such things still existed, my mother and grandmother always scorned such fripperies, but the pungent aroma is an effective assault to the sinuses and I struggle upright, with the lady's help, and am soon sitting up clutching a glass of water and muttering about the unseasonably warm weather. Milligan glances out the window where a chilly spring wind speeds white-capped waves across the harbour, but sensibly decides not to contradict me.

The lady returns her sponge to its container and the scent of ammonia disperses slightly. Warming to her self-assigned role as saviour and chaperone she sends a boy to hail a taxi and soon we are bowling along towards home.

Eleanor Gordon.

Who on earth is Eleanor Gordon? And who is Patsy O'Hanlon in this mystery? My grandmother swore on the stars and moon yesterday that she was a lone orphan, and yet now there are two sisters vying for a place – Patsy, who I have always known, and the mysterious Eleanor Gordon.

At the gates of the boarding house my saviour waves away my attempt to pay the cab driver. 'Nonsense, my dear, nonsense. I'm delighted to have been of help.' She places her hand on my arm to prevent me alighting. 'Let me recommend Doctor Winstanley, a thorough gentleman and an undisputed expert in ladies' problems.'

I promise to make an appointment forthwith and she allows me to descend. 'It's a man's world, my dear,' she adds, 'and how little they understand of how we suffer. At the very least you need a strong tonic. You know. To help with ... ' She lowers her voice. ' ... The Change.'

I wave vaguely towards her upraised hand as the taxi moves off at a smart trot. I might go and visit Doctor Winstanley when things return to some semblance of normality. Or I might not.

My grandmother and my great-aunt came to Tasmania, not as modest, hard-working immigrants seeking their fortune in the New World, but as convicted criminals. And of my mother there is no hint. It's going to take more than a strong tonic to deal with this change.

When my grandmother was raving with the fever, the name she called out more than any other was Nellie, and her voice was frail and full of terror. Nellie. Is Nellie my new-to-the-party aunt, Eleanor Gordon? I never heard her name in all my life. Nellie Gordon, she's the key to this mystery. If I can find her, I can unlock it.

Chapter Fourteen

The Curragh, County Kildare, Thursday, 30 November 1848

Nellie Gordon's nest was a palace. Thick sods of grass had been banked up inside the natural dome of the furze bush, making sturdy walls, over which was draped a thick waterproof tarpaulin of waxed canvas – the floor was drier than the inside of Sally's mother's cabin. Nellie didn't wriggle through a tunnel, catching skin and clothing on the sharp thorns, but strode upright through a doorway, hacked with great effort from the front of the bush and served for a door with another generous length of canvas, propped aside to allow the smoke to leave.

'I'm the Queen of the Wrens,' she laughed when she saw Sally's face. 'There's not many who lives like this, around here.'

For furnishings and utensils, her makeshift home was certainly better served than any cabin in Clonsast had ever been. She had three chairs, made by a joiner, and several creepie stools also. Pots and basins for every purpose; one to cook and another to wash your face. She added Martha's pot to the collection, 'It's a small thing, to offer as rent for three mouths, but it'll do for a start, and ye won't be here for ever.'

A stew was seething over a low fire and Sally squeezed Peggy's hand tightly as her stomach growled and whined. Nellie had four bowls, or maybe even more, and they were all able to eat their small portions at once, rather than wait one at a time for the empty bowl.

'That's enough for you, now,' Nellie said. 'There's meat in each of them bowls and I don't want you children shitting all over the place. You can have more maybe when I see how that settles.'

The children licked their bowls and sucked their fingers. Their eyes were round with excitement.

'Put them children down in the moss back there,' said Nellie, gesturing to where a thick pile of spongy moss and bracken made a good bed. 'Now, girl. Put that cap back on, and keep your britches tight around you. Let no one see your true nature till I have this worked out and planned proper in my mind.'

'I was calling myself Sam, and the children are growing used to that.'

'That's good. I'll go along with that.'

Nellie rummaged in the bosom of her dress and pulled out a small paper bag, teased a few threads of tobacco from it and stamped them hard into a clay pipe. She drew on the pipe till it lit to her satisfaction, then leaned back in her chair – Sally was on a stool, which she thought was wise, showing her respect for the queen of the wrens. Whatever had made Martha so wary of the wrens had yet to manifest itself. Nellie had treated Sally with the only kindness she had encountered since Patrick O'Loughlin had sent her on her way to the workhouse of Nás Na Ríogh.

A cloud of fragrant smoke drifted out of Nellie's pipe and that, combined with her full belly and the heat of Nellie's generous fire, had almost lulled Sally to sleep. She started and peeled her eyes back open as the wren spoke at last.

'Sally, tell me what you know about the world, and how exactly you were planning to make your way in it, with two children, and not two coins to rub together.'

She took the pipe out of her mouth and pointed the thick stem at Sally in a gesture of mild threat. 'I might as well tell you, here and now, that if you've any money on your person, you can hand it over. The Queen takes her tax, and she takes it from all the new girls.'

Sally flushed and looked down at the floor.

'I tax you, the ranger taxes me, the world goes on turning and no one's nest gets burnt out, 'less I agrees so.'

Sally realised that her hand had flown, unknown, unbidden, to her waist, where the folds of her old dress beneath the breeches still held twelve of Martha's pennies.

'Oh, you can keep yer coins, if you'd rather, Sally. But you'll be keeping them in the shelter of your old nest, and boiling nettles again. Until the day comes, and that's not far off, when you're scratching a shallow hole to put the little girl into, and wishing that you had paid me my dues.'

Sally slipped her hand inside the ragged shirt, fumbling around in the recesses of the twisted fabric, struggling and twisting until Nellie rose with an abrupt curse, 'Christ, girl, stand still.' Yanking the shirt over Sally's head and ripping the dress from round her middle, she soon had Sally naked as Eve in the Garden, and the few remaining coins slipped into the purse in her bosom.

'Dress quickly, and throw away that rag of a frock into the fire. You couldn't be seen dead in it. I wouldn't put a corpse into it. I'll get you a warm sweater tomorrow, I have a few friends owes me a favour. Yer a boy until I tells you yer not.' Sally scrambled back into her clothes. She had never been naked in front of another person, for her mother had always found her a blanket or cloth to wrap herself in when the clothes were being washed.

Nellie did not look away to spare Sally's blushes, rather she took a good gawk, and she smiled and nodded. 'That's good skin you have, Sally. No scars, no marks. Never been beaten much, I'd say?'

'I've never been beaten at all, may God forgive you. My father never lifted a hand to me.'

'Oh there's more than fathers do be beating young girls, and you need to remember that. But yer clean hide is a blessing, and will definitely help our cause, when we're out.'

She settled back down again, drew on the pipe, hiked up her skirts so the heat of the fire warmed her legs, and Sally sat down on the stool and waited.

'So you never answered the question. What do you know about the world?'

'I know enough, I think. I know more than my mother did, anyway. I had four years done in the national school before the potato blight put the thoughts of learning out of people's minds. I can write my own name and read most words if they're wrote clear enough.'

As Sally was starting to detail her skills in counting and figuring, Nellie burst out laughing.

'For the love of the divine, sure I don't care about all that shite. I can barely make my own mark, but here I am with the thick pot of stew, and there are you, starving.'

She gripped Sally's chin and stared hard in her face, her breath rank against Sally's cheek, the unmistakable smell of porter and whiskey underlying the thick greasy smell of the mutton stew. She shook Sally's face roughly.

'Don't tell me no lies and don't try to take me for a fool. What do you know about the workings of the body, the needs of men, the getting of children and all that sort of stuff?'

Sally laughed with relief, for she knew all about that stuff, she wasn't stupid. The couple knelt down and in their night-time Rosary they sent up their prayer to God, and the angel Gabriel (who was a man even though he had a woman's name) would plant a tiny baby in the woman's stomach, to grow until it was strong enough to come out.

'But the angel knows more than we do – and them who asks, doesn't always get. There's my mother on her knees for years, and only one child to show for it, and Brigid Deegan across the field from us with seven. Although she has buried three of them since the hunger came.'

'Seven now, isn't that a great family, right enough? And your poor mother with only the one, God love her.'

Sally nodded. 'Indeed, it doesn't seem fair, but the angel knows God's will.'

'It must have been a great comfort to your mother, all the same, to have you there to help her. And would you mind telling me, if you would be so good, how come yer mother was blessed with only one child, and yet here I am feeding my stew to yer brother and sister?'

Nellie swiped the cap from Sally's head and wrenched her to the ground with a fistful of hair wrapped round her knuckles. 'Didn't I tell you not to lie to me and not to treat me like a fool? Didn't I? The truth this time, or I will bring you to the ranger myself.'

Sally's scalp ached and her face was twisted inches from Nellie's feet – if she were to aim a kick, there would be blood and teeth on the floor of the nest. In Sally's mind the only thought was of Grainne, and of Martha teasing out the clumps of hair and flesh from the bloodied mess of her head. She didn't want to end up like Grainne. Nellie had a life of comfort and power and privilege, Sally could see that. The only choice was to throw herself on Nellie's mercy, if she had any. The whole story took but a few minutes.

Nellie tutted and sighed, cursed and threw venomous glances at the two children who slept still on the furze and bracken in the far corner.

'Sally, you are the stupidest girl it has ever been my misfortune to meet. And the worst liar too. If the Peelers comes looking for those children … ' Her right hand formed into a fist, although she seemed unaware of it. 'If the Peelers comes here to my nest on behalf of those two half-dead gutter rats, I'll strip that nice, clean hide off of you myself.'

Nellie stood up and took a turn or two about the nest; it was high enough to walk in comfort and she had a span of seven large steps. Sally watched and counted, seven to the left, swing about, seven to the right, swing about. Martha's money was tucked in Nellie's bodice in the tobacco pouch, and if she chose to throw Sally, Davey and Peggy out onto the face of the earth again, their destitution would be utterly complete.

'To hell with it. Yer as stupid as the day is long, but you have another qualification that is rare in the girls around here, and what is rare is wonderful. I've been waiting for this chance for a long time. Sit down now, till I fill you in a few bits and pieces about the angel Gabriel.'

She spoke at length and in detail until Sally finally jumped from the stool. 'No, it can't be. Sure that's like two dogs in the street. But it's different for people … the angel … the prayers.'

'I'm not going to say that sometimes there mightn't be prayers, but in this neck of the woods, the prayers is mostly for it to be over fast, and to get on to the next fella, and let him be fast too. Of course, you might pray not to catch the pox, but around here, that prayer's unlikely to be answered.'

Sally thought about Grainne, and the thumping and pounding, and her keening wails and the mats of blood caked into her thin yellow hair. 'And does it hurt much? And would my own parents … ?'

'It needn't hurt too much, if yer careful, and I daresay there's women takes pleasure in it. Of course, there's a lot of men who won't be careful. They can be right hurting bastards. And, of course, it always hurts when yer fresh.'

And the whole thing clicked into place, like a part in a mechanism, and Martha and Grainne's plan for Sally, and their reason for keeping her hidden and fresh.

'And that's what I'll have to do now? To earn my keep? I'll have to do that?' Sally's throat swelled up and the words died in her chest. 'But not Peggy? Not Peggy, she's too young. Davey thinks she's maybe four years old. She couldn't be big enough for to interest a soldier.'

Nellie threw back her head and roared like a banshee perched on the thatch of an enemy, awaiting a chance to suck away his soul. 'Too young? Catch yerself on, too young for that pack of bastards yonder in those tents?' She jerked her head towards the camp, which was a lot closer to Nellie's nest than it had been to Sally's furze bush. 'There's men in that camp would get up on a cracked plate, or on a newborn baby. Oh, she's well big enough to interest those boyos. Davey too, if I could get somewhere private for the act to take place.'

Sally leaped from her stool and spun on her heel with every intention of scooping the two sleeping bodies into her arms and fleeing back into the night. And she thought of Martha, hiding the children in the box each night, with threats to keep them quiet, when she could have sold them to the soldiers' appetites. And Sally knew then that, somehow, somewhere, buried under the hunger, under the whiskey and the porter, there had lurked some tiny vestige of a mother's love.

'Leave the childer be, Sally.' Nellie stood in front of the doorway, blocking any hope of escape. 'Let them rest. I've waited a long time for a girl like you to come along. I'll keep you safe. And if that means keeping the childer safe too, well, so be it. You and me are gettin' away out of here. You and me and that treasure between yer legs.'

'The treasure between my legs?' Sally looked down at the strange profile of the breeches that clung to her legs.

'Christ, I did say you were stupid. You've got a treasure that the other girls don't have.'

'But I'll only have it the once. Didn't you say, I've to pay my rent and my keep? And for Peggy and Davey too. You'll be selling me, just like Martha planned.'

'Yes, you'll only have it the once. So you've got to sell it some place where it's worth something. In the land of the blind, the one-eyed man is king, Sally. In the land of no women, you'll name your price. You're goin' some place where you can sell what you've got. And the price you're askin' is a home and a husband, and a place in the corner for your widowed sister, Nellie, until she finds a man of her own.'

'And the two little ones.'

'Yes, of course, surely. And the two little ones.'

'And is this place far from here?' Sally needed to get Peggy and Davey away from Newbridge. With the first friendly face and kind word, she had revealed the secret of the stealing of the children – they couldn't stay here. And although Martha might protect Peggy for now, if she got her hands back on her, sooner or later Peggy would end up joining Grainne and her mother in the squalid and dangerous work of the she-barracks.

Nellie looked into the distance and then down as she fiddled with her pipe. 'It's middlin' far away, all right.'

'And what's it called, this place?'

'Van Diemen's Land.'

Sally rolled the strange words around on her tongue. 'Van Diemen's land. And how will we get there? Will we walk?'

As Nellie opened her mouth to answer, a man's rough voice called out. Sally shivered and ran to stand in front of the sleeping children, blocking them from sight, but Nellie strode out, heading the man off at the entrance to the nest.

'Ah, there you are, Nellie.'

Through the half-open canvas curtain covering the doorway Sally could glimpse the soldier. His uniform was slovenly dirty and there was no shine at all on his black leather boots. Sally prayed his loud tones would not wake the children, willing them to stay at peace, for since the night of the riot in Martha's cabin, they were even more frightened of soldiers than she was. Sally had used all her powers of invention to convince them that soldiers were responsible for the fire that had killed their mother and sister.

For the first time, Sally looked at a soldier, not with a nameless dread gnawing at the back of her mind, but in the full and certain knowledge of what he wanted and why he had come. And she thought of her mother, reaching out her hand, on a good day long ago, to stroke her father's arm, and of her father raising his head from the lazy bed to smile back, or to take the cup of water his wife held out. In Van Diemen's Land, Sally must find a man like her father, a man who would protect her and the children, a man who would smile and then bend his head back to his work. A man not like these other ones.

Sally pulled her cap down lower on her brow and stared fixedly at the floor.

Nellie bustled forward to block the soldier's path. 'Not today, Jem, not today. I was just coming to tie the red rag at the door. Come back on Saturday, good man, I'll be back in action then.'

Jem sulked and kicked at the furze root closest him. 'Do you think I was born yesterday, Nellie? Sure you had the rag out not two weeks ago. Even I can count to four weeks.' He spat into the fire where the gobbet fizzed and spitted a moment. 'I could have saved myself a walk, if you had bothered to put out the rag. If you're busy,' he said, glancing into the dimness towards Sally, 'I wouldn't take long.'

Nellie put a hand firmly, but carefully, on his shoulder and gently pivoted him round to face the doorway again. 'There's a fine new girl over at the Athgarvan nest, in with Susan and Tess. Clean as a whistle, and she won't stay that way for long around here.'

'But, I'm here now, and I know you're just using the rag as an excuse.'

She lowered her voice and muttered, 'Jem, I'm not as young as I once was, and sometimes I don't get the full four weeks. Or I might be sickening for something …'

He glanced carefully up at her face, 'I might be better off in Athgarvan, so?'

'I think so, Jem, today at any rate.'

They could hear his muttered complaints borne back towards them on the breeze for a moment or two as he grumbled his way towards Athgarvan. Nellie stepped out and tied a strip of red cloth to a branch where it fluttered in the stiff breeze. Sally knew everything she needed to know now; the red-clothed bucket, the half-formed babies slipped early from the womb into the bog. All these things Nellie had explained to her. She was a grown, knowledgeable woman of the world at last, and how she wished she were not. How she wished she were back in Clonsast, whispering with Molly and wondering about the ways of men and angels.

'We still need to be careful, now,' Nellie warned. 'That rag won't keep us totally safe. There's men and there's *men*. Jem's not the worst, when he's sober. I've known him for a right while, but there's plenty of others who wouldn't take no for an answer like that.' She sighed and gently rubbed her temples with the flat pads of her fingers. For a moment she had the look of a frightened, tired woman instead of a queen. 'There's men would even take you in your bleeding, dirty animals that they are.'

She sat down with her pipe again and told Sally of the dangers. The men who wouldn't even pay the few farthings that was asked of them. The men who lay in wait in the darkness, with a stone in their hand, who would smash it into your head and do you while you lay dazed on the ground. The men who came so drunk that there was no reasoning with them at all, and the only thing was to give in or die.

For that reason, they needed to get out of the Curragh soon, before Sally's precious treasure was lost.

'It's time you had a blade. I take it you've none?'

'Nellie, you've seen me in my bare buff. Where would I have a blade hidden? And how would I know how to use it, if I had one?'

'Oh you'd know all right. Just stick it in and twist it.'

'And swing on the end of a rope?'

'Not at all, Sally. Who would care? The men in that camp are the sweepings of the roads. They're not like the men in Newbridge barracks, all counted and reckoned twice a day. They're more like rats in a granary. They come, they go. They take the Queen's shilling for a month or a year. They fall foul of the sergeant, or they fill their pockets with another man's coins, or their wife sends to say that the crop is ready. Then they head off into the distance, and are never seen again. Deserters, they're called.' She laughed, deep and throaty. 'I've helped one or two desert this life for ever.'

From a hiding place among the stores of her pots and dishes she pulled out an evil blade.

'I've no spare knife to give you, but this'll serve. I'll keep the knife myself, for I've more chance of using it right, and I'll never be far from your side.'

The blade in Sally's hand glinted dully in the faint glow of the fire. She turned it over and over and imagined thrusting it into the guts of a soldier — a wicked green triangle of bottle-glass embedded into a smooth handle of furze-branch.

'I made it myself, and it's as good as a knife any day, better in fact. Keep it safe, I haven't another one as good.' She showed Sally how to hide it in the pocket of the britches, and to keep a rag wrapped round the sharp edges. 'Make sure you twist the blade on the way back out, if you use it. Use it right, or don't use it at all.'

No wonder Martha and Grainne had feared the wrens. And no wonder they had admired them too.

'I don't think I could do it, Nellie. I think I'd nearly rather let him have his way, than kill him.'

'It's up to you, Sam. It's your choice. But I am going to Van Diemen's Land with a fresh girl to sell, and if it can't be you, it'll have to be Peggy. Your choice.'

Sally looked at Peggy, the innocence, the warm arms which crept around Sally's waist in the dark of the night, and the small hand which slipped into hers when the child was frightened. She looked at Davey, over whose mouth she had slipped a quietening hand as the soldiers rampaged in the she-barracks. If

Nellie could not have Sally, clean and virgin, she would have Peggy. *Your choice*, Nellie said.

And there it was, no choice at all. Peggy and Davey were coming to Van Diemen's Land, at Her Majesty's pleasure, and when Sally's time was served, and she was released and finding a husband, they'd still be younger than she was now. Young and safe, and ready to start a new life at the table of her man's kitchen. Sally put her hand into her pocket and caressed the smooth handle of the blade. She would use it if she had to, would kill to keep the children safe, if no other choice existed.

'When are we going to Van Diemen's Land, Nellie?'

'We start our journey tomorrow night.'

★ ★ ★

Not a bird moved in the inky blackness and for once the winter's breeze was still. The party of four had no moon or stars to guide their steps, but Nellie had a dark lantern and would pull aside the shutter from time to time to let the faint glow of the candle out. When she had her bearings, she closed the shutter again and they moved forward, holding hands in silence.

Before they left the nest, they had eaten every scrap that they could find. 'Drink it up,' Nellie said, 'for we'll not be back and we won't leave the good stew behind us for the foxes and the rats.' Davey and Peggy had eaten till their mouths glistened with grease and their bellies stretched out under their thin rags.

'Stop, in the name of God, stop, you'll make yourselves sick as two poisoned pups,' Sally had begged them, but who could blame two children who had never once had their fill before? They licked the last smears of fat from the wooden bowls and Nellie tucked the spoons inside her small bundle.

'And what about the rest?' Sally asked, looking at the collected finery of Nellie's nest. 'The pots, the chairs, all your clothes and trappings?'

'They are staying here, all except the blue and white basin, you'll see why. And we can't take the other stuff where we're going.'

In Nellie's blue and white enamel basin she carried a half-pint or more of lamp oil, bought at the Curragh market and paid for with some of Martha's pennies, and Sally had a full new box of Lucifers in her pocket alongside the blade of green glass. Nellie had made sure they that were seen together that morning buying their goods; a well-known figure of a woman and a streel of young children she had acquired from the Lord knows where. She had stopped to talk with the other wrens at the market, but had not answered their questions about the children. The children had kept their eyes on the ground, and their mouths closed as instructed.

In the enveloping dark, in the direction of Kildare town, a vixen screamed, and Peggy shivered and whimpered, clutching Sally's hand till she wondered at the strength in the child's tiny bones and feared her own might break.

Davey was silent and brave until, out of the gloaming night, a bat swooped down, so close they might have reached out and touched it as it sped past their shocked faces. Then Davey threw himself onto the ground, refusing to rise, and at length he continued the journey in Sally's aching, burning arms, while Peggy held fast to the hem of her shirt.

Nellie had chosen their target carefully, a standing rick of straw far from any stream or trickle on this dry plain, but close enough both to the army camp and to the farmer's house to ensure that the criminals would be captured and detained.

Nellie sprinkled the lamp oil as far up the rick as she could reach.

'You're Sally Gordon, my sister, you've travelled from King's County to join me, dressed as a boy called Sam to preserve your virtue in these dangerous times.' Sally repeated her words, as solemn as any oath, and she struck a match and held it, spluttering and guttering to the straw, until the oil caught and a snake of flame raced upwards in the dark.

'You're Peggy Gordon, brought to the Curragh at the bidding of your big sisters, Nellie and Sally Gordon, and you set fire to the straw on purpose. It's not a game.'

Peggy took the flickering match and held it to the straw. 'I'm Peggy Gordon,' she said, 'I've got two names now. Peggy and Gordon.' Nellie sighed and muttered, 'What did I do to be cursed with such a shower of half-wits?' She struck another match.

'You're Davey Gordon, you're six years old. Old enough to know better. You know that what yer doing is wrong. You know it's a crime and a sin. Your sisters Sally and Nellie made you do it. Your mother is dead.'

'Yes.' Davey nodded and held out his hand for the match, but she let it die away in the breeze until he had repeated his oath. After he had lit his portion of the rick, Nellie quickly lit a fourth match and pressed it close against the oil-soaked straw which was now blazing like a beacon under the clouded, starless sky. All they could do was wait.

'We're arsonists. We're foolish and unlettered people. We don't deserve to stay in Ireland with good decent folk, and we're going to Van Diemen's Land to pay for our crime and learn how to be better people.'

'What?' gasped Sally. 'Leaving Ireland? You said we were going to prison. You never said anything about leaving Ireland.'

Nellie sighed and shook her head pityingly.

'What a little fool you are, Sally. Didn't I say we were going to the land of no-women? Look around you here in Ireland, all you see is women and starving children, while the men are dead already, or on their way to America.'

'And is Van Diemen's Land in America? Reverend Joly sent all his Galway tenants to America in a big ship, to leave more room for his sheep. But not us in King's County; Clonsast is really too boggy for sheep. Maybe we'll meet them out there.'

'No, no,' Nellie soothed her gently, 'Van Diemen's Land is much, much closer than America, and now that we're arsonists we'll have free passage on a ship, and a chance of a life of ease in a few years' time.'

'Please God you're right.' Sally made the sign of the cross as she knelt beside the flaming rick and thought how to take her mind off the terrifying idea of leaving Ireland behind.

'Davey, Peggy,' she said, fake cheer in her voice, 'wouldn't this make you think of the thousand-year fire? We'll say a prayer to holy Saint Brigid, who it's well known still walks the plains of Kildare, all these hundreds of years later.'

The children stared blankly.

'How could you not know about Saint Brigid, second only in importance to Patrick himself?'

'Sure, what do we know about that? We know about not-enough-bread, and more-than-enough-cold, and the inside of the box late at night.' Davey blinked and rubbed his watering eyes. 'Nothing much else was ever told to us.'

She gathered the children into her arms, and while Nellie kept watch for the ranger and his men, she whispered all the old tales she knew of Brigid. Crafty as a fox, tricker of kings, she and her holy women had kept a flame burning in her monastery in Kildare, day and night.

'She ruled this part of the land, and her sisters ruled it after her, for a thousand years, until King Henry's men came and knocked her monastery to the ground. Now we've lit our own beacon, and we'll escape this cold, hungry land, with the help of God and Brigid.'

'With the help of Nellie Gordon, you mean. You'd be a long time waiting for fairy tales to save you.' Nellie's voice shook with anxiety and lacked its normal conviction. 'Where the hell is the ranger? Why doesn't he come?'

The children's eyes fluttered between open and closed, and their heads grew heavier and weighed Sally's shoulders down onto her chest. She clutched their stick-thin bodies tight and swore that no ill would ever befall them again while breath remained in her.

'You're mine now,' she breathed into their hair. 'You're the first things I ever had of my own. You're mine. I'll build a grand new life for us under the sun far away.'

Sparks spiralled up into the blackness as the flaming rick settled and sank in upon itself. For almost the first time in her life, Sally was too warm. As her head sank lower onto her chest and the children snored in her arms, she heard the sound of distant shouting and, in time, the beat of horses' hooves cantering across the plain towards them.

★ ★ ★

Donal Teaghan was the ranger's name. Nellie stood in front of Sally, obscuring his view, and, in the scant half-light of dawn and the fading embers of the charred straw rick, he barely glanced at her. Little as Sally knew about Curragh society, even she understood that Donal Teaghan was not a man whose cut-open body could be concealed in a ditch; he was an important officer with a uniform and a bright, sprightly chestnut mare. He must return to his office safe and well. If there was to be a payment of the body due for this night's work, Nellie would pay it herself.

Teaghan did not come alone, however; the landlord's man had been raised from his rest, and a straggle of thin, weak-chested farm hands too. There was no chance for Donal to demand anything of Nellie, except her confession, which she readily gave. The men poked and dragged half-heartedly at the smoking straw, but gave up the rick as a lost cause.

'Will you harness up your grey mare to the trap, Mr French, so we might take these wretches to the gaol in Naas?' Teaghan asked. The farm agent spat in their direction and cursed them with a complicated hand gesture.

'I will in my hole! Exhaust my mare on that fool's errand, and they after destroying a month's bedding for my animals? Let them walk, to hell.'

'French, come on, be reasonable. They're next door to walking skeletons. It'll be tomorrow before I get them that distance on their feet. What if they try to make a run for it?'

'I'll loan you my mastiff to herd them along the way, wouldn't he love nothing better than a chance to bring down and eat a little girl?' Peggy whimpered and buried her face in Sally's stomach. Sally gripped her shoulder and held her tight, nearly sure that the man was joking.

'Mr Teaghan, sir,' Nellie spoke with a quiet respect that Sally had not heard before, 'put the children up on the saddle of the horse and the other two of us will walk if needs be. We won't run. It's the gaolhouse for us, and the prison ship afterwards, with the help of God.'

And in that manner, the sorry party of hardened criminals made its way to Naas, French and his farmhands cursing and spitting after them.

The ranger walked quickly, leading his mare with one hand on the bridle and Nellie reached out and touched his other hand gently. He did not shy away or shake her off.

'Donal, you know me well?'

'I do, Nellie. I know you better than some might say I should.'

'You won't have such an easy time of it without me to help you keep the nests in order. I know I am after putting you to trouble with my little bonfire.' She chuckled deep and rich and Teaghan's lips twitched until he was smiling too.

'Oh, I daresay I'll manage.'

'I've left everything I had in the nest for you, Donal. As a class of a thank you. There's three fine pots and a dish. Chairs too, real ones, and the house I stole them from is far from here and they'll never be recognised.' They both laughed at that. 'Take the whole lot into Kildare, Donal, and sell them for whatever you can get. But, for the love of God, when we get to the gaolhouse, don't tell them I was *on the town*. They'll stick us in the special shed at the back of the workhouse with all the rest of them filthy whores, and there's a right few locked up in there who don't feel they owe me any favours.'

'Well, I won't say anything, Nell, but surely to God, someone in there will know you.'

'That's true, but I'll take my chances. And thank you, Donal.' After the shortest of pauses she continued. 'You know, there's some in the gaolhouse, and in the courthouse too, might be surprised to learn about our little arrangements. People who wouldn't understand that to have a solid, sensible queen ruling a few, friendly, tax-paying nests is better than to have dozens without a leader, who have the ranger as their enemy.'

'Damn you, Nellie, I said I would keep your secrets. You'd better keep mine. It's a sentence of transportation you're after, but if I told all that I know about you, you'd never feel that warm southern sun on your back. You'd end your days dancing the hemp fandango in front of a cheering crowd. Nothing excites the people as much as a good hanging, extra special when the murderer is a woman.'

'Donal, you'd hardly call it murder, ridding the world of a few pox-ridden soldiers, the dirt of the road. But we understand each other now. We've both got secrets. Let's keep them secret. And there's fifteen or twenty shillings extra coming to you from the sale of my stuff, if yer careful.'

Teaghan turned abruptly and swung himself into the saddle of his horse,

Peggy in front of him perched on the pommel, and Davey behind on the animal's wide flank, arms wrapped round Teaghan's waist. The two women walked on beside him, below Teaghan's attention, as was their rightful place.

There wasn't another word spoken all the long ten-mile walk to Naas town.

Chapter Fifteen

Hobart, October 1919, Saoirse

Outside my grandmother's window, a nest full of tiny wrens chirps and tweets, demanding the return of their parents, and the good fat insects they will bring. I envy them their certainty. Mother, father, flying backwards and forwards all day long, popping ants and gnats into the open beaks. No secrets, no lies.

'I'm sorry, Saoirse. I'm really truly sorry.'

'Is there anything I believe that isn't a lie?'

My grandmother puts her head in her hands and sobs. In my whole life I have never been more than a few hundred yards from my grandmother's side and I have never seen her weep. Pain, illness and grief have never before, in my experience, loosed one tear from her in public. She stood at the graveside like an alabaster statue as they lowered her sister, and then her daughter, into the soil.

'We didn't really lie to you. Don't say we lied to you.'

'What would you call it? A careful version of the truth? You came here as a prisoner! A convict. I don't know who you are any more. I don't know who I am. I've lost my aunt Patsy, she doesn't share your name. I've gained a new Aunt Eleanor who does …'

'No you haven't. That woman is none of your kin, or mine, that bitch.'

'But who is she? Where is she, this Eleanor? Is she the Nellie who haunted your dreams while you raved? How did you get away with this subterfuge for so long? Are you lying to me, or have you been lying to everyone else?'

My grandmother wipes her eyes and when she turns to face me I freeze in shock. She is dying. At last I see the truth, she is dying in front of my eyes. I don't know how much more of this she can withstand, this endless talking, the horror she is reliving.

'You don't understand. The whole city of Hobart is built on a tissue of lies, half-truths, kindly deceptions and outright self-interest.' She gestures weakly towards the window. 'Scratch the surface of any family in town, go back far enough and you'll find a prison ship manifest.'

'I don't care about those other people,' I say. 'I only care about the lies you told me.'

'You found Hobart society kind, did you, Saoirse, growing up a bastard? You think you would have found school easier being the bastard granddaughter of a transported criminal?' I gasp and start to protest, but she will not be halted. 'After the gold rush, with tens of thousands of people pouring through the country, half the populace on the move, records were blurred, lines were crossed. We had a chance, a fleeting chance, Patsy and I, for a new future, where our history was what we said it was. Don't blame us for seizing that chance.'

'And my mother? Why didn't she marry my father?' The question I have pondered so long, but never dared ask. But she is forcing it into the open, if she will insist on using that word. Didn't my mother know the cruelty of raising me in the world, fatherless, in plain sight? A choice no normal woman would make, surely?

'Why didn't she do the decent, the normal thing, and give me a father, like every other girl? And why won't you tell me where you buried my grandfather, your husband, if you married here and not in Ireland? Why was he not here, in his proper place, a man as the head of the house? Did you think the laws of God and man didn't apply to you?'

I have never spoken to my grandmother, or my mother, of this before. A lifetime of pain and shame is forcing its way out of my breast and into the very last days and hours of my grandmother's life. I don't know if I am giving her ease or killing her. But she started it, with her gravestone demands.

And a light comes on in my head, like the lighting of the newly installed gas streetlamps at dusk, dim at first, then spilling out and filling every corner of my brain as I scrabble to decipher the shadows.

'You're only eighty-five years old. You came here as a mere child, and yet you told me a pack of lies that you were widowed in the old country. I'll bet my mother is not in the ship's manifest. How could she be?' I clutch at my head, and I really believe for a moment that I will faint again. 'If I hadn't swooned I'd have asked the registrar for my mother next, and I'll wager she wouldn't have been there. You're only eighty-five years old and I spent my life believing you to be a decade older. When my mother died she was ... ' I start to count on my fingers, my brain so addled I cannot manage the simple arithmetic of deceit.

'I am only ten years older than your mother,' she says, 'and that means ...'

I scream. As I sink into a chair I whisper. 'You are not my grandmother. Who are you?'

But what I mean is, who am I?

Chapter Sixteen

Naas, County Kildare, November 1848–March 1849

Donal Teaghan was true to his word and had kept Nellie's secret, and although one of the gaolers had been an occasional visitor to Nellie's nest, he had the sense to stay quiet. The four new prisoners did not end up in the shed at the rear of the workhouse, with the other whores and nightwalkers, but in the common gaol, close to the courthouse on the wide main street of Nás Na Ríogh.

The smell. Oh, the smell. The stench of Naas Gaol filled the eyes with tears and the mouth with bile. The buckets and barrels overflowed day and night. The cesspool behind the gaol was filled beyond its level, seeping out over the ground. The respectable citizens of Naas town pulled their scarves well up over their noses and mouths as they passed by.

It was impossible to use the bucket without splashing your nethers with the leavings of others. The more experienced gaolbird women would shit, groaning and puffing, on the ground and then scoop it up in their hands afterwards and drop it into the bucket, rather than balance on the hard rim and risk slipping right in. As for those poor souls who suffered from the dysentery, they lay groaning in their filth on the cold, rush-matted floor and the stuff seeped out of them, beyond their control. Sally and Nellie didn't pity them, but cursed them and urged them to hurry up and get better, or else to die as fast as possible.

Men, women and children beyond counting crammed every corner of the gaol – hundreds in the women's section alone. There was neither space nor comfort. The gaol had sixty-two cells and the written rule was one inmate to a cell. Before the failure of the potatoes, the gaol had been half-empty nearly all the time, women and men kept separate – silent, clean and sorrowful. There had been prayers and discipline, there had been bunks and beds, but now the master had had them taken away, for the wards were barely large enough to accommodate the great crowd within them, never mind room for furniture.

'Here, Peggy, take my space,' Sally called up to the child, not rising until Peggy was halfway down to the floor. To stand up was to lose your space immediately, as the mass of sprawling, tangled human bodies spread and rolled, filling every inch.

'Get away out of it,' roared the woman beside Peggy, coughing and gasping with the exertion of speech, desperately stretching her cramped legs and arms, trying to push the child out of the tiny space Sally had just left. 'Would you take my grave as fast?'

'Ignore her, love, she knows fine well I was here first.' Sally stroked Peggy's forehead gently before turning to the wretch on the floor beside her. 'It's my space, and I'll rip the hair off your head if I see you budge that child one inch.' Oh, Nellie Gordon was a good teacher, and Sally was a fast student.

Peggy lay down obediently, the woman ceased her wailing and Sally clapped her arms round her chest over and over until some slight tingle of heat returned to them.

A loud clanging bell rang out and she seized one of Peggy's arms and one of Davey's, and they scrambled towards the door, youngest and fastest first, the old and infirm tottering in their wake. The prison was so overcrowded that the ration was dispensed in the exercise yard on dry days.

'Breathe in that air, Davey, take it into your lungs, it'll put hairs on your chest, all right.'

The air was thick with the stench from the cess, yet it was considerably better than the ammonia reek of the ward they had just left. The children lowered their heads and pushed their way forward as Sally and Nellie had shown them, elbows and knees digging into the bellies and hips of the mass of hungry women, the crush so great that the children had passed them before the women could even raise a hand to swat them away.

Peggy and Davey were both in fine fettle. They had been in gaol two weeks already, and neither child had ever seen as good a ration before. Twice a day they had hot food, just like Sally had had in her mother's cabin before the worst times came. Two pounds of potatoes weighed out per person, placed in a net, and the hundreds of nets boiled all together in a giant cauldron. And there was sometimes thin, well-watered buttermilk too, which the children were learning to like, even though Nellie told them it was dirty stuff, out of the tits of animals, and that they should leave it alone.

They fought their way forward, close to the table and the serving girl, who lifted a net full of potatoes, steaming, out of the drained cauldron and dropped it onto the first tin plate in front of her, which was held out, shaking and quivering, by an old crone, newly arrived that morning.

'Where did the praties come from?' the near-naked, shrivelled skeleton of a woman asked, 'I haven't seen a pratie this twelve months gone by.'

The girl laughed, 'Don't worry, mother dear, nothin's too good for the likes of you.' She spat into the old woman's tin dish and the thick green gob of snot glistened and melted on the brown skin of a steaming potato. 'There's food and to plenty, for criminals like yourselves. Sure it's only the Lumpers are blighted, the potatoes that the gentry prefer survived fine this year.'

The old woman twisted her free hand into the apron of the serving girl, her grip like a handful of twigs, twisted into a wizened claw. 'In the name of God, will there be praties every day?' The girl struck the filthy hand from her apron.

'Hurry up to hell,' roared a voice from the back of the milling, complaining crowd and a warden pushed through, clutching a birch rod, and restored a bit of order to the fuming, impatient prisoners with a few wild, slashing blows. The serving girl shoved the old woman away and thrust a net full of potatoes onto the waiting plate of the next person, which was Peggy.

The old crone didn't pause even to wipe the snot off the potato, just lifted it and crammed it whole into her beak. She sucked long, cooling breaths into her stuffed mouth through the few, yellow fangs that hung at strange angles from her raw gums like tombstones in the oldest part of a boneyard.

'Christ be praised,' she whispered to herself. 'Oh, Mary Saunders, in yer whole fifty years, you never done a wiser thing than when you stole that loaf off of the baker's wagon. Three months in gaol, until the assize court, and praties every day.'

In every inch of the yard women huddled beside their children, guarding their potatoes, and thanking God for their wisdom. Most were in for theft of small stuff – a loaf, two eggs, a ragged old dress off a washing line to cover their nakedness. And in a week or a month when they were pushed back out onto the street, they would thieve again to return to the gaol. It was prison or workhouse.

Workhouse was out of the question.

★ ★ ★

Sally, Nellie and the children had passed the gates of Naas workhouse two weeks previously, the women stumbling exhausted at the heels of Donal Teaghan's horse. Sally looked up at the high stone wall and remembered her father's last few words back home, when the typhus had him firm in its grip; 'Don't let them bring me to that greystone hellhole in Edenderry. Let me die in fresh air with my people at my side.' Although staying out of the foul air of the workhouse had done him no good, for he died hours later, his mouth stained green from the grasses and nettles she'd been boiling for him.

'Don't dawdle there,' Teaghan had roared at her and Nellie, as he trotted past the gaunt, three-storey building. 'Come on, in the name of God, the day is half done.' But Nellie and Sally had both slowed, staring, unable to drag their eyes away. A swarm of the homeless hungry lay, sat or squatted in the gutter outside the huge iron gate of Naas workhouse. At the first glance it was not easy to spot those who were dead already, lying disregarded among the near dead and the half quick.

'Sally, I don't want to come here,' screamed Peggy. 'Don't let him bring us here.' She struggled in Teaghan's grip, kicking and twisting. And even though she fetched him a couple of blows with her tiny fists, Teaghan, shaken to his core by the sights and smells, had decency enough to answer her, holding her tight against his body and anchoring her to the pommel of the saddle as she struggled.

'Shut your beak, child. Don't worry. It's the gaol for you, not the workhouse. The gaol will have to take you in, after what you done. You'll not be left outside to rot, like these poor bastards.'

Some of the rag-clad people half rose from the stinking ditch, hands outstretched, 'A penny, sir. A penny, for the love of God.' Teaghan swished his riding crop in their direction and they fell back into their half-crouch in the mire. 'Good mistress, in your fine dress and boots, a ha'penny even.' Nellie turned her head away.

'Shut your eyes,' Sally called up to Peggy and Davey, and they screwed up their eyelids so tightly they looked more like last year's apples than young children. But none of them could close their ears, and the keening followed them as they dragged themselves, weary step by weary step, all along the damp stone wall of the workhouse.

As Teaghan's horse drew level with the end of the workhouse wall, Peggy finally opened her eyes, just in time to see a stinking tower, a mound of dead bodies, blue-black and swollen with gas, not even hidden from sight. Four men in huge leather aprons and gloves laboured, scarfs drawn tight against their mouths and noses, swinging unshrouded corpses up and onto a cart to draw them away to a boneyard. As Teaghan's party passed the workers, they swore and kicked out at a scrawny collie dog which scampered off, red from nose to chest, the body of an infant child tightly gripped between its teeth, two tiny feet and two tiny hands dragging faint furrows in the mire of the road.

Two weeks later, on the heels of Christmas, safe in gaol and well fed, Peggy was still waking, screaming, in the dead of night.

★ ★ ★

Weak March sunshine struggled through the dirty windows of Naas court-house and over the spectacle of the spring assize court. Sally and Nellie had not seen or heard from Donal Teaghan for over three months, and now their futures hung upon his testimony at the spring assize session. He stood firm, facing the bench and cast them never a glance. Nellie avoided looking at him, but Sally kept her eyes fixed upon him and the judge, and prayed for a sentence of transportation. In gaol she had had confirmed what Nellie had promised, arson was an almost certain ticket to Van Diemen's Land.

Justice Crampton struck his gavel on the block and returned to the case in hand. Sally wondered if he was the distant half-cousin of Tom Crampton. Tom Crampton had saved her life with his crusts of bread, and now this fine, bewigged and black-robed Crampton gentleman was going to save it again, by sending the four of them overseas.

'Mr Teaghan, you say that the rick was utterly destroyed?'

'It was, your Honour, razed to the ground and, with your pardon, I might venture to add that after the wet summer and scant harvest we had this year, any straw, even of the poorest quality, was a thing of great value, and the miscreants would have surely known that.'

'And the accused persons made no attempt to escape or to deny their part in this crime?'

Teaghan looked over at last towards Nellie, Sally and the children, a careful glance with not a hint of recognition. 'They did not, m'Lord. They rested by the fire to warm themselves and held a box of Lucifers in their hands.'

Sally stared at Teaghan, willing him to continue, to damn them with his words. Ireland was now become a hell on earth, and all belonging to her were either dead or standing in the dock with her. Cromwell's curse was fallen upon Ireland, once again, and Van Diemen's Land was as good a new start as any.

In one arm she held Peggy, her sticky, musty hair tickling Sally's nose and partly hiding the judge from her sight. With the other hand she gently squeezed Davey's shoulder. Soon, very soon, they would be heading for the muster point, the prison where all transportees awaited their vessel, some with a heavy heart, torn from friends and lovers, some like Sally, eager to embrace their new life.

'And did you know these people, when you apprehended them?'

'I did not, m'Lord. I believe that they entered the Curragh with the sole intention of causing some sort of mischief. They appeared unable to give account of themselves in relation to the townland of their origin, beyond saying that it is from King's County they came.'

Oh, good man, Donal Teaghan. How well that Nellie filled your purse and collected your tithes, and that you had the honesty to repay her. Sally smiled. *Paint us as black as you will, Teaghan, we want no mercy from the court this day.*

Not that the court seemed inclined to show them any mercy, nor to any of the other poor and wasted spectres who had stood before the bench already. His Lordship's lip had curled, and his eyes wandered as beggar after beggar was hauled in front of him. Most had been sentenced and sent down in minutes. Those who had been in gaol a while, for serious offences, awaiting the arrival of the assize court, were well-fed and robust enough, but the newer arrivals were walking skeletons. From time to time, the judge had pulled a stiff, white square of cotton from his waistcoat pocket and brought it up to his nose, and it was no wonder, for even Sally, fresh from the squalid misery of the women's part of the gaol, could feel the filthy reek off some of the men prisoners clawing at her eyes and nostrils.

She risked a small smile at Nellie who stood before the court in her decent black shawl and the neat dress she had worn on her arrival in Naas, although Sally had not seen it since. When asked by what miracle her prison garb had transformed, she'd winked and held her counsel.

Sally mouthed at Nellie, *we're safe,* but she didn't return her glance, so Sally hugged the joy silently in her heart. Her blood pounded a joyous rhythm in her ears, *we're going away, we're going away, we're going away.* She put her lips close to Peggy's tiny ear and whispered, 'We're going away, my love.' Peggy nuzzled her face into the hollow at the base of Sally's throat and her arms, stronger and less bony than before, tightened around Sally's shoulders. Sally loosed her hand from Davey's grasp and slipped it round his waist, pulling him closer. His little head found her body and rested there, in the bowl of her belly. His eyes sought Sally's and he smiled, a tiny, faint movement at one edge of his mouth.

'Have the prisoners any person to speak for them?' The judge leaned forward, eager now to be done and away from the stink and the solid press of humanity.

'They have not, your Honour.'

The judge nodded. 'The case is clear. No defence has been made and none is possible. Crime against property, with or without violence, is a heinous matter. Seven years' transportation for the whole lot of them, on the next available vessel.' He leaned back in his seat, wiped his brow with the cotton kerchief. 'What's next, Mister Clerk?'

A gaoler gripped Sally hard by the upper arm, almost sending Davey sprawling, and pushed her towards the door of the courthouse. From the corner of her eye, she saw another wretched woman, who she half recognised from the ward of the gaol, moving slowly to occupy the dock they had just left. Sally hoped the other woman would fare as well as she had.

'My Lord, my Lord, honourable Master!' A shriek rose from the floor behind her and the whole crowd, gaolers, wardens and prisoners, gasped and craned their necks. 'Mercy for the childer, my Lord, I'm begging you in your goodness.'

Nellie had thrown herself to the floor in front of the bench. 'My Lord, I am a foolish and wicked woman, but I am not so far gone as to destroy the poor, dear childer.'

'For heaven's sake, woman, comport yourself with respect in this court, or I'll have you in the stocks.' The judge's beefy, ruddy jowls trembled with rage. 'Your brother and sister were old enough to commit this terrible crime, they're old enough to pay the price.'

A blood-chilling shriek rose from Nellie's gaping mouth. Several women in the room crossed themselves, or reached for their rosaries.

'That's what I'm telling you, worshipful Master. The poor childer, they're no relation of mine, or hers. The poor little mites are stolen away from their mother.' Nellie rose and pointed her finger, shrieking and spitting in Sally's direction, 'Sir, they were kidnapped by Sally, for the purposes of abusing them and profiting from their labour. Their real mother lives only ten miles away, in Newbridge, and is seeking the childer in every corner of the town, so I have just recently heard tell.'

Several well-dressed gentlemen whipped out their pencils and started scratching on small pads of paper they had hidden in their pockets.

'What's that she said? What's happening? Kidnapped!' Angry cries rose up from every corner. The gaoler drove his fingers into Sally's arm until her will left her, and she sank to her knees upon the stone-flagged floor.

'Nellie, in the name of God. Nellie, what are you saying? Sure, don't you know their mother is dead?'

'It's a lie, your honour, a wicked lie. The mother lives. Until I discovered this fact, just a day or two ago, I thought my sister was saving them, and they were alone in the world, or I should have told the truth earlier.' Nellie drew herself up from the flags and stood at full stretch, short and slight, but a fine figure of a woman. 'Don't let me take this sin upon my shoulders, my Lord. Don't send me over the seas knowing I could have saved the innocent childer from this wanton girl and her schemes.' Nellie wrung her fingers and rent her shawl. 'Send me away, your Honour, as I deserve, but save the poor babbies.'

A cry went up around the courthouse, nervous at first, but gaining in power by the moment, 'Shame, shame. A kidnap. Shame.'

'Silence,' roared the judge.

'Silence,' bellowed the clerks and the wardens.

'Get those screaming harpies out of here,' shouted the judge. Some of the loudest keening women were hustled bodily through the big double doors at the back of the chamber and flung onto the street.

'Child, approach the bench.' The judge crooked a thick, meaty finger at Davey.

'Your name, boy?'

'Davey, sir,' a shaky whisper.

'Your second name?'

'I don't know, sir. I don't know for sure what to say.' Davey looked at Sally, desperate for reassurance, but her face was as blank as a fresh-painted wall and she knelt on the floor witless and silent.

'I can't remember my second name, Sally.' He looked back at the judge. 'Is it Gordon?'

'Well, I don't know, lad. Is it? Is it Gordon? Is your mother dead, boy?'

'I don't know.' So quiet the newspaper men had to strain themselves to catch it, though the courtroom was now as hushed as a church at midnight.

'Your name is Davey Gordon. Don't you remember, Davey?' Peggy's bright lisping voice rang across the hushed court-room. 'Don't you remember when Sally held the burning matches and we set fire to the big straw, she said I had two names now, Peggy and Gordon?' Peggy struggled out of Sally's grip and ran to Davey, grasping his hand. 'No more Mammy, no more Grainne. Sally's our new sister now.'

'Witch! Kidnapper! Murderer!' The court was in uproar. Sally struggled back up off the floor and gathered the two children in her numb arms.

'As God is my witness, these children are my very own sister and brother.'

'As God is *my* witness,' Nellie shrieked, 'your honour, they are not.'

The judge stood and banged his hammer upon the desk over and over, adding to the fearsome din. 'Take these children to the care of the matron of the workhouse and see that they are well provided for until their mother can be found.'

Sally's screams rang up to the very rafters of the courthouse.

'Not the workhouse. Not the workhouse. They'll die surely.'

'The workhouse?' Peggy screamed. 'With the bad dog who eats babbies?'

Sally kissed Peggy's hair, cheeks and hands, but the child continued to scream, eyes closed, breathless and weeping.

Donal Teaghan rose to his feet. 'M'Lord, the workhouse is bursting at the seams and inmates are dying daily from cholera, faster than they can be buried. They won't take the children.'

A thwack of the gavel. 'They will take the children on the instruction of this court, or be held in contempt. The workhouse is funded and functioning. Wardens, take them away.'

Two wardens appeared at the bench, and each one took a child. With an arm round the middle of each small body they carried the children, kicking and scratching, towards the door. Peggy smashed her head backwards with all her small power into the chin of the gaoler carrying her, who raised his free hand and slapped her hard across the mouth.

'You filthy little hussy,' he roared, grabbing a handful of her hair. 'You'd best not do that again.'

As he carried her, silent and limp through the door, Sally took a last look at her and at the boy she loved.

'Don't cry, Peggy, don't cry. I'll find you,' she screamed into the doorway, 'wait for me, Davey, I'll find you.' Her gaoler spun round to face her, fist raised. The room went mercifully dark.

Chapter Seventeen

Hobart, October 1919, Sally

It's dark now, the wrens outside my window are silent and sleeping and the moon looms large through the window pane. It would be a good night for a dying soul to slip away, but I can't leave until I dredge up the strength to finish my story.

I wish Saoirse had stayed with me, to speed the passage of the hours, but how can I blame her for leaving? Every night for a week now she has spread an eiderdown over her knees and dozed uncomfortably in an armchair by the embers. But tonight she has returned to her own chamber and to her own bed, telling Josie and the serving girls that I am out of danger. Josie offered to toss and turn in the armchair in her place, but I heard Saoirse decline. She is afraid of what I will say, what secrets I will reveal. But she is wrong, this story is for Saoirse's ears only.

Now, I might think, she knows enough. She knows her grandmother is a fool and a liar. She knows enough. I could spare her the rest. I could tell her a fairy story now, a joyful vision of her mother's early life, happy under the warm sun of Tasmania, and how she came by chance to rest under my roof until I thought of her as my own child and gave her my name.

But, whatever else she might be, my granddaughter, for I will always think of her that way, is not stupid.

I will tell her the whole truth if I am spared long enough to do so. I am hoping to free her from the cage of respectability into which she has cast herself, free her from her cage of despair and self-loathing.

I will try to show her how a woman might make her own destiny, and something of the choices she can make.

I shiver under my eiderdown, although I am not cold. It's so dark. What wouldn't I give to see a loving face at my bedside?

Chapter Eighteen

Grangegorman, County Dublin, March 1849

Above Sally's head, a semi-circle of moon-like faces gazed down. A group of strange women and girls. She didn't fear them. She didn't feel anything at all.

'What ails that child, does she ever move or speak at all? Is she a defective?'

'Maybe she's a lunatic, or a mute.'

'She shouldn't be coming with us.' A tall, gaunt woman with faded red hair and the remnants of a faceful of freckles sniffed, and prodded Sally with her finger. 'There's no place for a mute lunatic on a ship crossing the ocean, dribbling and raving and killing the lot of us in our beds.'

'Well, Catherine, you would know more about that than the rest of us,' snapped back a younger, sad-eyed woman wrapped tightly in a blue shawl, her thin, yellow hair scraggled back into a braid. The red-haired woman turned on her heel, while the others hooted with laughter and mimicked her flouncing away.

'Sure, poor Catherine never killed that old biddy. Catherine's the only innocent woman in Grangegorman, apart from myself,' hooted a young girl, no older than Sally.

'She's damn lucky she's here in Grangegorman, and not swinging on a gibbet,' said Blue-shawl.

Sally closed her eyes again and let the darkness swallow her.

★ ★ ★

'Sally. For the love of God, Sally will you wake up and come back to yourself.'

Out of the dark black inside her head, Sally could hear words buzzing, but she never knew the sense of them, and she couldn't have cared less. Sometimes the words were kind and gentle, sometimes harsh and brutal. Sweet tunes and old lullabies sung close to her ear did not raise her, nor did curses or threats. She was hidden inside herself. Alone.

Alone.

★ ★ ★

Cold. Bitterly cold. Wet. And the musty reek of feathers burning. A sensation of heat. Pain.

'It's working.'

'It's true. Her eyes are opening, and I'd swear she sees me.' A familiar voice. 'Sally, little Sally, dearest sister. Say something, Sally, quick, before you're burnt for real.'

A searing agony shot through one of Sally's feet, the smallest toe smarting and throbbing. She struggled to raise her head off the bed, and saw her right foot in the grip of a strong, decently dressed woman. Wedged between each toe was a long, smouldering hen's feather. The pain ate into her foot and she gasped and raised herself slowly into a sitting slump, supporting her weight weakly on shaking elbows. The woman quickly dashed all the burning feathers onto the floor, grinding them beneath the heel of her sturdy buckled shoe.

'Oh, Mistress, you've done it, where all before you have failed. I see the light in her eyes.' Nellie Gordon rose from the side of Sally's pallet bed and grasped the hands of the other woman. 'Praise be to God, you're after bringing my sister back to me.'

'A weak broth is what she needs now,' said the older woman, 'A weak broth and a rub with these warm cloths. Get her out of those wet rags and I'll return directly with a broth and a shift.' She paused with her hand on the door frame. 'How long since she's eaten would you say?'

Nellie wrinkled her brow. 'She had her potatoes for breakfast the day we left the gaol for the courthouse.' She counted on her fingers, paused and added, 'That's three days since.' The other woman pursed her lips and bustled off, skirts rustling.

Nellie turned to Sally and started dragging at her clothes, which Sally clung to, and held close to her body in fear. 'Come on, you little imbecile.' She wrenched the dress over Sally's head, twisting it on the lugs of her ears, with a fearsome pain, and catching her wet, matted hair in one of the buttons till she shrieked. 'Get out of that wet dress, we're after dousing you with a bucket of water straight from the well, to help bring you back to your senses.'

Now Sally lay naked and shivering, on the coarse palliasse of the pallet bed, too tired and weak even to care about her lack of modesty, or to raise an arm to cover her breasts. Her breath soughed with a rasp in and out, slower now, and steadier. Nellie fell to rubbing her with a length of coarse calico cloth that lay nearby, chafing and bruising her, but finally driving some warmth and feeling back into her frozen arms and feet.

'Ow! Mother of God, that hurts,' Sally shrieked, as Nellie rubbed the rough fabric over the swelling burn on her little toe. 'Go easy, Nellie.'

Nellie stopped her rubbing, puffed a strand of hair off her face and stood back to look down at Sally, scowling. 'So you know me, then. Well that's a mercy. I thought you were after turning yourself into an imbecile. I thought the mind had snapped inside of you.'

She grabbed Sally's foot and examined the burn carefully. 'I'll get Mistress Jonathon to put some salve on that burn. I can't have you losing the toe, landing in Van Diemen's Land as a limping cripple, and what man'd look at you then?'

'Van Diemen's Land? Are we on the ship?'

'Don't be an óinseach! God give me strength. It could be months before a ship is ready for us. We're here in the women's prison in Grangegorman, in a muster for the transportation. There's a hundred and fifty of us convicted, some here, and some scattered round the country. And fifty more convictions will cause a ship to be summoned for us.'

She lifted Sally's right arm and joined her thumb and middle finger around the wrist. She slid the whole of Sally's hand through the loop of her fingers without difficulty.

'Christ, you're away to skin and bone. You've lost every bit of condition you gained in the gaol and more along with it. I thought you were for leaving this place in a box, and leaving *me* here, to start all over again with another girl, instead of my own dear sister.'

Sally's hand in Nellie's grasp swayed in the air in front of her face. The fingers were long, pale curved claws and she remembered the old woman with the spittle melting on her potatoes clinging to the serving girl's dress. She remembered the other women, all lining up to walk to the assize court in Naas.

'Nellie, what happened to the other women from the gaol in Naas? Old Mary Saunders, is she here?'

Nellie laughed and shook her hair down her shoulders. 'Don't you remember? No, she was sentenced after us, you were already dazed.'

'I don't.' Sally shook her head. 'She was sentenced, so she's here somewhere then?'

Nellie chuckled. 'Oh, she's not here. She cooked her own goose all right, shouting in the courthouse. Roaring and shouting at the gentry never gets you anywhere, *I'll be guilty of worse when I get out of here, My Lord*, she let rip, stamping and shaking her old fist, *if I don't get what I want. I'll thank your Lordship for seven years' transportation.*'

'And what did she get?'

'Two months' hard labour and solitary confinement, in Naas, and Judge Crampton telling her he'd cure her of her wish for life across the seas.'

'And what about the serious crimes? The other arsonists? Eliza Guilfoyle, Anne Daly, Kitty Nolan?'

'Oh they're here with us, back in the dormitories. Oul Crampton said to them he'd never seen a day at the assizes with so many arsons to come before him. He didn't give them solitary though, he sent them along here.'

Nellie sucked in her cheeks and then blew a loud, rasping fart through her red lips. 'No, he sent them along here, to wait for the ship, like us. I daresay he thought we'd be more use to the men of Hobart than an oul' wizened, dry apple like Mary Saunders. Kitty Nolan went down on her knees in the courthouse and thanked him kindly.'

A sudden fit of the shivers rippled across Sally's naked skin and her hairs stood up out of thousands of goose pimples. She had almost forgotten about the men of Hobart, far away in Van Diemen's Land, and of the one who would be waiting there, waiting for her, in the fullness of time. She crawled back onto the bed and drew the scrap of blanket across her middle. Her eyelids grated down over the burning, aching orbs of her eyes.

'And the children, Nellie,' a huge yawn interrupted her, almost splitting her face in two, 'will you go now and tell them I'm better from whatever ailed me? Have you been taking good care of them angels, and me sick in here, three whole days?'

'Never worry yourself about the childer. Sure they're in good hands, in the right place. We'll talk more about the childer later when you're stronger.'

Nellie sat gently on the pallet beside her and rubbed her shoulder, round and round, soothing and warming. It was the first kind touch Sally had had from Nellie in the four months of their acquaintance, and she was asleep before Mistress Jonathon returned from the kitchens with her broth.

★ ★ ★

Sally struggled up off the pallet and then sat down again heavily on the edge of it, head swimming, eyes flickering, and panting like a steam engine.

A young girl, wan and washed-out looking with bulging frog eyes, sat down beside her. 'You may houl' yer horses there, wee girl. You'll not be leppin' up out of thon bed any day soon.'

'That's right,' agreed a red-haired woman Sally remembered seeing in the days or hours of her delirium. 'We all thought you were dying, or 'changed by the fairies.'

'Aye, fairy-changed or mebbe hag-rid, that's what I thought, when I heard you shouting out in the night,' said the girl.

Sally wiped her hand across her brow, cold-clammy, and wiped it then on the rough woollen blanket. 'But who are you?'

The girl laughed and her big pop-eyes disappeared into a bright, deeply dimpled smile. Mischief and good spirits washed off her in waves and Sally found herself smiling back.

'Jesus, you're like a corpse with all its teeth on show,' muttered the red-haired woman, shivering and drawing her shawl tighter around her.

The girl hit the woman a good-natured slap on the shoulder.

'Leave the wee girl alone, can't you see she's half-starved? Don't worry, Sally, they'll soon fatten you up in here, the best of everything for the ladies of Grangegorman.'

'But, who are you? And where's Nellie and the others?'

'Where's me manners?' the girl laughed. 'Well, I'm begging your pardon, madam, I'm sure.' She leaped off the bed and dipped a sweeping curtsey while the other women laughed. 'Patsy O'Hanlon, lately of the parish of Drumcree in the Orchard County, at yer service.'

'And I'm Catherine Colligan,' said the thin, red-haired woman. 'I seen you the day you came in here, and I swore you'd never leave, except to go to the boneyard.'

'That's enough, now.' Nellie approached the bed from the corner where she'd been hidden from view. 'Don't be crowding round gawpin' at my poor sister like she's a crowing hen, give her some air. And you, Patsy, take yerself to Mistress Jonathon's room, tell her Sally is awake and sensible at last, and ask her for the broth.'

Patsy skipped off, just pausing on the threshold to flash Sally a wicked smile, and the other women drew back slightly too. Nellie sat on the pallet. Her smart shawl and her tight-bodiced dress were gone and she wore the same uniform as all the others, a loose, drab blue frock, more like a nun's habit than anything else. But Sally noticed she had kept her fine, many-buttoned boots, while the other women had poor, thin shoes on their feet. Under the warmth of the coarse woollen blanket Sally wore a long white cotton shift, much patched, the best piece of clothing that had ever covered her bones.

'Hush, little sister, let me tell you a story.'

Nellie took Sally's hand in hers, looked straight into her eyes, and stroked a few tendrils of hair away from her face. And in that position, one hand crushing Sally's bones, and the other discreetly pulling a clump of her hair so that she could hardly hide the pain from the watchers, Nellie spoke in a flat calm whisper that chilled every fibre of Sally's being.

'Now little sister, here we are in the muster at Grangegorman, waiting for the ship with these fine ladies. Whores and thieves the half of them. We got what we wanted, transportation to the hot side of the world, lucky you to have me to guide you.' She paused long enough to rub a forefinger gently down Sally's right cheek, and to take a firmer grip of her hair surreptitiously. 'What is done is done, and can never be undone, Sally. Stick to me and pay attention to everything I say and do, and life will be fine and easy, from this day out.'

Just the smallest movement of her little finger brought the pain in Sally's scalp to such a height that there was no choice but to lie motionless, and she shuffled closer still, so that the two girls appeared locked in a fond embrace. 'Spoil this for me, Sally,' she hissed, quiet as a prayer, 'spoil this for me and yer life from this day on will be a walking misery, a living hell. As God is my witness, I will ruin you, if you try to thwart me.'

She crushed the twig-thin bones of Sally's hand hard enough to draw a gasp, then released her and smiled at the other women.

'It's the will of God,' she said to them. 'A new life for me and my sister under the bright southern sun and three meals a day for the rest of our lives.'

'And the others?' Sally asked, craning round for a glimpse of the bright, shining faces she loved. 'Are the children in another ward?'

With her hand on Sally's shoulder, pinching so as almost to tear right through skin and sinew, Nellie smiled and whispered, 'Let's be quiet now for a moment, pet? Let me talk to you later and tell you all you've missed.'

Sally was silent and nodded her head until the brutal grip upon her shoulder loosened. Fear, confusion and pain in equal measure raced through her mind.

'Ah, lovely, here's the good broth now,' Nellie said. Patsy burst through the door followed by Mistress Jonathon, who bustled and creaked like a ship under sail.

'Praise be, *the dead arose and appeared to many*, as the Good Book says,' Mistress Jonathon cried. And then there was no talk, no thought at all as the spoon scraped the bowl and the warmth and the flavour spread out through every inch of her, and she never remembered Peggy and Davey again until every morsel was licked from the wooden bowl. And that shame haunted Sally for ever.

Chapter Nineteen

Hobart, October 1919, Sally

The rosary beads have at last dropped out of Saoirse's hands and she stares at me in horror.

'My mother was not your daughter. Margaret Gordon was not your daughter? She took your name, and yet now you tell me it's not your name either.' Saoirse's voice rises and shakes. She clutches at her head as if she will pull the hair out by the roots. 'I'm so confused, I can't make head nor tail of it.'

I close my eyes for a moment. This is even more painful than I had feared.

'I'm sorry, Saoirse. I'm truly sorry that we kept this from you. We thought we were protecting you.'

'My mother spent my whole life lying to me, and keeping up this pretence. What gives you the right to tear it all down now? In a few days' time, I'd have been none the wiser.'

'When I'm dead, you mean?'

'Yes, when you're dead.' She flushes, but for once she doesn't drop my gaze, and I am glad of that. 'You're the one says you come from a place and time where people talked about death, gathered round all singing and drinking,' she snaps, 'but I'm not allowed to say the obvious, that you're dying and that soon what you want, or what you need, won't matter any more?'

'I thought you were a Christian?'

'What?'

'Doesn't Jesus preach forgiveness?'

'Repentance is what he preaches, and I see precious little evidence of repentance, for anything you've done, in your crazy story so far. If you don't repent of raising me in a tissue of lies, don't you at least regret taking up with that harlot, Eleanor Gordon? Don't you repent of having those two poor innocent children sent to the workhouse?'

'Have you understood my story, I wonder?' I look in her eyes, snapping harsh and bitter under their heavy lids. 'Do you understand that Peggy and Davey were destined for a life of violence and misery? Do you understand that they never could in a hundred years in Newbridge have hoped for the life I planned to make for them here?'

'It was not your choice to make.' She turns from me and dashes angry tears away. 'They were four and six years old. You killed them.'

'Choices. There's that word again. I made so few choices in my early life, most of my decisions were made for me. Women had so few choices then; starve or steal, graveyard or gaol yard, lie or die. My story's not so remarkable.'

'Compared to whom?'

'Compared to the rest of them. The respectable grandmothers of Hobart. Seventy years ago, this town was full of the sweepings of the gaols of the British Empire. It didn't take much provocation to end up out here. For every one hardened criminal there were fifty girls like me; larceny, petty theft, motiveless arson. And women were needed. Fill the cradles of Hobart and empty the gaols of England and Ireland at the one time.'

Chapter Twenty

Grangegorman, County Dublin, May 1849

Convicts were flooding into the women's prison in Grangegorman, hidden in the rich farmland of north County Dublin. Every woman who arrived brought the time of embarkation closer. It would not be long before Sally and Nellie began their voyage. Nellie counted off the days with impatience, Sally plodded through each day, disconsolate and mourning. Her nights were disturbed by horrifying dreams of the children swelling and blackening with typhus in the workhouse ward, or of their stick-thin bodies lying on a pile, rat infested and dog gnawed.

Although she barely spoke and never smiled, Sally grew in strength of body if not of mind. Nellie saw to that. She watched every mouthful of food Sally was given with a jealous regard, and pinched or slapped her if she tried to push it around her plate. If she could have chewed the morsels before they went into Sally's mouth, she would. Sally chewed and swallowed under her instruction, tasting nothing and caring not at all. Three or four times a day Nellie took a firm grip of Sally's arm under the oxter and dragged her, stumbling and staggering in the fresh air, until the girl was strong enough to walk on her own. Then she released the grip she had on Sally's arm, but not on her mind or on her tongue. It was her constant employment to ensure that Sally was never alone with another woman or girl, even coming into the jakes with her and driving out the others if they wanted to piss at the same time.

'Sarah,' Mistress Jonathon said to Sally a dozen times a week, 'you have been blessed by God in the sister he has given you.'

'Yes, mistress.'

'I hope you are grateful, for the love and attention Eleanor lavishes upon you?'

'Yes, mistress.'

'Never forget to include Eleanor in your prayers, for I cannot imagine you recovering your health and wits without her loving attention.'

Nellie smiled and helped Sally out into the exercise yard once more.

'What's done is done,' Nellie told Sally at least once each day. 'Here we are in the warm and dry, potatoes and milk three times a day.' She grabbed Sally's uniform dress and rubbed it between her fingers. 'Look at the cut of you, the fine frock you have on you. You belong to Her Majesty now, you're a valuable piece of gear, to be protected and kept alive at all costs.'

'And the children, Nellie. In the workhouse. I'll never forgive you, if I live to be a hundred years old.'

Nellie tightened her grip on Sally's upper arm. 'Forget the childer, Sally. Them childer near killed you once already. When the gaoler belted you in the courthouse and you fell and dashed your head off the stones of the floor, I thought you were dead and gone. I nearly died myself with the fright of thinking I'd be stuck in Van Diemen's Land with no sister.'

'Why do you even need a sister? What difference would it make if I died now?'

'I need a sister. I need a clean, young sister. When I have my seven years' servitude done I'll be thirty-six years old. You'll only be twenty-one. A husband wants a young, child-bearing wife. I'll find a respectable, decent husband for my nice young virgin sister, and a home for myself along with her, a hell of a lot faster than for myself alone. I'm not marrying any convict, and the free men are few out there. And listen to you complaining, after I saved your life. You'd be dead and gone without me.'

'I wish I *was* dead and gone. I never should have left Clonsast, I'd be under the ground now with my own people.'

'Well, you're not. You're not dead, and you're not lying on a bed of prickly furze while some soldier rams into you over and over, and spits in your mouth when he's finished.' She swung Sally round to face her and grabbed her shoulders. 'Now listen, what I've done for us is a near miracle. We're clean and fed and I have that whole bunch of scrawny hens in there thinking I cured your illness, and that I'm a miracle worker, near enough. And it's that oul' bitch Jonathon who saved you, when all is said and done.'

'But Peggy and Davey. I stole them away from their mother and now they're in the workhouse.'

Nellie drew herself up. She wasn't a tall woman – already Sally reached nearly to her shoulder. 'Forget the childer. Peggy is dead. Davey is dead. You know that as well as I do. Without you to fight their corner in the workhouse, to elbow them forward, to shout out for them, they wouldn't have lasted a fortnight and you know it. Typhus, cholera or hunger, take your pick, whichever bothers you least.'

She put her lips close to Sally's ear and whispered the lesson Sally refused to learn.

'They're dead.'

Sally bowed her head, and not a drop came from the eyes that were cried dry, nor from the heart that had turned harder than an altar stone. Nellie was right, they were dead, and Sally knew it.

They turned from the exercise yard and walked together back towards the ward. Ten yards from the gate, they looked at each other and began to run. They burst through the door to the howls and whoops of a dozen women, and there, tangled on the floor in a mess of arms and shoes and hair and nails was Catherine Colligan, beating the face off another woman, Lucy Smith from the far north of the country.

'I won't say it again. I never took the shovel to that oul' baggage, Marge Foran.' Catherine paused for breath and shook Lucy like a good terrier bitch will shake a nearly dead rat. 'I never stoved in her head and left her lying in her own kitchen where she'd be sure to be found, but I swear to Almighty God to be my judge, that I am sentenced as a murderess, and if one more of you gives me cause, I will live up to my reputation and kill that woman – and any who aid her.'

Lucy whimpered. 'God Almighty, Catherine, I'm sorry, sure I was only looking to pass the time with a bit of fooling.'

'Fool with someone else. I've had my fill of fooling, and I won't take another second of it.'

The flaming colour faded gradually from her once-pale freckled cheeks and she smoothed her red hair and rose slowly from the floor, reaching down a helping hand to Lucy, who seemed even more fearful of Catherine now, than when she had been flaking her.

'It's all right for youse, the half of youse are here on purpose. Half of Ireland is aflame these days with the arsonists, and a body can hardly dare close their eyes under their own thatch for fear of the likes of youse.' She glared at Nellie and Sally, and some of the other arsonists, who coughed and looked down at the ground. 'Oh it's a fine adventure for youse. But I'm branded a murderer, and torn away from my only child, and you know damn rightly I'll never set eyes on her again. Oh, Mary-Anne, Mary-Anne, God help you, motherless child.' She threw her apron over her face and rocked to and fro – silent and terrifying.

Sally slipped down on the bed beside her and risked putting her arm around her, though her father had warned her over and over of the bad luck that followed red-haired women and of their wild rages. 'I know how you feel, Catherine. God help us, maybe you'll meet her again in this world, and in the next.'

She struck Sally's arm away.

'How would you know what I feel, little óinseach? How could you know what a curse and a heart-scald it is to be torn away from the child you love, the pulse of your heart?' Sally opened her mouth and saw, just barely in sight, Nellie, shaking her head slowly. She clamped her lips shut.

Lucy Smith rose up from her knees then, and to the surprise of the gathered women leaned across and took Catherine's hand. 'Take heart, love, sure the child is with her father, and with the help of God, ye'll be together again in time.'

'That bastard!' Catherine sniffed and wiped a long snail trail across her cheek with the back of her right hand. 'That cur! And who do you think it was killed the old woman? It was himself, I'd stake my soul on it. We'd been lodging there with her four months, and he hated her. God knows she was a difficult woman to like.'

'And what about the neighbour woman, Mary Hurley? She said she heard you make threats to the old Foran woman, and declare that, only for fear of the rope, you'd kill her and have the whole house to yourself.'

'And who do you think put Mary Hurley up to that trick? That bastard Samuel Colligan, may he burn in the eternal fires of hell for what he done to me.'

She stood up, enjoying her audience.

'I'd say now, that if you knocked on Samuel Colligan's door in the dark of night, you might find him naked and not alone, neither,' Nellie said quietly from the back of the group.

'Oh, never a truer word spoken. What other reason would Mary Hurley have to be saying those things about me, and me that never done her a bad turn?' Catherine stamped her foot. 'Oh that's a bad whore of a new mother that my Mary-Anne has got for herself, God be good to her.'

Catherine walked out of the room and leaned her flaming cheek against the cold wall of the yard.

'You know she was to swing?' Lucy said quietly. 'Sentenced to the hangman, but she pleaded the belly, and the judge changed the sentence to be sent out, not for seven years, but for life. It was Justice Crampton himself wrote the petition for mercy – make of that what you will. Caused a big stir in Naas. It was in the newspapers and all. There was plenty who said she should swing anyway, once the baby was weaned.'

'Pleaded the belly?' Nellie said, 'Well, the husband was dipping in both bowls at the same time then. And she should start to show, by-and-by, so we'll know soon enough.'

Lucy laughed. 'If every woman in here who had pleaded the belly was really up the pole, we'd need a midwife in the boat with us. There's only one is truly pregnant, to the best of my knowledge, Mary Gandon by name, and a few, like me, with babes at the breast.'

'So did she kill the old woman or not?' Sally asked. Sally wanted a friend and she wanted an ear to pour her sorrow and loss into, but not so badly that she'd take up with a murderess.

'Who knows? Who cares?' said Patsy O'Hanlon. 'The judge has sentenced her, the Peelers has solved the crime so they're happy, the oul' bitch that is in the ground probably deserved it – I never met a boarding house woman yet who could keep a civil tongue in her head to those below her.' Patsy sniffed and winked at Sally. 'We're all criminals here, and you'd do well to bear that in mind.'

The stern tones of the prison bell tolled through the building, signalling the end of leisure and the start of chores. Sally was due a lesson in the laundry, and this was one of the few times in the week that Nellie could not accompany her. Patsy O'Hanlon and some of the younger girls joined her as she hurried toward Mistress Jonathon and the next lesson in the skills they would need in servitude.

'Now ladies, take the shift in your left hand and lay it out on the table.' Mistress Jonathon swished around the small room, tutting and correcting the dozen girls who stood in front of her. 'Now pick up the smoothing iron in your right hand and glide it up to the neck.'

The iron weighed heavy in Sally's hand and sweat trickled from her armpit, making her itch and squirm. She laid the iron on her shift and dolefully pushed it forward, but it stuck and the fabric puckered and wrinkled. Mistress Jonathon tutted and puffed, pushing her aside, then lifted the iron and spat on the sole plate. 'It has to be properly hot, Sarah. A drop of water should sizzle on a hot smoothing iron. Look at the state of your good shift. Still, it's better than burned, I suppose.' Sally stuck the iron back into the glowing coals.

'I've never heard the like of it. The shift and the uniform to be washed once a week,' muttered Patsy quietly, '*and mended if necessary*. In the name of

God, whoever heard of washing clothes once a week? Who would have the turf to heat the water, and what could you do to a shift in a week anyway, that would warrant washing it?'

'Cleanliness is next to godliness,' Mistress Jonathon said, and those same words were worked in coloured threads on a piece of cambric that hung on the wall of the laundry.

'Mistress Jonathon,' Sally asked, 'd'you know that in Naas Gaol, the women washed themselves just the once, on the day that they came in, and it was done in the kitchen, beside the plates and cups. By the time it came to my turn, the water was as dark as ditch water. If you'd dropped a potato into the bowl, you'd never have seen it again.'

'Disgusting,' Jonathon snapped. 'I've not been inside a common gaol, and I don't care to talk about it. It's my job to get you ready for life in the colonies, doing something useful for a change.' She handed Sally back her iron. 'Spit!' The drop of slabber fizzed and sizzled, little bubbles bouncing round and round on the hot plate. 'Now press that shift, and do it properly, or you'll end up on a farm in the back country, feeding swine and sleeping in the sty too.'

Patsy chirped up from the other side of the big table. 'Isn't it a crying shame no one ever thought to teach us anything useful when we were on the outside? Maybe we could have stayed outside, and not had to be robbin' and burnin' down half the countryside to get in here.'

Mistress Jonathon walked over and inspected Patsy's shift. 'That's excellent work, Patricia,' she said, 'I'd hardly do it better myself.' Then she turned and belted Patsy across her smiling face, so hard that a little grunt escaped her lips with the effort of it. The sound of the blow echoed round the laundry and the girls gasped.

'How dare you speak to me like that? I'm matron of this establishment. I'm not your friend and I'm certainly not your equal. Never raise that saucy face to your elders and betters again, if you want to make a life for yourself. You are being given the wonderful gift of a second chance, at great cost to the Poor Law ratepayers of this land.' She glared around the kitchen.

'You won't get a third chance. Criminals and streetwalkers, the scum of the earth. Stealing bread and opening your legs, when the safety of the work-house is provided for you, at great expense to the Unions, but you won't go in. Animals.'

She stormed over to the door and wrenched it open.

'Get out! All of you!'

The inmates grabbed their shifts and fled.

'Her soul to the Devil, Patsy, that was some quare smack she gave you,' said a girl called Eliza Guilfoyle when they finally stopped running. On the left cheek of Patsy's face, clear as the nose upon it, was the imprint of four fingers, fiery red. 'I wouldn't have thought she had it in her.'

'And to use words like that,' sniggered little Liz Curry. 'I wonder where did she learn them, was it in the big Protestant church?'

'Ach, don't give it another thought,' laughed Patsy. 'I'd say it's a long time since she was asked to open her own legs, and she's just jealous.' They laughed.

Patsy touched the red skin of her face and winced.

'I have a pot of salve from Mistress Jonathon,' Sally said. 'It's for my burnt foot. Come away with me and I'll give you some for your poor face.'

'Oh, it's *Mistress* Jonathon is it? Thon oul' carn.' But Patsy laughed to show that there was no hard feeling and she linked her arm through Sally's. 'Come on so, and we'll use up the salve till I'm gorgeous again.'

Sally laughed, for a blind man couldn't call Patsy gorgeous, or even pass-ably well-looking, with her bulgy eyes and small nose, but her smile was the light of the sun streaming through a patchy cloud, bringing beauty even to a winter sky. Sally squeezed her arm, gently, and she pressed back again and slipped her arm round Sally's waist. At the door of the ward, Sally paused and shook Patsy's arm off.

'Better not let Nellie see that we're friends. She's fierce jealous, after prom-ising our mother to protect me. Doesn't even like me going to my lessons in the laundry without her.'

Patsy raised up her big pale-green eyes and stared straight into Sally's until she felt the colour rise up in her cheeks and her own eyes sought the paved floor.

'Listen, Sally. I don't know you and you don't know me, but this much I can tell you. There isn't one person in this place, barring Jonathon, who's blind enough to think Nellie Gordon is your sister.'

'But she is.' Sally's story was straight. Nellie had thought of everything and had coached her carefully. 'I know we're different on the eye, and the gap of years between us is big, but that's because my mother's first husband died, and she was a widow a long time before taking up with my own father. Nellie was older than I am now when I was born. She's like a second mother to me.'

Patsy put her finger to her lips, and pulled Sally past the door of the ward and out into the yard. 'Sally, you can lie to me or you can speak the truth, but we all know fine rightly that thon woman is none of your blood. It's not the look of her, there's many pairs of sisters look less alike than you do.' She sighed and glanced away. 'It's not the way she doesn't look *like* you, it's the way she looks *at* you. You pretend that she guards you like a cat guards her kitten, but it's not that way at all. She's more like a dog with a bone. There's not a hint of love in her eyes, just hungry greed. Not one kind word have I heard fall from her lips towards you in all the weeks since you regained your senses.'

'You're wrong, Patsy. You have her wrong. She's stern, is all. She gave her solemn word on our mother's deathbed to protect me.'

'Did no one ever tell you that you rub at your chin when you're lying?' Patsy asked. 'I seen you do it loads of times before. Ach, well. It's no skin off my nose if you want to keep your secret.' She stood up and turned before leaving. 'I won't ask you again, wee girl, and if you're happy, you're happy. But if you're not … you know where to find me.'

Her thin shoes crunched across the sharp gravel of the exercise yard and two tears slipped out of the corners of Sally's eyes and slid down her cheeks. The fear of Nellie fought with her loneliness and with her sudden liking for this ugly, strange girl from the far north of the country, and with her need for a friend.

Fear won.

★ ★ ★

Screams and shrieks echoed down the cold, stone corridors of Grangegorman, mixed with the frantic bawling of small children. Nellie and Sally rushed to-gether to see the source of the new excitement. All the women were truly sick of the sight of each other, and they ran towards the screams, rather than from them, as they would have done a few weeks earlier.

They paused at the door of the washroom and leaned against the door jamb, panting.

'Eleanor, Sarah, come in here at once,' ordered Mistress Jonathon, 'and restrain this woman. Eliza, run to the dormitories and find someone who can gabble to this lunatic in her own heathen tongue.'

Nellie and Sally advanced slowly into the room, for they wanted no hand, act or part in this drama. Two small, naked children stood by the side of the big washtub, which was steaming with plenty of clean, warm water. Sally longed to slip into it. She had had two hot baths since her arrival, an extra one on account of how sick she'd been, and she had lain for many minutes in that glorious heat, and wondered at the wasteful luxury of it all.

Between the children and themselves crouched the most wretched wreck of a woman Sally had ever seen. Her lips were drawn back from big yellow teeth on gums of shocking, weeping red. Her bones were held together by skin and fury – in this land of woeful want, Sally had never seen a thinner body that still breathed.

'Seize her, and hold her fast till the children are washed,' ordered Mistress Jonathon, but Nellie and Sally took one step backwards instead.

'I'm afraid she'll bite us, mistress, begging your pardon, or else I'd do your bidding,' Nellie said. At Jonathon's urging they took one step closer and the pitiful hag opened her mouth and hissed like a tortured cat. They leaped back. A string of abuse issued from the woman's mouth, and they didn't need to understand the words to know exactly what she meant.

Eliza arrived back, with Lucy Smith close behind. Lucy slipped into the room and crooned and chirped to the wild woman, in the old tongue, back and forth, while the rest stood like imbeciles, not a bit the wiser.

The woman rose from her half crouch and stood upright, to the best of her abilities, for she was stooped and crooked in the shoulders. The light of terror shone in her eyes and she wept as she spoke with Lucy.

'Begging your forgiveness, mistress, but she says she has suffered great pains and broken the laws of God and man to reach this place. All belonging to her have died by the roadside, barring these two young ones, which she believes it is your intention to drown in this here giant cooking pot, and serve for supper.'

Mistress Jonathon swelled like a bantam cock and her voice was as cold as charity.

'And would you be so good as to explain to her that Christians do not eat children, and that those filthy pups must be washed and deloused with no further delay.' She rubbed her hair distractedly where it peeped out under her cap and added quietly, 'I'm itching all over, and I haven't even laid hands on them yet, filthy things.'

A flood of language – fear and protest from the strange woman, soothing and cooing from Lucy. 'Mistress, her name is Áine, that's Anne in these parts, and her Gaelic is from the west, whilst mine is of the north, but as I understand her, she says she has raised nine children so far, and ne'er a drop of water has touched any of them.'

'Or herself, it would seem.' And indeed the stench from the three of them was an insult to the senses. 'Ask her, Lucy, would she like three generous plates of potatoes, a little broth and some milk, or water. Or would she like to be turned onto the street to die of hunger in a land where no one will understand her final confession?'

The baths proceeded with much screaming and terror. 'She thinks the skin is after peeling off the children,' Lucy explained, as layer after layer of black scum rose up from the lather of the carbolic soap.

After the excitement Mistress Jonathon went to lie down and loosen the stays of her dress. The three new inmates were taken to a pallet in a ward with two other Gaelic speakers, and Nellie, Patsy and Sally were left together, picking up the new arrivals' discarded rancid rags with tongs and dropping them into a sack to be burned.

'Mark my words, girls,' Nellie nodded and smiled, 'the time of leaving is close. That's the tenth new woman this week. They're sending them from every corner of the land, thick and fast. The gaols are emptying into Grangegorman. It can't be much longer.'

Patsy and Sally looked at each other, and although they didn't answer, they smiled. They were ready for the journey. It was time to put Ireland behind them.

Chapter Twenty-one

Hobart, October 1919, Saoirse

The woman who used to be my grandmother has asked me to bathe her. She says she longs to sink for one last time into a warm canister of water and let the heat soak into her bones. I stoked the fire for her instead. Her chamber is warm enough, and spring is well advanced. If she thinks I am putting Honora and Joanna to the trouble of heating and carrying buckets of water, she has less wit left than I think she has.

She tried last night to tell me a story about a bath, about a bath in the prison. I don't want to hear about prisons.

I wash her face and moisten her lips. That's good enough. It isn't easy to touch her. I shrink from the flesh that last week I stroked and dabbed and wiped, in love as well as in duty.

'Saoirse, my pet.'

'What is it?'

'Have you time to listen to the rest?'

I do not recognise the wheedling tone that has crept into her voice. Where is the strong proud woman I have lived with all my life? The woman who would have commanded that I sit and listen?

'I am going back to the registrar to look for the record of my mother's birth. '

'You won't find her that way, but if I'm spared ... '

Her voice cracks and trembles and abruptly I leave the room. I can't bear this new cravenness in her character. She knows she has lost me and can only have my company by stringing out her story, with the promise of revelations to come.

I must make her understand that I no longer care about her story. It is my story I want. My mother. My father. If I can't have a grandmother, I need someone else.

I pull on my coat and hat, walk out into the bird-bright morning and head for the dock.

Chapter Twenty-two

Kingstown port, County Dublin, Tuesday, 26 June 1849

The dockers roared and cursed, the gulls shrilled, the ropes securing the sails flapped and snapped in the stiff onshore breeze. Two hundred women and twenty-eight children stood and laughed or wept on the quayside. Kingstown in the south of the county of Dublin thronged and heaved with sailors, chandlers, chancers and hawkers. On every corner, at every door and following the heels of the workers and gentry alike, crowds of starving children, hands outstretched, wept for bread or a penny. The children drew back a yard or so for each curse hurled in their direction, but only a swift boot, or a slash with a walking cane made them retreat completely.

After the fresh countryside of Grangegorman, the reek of Kingstown made Sally's breakfast of potatoes and milk stir in her stomach. She clapped her hand over her mouth, the filth of the port being almost as bad as the gaol in Naas. Steaming piles of horse shit littered the roadways, and muckrakers dashed between the hooves and the rumbling wheels, scooping the dung into buckets with their bare hands.

With a sudden stabbing anguish, Sally remembered the last time she had carried the brimming pisspot to the tanners in Newbridge, and she hardened her heart against the fierce pang of grief for the sorry end of Peggy and Davey, and against the guilt she felt even for their mother, who, when all was said and done, had fared much worse from Sally's stay with her than Sally had.

Nellie was right, it was time to look forward, not back. The children were dead, her parents were dead, but she was alive, and when the summer had hit its height last week on Midsummer's Day she had celebrated her fifteenth birthday, better fed and dressed than ever before, and ready to leave this living hell behind.

Little Liz Curry leaped from foot to foot, stretched on tiptoe and craned her neck around until it seemed the sinews of her throat would snap and her eyes would fall out from the exertion of it all.

'What the hell ails you, girl?' Nellie snapped at Liz. 'Could you not stand at peace and quit your stamping all over me?'

'I'm looking for my father.' Liz strained upwards and took a long slow sweep of a glance round the quayside. 'I spoke out the words I wanted to say to him, and Mistress Jonathon took the letter down and promised to give it to the message carrier. He should be here. If he still lives in the same house, he would have got the note in plenty of time and Missus Cassidy in the victuallers would have read it to him.'

'Well, now,' sighed Nellie, 'and what would your father be doing here? Wouldn't it cost him a clean fortune to get here from Naas, even if he wanted to? And he never wrote to you, nor sent a memorial or petition to the Convict Board for to get you released, and you a bare child and on your first offence of larceny?' Nellie smiled a slanted, cruel smile as she rubbed salt into the wound. 'You'd have been a prime girl for a pardon, if yer father could get off his arse and petition for you. That oul' bastard Crampton never should have transported you in the first place. I'd say yer father's glad to see the back of you.'

Sally reached out a hand and gave Nellie's arm a gentle squeeze, asking her to stop her needling, but she shrugged Sally off with a snarl and turned back to bait Liz again. Liz, only four foot tall, and alone in the world, was a match for Nellie and ready for her.

'Well, yer right and yer wrong, Nellie.' Liz rested a moment from her search to turn to face them. 'My father's not glad to see the back of me, but he's hopeful for me and that's how I can't give up hope myself. After the sentence was passed, he came to the prison and said he would move heaven and earth to be on the quayside to wave me off.'

'Hopeful? How would he be hopeful and his daughter sent across the seas to the other side of the world?' Sally asked.

Liz sighed and rubbed her forehead with the back of her right hand, and Sally noticed how clean she was, how clean they all were, scrubbed and smelling of carbolic soap to pass their inspection with the surgeon.

'He's hopeful for me, Sally, for my brothers William and Andrew are sentenced to seven years as well. For all I know, they are gone out already. It was the twelfth day of March when we were arrested and here it is past Midsummer.' She jumped up on the balls of her feet again and took another look around the milling crowds. 'It'll be a fine thing for me to reach Van Diemen's Land and to know my brothers are there too. Maybe it's not such a big place. I daresay we'll find each other, soon enough.'

'All three of you arrested?' Sally gasped. 'Is it a whole family of criminals you were?'

Liz laughed. 'A family of criminals? Well, that'd be your own situation too. Sure aren't you and Nellie a family of criminals?'

Nellie turned like the crack of a drover's whip and looked as though she would strike Liz's smiling face. 'Indeed, and we are not criminals. We're decent, well-bred sisters fallen on hard times who set fire to a straw rick with no malice at all, just to escape the trouble that the country is in. And we end up in this company; thieves and streetwalkers.'

But Liz just pealed a long trill of giggles and answered, pleasantly enough, 'Oh, I do beg yer pardon, Lady Muck, here's me forgetting meself, and cheeking me betters. I'm not a thief, not really, and if that oul' bitch Grace Magee hadn't been so drunk, I wouldn't be in this position.'

Some of the other women crowded round, and when Liz had her audience settled and quiet she took up the tale again.

'My poor mother is under the sod this many a year, God rest her.' They all blessed themselves and murmured the response, *God and Mary rest her.* 'And my father, John Curry, of New-Row, Naas, in the county of Kildare, has married a new wife.'

'Ah,' burst in Eliza Guilfoyle, 'and it is the witch of a stepmother has you sent away, to save the few pennies for her own children?' The women nodded – it was an old familiar story.

'Houl' yer whisht, and let me speak.' Liz's eyes were dancing, she had the air of a seanachie about her. 'My stepmother is a good and Christian woman, at least she is up to this point, and she has no child of her own yet, and no sign of one. She treated myself, the brothers and the sister, Mary, as good as could be hoped for, and we had no cause for complaint on that score.

'Now she runs my father's house in New-Row as a rooming house, and things were not going well for us, as the blight and destitution has the travelling people so short of money, and no journeys being made unless there is no choice at all in the matter.' The women nodded.

'Well, I won't lie to ye, ladies, at the close of a market day last March, in comes an oul' peddler woman, Grace Magee, and she was a stranger to us, and wall-falling drunk. *Sit down to the fire, my good woman,* says the stepmother, meaning to treat her well and to lighten her purse with kind words. But no, up rises Magee and says she, *Where's the fire? You can't mean that miserable spark over there?*

'*We haven't the money for turf,* answers my stepmother, and doesn't Magee produce from inside in her bosom, a drawstring purse, and shakes out three ha'pennies and sends my brother William running for turf. And when the fire is well stoked, Magee raises up her head and says, *What'll we ate?* And we've scarcely a crust in the whole of the house for the family, never mind to share with the stranger.' Liz paused and put her hands on her hips, a passable imitation of an old woman.

'Well. On my soul, out comes the drawstring purse again from deep in the bosom and more money given to Andrew to go and buy a pound of Indian meal, which in truth is better than nothing, but not much.'

'Indeed, indeed, that's the truth,' the women whispered.

'Well, we ate the meal once it was halfway cooked, which was an hour or more, and Grace Magee was supping from a brown bottle all the while, although she was already fluthered, and never asked the stepmother nor the father if they had a mouth on them at all.'

The women tutted and shook their heads at this shocking display of greed and ill manners.

'She was pissed as a lord when she stood up, swung on her travelling cloak and disappeared out into the night. Well, we didn't know if she'd be back for a bed for the night, or not, but hadn't we the roaring fire and the half-cauldron of meal inside us, so we were happy enough.'

Liz paused and looked around her audience. Every woman close enough to hear was silent, hanging on the words as they dropped from Liz's mouth. It was obvious she was the daughter of a rooming house – she must have heard many stories, and learned how to tell one, in the long evenings beside the fire with the weary travellers.

'Well!' roared Liz, and they all jumped, then laughed nervously. 'Didn't she rush back in five minutes later with a constable. *That's the young strap who stole my purse*, says she, pointing straight at me. *And them's the boyos emptied the coins from it and knocked me to the floor when I begged them to give it back, as God is my witness*, and she pointing at Andrew and William. And how, I might ask you ladies, would a girl as small as me reach down deep into the bosom of a big peddler woman and take her purse out from there?'

The women nodded and clucked their tongues.

'My brother Andrew went down on his knees in the court in front of Justice Crampton at the March assizes, and begged him to spare me, and me only thirteen years old at the time, and of good character. Oul' Crampton says, *Give me until tomorrow to think about the girl*, and when we came back on the morrow, he give me the same sentence as the brothers – seven years.'

'Shocking, shocking, and you as innocent as the babe unborn,' Eliza burst out, 'Hell's curse on that disgraceful, drunk oul' baggage, making accusations and bringing trouble onto the heads of innocent, decent folk.'

'Aye,' laughed Liz, 'that's the very truth of it, a disgusting oul' liar she was. Although,' she broke off and nudged Eliza in the ribs, 'although, when the constable came in the house, he found the purse tucked into my dress and two shillings in coins in Andrew's pocket.' She screeched with delighted laughter. 'It's a mystery to be sure.'

Some of the women laughed with her, some, like Nellie, let on to be shocked and annoyed, and others just looked at the ground and tried to work it out in their stiff, slow minds.

'Ah, lookit,' Liz finished, 'the Da came into the prison to talk to me and the plan is made. When me and Willie and Andrew is finished our time out foreign, there'll be three of us earning. It's only seven years. We're to send for him and my sister and stepmother and, God willing, we'll be together and set up for life. That's the reason there was no memorial nor petition made to the penal board. Who, or what, remains for me now in Naas, after what I done? Or didn't do.'

A whistle shrilled along the quayside. All chatter died away as the women watched while slowly, slowly, a small rowing boat was lowered from the side of the barque *Australasia*. With four men at the oars it creaked across the bay and was secured to huge stanchions on the quay. The two hundred prisoners stood, each clutching a small canvas bag with a change of uniform, two pairs of woollen stockings, a shift and any small possession she might have of her own. Some women had a prayer book or a bible, Nellie had her fine black shawl and button boots. Sally had nothing of her own, nor did Liz Curry, Patsy O'Hanlon, Eliza Guilfoyle or Catherine Colligan.

Under Mistress Jonathon's instruction batches of women marched, some smiling and eager, some weeping, down the plank into the boat and were rowed out, towards the deck of the vessel which would be their home for three months or more. A terrible mournful shriek rose up from the mouths and hearts of many of the women, and those from the west of the land wailed and keened in their own tongue, like so many banshees.

Liz Curry ran to the harbour wall, knuckles white as she clenched the railings and sought in vain for the face of her father among the crowd who had come to weep, to cheer, or to spit upon the ship full of female criminals bound for the far shores of Hobart. She never took her eyes off the milling crowd, until her fingers were prised loose, not unkindly, by Mistress Jonathon, who led her to her place in the muster of women on the boat. Not a tear escaped her, but her face twisted with the pain of keeping them behind her lids and she blinked furiously.

'Don't blame yer father, love,' whispered Patsy, 'sure it's fifty miles to Naas, if it's a mile. And it's a hundred more to Armagh, where all belonging to *me* think me dead.'

'With the help of God, Liz, you'll find your brothers on the other side,' Sally muttered. 'That's more than I can wish for, for I'm alone in the world.'

'Except for your sister,' Liz said, with a curious stare. Sally glanced at Patsy who widened her eyes in warning, and shook her head a fraction.

'Except for Nellie, of course,' Sally agreed. Sally slipped one hand into Liz's, the other into Patsy's and the three of them clung together and watched from the rocking, rolling boat as, on the shore behind them, Mistress Jonathon took the hand of a car-man who helped her up into a brougham. He clicked his tongue at the horses and she was borne away from the inmates without a backward glance.

★ ★ ★

The women, hampered by the long skirts of their navy blue uniforms, boosting their children from behind, or with infants tucked inside slings fashioned out of shawls, climbed the long, swaying rope ladders from the belly of the small boat up onto the wide expanse of the deck of the *Australasia*, a small, modern three-masted ship that was to carry them away.

'Did you ever think you'd be sorry to see the back of Jonathon?' asked Patsy, touching the face that had been so soundly slapped weeks previously in the laundry at Grangegorman. 'Better the devil you know,' answered Liz. 'God help us all now, and us trapped on a ship full of hardy sailors, without Jonathon to stand between us and all harm.'

They turned to the front of the ship, where a tall, elegant young man stood beside the captain. Behind and to one side was a stout, soberly dressed woman. 'Look at the size of them tits,' whispered Patsy. 'She's not seen much hunger. She won't break her nose if she trips over, that's for sure.' Sally sniggered, and even Liz shook off her disappointment and heartbreak for a moment and managed a small, twisted grin through her sorrow.

The young man cleared his throat. 'I am Mr Alexander Kilroy, surgeon, employed by Her Majesty's Department of Convicts to escort you to your new home in the colonies and to get you there as well and in as healthy a condition as can be managed.'

The surgeon gestured behind him and the woman stepped forward slightly, her dark eyes squinting into the bright June sunlight adding to her severe appearance, partly created by the tight bun of black hair at the nape of her neck. Sally didn't see one ounce of compassion in her face.

'This is Mistress Richardson, the matron employed to assist me in my medical duties and to supervise your continuing education, moral conduct and appropriate behaviour.'

He turned then to face the captain of the ship and bowed slightly. 'Captain will communicate with me, I will communicate with Matron, she with you. No woman or child on board is to speak to, linger with, seek the company of, or in any way interfere with the captain or with any one of his crew.' He surveyed the two hundred faces, each one shining and clean, as they stood before him. 'There will be no corporal punishment of any woman on board this ship, a promise that would not have been made to you as recently as one decade ago, but any woman or child breaking the ship's rules will have her rations curtailed. Do you understand?'

'Saving your pardon, Doctor, sir, but I don't understand some of them big words,' replied an old woman at the front of the muster.

'And begging your pardon also, Doctor, sir,' said Lucy Smith. 'There are women and children here, sir, who speak not one word of the Queen's English, being from the west and the north and having knowledge only of the old tongue.'

'Be quiet, all of you,' snapped Matron. 'Mr Kilroy does not expect an answer to his question. All that is expected from you is silence and obedience. Those who cannot understand must be made to understand. There will be no place in Van Diemen's Land for those who cannot follow simple instructions.'

Kilroy nodded and cleared his throat. 'Indeed, thank you, Matron. And now we shall proceed to draw up the muster.'

They sat on the deck. The captain went to watch over the loading of hundreds of barrels, which were hauled from a flotilla of small boats by crew and dockers, and then carefully lowered into the bowels of the ship. Kilroy sat at a round table to one side and dipped his pen into a small bottle of ink.

One at a time, or in family groups, the women approached the desk and stood, twisting their hands together in shame, or staring him boldly in the eye, according to their nature, and answered his questions. The sounds of the quiet murmur and the scratching of the pen on the paper were swamped among the shrieks of the gulls, crying *iasc, iasc*, the crashing of barrels as they were stowed, the piping whistles of the mate and the captain, and always the gentle slosh of the small waves against the sides of the ship.

'This is not so bad,' Sally murmured to Nellie. 'I had fears of the seasickness that the other women talked of, but this is grand.'

'God spare me, but you're an awful óinseach, Sally. This is the safe and tranquil harbour of the best port on the eastern coast of Ireland. Wait until we're out in the wilds of the ocean, winds howling and waves battering the side. We'll see how grand it is then.'

Nellie already looked pale, the green tint of her face not unlike the colour of the waves beneath them. Sally prayed that Nellie might be laid low for the journey and let her out from under her notice. 'Oh, I'm sure it'll be grand, with the help of God,' Sally told her, smiling.

After an hour or more had passed, Nellie and Sally stood in front of the surgeon. He dipped his nib again and addressed Nellie first.

'Your name and age?'

'Eleanor McMurrough, but sentenced by my maiden name of Gordon, twenty-six years of age.' Sally wasn't surprised to hear Nellie lopping a few years off her age. She had no way of knowing whether Kilroy considered twenty-six to be old or young. To her, Nellie was old and hard.

'Occupation?'

'Widow.'

Kilroy laid down his pen and looked up at Nellie for the first time. ' "Widow" is not an occupation. How were you employed before your marriage?'

'I was not employed, sir. There is almost no work left in the land for men, never mind for women. When I was a young child, my mother used to spin and card wool for to be sent to the weavers in the mill at Celbridge, but the mill has been closed this twenty years since, after the big machines came to the factories in England. That's when the bad times came for the women, and the wives' laying hens and pigs disappeared from the small cabins.'

'But you must have spent your hours at something? Did you work on the land?'

'Well, sir, after the landlord ripped out the corn and oats and turned near the whole estate over to pasture and grazing, there was little enough work offered even to my father, never to speak of my mother and her children. Before that, she used to get seven pence a day, for a week or two during the harvest, to help the men, and I would get fourpence a day – when the men would permit the children to work.'

Kilroy smiled and turned to his page again. 'Well then, you are a country servant.' He inked the words into the column. 'Crime?'

'I beg your pardon, sir?'

'What was the crime for which you were sentenced?'

'Oh. Arson, sir, but driven by starvation and poverty after the death of my husband, and me with my young sister to provide for.' She pushed Sally forward and she smiled shyly and tried to look like the innocent young girl of Nellie's story, but Kilroy did not raise his eyes.

'There is no space for elaboration. Arson will suffice.' The pen scratched on the page. 'First offence?'

'It was, sir.'

He lowered his voice and spoke over the top of Sally's head, as though this would cause her to be struck deaf. 'And may I know, were you ever on the town?'

'Indeed, sir, I don't understand the question.'

He sighed and laid down the pen, rubbing his eyes. 'Mrs Gordon, I have two hundred manifests to make before the women can be accommodated in their quarters. I doubt that you do not understand the question, and for delicacy, I will not explain myself further. Have you ever been on the town?'

'Certainly not.'

'Then you have no … *ailments*? No diseases of a private nature?'

Nellie shook her head with a look of disgust. Kilroy made a further entry on his page and then turned to Sally. With Nellie answering, he filled Sally's columns, she being also written down as a country servant.

★ ★ ★

The piercing whistle that controlled and measured the *Australasia*'s days shrilled out, three long blasts, three short. Sally jolted awake and sat upright with a gasp. It was black dark, and the hum of the air was thick enough to cut with a knife. Ten days into the voyage and the horror of waking in the dark hold of the ship had not in any way abated.

Still drowsy, and uneasy in her mind after a night spent dreaming of the ghosts of Peggy and Davey roaming the long stone halls of Naas workhouse, she reached out a hand blindly in the gloom. Her questing fingers touched a warm, wet object clotted with hair, and panic seized her. Scream after scream echoed through the hold until suddenly she felt a sharp blow to her right cheek and heard Nellie's voice furious beside her.

'What the hell ails you now, Sally? Houl' yer whisht or you'll have every child in the boat awake and screaming too.'

'A rat, a rat. I stretched out my hand and there was a giant rat right beside me.'

'Ah, for crying out loud,' laughed Patsy. 'Sure that was me. I thought you'd blinded me, pulling my hair and poking me right in the eye like that.'

'What did I ever do? What did I ever do,' muttered Nellie, 'to be lumbered with such an imbecile?' Nellie's face suddenly appeared out of the darkness close beside Sally as, way up above their heads, a sailor lifted the lids off the hatches, allowing light and air to flood down into the prison ward of the ship.

'Five bells and all's well,' the sailor shouted down. 'Cooks up on deck, look sharp about it.'

Nellie struggled to her feet off the hard boards of the bunk and straightened her shift before slipping her blue uniform dress on over her head. Sally helped her tie her laces and fasten her buttons, blinking as her eyes acclimatised to the half-light.

'Right, I'll away up now to start the breakfast. Sally, get that pot emptied, Patsy, start wrapping up the beds.' Nellie turned and moved towards the ladder, which was nailed to the wall of the prison ward, under the hatch.

'Who died and made her queen?' asked Patsy. 'You know she only wanted to be cook because it means the food is under her control. It's not for the love of giving us extra time in bed.'

'Lookit, just let her get on with it, doesn't it give us a few hours' peace from her,' Sally said, and Patsy smiled in reply.

'Not much love lost between you two dear sisters.'

Sally shot an anxious look at the other women lying close beside her, still shrouded in their thin, coarse woollen blankets, but awake and doubtless listening. 'Maybe if we find a few quiet minutes up on the deck, I might talk to you about that.'

'Well, you might as well. Whatever divilment you two have cooked up between you, they're hardly likely to turn the ship back to Kingstown now to sort it out, and us eight days clear of the coast of Ireland.'

The last of the cooks struggled up the ladder and clambered out on deck. Apart from the two or three women with sucking babies, which clamoured and whimpered until finding the nipple, the rest of the inmates rolled over in their blankets and tried to close their eyes again.

Each square wooden pallet bed held a group of six women or children, which they had learned to call a mess. Mr Kilroy had called the names of each mess when his muster was complete – families together, and then others added on to the group until each woman had been allocated a spot. Sally had held her breath and listened as the muster was read out. No woman wanted a baby in their mess, shitting and puking and wailing all night long. Sally's luck had held and, along with Nellie, she had Patsy, Liz Curry, Eliza Guilfoyle and Catherine Colligan. Catherine's melancholy grew with every hour they travelled further from the coast of Ireland and from her precious, lost daughter, but, leaving aside her silent tears and her taciturn ghostly presence, otherwise they made a right merry group. Catherine and Nellie, as the oldest, had struggled for control of the group, but it was no surprise to anyone when Nellie came out on top; the cook, and therefore the controller of the food and water for their mess. Catherine had sunk back into her sorrow and grief and given up the power to Nellie, and, in a truth rarely acknowledged, and then only in whispers, the other girls were happy with the outcome. Nellie would fight like a tiger for any scrap of extra, or any moment of luxury that might come their way.

'God, I wish I was cook,' said Eliza. 'It's well for Nellie, with two hours more on deck, in God's fresh air, and us stuck down here in this stinking cesspit.'

'Oh give over with yer moaning,' Sally answered the unspoken reproach. 'I'll empty it in a minute.' It stuck in her craw that Nellie had given her the job of emptying the mess's chamber pot. Every morning when Sally hoisted that pot and carried it carefully to the privy, guarding against the rolling and pitching of the ship, a vision, as real as a hallucination, flashed across her inner eye, of Peggy and of Davey, setting off bravely beside her, with not a backward glance at their mother as she soothed the broken, bloodied body of her oldest child.

'Did you give me this job on purpose to break my heart each and every day?' Sally had asked Nellie, but when she explained the question, the older woman just laughed. 'Jesus and his holy mother, are you still going on about them two sewer rats? It never crossed my mind. You're the pot carrier and that's all there is to it.'

All around, women were stirring for the day. Sally never could clarify in her mind whether the messes in the upper berths were better or worse off than the lower. The women berthed above had to climb a ladder to reach their wooden platforms, swaying and clinging like monkeys in the rolling darkness, but once up there, they were closer to the hatch, so they got the benefit of the fresher air.

Down below them, Sally's mess was steadier and had less risk of an accident, but three times already she had been wakened from her sleep, to find the hot, stinking vomit of a woman in the berth above splattering down onto her face. On those bad nights, when the seasickness got the worst of the weakest women, they had not even the strength they needed to hang their faces over the piss-filled pot, but simply vomited out the side of the bed. The women in the upper berths had been warned not to bring their pots up with them at night, but in truth even Sally couldn't blame them, for the clamber down the ladder in the dark of the ward, with the hatches battened down, was dangerous and full of terror.

'Get up outta that, Sally, ya lazy hallion,' said Catherine. 'The smell in here would kill a billy goat.'

Sally sighed, rolled out of her blankets and seized the pot. It wasn't too full, for none of them had been sick in the night, for once, and she managed to carry it to the privy without splashing herself. She lined up at the privy with the other women. The sailors called it a latrine, but it was nothing more than a cupboard with a barrel, and the stuff from the barrel flowed straight out the side of the ship and into the waters around them. She took a deep breath when her turn came and though her eyes watered and her cheeks reddened with exertion, she managed not to breathe again until the stomach-churning job of pouring the contents of the pot into the barrel, swilling out the traces with a cupful of water and adding the rinsings to the barrel also, was completed and she was out of the cupboard and back into the ward again.

Back at the mess, Patsy was scolding. 'Liz, get up, ya lazy looderamawn. You're the idlest child I ever set eyes on.' Liz rolled over and yawned and Patsy reached out, took a firm grip of Liz's hair and dragged her from the bed. 'Strap 'em up girls, and hand 'em over.' It was Patsy's job to ensure that the six bedrolls and blankets of her mess were properly rolled and stored away for the day.

A head appeared in the hatch once more and they squinted up against the bright light streaming in through the square opening high above them. 'Seven bells and all's well. All souls able come up on the deck. Walking wounded to the hospital. Look lively.'

'Pick up them beds, girls,' Patsy said, and they lifted the carefully tied bedrolls and tucked them under their oxters. Then, more or less one-handed, they climbed the ladder to the deck. Patsy carried Nellie's bedding as well as her own, and she climbed slowly and carefully with her awkward, bulky burden. After her, Catherine Colligan flew up the ladder like a rat up a pipe.

'She's no more pregnant than I am,' whispered Liz Curry, and Sally nodded her head.

Once their names were ticked off the register, they walked to where a sailor stood by the rigging and, as they handed over their bedrolls, he strapped them tight and safe into the rigging for safe keeping, six rolls to a mess and a careful watch kept to ensure no confusion. Sally made sure not to touch his rough hand by chance, nor to draw his glance upon her.

Any sailor found consorting with a convict will be lashed, ten strokes, Mr Kilroy had warned on the first day aboard.

'That's nothing,' Nellie had pinched Sally's arm and hissed in her ear. 'If I find you tucked away in a corner with anyone of those men, you'll be no value to me anymore, and I'll clap my hand over yer mouth and nose while you sleep. One less mouth to feed.'

Sally didn't doubt Nellie's words, not after the way she had thrown Peggy and Davey to the workhouse without a backward glance or a second thought. *Houl' yer whisht or I'll hit you a slap in the beak,* she had hissed in the hospital ward in Grangegorman when Sally had finally realised that the children were gone to the workhouse. Her screams had echoed along the passageways and, outside, she could hear footsteps ringing off the granite floor of the corridor; women hurrying towards the din. *Quit acting like a fool, what man in his right mind is going to marry a woman who comes along with two extra young beaks gaping to feed?* She'd turned her face to the wall and moaned the piteous wordless groans of a sick animal. Nellie had forced her back to face her, *Yer mine, to be bought and sold. I bought you with a fine, safe nest and plenty of my own hard-earned food, and I spared you from the soldiers. I'll pass you on to a decent, respectable man, with a space in the household for me, when it suits me, and them childer are none of my concern.*

Sally pulled her mind back to the present. For the hundredth time since she had come on board in Kingstown ten days ago, she glanced over to the rolling, dark blue sea and shielded her eyes from the dazzling glare thrown back. Would God forgive her if she leaped over the side? Nellie called for help, and Sally shook herself and turned away from the sailor and back to her mess.

After the maize gruel she helped Nellie wash the six bowls and spoons. Eliza groaned and wrapped her arms around her belly.

'Christ, I'm fierce blocked up. I haven't gone for days. The pain is savage this morning.' The women nodded. They had become accustomed to good food in Grangegorman – potatoes every day, bread to spare and plenty of buttermilk. The change in their diet was the biggest gripe they had with life on the ship so far.

'What's for breakfast?' Patsy had asked on their first morning, when they had awoken a few hours distant from Kingstown and the excitement of embarkation was already beginning to morph into the monotony of life at sea.

'You know damn rightly what it is. It's called cornmeal,' snapped Nellie. 'It looks like food for horses – I don't know what the hell I'm supposed to do with it.' The women of Gordon's mess stared at the thin gruel with lumps of grains floating here and there in their bowls. 'I had the devil of a time getting the fire alight under the cauldron, out here in the wind,' said Nellie. 'Mebbe it could have done with more cooking.'

They looked over at the small cauldron. It hung from one of many iron chains above a long fire of smouldering charcoal. The fire was contained in a wooden box, scores of feet long, lined with bricks and with a latticework of iron bars along one side for poking and prodding the stubborn coals. There were several of these fireboxes on their half of the deck, and Nellie said they would have to guard their cauldron carefully against those who might try to dip into their share.

Liz lifted her bowlful and laughed. 'It's just Peel's brimstone, Indian meal, from America, same as we had at home, unless Nellie is pretending she was never hungry enough to resort to this oul' muck.' Liz sighed. 'The last time I saw a bowl of this was the last night I spent under my father's roof in Naas.' She tasted it carefully. 'God almighty, it's terrible, worse than at home, even. Nellie, did you put any salt in it?'

'Salt? Oh, I did to be sure, I pulled a small sack of salt out from between me tits where I always keep some, and I sprinkled it in.'

'It's fine, Nellie,' Sally soothed. 'It's grand and we'll soon get used to it. Thanks very much for making it, and isn't it better than nothing?'

'True, true, half a loaf is better than no bread,' said Catherine despondently, sucking up the gruel. 'There'll be potatoes for the dinner, sure isn't there potatoes and to spare in the land this year by all accounts, for those who can afford them, so they say?'

But there were no potatoes.

'It's unfortunate to be sure, the apple potatoes did not arrive on time,' Matron told them that first morning after they had finished or rejected their breakfast of Indian meal. 'The apple potato is a very powerful remedy against scurvy and each convict ship is assigned a portion. Mr Kilroy and I begged Captain to wait, in case the belated delivery would come, but Captain said that time and tide wait for no man.'

She held up her hands against the sudden horrified clamour. 'If we did not sail on the tide as calculated, we would have missed the winds that will carry us from the Cape of Good Hope to Van Diemen's Land.'

The prisoners looked at each other, horror dawning on their faces.

'Will there be hunger, then, mistress?' a woman asked. 'Did we break the laws of God and man, just to starve on the ocean instead of on the dry land?'

'Nonsense,' Matron snapped. 'Captain took the wise course of filling the hold with salted provisions when the delay in the delivery of the potato stores became known to him. There will be no hunger.'

And they were not hungry, but the change from fresh potatoes and milk to cornmeal, salted bacon and brackish water caused a huge problem amongst them. There wasn't a woman on the ship could shit without pain and groaning. Some couldn't manage at all. Each morning at the breakfast hour a trail of woman stood outside the hospital ward, leaning against the wall, moaning and clutching their guts, doubled up.

'Obstipation, that's what it is,' said Kilroy, pulling corks from a collection of huge brown glass bottles and mixing a few drams of their contents together, 'I hope to God I have enough oil to last the journey.' The women coughed and gagged on the measures of oil as it slipped down their gullets.

'By God, I think the cure is worse than the ailment,' Eliza had gasped after her first dose, and now she suffered on, but not in silence – the mess were sick to death of hearing about her bowels.

'Oh, quit yer griping,' muttered Catherine. 'It was yourself put a lit match to yer rights to good food. I done nothing to deserve this.'

'Tell us what you done, Eliza,' asked Liz. 'We all know my story now, and the whole bloody ship knows that Catherine Colligan is the only innocent woman ever sent to Van Diemen's Land.' They sniggered, but Catherine didn't rise to the challenge, pretending to accept the words for what they were.

'Ach, well, there's not that much to tell,' Eliza started. 'You wouldn't have any interest in my story. ' She smiled and they clamoured for more.

'Well, now, to start back at the very beginning. One day in the *Leinster Express* last spring, I read a letter by a man called Flood.'

'And what would you be doing buying a newspaper?' sneered Nellie. 'How could you make head nor tail of a page of letters like that?'

'What would you know? I was at the national school, from age six till age twelve, and I can read fine rightly. As would you be able to if you were so goddamned smart as you let on to be … But if you're not interested … ' They begged her go on.

'Well, that day in the street, I found a page from the *Express* that had been wrapped round a scrap of meat, and I picked it up and sucked the blood out of the paper. When I was finished, through the bloody stains, I could make out the words, most of them. Well, this man Flood had gone from Naas to Australia, to a town called Adelaide, and isn't that the prettiest name for a place you ever heard?' They nodded.

'Well, Adelaide is a beautiful place, says he, and the sun shines in Australia, and the work is plentiful. *Come out*, says he. *Have no fear. Leave Ireland behind to hell, to rot in the rain and come on out to Australia.*'

The women smiled and hugged each other tight and gloried in the cleverness of their decision, all except Catherine, who sighed and rocked backwards and forwards on her hunkers.

'Well, the seed was planted.' Eliza was rushing now, words tumbling from her mouth as she reached her climax. 'I couldn't stop thinking about them words. I'd spent one month in the gaol in Athy already, for the stealing of a basket of bread back in '47, and I knew that there'd be no mercy shown me if

I ended up in the courthouse again. Even though I was as good as gold in the gaol, and the gaoler told me I was a model inmate.' She took a deep breath and they all huddled round closer.

'Well, I waited till I knew the spring assize was coming up in Naas, and I asked, and I made sure that it would be Justice Crampton on the bench. Oh, I knew what I was doing, I wanted that oul' bastard, just to be sure there'd be no mercy. I chose my day carefully. I didn't want to spend too long back in the gaol in Athy, for though the prisoners got their allowance of food twice a day, there was a hundred people crammed into thirty cells, no roof on half the building, and cholera after breaking out in the town. I knew it wouldn't be long before the cholera made its way into the gaol, for the pump on the well was broken, and the whole place was as dirty as the arse of a pig.' Catherine Colligan snorted, and gave a loud tut, but she listened carefully all the same.

'On a dark Tuesday night this March gone past, just a week before the assizes, I crept out into Barrack Street in Athy and I set a hot sliver of turf into the thatched roof of the outhouse of an old widow who lives there.'

'And what grudge had you against the poor misfortunate woman?' snapped Catherine.

'Never a grudge at all. I barely knew her. I chose her roof for it was only an outhouse and I reckoned she could live without it.' Eliza dropped her eyes for a moment before forcing her head back up defiantly. 'Now it was my misfortune that the night was wild and windy, and March-of-the-many-weathers took a hand in the crime. The gale licked the flames round and round like a storm from the pit of hell, and when all was said and done, five buildings were ablaze, and four of them were dwellings.'

Her audience, as one woman, blessed themselves.

'The door of one house on the lane behind Barrack Street had to be broke down by the Peelers from the barracks, and the man within dragged from his bed and he buck naked.'

'It's a blessing it's not his murder you were charged with,' Sally said. 'You should have chosen a hay rick or something out far in the country, like me and Nellie.'

'But, I wanted to do it in Barrack Street, so that I could give myself over to the Peelers straight away and say it was me that done it.'

'You're lucky you didn't swing,' said Catherine.

'I am, I suppose, but I swear to God, I'm in such pain that if I don't have a shit soon, I might hang my own self from the rigging, just to be done with it.'

They laughed, even Catherine, and the whistle blew for cleaning time. Patsy and Sally took up pails of water and chloride of zinc and climbed back down the ladder, to scrub the floor and berths of the ward with sandstone scrubbers. The smells of vomit and piss clung around them as they headed down into the half-light.

Chapter Twenty-three

Hobart, October 1919, Saoirse

Sally Mahon soiled herself last evening. It is not the first time, although it will probably be one of the last. She is eating so little, there cannot be much left within to come out. She cried out for water and as I leaned over her with the cup, the smell arose from the bed, like a punch in the solar plexus.

Before, when she was my grandmother, I'd have smiled and hugged her, begged her not to upset herself and have cleaned her in silent good will, as befits a Christian woman. But last night, I stared in horror at the stranger in my home, and I could not bring myself to wash her.

Josie Hendron washed her instead, slipped the soiled sheets out from under her with the help of Deirdre, the calmest and most sensible of the serving girls. Through the closed door, I could hear Josie chirping and chatting to the old woman in the bed who answered in monosyllables or not at all.

Josie found me in the hallway, when she left the bedchamber, and there were tears in her eyes. 'God bless the old mistress,' she said. 'A kinder, better employer doesn't exist in this city. But you know that already.' I nod, close-faced.

'Josie,' I ask abruptly, 'what did you think of my father? Did you know him well?'

She shakes her head. 'You were already born when I came to help. I came because your mother was unwell after your birth. But you knew that of course, Mistress?'

Now it is my turn to shake my head.

'I didn't. Was it a difficult birth?'

'Not specially, I think. Your mother was well enough in body.'

'But in mind?' I breathe. 'She was unwell in her mind, probably as a result of being deprived of a husband.'

Josie looks uncomfortable, and it is no wonder, for though she worships my grandmother and hangs upon her every word, she and I have not been close since I started to wear long skirts and put up my hair. I am ashamed to broach these questions with Josie, but who else can I ask?

'I don't know, mistress, I never heard any such talk about pining for a man. All I know is that by the time I got here, your mother had turned her face to the wall. She lay in bed weeping, or silent, for months, while your grandmother sat, holding her hand, stroking her hair. Your great-aunt and I had the minding of you, and the work of the house besides.'

'Thank you, Josie, I know you always did your best.'

She bobs her head, which she has never done before, and only after she leaves do I realise that she called me 'mistress'. And I understand that Josie fears for her future, a woman of sixty years, with nothing standing between herself and the street other than whatever she has scrimped over the years, and her destiny entirely at my whim. While I am about to inherit a boarding house from a woman who is not even my kin. How lucky and how sheltered I have been. And how cold and hard Josie must think me, not to know that she will be welcome in the Australasia until she dies.

A fine kind of a Christian I must be.

I force myself back into the bedchamber and begin my prayers.

Chapter Twenty-four

Prison Ship Australasia, July 1849

Hail Mary, full of grace, the Lord is with thee, Blessed art thou amongst women and blessed is the fruit of thy womb, Jesus.

Women's and children's voices trembled and shook as they answered.

'Holy Mary, mother of God, pray for us sinners, now and at the hour of our death, Amen.'

Hail Mary, full of grace ...

The ship lurched left, shuddered, trembled and heaved upright again. They screamed and the words of the prayer were lost among the roars and howls of terror.

It was black as the depths of hell. The hatches had been battened down at the first squall of wind, and all their oil lamps had been taken above decks and stored away to prevent them burning themselves to death by keeping them alight against orders.

The pots and buckets were stored away also, to keep them intact and not have them smashing through the air as the ship leaped and bucked on the breast of the ocean. The floor was awash with piss and vomit, deep enough to cover a child's foot.

Hail Mary, full of grace ...

The wooden bunk creaked and shifted slightly.

'It's coming away from the wall,' screamed Liz.

'Hold on tight, don't let go for the love of God. If it shifts from the wall, we'll be dashed through the ward and killed.'

The six women from the berth above had clambered down from their bunk and climbed onto Sally's, as they'd been instructed when the storm began.

'Get those other bitches off our bed,' screamed Nellie.

'Have a heart, Nellie! Where are we to go?' begged Anne Daly, one of the new women. 'If the bunk comes off the wall, it won't matter how many of us are on it – we're all going to die.'

'If I could see your face, Anne Daly, I'd scratch yer eyes out,' shouted Nellie. 'The weight of you heifers is loosening the nails.'

Glory be to the Father, and to the Son and to the Holy Ghost, Amen.

A shriek rang through the ward, piercing enough to quell all other noises for a moment, even the shout of the rosary-caller.

'It's a banshee,' Sally whispered, her teeth chattering so hard that she could hardly hear herself. 'A banshee, and we all heard it. We're all going to die.'

'My baby! Peadar, love, where are you? Help me, for the love of God. I've lost hold of Peadar.' They could hear a woman scrabbling and sloshing around in the filth. 'Peadar? … Help me, you shower of bastards. Will none of you leave off yer prayers and help a body?'

'I have him, Norah, love,' cried out a voice, sing-song, sharp, northern. 'I have him here. Stay where you are, Norah. Don't set foot on the floor – you'll be kilt. I'll houl' him as best I can.'

'Is he alive?'

'I don't know. He's just lying here. I'll give him a slap.'

The sound of flesh on flesh echoed through the hold like a pistol shot across the Curragh of Kildare, followed by the lusty screams of a baby. Until Sally breathed again she didn't even know she'd been holding it.

Hail Mary, full of grace, the Lord is with you …

A strange squealing noise and a thudding echoed through the ward, an insistent rhythm, like a musician thrumming a bodhrán. The howling gale had worked its way under one of the hatches and was screaming and heaving against the bottom of the boards, as well as hammering them from above. Then, with a high-pitched tortured sound, the huge invisible hand of the wind ripped the nails from a plank and it flew upwards into the night, leaving the hatch partially uncovered. Cold, fresh air streamed down over the women, which was a mercy, but it brought the rain with it, each drop flung so hard at them that it stung worse than hail.

… thy will be done, on earth as it is in Heaven …

Through the damaged hatch they could hear the distant shouts and whistled commands on deck.

'Will they save us, Nellie?' Sally whimpered. 'They know what they're doing, don't they? They've done it before?'

'Shut yer beak.'

But through the darkness Sally felt a hand reach out and take hers. They wrapped their fingers together, then gripped the raised lip of the bunk once more, clinging on together. *Thank you, Nellie. There's a heart in there somewhere, and there's a whisper of care in it for me.*

She clung to that hand the rest of the night, even after the rolling subsided, even after they knew that the ship had survived this time. Though the screaming wind abated and, in the tiny patch of sky they could see above them, an occasional star appeared, Sally never let go her grip. She clung to that warm human contact in a tight mesh of fingers all night.

The sailors sat straight-legged on their half of the deck, and the thimbles they wore on the balls of their thumbs flashed and sparkled as they drew coarse, waxed threads through the strips and shards of torn rigging and sails. The storm was almost a week behind them and the massive damage wreaked on that night was still far from being completely repaired.

The worst consequence by far was the loss of drinkable water. Some of the casks had broken to splinters, spilling their precious contents into the hold. Others had been swamped with salt water from the giant waves that had washed over the deck time and again. These particular barrels had not smashed open, but a taint of the salt water had travelled through the thick staves and the already stale and brackish drinking water tasted worse than ever. The sailors mixed this foul water with their rum and seemed not to care overmuch, but the women could hardly choke it down.

They sat in the brutal glare of the sunshine on the female half of the deck – in the pause between breaking their fast with the gruel and starting the daily cleaning, Matron read aloud from her bible. Since the storm, she tended to choose a lot of watery stories. Their Saviour had walked across, or otherwise stilled, the choppy waves of the Sea of Galilee three or four days in a row now. Sally wondered was there any point in telling Mistress Richardson that the women had prayed throughout the whole terrifying night of the storm, and she wondered if the matron had done the same in her own cabin, wherever that might be. She probably didn't think Catholic prayers counted for much.

Matron and Mr Kilroy had been busy in the days since the storm. Sally looked around at the two hundred women and saw bandaged heads, black eyes, arms in slings, and women hobbling, their knees and ankles strapped up under their dresses.

Baby Peadar was famous now, passed from hand to hand as a good luck charm while his proud mother looked on. Even so many days later, women still reached up to touch him, in the hope that his luck might rub off on them. Not one of the inmates had died. Sally offered up a prayer of thanks.

At the whistle, Sally and Patsy took up their buckets and scrubbers and climbed down into the ward.

'Christ, it would choke you in here,' Patsy gasped.

'I know, and it feels worse when you come back down off the deck. It wouldn't be so bad if you were stuck in it all day long, like when me and Nellie were in Naas Gaol. You'd kind of get used to it.'

'I'll do the bunk, if you'll do under it.'

'Right, so.'

They scrubbed in silence. The joyful ease and carefree nature of the friendship was ended. All talk between them since the storm was superficial and short, never touching on matters beyond the immediate. More was never said between them than was strictly needed, and all the joking and laughter had stopped. The enforced hours of scrubbing together were now the only time they spent alone in each other's company. Sally blamed herself.

She had prised open her grit-filled weary eyes on the morning after the storm, looking for Nellie. Her fingers ached and stung from clasping all night long to Nellie's fingers. The first stirrings of love and gratitude had awakened in her breast, as the hard older woman gave generously the only solace she could, the warmth of human touch in the terror of the night.

But Nellie was nowhere to be seen. It was Patsy who had clung to her all the night. Patsy who had reached out in the depths of the valley of death and cheered her with her silent touch. Sally stared down at her friend, and reached to brush the matted, tangled hair from her face. She leaned closer and ran the fingers of her free hand across her friend's swollen, bruised cheek, wincing at a fresh gash she saw there. Patsy muttered from within the dark, filthy nest of her soaked-through blankets and her eyes flickered open, just inches from Sally's mouth.

'What are you at, Sally? Let go of me, to hell.' Patsy had struggled upward and dashed Sally's hand from her face. She tried to release her other hand from Sally's grasp, but their fingers were so tightly knit, so stiff and cramped that they had had to pry them apart, one finger at a time, and both girls gasped at the pain as the blood started to flow back into them and they throbbed and ached.

'Keep yer paws off of me. You've no business to be mauling me in my sleep.'

That's what her mouth had said to Sally. The flashing, snapping green of her big, gooseberry eyes, even more swollen than usual after the awful night they'd shared, said something else. But Sally didn't know what it was.

★ ★ ★

Hard on the heels of drought came the worse fear. Fever.

Shipping fever. Road sickness. The swelling stink and creep of disease. Matron seemed nearly as frightened as her patients. Kilroy bustled around on deck, whispering in the captain's ear, fussing with his books and his fine pen while casting anxious glances over his shoulder at the women's half of the deck.

A woman from the mess above Gordon's, Anne Daly, was the worst case of fever yet seen on the water, and they knew that she might be the start of a plague that would sweep through the ward and decimate all who came into contact.

'If she doesn't die, I'll kill her myself when she comes back up from the hospital,' Nellie declared, and many of the women nodded, while the others didn't even pretend to be shocked. Anne had done a bad thing, the worst thing, the crime unforgivable. Not two weeks since recovering from a bout of ordinary fever and a terrible crippling headache that had kept her confined in the hospital for eight days, she had hidden her new sickness for days, moving among them and tainting their air.

'Oh she's a bad one and no mistake,' said Liz Curry in hushed tones. Anne was not part of their mess and they felt free to blacken her reputation and damn her.

'Hiding her sickness, all for the sake of her bloody hair! When I see her next, I'll pull the hair out for her, if Kilroy hasn't already done it.'

Nellie once more put into words what everyone else was too mealy-mouthed to breathe aloud. Anne Daly had been lucky to recover from her first fever with her long dark hair intact. She was never done playing with it, plaiting it into complicated patterns and twists, and tying it with blue threads pulled carefully from the hem of her dress. Other women had not been so lucky on their trips to the sick ward.

Sally's eyes strayed over to glance at poor Mary Regan, a wreck of a young woman sitting with her own mess, listlessly picking at the ragged skin that wept and peeled at the edges of her weak, soft nails. Mary Regan's hair stood in clumps and tufts from her scalp, a quarter of an inch in length. Kilroy had cured her, but at barely twenty-one years of age, she looked a wretch who would near as soon be dead. With her fever climbing higher and higher, until one of her mess reported that her skin burned to the touch, all of Kilroy's potions and purges had done nothing for her. At last, the surgeon had ordered her brought to the hospital, where, in a state of delirium, she'd been shorn like a sheep.

'Christ, she's a fright,' whispered Patsy, following Sally's gaze. 'Lucy told me it took three women and Matron to houl' her down while Kilroy took all the long locks off of her.'

'Did he cut it with a knife and fork? He has no skill as a barber, that's for sure,' said Eliza.

'It's the blister he done on her that has it so bad looking. First he put cold, wet cloths on. He hoped that would break the fever. If she was a rich woman on a passenger ship, he said, he'd have packed her in ice, that's how hot she was.'

'Ice?' Sally asked. 'Ice in the middle of the ocean? Don't be stupid Patsy.'

'You don't know much about the power of money, girl,' laughed Eliza, 'you can have ice packed tight in sawdust in the middle of the ocean, and hothouse fruit at Christmas if you have the money to pay for it.'

'Well, according to Lucy,' said Patsy, 'the cold cloths don't work, the fever climbs higher, Mary Regan's raving now, and next day, out comes the blister. A big thick paste of mustard and water, and God knows what else, and Kilroy slathers it onto Mary's bare scalp with a brush, like lime-washing a cabin.' Patsy stopped and made a sign against the evil eye. 'Lucy says the screams and roars out of her would have deafened an ass, and this from a woman who was barely sensible a minute earlier.'

They all shook their heads and glanced over the deck at Mary Regan again.

'She barely looks sensible now,' muttered Nellie.

'Sure her story is only half told, poor wretch that she is,' Patsy said. 'Next day, Lucy goes in after breakfast to help in the hospital and there's poor Mary lying yonder on the pallet, and she looks half dead. The whole of her head is covered in big swollen blisters from the paste and Kilroy takes a wicked looking spike and plunges it deep into each blister.' Patsy's audience winced and sucked in its breath as she made a gulping, gurgling sound deep in her throat, the onomatopoeia of horror.

'Then all this stinking, sticky pus comes glop-glop-glopping out of each blister and Kilroy is right and pleased with himself. *The poison is drawn off, thanks be to God,* says he, and Lucy herself says it was all she could do not to boke down on top of the poor woman's ruined scalp.'

'By Christ, and here's me and Patsy thinking we had it hard, being on the hold–cleaning detail,' said Sally. 'Mind you, there's days we're nearly boking ourselves, down there.'

Gordon's mess all looked at Nellie, but none said what was in all minds, that Nellie had the best job of the lot, and wasn't it just like her to have come out on top of the heap.

'Well, that's still not the end neither,' Patsy continued the gruesome story. 'For after the pus and mess is cleaned away, Lucy dabbing as gentle as she can, Kilroy takes a giant hollow needle and sticks it straight into Mary's arm and starts drawing off cup after cup of blood. Well by this stage, poor Lucy is feeling faint and starting to weave on her feet and Kilroy bids her sit on the floor and then tells her that the overheating in Mary's blood will be relieved by the blood–letting.'

They all looked over at the poor misfortunate woman again. 'Well, she's alive, and isn't that the only thing that matters, really?' said Nellie, finally, drawing her arms across her shawl with vigour. 'But I'm warning you all, don't cross me on this. There'll be no Anne Dalys among you. The first sign of a fever in our mess and it's the hospital for you, and whether you hang on to yer hair or not is no concern of mine.'

'Couldn't they even give poor Mary Regan a bonnet to hide the mess of her hair?' Sally asked.

'She's a convict, Sally, a bloodthirsty criminal, like yerself and Nellie,' teased Patsy. 'D'you think Kilroy or Matron cares how Mary Regan feels or looks? Once she reaches Van Diemen's Land alive, to be worked like a horse for the next seven years, that's the sum total of their interest in her.'

'Or in any of us.'

'Well, I hope to God that Anne Daly comes back in one piece,' said Eliza, 'for she's a Kildare woman like the rest of us, although she's in a different mess. She stood in front of oul' Crampton and answered for her crime on the same day I did, and I reckon that makes her no more a real criminal than I am.'

In all the long, sweltering days of the voyage yet to come, Anne Daly never set foot on the deck of the *Australasia* again, but was carried off the vessel on a stretcher and borne to the hospital in Hobart.

★ ★ ★

'Oh, Lord God, kill me now. Have mercy on me, someone, and kill me.'

Catherine Colligan's groans of pain were pitiful and would have melted the heart inside a stone. Clutching her belly, doubled up on the boards and keening, she would have been a frightful sight, but in the pitch dark of the night the other women of her mess couldn't see her, though she lay on the same pallet and they could feel the fever-heat scorching off her skin.

A terrible stench rose from Catherine's skirts as she farted and belched and muttered prayers. Her rocking and swaying set Sally's nerves on end, until she wanted to scream at Catherine and curse her and damn her to hell and back, but she pretended that she didn't mind and kept the fearsome oaths clamped safely behind her teeth. Sally knew enough to be ashamed of herself, and that made her angrier still with the helpless woman who tossed and turned and wailed beside her.

'Oh, get me the bucket, for the love of God, it's coming,' Catherine said.

The other women scrambled round, trying to give Catherine some space, until Nellie's voice rang out, sharp and angry, and the only surprise was that it had taken her so long to come to her decision.

'Right, get that woman out of my bunk, before she shits all over us.'

'Mother of God, Nellie, have a heart,' answered Eliza. 'She can barely move, she can't stand up all the night long.'

'Let her lie on the floor, so. Her time in this bunk is finished, until Kilroy cures her or kills her,' Nellie said. 'Someone get a hand under each oxter and heave her out onto the floor, be as rough or as gentle as ye want, but be fast.'

No one moved. Nellie was terrifying and, more importantly, she had the control over the food ration for the mess of six, but even so, to dump poor, sick Catherine onto the rough, vomit-damp floor was a merciless act for which no one wanted to accept responsibility. They lay still and waited.

'Get her off the bunk, I said, or ye'll feel the back of my hand.'

'Well, dare you try,' replied Eliza. 'I'm a grown woman, and you're no mother of mine. Try lifting yer hand to me. You won't try it twice.'

'Shut up, for the love of God!' echoed a voice from further down the ward. 'Have ye no consideration at all for the sleeping and the ill?'

There was a chorus of agreement from nearby bunks.

'Right.' Nellie shifted and moved and Sally could feel that she was rising, carefully lowering her feet onto the floor, searching out the dry spots. By the shuffling of her feet and the quick, dragging movements that followed, it was clear that she had found poor Catherine and was hauling her onto the floor. Catherine moaned and whined and then gasped as she hit the floor with a dull thump.

'Oh, as God is my witness, Nellie Gordon, there isn't an ounce of human kindness in your whole body,' she gasped. Nellie clambered back up to the bunk.

'First thing in the morning,' Nellie said, 'when I go up at five bells to start the fire lighting, I'll try and get word to Kilroy or to Matron, that Catherine Colligan can't wait until the hospital opens at seven. But, in the meantime, on the floor is where she'll stay.'

With a moan and a wail, Catherine lost control of her bowels, and the patter could be clearly heard of the liquid poison bursting out from her and pouring onto the floor where she lay. The reek and acid of it rushed up from the floor towards the berth. Sally clamped her hand over her mouth, retching and belching.

'If yer going to be sick,' ordered Nellie, 'it would be decent to boke out the other side of the bed, and not down on top of Colligan, she's in a bad enough way as it is.'

'Oh, yer a real Christian, right enough, Nellie,' said Eliza, 'how kind of you to spare a thought for the poor sick woman you've just dumped onto the floor.'

'Shut yer beak, Guilfoyle, or I swear I'll shut it for you. If I hadn't acted when I did, we'd all be lying here, covered head to toe in the dysentery, and by Friday breakfast, there'd not be one of us that wasn't sick ourselves.'

They knew she was right. And Sally knew, as she lay there, that the other three were feeling just like she was, thanking their lucky stars that their mess had a bitch like Nellie in it, to do what was necessary and to take all the blame on her own broad shoulders.

Catherine lay and shivered all night, her guts pouring out hot and steaming onto the dampness of the floor. When Patsy and Sally went down again in the morning after breakfast, with pails and chloride of zinc, vinegar-soaked rags pulled up over their noses and mouths, their eyes burned with guilt, and with relief, as they swilled away the filth.

They'd never imagined anything like it before, blood and slime and shit all mixed, and long tubes of a pale glistening jelly, not unlike the frogspawn that grew each spring in the corner of the bog in Clonsast.

'It's like the whole innards is coming away and coming out of her,' Sally said.

'I was feared for Catherine,' whispered Patsy over the sound of the scrubbing and swilling of thirty women working. 'I thought she might die, right there and then. That sister of yours is a monster. I'm heart afraid of her, and I'm not easy scared.'

Sally reached out, afraid that Patsy would strike her away, but she let Sally's hand rest on her upper arm for a moment and she squeezed it gently.

'You've a right to fear Nellie, but, please God, in the new land you might be far away from her. She'll be just another servant woman like the rest of us.'

Patsy smiled and they looked at each other properly for the first time in days.

'But if I'm far away from her, I'd be far away from you too, mebbe.'

'And would that matter?' Sally held her breath waiting for the answer. 'I thought mebbe things weren't that great between us? I thought mebbe I had done something on you?'

Patsy drew a shape on the floor of the hold with her thin shoe, then glanced back up to catch Sally's gaze again.

'You just gave me a shock, that morning after the storm, that's all. After the night we'd put in, it's no wonder a person might be feeling a bit crabbed.'

'You know I wouldn't do anything on you.'

'Ach, Sally, catch yerself on. I was nearly out of my mind with fear, I said the first thing that came into my head.' Patsy blinked furiously and drew the back of her hand across her eyes. 'It's not the first time I woke up to find a hand on my face, and the last time wasn't something I ever want to think about again.'

Patsy drew herself up with a visible effort and straightened her shoulders. 'It could have been worse,' she said with a wry smile, 'I could have woken up with Nellie's face two inches from my own. I think I would have died of fear on the spot. How the pair of you thought you could pass yerselves off as sisters is a mystery to me. You're everything she's not.'

'But she's everything I'm not, as well. She's clever and brave and does what needs to be done and she doesn't care a damn what people think of her.' Sally gave a few more strokes of the stone scrubber at the rough planks of the floor. 'Tell you the truth, I was glad when she dragged Catherine onto the floor, to keep the rest of us clean.'

'But you wouldn't have done it yerself.'

'No, I wouldn't have done it myself. But I was glad when someone else done it.'

'So sometimes good comes of a bad deed?'

'It may be so. I don't know. I'm too tired and stupid to think about these things. I'm glad to know that Catherine is in the hospital and I hope she comes back to us well and fit. But I'm even more glad that I didn't spend the night lying in her scour.'

'Tell me the real story about yerself and Nellie. You can't fear her down here, and I'll never tell. What is it that she has on you?'

'If I tell you, she'll kill me.'

'Not if I kill her first.'

Chapter Twenty-five

Hobart, October 1919, Sally

The mother wren, or perhaps it is the father, is back at the nest outside my window. Darting between the branches, he bears a large butterfly in his beak to the nest of hungry fledglings. Wrens are beautiful. But so are butterflies. Why is the world so designed that the strong prey upon the weak, and the weak upon the even weaker, until the whole planet is a seething, boiling indecipherable mass of death?

The butterfly brings beauty and joy, but the caterpillar is the enemy of the market gardener, who plucks him off the tough outer leaves of the cabbage and grinds him beneath his boot. The lamb is gentle and eats only the grasses amongst which she frolics. And then we hit her on the head and tear her limb from limb.

Our children are born soft and loving. So we harden them with words: bastard, amadán, whore, óinseach, coward, until they are hard enough to kill. The king sends his men with bayonet and grenade against the Boche, and his cousin, Kaiser Bill, sends German men back again with gas and rifle. And then the men come home to Tasmania in pieces, carrying the Spanish flu, this generation's road fever.

In the months long, long ago, before the stranger brought typhus into our cabin, my father earned handfuls of Indian meal, half a pound at a time, by dragging a handcart full of crushed stones to Hollywood House. Reverend Joly's new piano had arrived from Dublin, at the cost of forty-five pounds. Forty-five pounds, seventy years ago. How many wedding gifts would that furnish in 1919? And in all the many-roomed vastness of Hollywood House, there was no corner spare to accommodate the new instrument. As his tenants ate grass, Reverend Joly had his new music room built to hold a machine made of precious, waxed ebony and the teeth of dead elephants. *Much wants more,* my mother used to say, and *little gets less and less of his fair share until at last he is driven to the workhouse or the boneyard.*

And – workhouse, war or winding sheet – women are in the midst of all. Women, and the way in which the world treats us, and the children we bear.

Would we be better off drowning our daughters at birth? Patsy asked me once. But we didn't drown Saoirse, and we didn't cast her into the asylum. How could we? We knew what we knew about the asylums. We knew better than most.

Chapter Twenty-six

Prison Ship Australasia, August 1849

'May God almighty forgive you, Patsy O'Hanlon, you're heading straight to hell.' Sally's voice trembled and shook, while Patsy scowled fiercely into the sunset.

For good or ill, Sally had summoned the courage at last, found a quiet corner and poured the whole story of her recent life into Patsy's willing ear – from Patrick O'Loughlin and Tom Crampton to Grainne, Martha, Nellie hanging the bloody rag on the furze bush, Peggy and Davey in the workhouse – the lot of it.

She stared at Patsy and then gave a small laugh. 'But, sure you're only joking? You're making a big fool of me again, and everyone knows I'm a terrible eejit who would believe anything.'

Patsy grabbed her arm and twisted the flesh until she winced and brushed her off.

'Listen to me. There's not a hint of a joke or fun about it. I'm deadly serious.'

'You're serious?' Sally lowered her voice even further. 'You're stone crazy, Patsy. You're sunstruck, or otherwise sickening for something. It's one thing to talk about sticking a blade into a drunken soldier, when your back is tight agin the wall. You're making jokes about murdering a woman. You'll go straight to hell, for even letting the words past your lips.'

Patsy's angry stare held Sally's until Sally gave in and had to lower her gaze from her friend's bulging green eyes, which started out from the angry glow of her cheeks. Her pop-eyes were even more prominent now, surrounded as they were by deep black hollows from the poor food and the nights spent tossing and turning on the thin bedrolls laid on the hard bunk. The shafts of her cheekbones flared out under the black shadows and a hectic red flush made her uglier than ever.

Sally longed to stretch out and smooth away the anger and the fear from her face, but she kept her hands still by her side. Sally never knew when a word or touch would comfort Patsy and when it was best avoided.

'She deserves it,' Patsy said. 'You should kill her. She's a bloody monster. She killed them two childer as much as if she strangled them with her bare hands.'

Sally nodded and lowered her eyes to hide the tears welling up behind her lashes, but Patsy took her chin in her bony fingers and forced her face upwards.

'Well might you cry. Why wouldn't you cry for them two dead childer? Don't be trying to turn yerself into a block of stone, like Nellie. Do you remember them every day? Do you pray for their souls at night?'

'I do pray for them,' Sally gasped, and suddenly the tears were out, like a rat escaping from between the jaws of a terrier, fierce and angry, and all the more so for being trapped such a long time. She howled and wept and pressed her mouth into Patsy's bony shoulder and she drew an old piece of sailcloth, on which the girls were supposed to be practising their hemstitch, up high, around her face, for whatever shelter could be maintained from the curious gaze of the eyes all round. Nellie was below in the storeroom, in a long queue, getting the rations for tomorrow, or Sally never would have dared make such a scene.

At last, Sally started to gasp and choke out a few words in between the sobs. 'Well, no matter what Nellie done to Peggy and Davey, we can't do *that* to her. It's a sin.'

'It's a small enough sin, I'm thinking. We can do it and we will.'

'Why would you take such a risk to be revenged on Nellie? Sure you hardly know her?'

Patsy looked down and spat on the floor, rubbing the small moisture into a complicated pattern with her finger, before the heat of the midday sun dried it up, disappearing in front of their eyes.

'What do you know about the workhouses, Sally?'

'Well, I know enough to stay out of them, and isn't that enough?'

'D'you know how long it takes to build a workhouse?'

'Of course not. Ten years?'

'Not at all, it doesn't take even ten months, every workhouse is the exact same and the plan is sent from town to town, and the list of necessary materials with it. It's put together like one of Mistress Jonathon's recipes.'

Patsy glanced up and smiled a twisted grimace. 'Didn't my father help with the building of the workhouse in Lurgan, back in the year '36? The wages wasn't great, but it was better than he could get in the landlord's fields. The plans was sent up from Dublin, and everything was laid out, right down to the number of nails in a door.'

'And why are you telling me all this?'

'D'you know what was the hardest thing of all, for them who were charged to design and oversee the building of the workhouses?'

'No, Patsy, I know nothing about anything, I think.'

'Them workhouses should have been built ten years earlier, like they were in England, but the Englishmen sent over to plan the thing had a big problem. The government in London says to the men: *'Be careful and make sure that nobody goes into them houses unless they are really desperate, make sure they're less comfortable, and the inmates less well fed, than they would be on the outside, or else them workhouses'll be filled with corner boys who are too lazy to work for a living.'* That's what has happened in the English workhouses, so they say.'

'And what's the problem?'

'What's the problem? Mother of God, Sally, are you stupid? The problem is, the men sends word back to London: *'Honourable Government, here we are trying to do your bidding, but it's not possible to make the Irish tenant one iota less comfortable or less well-fed than he is right now, not if you plan on keeping him alive, anyhow.'* '

Patsy snorted and tossed her head. 'But them bastards in London went ahead anyway and told them to build the big grey houses, and for the year of the building work at least, my father was able to feed himself and take himself a wife.'

She laughed. 'And here I am. And them both dead, to the best of my knowledge. And all belonging to me thinks me dead too.'

'And why do they think that, Patsy?'

The colour seeped away from her friend's face and she tugged on her lower lip with the sharp buck teeth that stuck out from the front of her mouth.

'Because, in the year '47, my poor father finally gave in.'

'Gave in?'

'Gave in. Took me and my mother by the hand and went to the warden looking for a ticket, and all of us, and the brothers and sisters besides, walked up to the gates of the big house in Lurgan.'

Sally gasped and gripped Patsy's elbow tight. She was as cold as ice in the bright sun of the midday, and Sally wrapped the length of sail close around her. Patsy didn't move or make any reply, just gazed away into the distance, where the sunbeams glinted off the caps of the waves, enough to nearly blind a body.

'You went into the workhouse?'

'We did.' A silent tear slid out of the centre of Patsy's right eye and traced a line down the black smudged hollows carved under her lashes. When it reached the tip of her chin, it hung motionless and the sunlight shone through it until it sparkled like a diamond. Sally thought about diamonds, how she had heard they were formed by all the weight of the world pressing down, and she saw how the weight of the world might press a girl like Patsy, until she too was hard and sharp and strong enough to cut through a sheet of glass. Sally touched the tip of her forefinger to the solitary tear and then pressed it, salty and precious, against her lips. If Patsy noticed, she made no remark.

'And then?'

'And then I never saw hide nor hair of most of them again.' She sucked a huge shuddering breath into her lungs. 'They ripped my mother from her husband's arms, and both of them crying like babies. And we, children that we were, were hard pressed to try to comfort them. My brothers went to the men's ward with our father, I went to the women's ward with our mother, and the little ones went to the children's ward.'

She started to gnaw on the nail of her right thumb, which was worn down to the very quick.

'For a few days, we would stand, my mother and me, at the wall of the women's exercise yard at breaktime, and we screamed their names over the top of that wall, until our throats were raw and our ears rang with our own noise. But we never heard an answering call. Not one we recognised anyways. And then the trustee came to us on the third day and said that we would get a few stripes of the cat if we didn't stop our hollerin'.'

'But, you were fed, and you have survived and look at you now. There's a chance that the rest of the O'Hanlons were fed and looked after too?'

'They died, Sally. For my mother saw it in a vision, and she woke up in the middle of the tenth night, screaming on a pallet beside me. I asked her, *What is it, mother?* and says she, *I saw them carry Joan and Michael out, and Brid and Daniel too. And I'll be next, with the help of God, for Joan held out her hand to me and beckoned me to follow.*

'I took my mother in my arms and gave her a little shake. Says I, *It's only a dream, mother, sure we're not here two weeks, that's not long enough to lose four people.*'

Patsy dragged her sleeve across her face, and when she turned, her eyes were as dead as those of a plaster statue in a church. 'Within twelve hours, she started to blacken and swell, and three days later she was dead.'

'Typhus.' Sally breathed. 'Road fever, same as my own parents.'

'Typhus, right enough. There was no Kilroy there to slap a blister on her scalp, whether that might have helped or not, who knows? She died untended and unpoulticed, like a dog at the side of the road, and was tumbled into a pit.'

'And how do you know that, Patsy? Maybe she had a fine Christian burial, alongside her husband and children.'

'I know because when the men came round and swung her up onto the cart, I crept in deep beside her, when their backs were turned, and I lay under a pile of corpses to get out of that place.'

Her voice shook, 'It's hard enough to get into the workhouse these days Sally, but I'll tell you, there's only one way out. And next time you ask me why I hate that *sister* of yours, think of me, holding my breath under the pile of the dead, while they dribbled and leaked, and me crawling my way back up to daylight and away, when the sound of the cart grew faint in the distance from the boneyard. I had to climb out of the pit and run before they came back to sprinkle the burning lime on top of the unshriven, unwaked corpse of my mother, for to make her melt faster.'

Patsy took Sally's hand and squeezed it.

'Nellie Gordon's a murderess. You think of what I said to you. A six-year-old boy and a four-year-old girl, separated, in the workhouse in Naas. They came out of it in a cart, you can be sure, and they weren't holding their breath.'

Sally gazed back into Patsy's eyes and saw the hint of madness in them. And Sally wondered was she mad enough to join Patsy in her plan.

Chapter Twenty-seven

Hobart, October 1919, Saoirse

My grandmother was right about one thing. I might have spared myself the trouble of attending the registrar. We tried every permutation, every combination of Margaret, Gordon, O'Hanlon, Mahon, until I thought Mr Milligan was going to explode with impatience. My mother's birth is not recorded in the ledgers of Hobart.

What choice do I have now? I will have to listen again to the ramblings of the woman in the bed before me, punctuated with paroxysms of coughing, digressions, tales of the other filthy convicts, tales I would rather not know. I am reduced now to be the captive audience of my grandmother. The dregs of an Irish gaol. A thief and a kidnapper and an arsonist, at the very least. Consorting with prostitutes. And my mother. Of my mother there is still not a word.

My grandmother – the woman I have always thought of as my grandmother – shifts a little in the shroud of her blankets and moans.

'Water.' It is the barest whisper and the effort is visible on her face. I cross the room and pour a fresh glass of water and hold it to her lips. A rivulet dribbles down her chin and onto her nightdress, but she manages to wet her lips at least.

'Water, water everywhere, and not a drop to drink.'

'What?'

'It's what they say on the ocean, when times are bad and the drought is upon the vessels.'

I toss my eyes to heaven and sigh. 'And what do they say in the prison? What, I wonder, does a child say when a girl she trusts steals her from her mother, and condemns her to the workhouse, never to see daylight again?' I fix Sally with a bitter gaze. 'You have robbed me too. You robbed me of a father all my life, and if you die now before the whole of your tale is told you will have robbed me of my mother too. Why did you wait until now to tell me?'

'You never asked. If you had have asked, we might have told you.'

'Asked? Woken up one bright summer morning, looked at the shearwaters dabbling on the sand and thought to myself, *I must ask my mother if by any chance she has spent my entire life lying to me?* Why in God's name would it ever have occurred to me to ask?'

'You're not blind or stupid, you know something of your country's history. You must have known there are still convicts in Hobart. Not so many left now, not so many as old as I.'

'A child believes what she is told by the people who love her.'

As soon as the words are spoken I know what I have said. I have handed the conversation to her and all she need do is agree. *Yes, we lied for love.* But she does not take the easy way out. My grandmother – or Sally as I try now to think of her – has never taken the easy way out. She beckons for the glass again and draws another trembling, dribbling sip into her parched throat.

'Tell me,' she whispers, 'what do you know of water?' I stare at her, bewildered. 'What can you tell me about water?' I am silent so she shakes her head and answers her own question. 'I know what you know, for I sat with you as we read the encyclopaedias in the city library and I tried to fill you up with all the knowledge you should have gained in school.'

I tap the drinking glass to make a chime, but the glass is thick and dull, not like the fine tumblers we used to serve the gentlemen their whiskey in. My tapping makes the surface of the water shiver, but does not make the glass sing.

'I know the boiling temperature,' I say at last, 'I know that it is neither acid nor alkali.'

Sally interrupts me.

'You might think you know the essence of water. You might be a professor in the agriculture college, with your fine-ground lenses, revealing the secrets of water, one drop at a time. You might be the most celebrated scientist in all the world. But you wouldn't know what I know.'

She pauses and the silence draws out between us until, against my will and against all my best judgement, I finally ask. 'What do you know?'

'I know the true meaning of water.'

'And what is it?'

'You cannot know, until you thirst.'

Chapter Twenty-eight

Prison Ship Australasia, August 1849

Seven bells and all's well. All souls able up on deck. Walking wounded to the hospital.

Up they went, swaying and rocking up the ladder to the blue sky and the blessed smell of saltwater and gruel and charcoal.

'This must be what heaven's like,' muttered Eliza. 'Coming up out of the stink and misery and torture of purgatory and arriving under the sunlight in heaven.'

'You'd look well turning up to Saint Peter, the state you're in. Maybe they'd give you a bath first,' said Patsy.

'Maybe they would. A big hot barrel full of water, like in Grangegorman, and me the first to lie in it, before all you dirty bitches turns the water black.'

'Well there'll be no more bathing here, for the salt water makes you more dirty than you were before,' Sally said.

The water situation was perilous. For weeks now the women had been cooking the meal and trying to wash with salt water, drawn up from the sea by sailors hauling buckets hand-over-hand from over the ship's rails. The drinking water ration was down to a few mouthfuls per woman and the hum off the water in the tin cup would make a body heave and retch. The captain had given them tea leaves out of his own rations, and Sally was learning to drink it, but she didn't know whether it was the odd notion of drinking a boiled leaf, or the simple fact of the spoiled water that made the strange black brew so foul.

The previous week Nellie had made up a party of mess-leaders and cooks and they had taken their complaint to Kilroy.

'Look at this, if you would be so good, sir,' she had said, bobbing a curtsey and pointing her chest straight up at him, managing somehow to be lewd and servile at one and the same time. 'The water in this bowl has been settling overnight, and look at the state it's in, begging yer pardon.'

Kilroy took the bowl and stared gloomily into it for a long minute. He sighed, dipped a finger in and tasted a few drops.

'By Gad, it's foul indeed.' He looked around at the half dozen or so women. 'And what does Mistress Richardson suggest?'

'Mistress Richardson, saving your pardon, says we're lucky to have it at all, and must be grateful for Her Majesty's kindness.' Nellie flashed a glance up under her lashes. 'But Mr Kilroy, sir, the women who are sick in the ward, but not sick enough for hospital, are crying out and weeping for water, and this foul stuff is not aiding them.'

'Indeed. It is possible, and likely, that it's making them worse.' He took the bowl of settled sediment and rank water from Nellie, and if his fingers brushed hers, well, he was only human. 'I'll speak to the captain.' He turned and strode away and Nellie returned, surrounded by an admiring crowd of women.

'Fair play to ya, girl, speaking up to the gentleman like that.'

Nellie shook her hair and laughed, 'You seem to forget that I am a well-born woman, fallen on hard times, not the sweepings of the gaol, like some I could mention.'

'Oh leave it alone, Nellie,' Catherine replied. 'Has the best part of two months at sea not wearied you of the same jibe, over and over?'

'Well, it would only be a jibe if it wasn't true … '

Catherine sighed and took a few steps away, all the fight gone out of her since the terrible scouring dysentery had stripped the flesh from her bones.

'Nellie, could you not go easy on poor Catherine?' Sally whispered. 'Sure she's sick as a dog and she feels the loss of her daughter something terrible. She's a shadow of the woman she was in Grangegorman, and God knows she was bad enough back then.'

'And not to mention the babe unborn that was ripped out of her by fever during her sickness, better not forget that,' added Eliza with a wink and a cruel nudge.

'Well, she may get over it, and aren't you all lucky that I'm the one heading up this mess and not that damp rag of a waste of a woman?'

And there was some hint of the truth in that, all right.

Later, Mistress Richardson appeared on deck. In one hand she held a massive metal funnel and a bucket; in the other, Nellie's basin of foul water.

'Look sharp! Captain says some of the convict water has been sent out stored in old wine barrels and has been tainted by the must from the grapes. It is misfortunate, to be sure.' She looked around, daring any woman to raise her voice in complaint, but they were respectful and silent, even Nellie. 'Patricia, run to the store and bring a sack of charcoal, and don't delay.'

Matron lined the funnel with clean muslin, taken from the hospital stores, and then set twenty women to crushing and powdering the lumps of charcoal, which she fed into the funnel.

'Now, then, pour the water gently into the funnel. Don't disturb the charcoal. The water that drips through the charcoal and the muslin out into the bucket will be cleaner and have less of a tang, so the captain assures me.' She looked around, then pointed her finger.

'Elizabeth Curry, you are the laziest child that the good Lord ever placed on this earth, so it will be no hardship for you to sit all day beside the filter. Keep it topped up, and keep a tally on the clean water, one gallon per mess per day, for all cooking and drinking purposes.'

Liz's face was a picture of woe, 'How long will it take, Matron, if I might ask?'

'All day, every day, if it be necessary.' Matron swirled her stiff skirt around, caught Nellie by the arm and said, 'A word in private, Eleanor.'

And that was the last time Nellie spoke to a man on board the *Australasia*.

★ ★ ★

The cleaning of the water was a fearsome, slow and heavy task. If Liz was too rough with the pouring, the filth and silt rose up and disturbed the filter, and all through the daylight hours the slow drip–drip and ping of the cleaned water falling into the gallon jars was a torment.

'Jesus, I'm parched, let me have one mouthful only, Liz, for the love of God,' said Sally.

Liz shook her head. 'Get away out of my sight. Sure I'll cause a riot if I'm seen to be favouring my own mess over another. If you think you've a drouth on you, you'd want to try sitting here all day like me, watching and listening, and afraid to taste even one extra drop on the end of my finger.' She looked around at the groups of women, stretched listlessly on the rough boards around the fire boxes. 'I don't know who I fear most, Nellie or Richardson, and if I was to risk my life giving a secret sup to anyone, it'd be to Nellie, not you.'

'Why, am I not scary enough? Do I not put the fear of God in you, like Nellie?'

'Jesus, Sally, yer a creeping whisper of a thing. There's even less spirit in you than before the journey started.'

Sally hugged her knees and wondered if Liz was right. Since Patsy had devised her terrible idea, her plan for revenge, Sally had been quiet, pondering and turning it over in her head.

'Better watch out for Sally, Liz,' said Patsy from close at hand. 'It's the ones make the least noise cause the most trouble. Still waters run deep.'

'Here comes that lazy hallion Ellen at last, with the new barrel,' said Liz.

They turned and watched as a woman on the water detail, Ellen Doyle, hauled a drum of water out of the stores and started half-rolling, half-carrying it towards the filter.

'That's bloody madness, so it is,' said Patsy. 'Sure one of the sailors could throw them barrels under his arm and never notice the weight of them at all, instead of making us women drag them around.'

'Oh, but Richardson wouldn't have a man over here on our side. I don't know if she fears for us or for them. Considering she thinks we're all whores, though there's not twenty women on the whole ship written down as that.'

'Nonetheless, dragging them barrels is a penance,' Sally looked at her hands which were red raw from the daily scrubbing of the ward and now had new, deep welts in the palms from her stint hauling barrels the day before.

'Jesus, Mary and Joseph,' shouted Liz. 'Houl' on tight.'

The ship took a violent roll to the left and pitched them all over onto their sides. The women never knew why these things happened, and the sudden terror of it never left a body, nor got less. An unexpectedly large wave would come from nowhere, or a sailor would let slip his rope accidentally, and the whole ship would flinch like a whipped dog. A moment after the lurch, the ship would right itself and carry on as before. But not today.

'Save the filter, for the love of God,' shouted Liz, and they leaped to grab bottles, jars and all the accoutrements of filtration.

From the doorway of the storeroom came a sickening howl, and, with a noise like a thunderstorm in full voice, Ellen Doyle's dropped barrel of water hurtled down the deck, rolling straight towards a mess of resting women. The women scattered, screaming, and the barrel sailed right through the ship's rail and out over the side, accompanied by the splintered and shattered railings.

'Well bad cess to that, there goes ten gallons of water we can't afford to lose,' said Patsy.

'Never mind the water,' said Catherine Colligan. 'What the hell is after happening to Ellen? She's roaring like a bullock with notions pastured beside a herd of springing heifers.'

Ellen Doyle writhed on the deck, half in and half out of the doorway of the storeroom, and women rushed to help her.

'My leg, my leg.' Her face was grey and twisted, and beads of sweat started out on her forehead. 'Don't touch me!' she screamed, as a strong, hefty woman gripped her under the oxters. 'Don't move me, isn't the leg broken under me.'

'Run for Mr Kilroy, and ask him to come at once,' shouted Catherine, and three small children darted off to do her bidding.

'A wet cloth, someone, hurry.' Catherine gripped Ellen's hand and crooned, 'Don't worry love, Kilroy will have you on your feet again in no time, and you a fine young girl, strong and not yet twenty years old. You'll heal.' She wiped Ellen's face with the cloth and lay down beside her, holding her still against the rolling and pitching of the ship.

'Gordon's mess, get back to the filter at once,' ordered Mistress Richardson, as she bustled up, skirts swishing and stays creaking. 'There's nothing you can do here.'

And when they got back to the filter, half a pint of clean water was gone.

'Who would do such a thing?' asked Nellie, appearing from close by. Sally hadn't seen Nellie in the crowd gathered round Ellen, but she hadn't been looking for her either.

'Indeed, who would be so low as to steal the drop of water away from the rest of us?' asked Patsy. She locked stares with Nellie, her upper lip curled in disgust and her big eyes full of scorn, and it was Nellie who coloured and looked away first. Sally had never seen man, woman or child of an equal station defeat Nellie before, and yet Patsy did it, with just the power of the hatred in her glare.

Ten minutes later, some men did enter the women's half of the deck after all. They strapped Ellen Doyle to a wide board and carried her, howling and screeching like a soul in hell, to the hospital ward below. Her hip had parted company with its socket, and though Kilroy did his best, and splinted and re-splinted and gave her a few precious drops of laudanum, while he heaved and strained and groaned and pushed, the hip never went back in. Even through the fog of the laudanum and the thick wooden planks of the hospital door and the deck beneath their feet, Ellen's screams and prayers and curses rang out across the ship, causing the women to bless themselves and shiver.

'I wish she'd give over, in the name of all that's holy. It's a terror listening to that,' Nellie growled after half an hour.

'Christ, your heart inside of you is a piece of Connemara marble. I wouldn't swap my loving soul for all yer good looks,' said Catherine. 'The screams of that girl is like a knife in my heart – have you no pity for her, at all?'

'Pity is a thing of the past.'

Sally looked at Nellie and thought of the two precious children, dead back in Naas. If there was ever one grain of pity in Nellie's body, it was a long time past, indeed.

★ ★ ★

The days wore on. The water ration no longer stank, but no one was ever sated with the few drops they were spared. The sun beat down on the rough sailcloth shades and the women huddled beneath them. In the hospital and the prison ward, the heat made every scorching breath a torment, and the smell made eyes sting and gorges rise.

Nellie turned in fury and clapped her hands across her ears. 'Christ, can nobody shut that child up? It's been roaring this three hours or more.'

'*He's* been roaring, Nellie,' Patsy said. 'He's not an *it*. And why wouldn't he roar? That's Lucy Smith's baby, Liam, and I'd say his belly thinks his throat is cut, it's so long since he's been fed.'

'Well why doesn't she feed him then, and not have him wailing away over there? It's enough to put a body astray in the head.'

'Feed him? Have you seen the state of her lately? She's not even on the deck, can't get out of her berth at all, never mind climb up thon ladder. She has the dysentery fierce bad and not one drop of milk in her tits,' Eliza said.

'She was begging for an extra mouthful of water this morning,' said Liz, 'but her mess wouldn't spare it to her, she's just getting a sixth of a gallon, like the rest of us.'

'Has she no hope of getting better?' Nellie said. 'Then we might as well put our hands over yon baby's mouth and nose, and stop his squalling once and for all.'

'You're a walking disgrace, Nellie Gordon, I'm sure Lucy'll get better in time,' Sally said, brave enough because Patsy, Liz and Eliza would surely back her up. 'And isn't life hard enough without talking about murdering little babies?'

'It was only a joke, for God's sake,' snapped Nellie, refusing to meet her eye.

'You're King Herod's daughter,' laughed Patsy.

And that was how Nellie got her new nickname. She was growing more careless of her reputation, of her pretence at decent respectability, as the torturous voyage drew ever onwards. All through June and July she had kept up a pretence of dignified sorrow at the predicament she found herself in and, in public, had treated Sally with a semblance of sisterly care, but now she said whatever she thought and made no bones of how sick of the sight of the other women she truly was.

The deterioration in her temper was not unique, for they were all half-starved and cranky and wild with thirst. The tongues stuck to the roofs of their mouths all the day long. At night the young children wailed and moaned, while their mothers lay listlessly beside them, too worn out to comfort them.

Lucy Smith's child was like a bundle of twigs wrapped in a shroud. His skin had a sickly yellow hue and the whites of his eyes were muddy and brown. His cloths rarely needed changing and his piss was dark and sticky. He had shrunk to a wisp, with his giant, heavy head lolling on his shoulders, beyond his power to support it. In Grangegorman, Sally had sometimes cared for baby Liam when his mother was called upon for translations; he'd been two months old and a bonny, smiling lump of a child. Now, the hunger and the lack of care had shrivelled and aged him, and the women feared for his future.

'You know, you'd swear he was a changeling,' said Eliza. 'I know a woman whose child was changed on her, back home. One day he was a bright, bouncing babby and by the end of the next week, it was clear and plain to see that he had been changed in the night-time for a fairy child, weak and fretful. He never thrived again and walked with a limp all his days after.'

'Oh don't be stupid, Eliza,' said Patsy. 'Everyone knows that fairies can't cross running water, and how would a fairy have hidden here unnoticed for the best part of eight weeks?'

Nellie rose to her feet. 'I swear to God, I don't know what I ever did to be cursed with such a shower of fools. Fairies and hags. Don't you know there's no such thing as fairies? No more than there is a leprechaun with a pot of gold at the rainbow's end and no more than there is a God in heaven. The sooner you imbeciles realise that the better.'

She strode off and stood at the ship's edge, knuckles white as she gripped the rail. She spent the best part of each day there now, glaring off into the endless expanse, leaving the care of the fire and the cauldron to Sally, for she knew Sally was far too terrified of her to dip into the gruel.

Eliza and Sally crossed themselves against Nellie's blasphemy, and Eliza also made a sign to ward off fairy evil, but Sally didn't, because her mother had always forbidden it. Patsy looked solemn, though, and leaned forward, placing her hand on Sally's knee.

'I think she might be right, to be honest,' Patsy said. 'You know, I'd sooner believe in the fairies, watching and waiting to do you a bad turn if you let your guard down. Or in the banshee herself, waiting to suck the soul out of you — than believe in God.'

Eliza blessed herself again and pulled her rosary out of her pocket, ten smooth river stones threaded on a strip of hide.

'Patsy,' Sally said, 'will you houl' yer whist, for the love of God. The middle of the ocean is hardly the place to be blaspheming and talking all that kind of wickedness.'

'Well, aren't you just after making my point for me?' Patsy leaned over and grasped her arm excitedly. 'Just think about it. The fairies are *supposed* to be wicked and evil scheming things. They never pass up a chance to lead a man astray at night, until he falls into a bog-hole and drowns, and they suck the souls of the dead, if the kith and kin don't stay alert during the wake and keep them at bay.'

Sally shuddered, remembering how her own eyelids had drooped and scraped across their eyeballs while she tried to wake her mother and father.

'But,' Patsy continued, 'God is supposed to love us like a father, right? He watches over us and forgives us our sins. He cares for the sparrows of the air and the least of his children?'

'That's right,' Eliza spoke quickly, leaving off from worrying her beads.

'Well, then. Where's God now? Where was he in the workhouse when my parents and all belonging to me died of the hunger and of typhus? Where is he now when Liam Smith is teetering on the brink between life and death? If Lucy ever gets up out of that delirium again, she may find she has no child to wake up for.'

'Will you quit, for the love of God, Patsy,' Sally begged. 'You'll bring down a storm on us, or worse, as His punishment.'

'That's right. That's God for you. A bogeyman to scare the childer with. A lucky charm to keep you safe on the ocean's tides. You no more believe in a kind and loving God than I do. I don't know what kind of magical tyrant you believe in, but it's not the kind of God would send his only son to die for to save us.'

She took Sally's shoulders in her hands and shook them gently. She touched the back of her hand to Sally's cheek, whisper soft.

'The God you believe in is like the landlord's agent, come with his whip and the wrecking crew, to drive you off the face of the earth if you can't prove your worth.' She stood up and stretched her arms to the sky. 'Well, I'm finished with God, Mary, Jesus and the whole boiling lot of them. It's the only thing your precious sister is right about. It's every woman for herself.'

'Every woman for herself?' Sally whispered.

'Every woman for herself.' Patsy paused and looked at her, a slight blush rising on her cheek. 'And for those she loves.' She shrugged and disappeared below decks, breaking all the rules, where she knew Sally wouldn't follow.

★ ★ ★

The next day dawned bright and blistering hot. The women sat on the deck under shades of cloth lashed to the ropes and railings and tried to shelter their eyes from the blinding glare off the water. Mistress Richardson tried to get a needlework class going, unpicking and restitching the same seams over and over, training them up for useful and productive lives in Van Diemen's Land, but they were so sullen and surly that she gave up and went to lie down in her cabin.

The only sound on the women's half of the deck was the slow torture of the water dripping through Liz Curry's filter into a jar below and the fretful cries of a few infants. Liam Smith had been carried into the fresh air by one of Lucy's mess-mates, but he lay still and silent, barely twitching under his covering of calico.

'Shark! Shark to port astern.'

The lookout's voice rang out loud over the deck and the sailors rushed to the ship's rail, hanging over, shielding their eyes until they caught a glimpse.

Then they turned away, spitting and crossing themselves and making all manner of strange hand gestures, known only to the men of the sea.

'What's a shark?' Liz asked. 'Is it the same as a dolphin?'

Sally shrugged, 'I don't think so, for the men were right happy to see the dolphins, when they followed us out of the harbour at Kingstown, and they smiled and blessed them. They don't look too happy now.'

'It's a sign of a death on board, that's why.' Patsy spoke sharply. 'I heard it from old Mamie Johnson when we saw the dolphins. She comes from a far corner of the County Mayo, under St Patrick's mountain, and all belonging to her have been fishing on the water for generations past.' Patsy sat down beside Sally and continued, 'She was happy as a lark to see the dolphins, for she said to me *the sea-men believe dolphins to be the souls of drowned sailors, come for to protect the ship and all hands on her. But the shark, the shark is a sorry sign altogether, and if he is not caught and killed, there'll be a death on board before nightfall.'*

'D'you think they'll try and kill the shark, Patsy?'

'How would I know? Come with me over to the side, and we'll see can we find it.'

A small crowd had gathered at the rails already, but most of the women stayed beneath the shelter, shrouded in hunger and apathy, barely moving.

'There. Yonder. It's yonder!' shouted a young girl, pointing into the distance. They followed her finger. At first they saw nothing, then between the rise and fall of the waves they saw a black triangle, slicing through the spume. It sped alongside the ship, thirty feet or more off the port side, neither gaining nor losing speed, but keeping constant alongside.

'There's another,' cried a voice, and behind it a smaller, notched triangle sped through the water. The small knot of women and children watched for many minutes, but nothing else happened, the sharks neither leaving their sight nor drawing closer.

'Well, there's no sign of a boat being lowered,' Patsy said eventually, 'so they aren't going to try to kill them. There'll be a death on board tonight.'

'Ach, Patsy that's rubbish. How could you believe an oul' tale like that, if you won't believe the words of the holy Bible, when the whole world of your betters is telling you it's the truth?'

'I don't know what I believe in. All I know is that I don't believe in such a thing as *my betters* any more, or in such a thing as a God that loves me, or loves any of us for that matter. It's little enough love we've seen in our lives.'

'I love you, Patsy, if that's any good to you.' Sally stretched out a finger and touched it on the rough, tanned skin of the back of her hand. Patsy didn't strike Sally away, or look amazed. She just sighed and smiled sadly.

'It's not much good, to be perfectly honest. Two girls who'll be separated and sent the-Devil-knows-where when we get to Hobart. We'll probably never see each other again, if Nellie has her way. It would be all the world to both of us if we just had one sister each to love us.'

'But a friend is better than nothing, surely?'

'It is,' Patsy smiled, blinking away the tears that had gathered behind her lashes. 'It's better than nothing.' She rubbed the back of her hand against her eyes and said, 'Come on, let's get back to the others. This sun is cutting the eyes out of me.'

★ ★ ★

The sharks slid back down beneath the waves under cover of the darkness, but their prophecy was fulfilled. There was no great surprise when Lucy Smith's child slipped away in the night.

'He didn't even cry,' whispered Liz in hushed tones. 'He didn't make a sound. Susan Jordan was holding him in the night, as Lucy is still too weak to bear his weight, and when Susan woke up, he was as cold as a stone in her grip. She says she feels the cold of him in her arms yet.'

'How would the child find the strength to cry?' asked Nellie. 'Sure he hadn't been fed this four or five days past. Eileen O'Sullivan has been taking Lucy's rations this week, for she told Lucy she'd suckle him, along with her own child, but I'd bet she just tucked him under her shawl and never let him near the tit at all.'

'Jesus, listen to Herod's daughter, you really are a rock of a woman, and no mistake,' said Catherine. 'If she said she'd suckle him, I'm sure she did. Wouldn't that be the Christian thing to do?'

'She did and my arse! Or if she did, she's an even bigger fool than she looks, wasting her precious milk on another woman's child, and her own one hungry enough, I'd say.'

'Well, you got yer wish, didn't you, Herod's daughter?' snapped Patsy. 'For only yesterday you were making plans to murder the poor child, and now he is after sparing you the trouble.'

'Don't be stupid. Is there no one left here who can take a joke?' Silence fell.

Within minutes, Nellie was back at her solitary place at the ship's rails.

'I swear she thinks she can make the ship sail faster, just by staring out towards Van Diemen's Land,' Patsy said. 'If it's even to be found in the direction that she's looking.'

It was true that the women could no longer reckon which way the ship was headed. The wind had fallen to the faintest of breezes and the ship would be entirely becalmed if the men were less good at their business. All day long, and even through the star-filled watches of the night, the crew heaved and strained and swore, tacking the ship from one side to the other, eking out the tiniest surge from the slack winds. Sometimes they sailed into the sun, sometimes away, and although Mistress Richardson assured the women that they were making slow progress in the correct direction, it seemed that they just covered the same stretch of ocean, over and over again.

'It wouldn't be so bad, all this sailing backwards and forwards,' said Liz, 'if it didn't make the men so bloody hungry.'

'It's a torment, that's what it is,' sighed Catherine, 'a torture to the soul to smell the food and yet not have any of it.'

The men were so hard-pressed, and making do with so little sleep, that the captain had ordered their ration increased. Each man now received three pounds of beef a day, instead of two. The fires in the galley were never idle, and the scent of roasting and boiling meat pervaded the deck from sun-up until the women descended into the prison ward at dusk.

'D'you know,' said Eliza, 'I heard that oul' Richardson asked the captain for a few pounds of beef for the hospital ward and he told her to take herself to the Devil.'

'It's true, for I was nearby when she asked him,' said Catherine, 'and to be fair to her, she begged him for it. She all but went down on her knees. *Beef tea, says she, It's the best cure of all for the dysentery, if I could prevail upon you for just one pound of beef every second day.'*

'And what did he say?'

'Says he, *You can lose as many of them oul' biddies as you wish, and it'll do nothing to worsen my humour. But, if only three or four more of my men goes down with the shits, or scorbutus, the ship's sunk, and we'll none of us reach Hobart, for the wind has failed us.'*

Catherine sighed and dropped her voice, beckoning her listeners closer. She put her finger to her lips. 'I shouldn't have said that, for I swore to myself I wouldn't breathe a word of it, and worsen the spirits of the women even further. But between those of us who are here, he said, *I can't spare one morsel of food, nor one drop of water to succour them criminals. If the Department of Convicts has sent inadequate fare, write a report when ye get home, if ye get home. See how far that'll get you.'*

'If she gets home?' whispered Eliza. 'If she gets home? Well, Patsy, I'd say that's the kind of news would make a girl change her mind about God, eh?' She fished in her pocket for her rosary and started telling the beads, one by one.

'Put them away,' snapped Catherine, 'and don't let on one word of what I told you, for what this ship doesn't need is two hundred women weeping and wailing.'

'Indeed, that's true,' laughed Patsy. 'Nellie's nerves wouldn't take it, she'd kill us all in our sleep.'

'That's not funny, Patsy,' said Liz, and tears started from the corners of her eyes. 'I'm here to set up in a new life with me brothers, until me Da is able to come out. Dying of hunger or dysentery isn't part of the plan.'

'Nor a hand over your nose and mouth in the dead of night, and you snoring in the same berth as Herod's daughter,' laughed Patsy.

Catherine leaned over and slapped Patsy right across the mouth.

'That's enough.'

Patsy leaped to her feet. At that moment, a mournful wailing arose from the far end of the women's deck and they all forgot Patsy and turned to stare.

The keening grew louder, led by some of the wild women, in their own tongue, and though Sally didn't understand the words, it was the saddest, most plaintive song that ever she heard. Underneath the high-pitched keen came the solid patter and response of the rosary, women answering in whichever language suited them best.

'On yer knees, for God's sake,' said Catherine. 'You too, Patsy, and I won't hear no for an answer.'

They sank down onto the deck and tried to hide their eyes from the sight of a small cloth-wrapped bundle, as light as a sack of bog-cotton blossom, borne across the deck by Eileen O'Sullivan.

'It's proper and right that the foster-milk-mother should bury the child, when his own mother is still prostrate,' whispered Catherine. But, as though an apparition, and in seeming defiance of the laws of medicine and of gravity, up through the hatch of the prison ward rose Lucy Smith, pushed and supported from behind by two women of her mess. The skin of Lucy's face was brown and dry as an autumn leaf and a dull glaze filmed each sunken eye, which sought no friendly face, but remained fixed on the bundle in Eileen's arms.

'Christ,' breathed Catherine, 'look at the state of her. She'll be next, I'd say.'

The noise had reached such a pitch that even the men paused in their labours for a moment, and the mainsail billowed emptily for a few seconds until a roar from the mate set the sailors back about their tasks. The captain strode over to see the source of the disturbance.

'Captain, sir, begging yer pardon, won't you say a few words over the child, before the sea takes him?' asked Eileen O'Sullivan, shaking at her own daring and dropping an awkward, heavy curtsey.

'Is that the cause of all the bloody commotion? Get on with it woman. I'm paid to transport convicts, and if they choose to bring children and babes-in-arms with them, that's none of my concern.' His voice shook and his eyes didn't meet Eileen's or any of the rest of the gathered women's. As if of its own volition, his right hand stretched out, not touching the coarse shroud but hovering over it.

'Into your hands, oh Lord, I commend this soul until the judgment day when the sea gives up her dead.' He snapped back his hand and stared at it in wonder. 'Any further funerals are to be carried out at first light, and in silence.'

He turned on his heel and stalked away, without a backward glance.

Eileen moved towards the side of the ship and, supported by her two friends, Lucy was half-dragged, half-carried in her wake. She was entirely silent.

'Is she right in the head, I wonder?' said Nellie, reappearing beside Sally. 'Or does she know what's happening at all?'

'I hope she doesn't,' Sally answered.

Eileen reached the side of the ship and paused, waiting for Lucy to catch up. Mutely, she offered the bundle to Lucy, but Lucy shook her head. Reaching out her right hand, Lucy gently pushed the tiny bundle out of Eileen's grasp and it fell out of sight. The women held their breath, waiting for a splash, but the corpse was so light that the sound of its entry into the sea was drowned out by the everyday creaking and cracking sounds of the ship.

Lucy slipped from the supporting hands of her friends, and fell senseless upon the deck.

'Well, that's the first funeral,' said Nellie. 'I doubt it will be the last.'

★ ★ ★

Sally lay on the deck, sweat standing on her forehead and prickling and itching in the seams under her arms. The water drip-dripped into the gallon jar, the sun beat mercilessly through the weathered strip of canvas above them, and the ship drifted aimlessly despite the best efforts of the crew. Mistress Richardson had stopped assuring her charges that the ship would reach her destination on time and with a full complement, and instead spent the hours that she was not needed in the hospital resting in her own cabin.

'Christ,' muttered Patsy, sighing as she rolled over, trying to find some comfort by rearranging her skirts between her and the dry, hot boards of the deck. 'Christ on his cross, we'll never get there.'

'Of course we will,' Sally said. 'What choice do we have? We're heading off to the unknown and it may be there's none would miss the likes of us, but the captain and the crew, they have wives and children waiting at home, and they'll not give up the fight to reach Hobart, not while one ounce of strength remains in them.'

'Wives at home?' laughed Nellie. 'Men like that, they have a wife in every port in Ireland, England and beyond. You hardly think that the streets of Hobart are free from night-walkers and houses of ill repute?'

'Well, whatever is their reason, they won't give up,' Sally said. 'And Richardson says there is no shortage of water or meat for the men, and a three-week surplus besides.'

'And what about us? Has the Department of Convicts sent us a three-week surplus?'

'Oh, shut yer beak, Nellie,' said Patsy. 'Sure they sent barely enough water, and it completely spoiled from the cheap, re-used wine barrels, never mind three extra weeks of provisions. If we're delayed three weeks, we'll starve and that's the height of it. If they didn't even send the potatoes, what hope did we have?'

They lay a few minutes longer, too exhausted and weak even to bicker. Nellie didn't notice or care that Patsy had told her to shut her face, and Sally couldn't tell if that was a good or a bad thing. It was a new thing, that's for sure.

'You know,' said Patsy, 'if a woman, or a small girl, could cling onto that rope tight enough, I think she could follow it down to the galley stores.'

They followed her gaze to where a sheet of rope stretched down through a gaping hatch in the centre of the main deck.

'Don't be bloody stupid.' Nellie's voice was low and full of scorn. 'You'd set the whole ship's crew against us. If any member of my mess does such a stupid and a reckless act, I'll strip the hide off her back. And that's before Richardson and Kilroy get their hands on her.'

'It'd be a damn sight better than starving to death here, or dying of the drouth.'

'You'd want to be well sure that you'd not be caught. I'd say there's easier ways for a girl like you to get a bit extra round here.'

'A girl like me?' Patsy raised herself on one elbow, groaning, and turned to face Nellie. 'A girl like me? What's that supposed to mean?'

'Oh don't play the innocent with me, O'Hanlon. I seen your manifest when Kilroy was filling out his book. How else would a girl your age survive and get herself all the way from Armagh to Grangegorman alive, and with flesh still on her bones?'

'What are you talking about, Nellie?' Sally watched the colour rising on Patsy's cheeks and though her lips trembled, the look she turned on Nellie would have curdled milk in the churn.

'Oh now, Sally, don't be playing the fool. Are you telling me your little friend here hasn't told you all about her great experience in the oldest profession? Turning tricks and tumbling drunks on the town each night.'

'On the town?' Sally gasped. 'A nightwalker?'

Patsy turned to face her and there was a hint of desperation in her eyes as they bulged and fixed Sally in their glance. A hint of a tear shone behind her lashes, and Sally thought this one might actually spill out, as had happened the day she told her workhouse tale. Sally wondered did Patsy remember her lifting that tear to her lips, or had she even noticed.

'A nightwalker. Yes, I was. I'm here for theft, for they don't send women out for walking the streets, as long as they do no other crimes. But, yes, I was a day- and nightwalker. I never said I wasn't.'

'But you never said you was,' said Nellie triumphant. 'You might find my sister less keen to share your company now, little whore. You'll have some job finding a man to marry you in Hobart, with that written on your record for all to see for ever more.'

'A man! A husband. The Devil take any man who thinks he'll marry me, for I have had enough of men in one year as will do me for the rest of my life.' Patsy spoke more quietly, turning to face Sally, her shoulder and arm blocking Nellie from the sight of Sally's face. 'I have lain down, and stood up, and kneeled for the last man in my life, Sally. My plan is to die alone in a spinster garret.'

'But, children, Patsy?' Sally asked. 'You'd never live a life without children?'

'I'd live alone in the branches of a tree, like poor mad Sweeney, before a man will thrust himself in any part of me again. I bought my life with my body, and it's mine now to do with as I please.' She blinked again and again, and to her credit not a single tear escaped her. 'As for children? I'd never bring one into this world, for fear it might be a girl, for wouldn't the most of us be better off drowned in a barrel like kittens, than allowed grow up to be used as nightwalkers?'

There was nothing to say, so Sally leaned against her and tried to take her hand but Patsy shook her off and rose stiffly, walking over to the ship's rail, where Nellie was wont to stand, until the heat drove her back under the shadow of the canvas with the rest of them.

'Now, little sister, there's yer precious friend for you. A well-used young woman, I'd say.'

Sally turned to Nellie and gripped her hand in her own small fist, squeezing and crushing and trying to force some sign of pain out of her.

'Nellie, have you gone stone mad? Have you forgotten who you are and where we came from?'

'Listen, little fool, the truth is what you make it. The truth is what Kilroy has writ in his book. I'm a country servant, and a widow. And you, my little one, are as fresh as any woman who ever set foot in Van Diemen's Land. And so you'll remain, for seven years, and don't fear, I'll be watching every hour of the day.'

Sally clambered up and joined Patsy at the rail and put her right hand over Patsy's left, where it gripped the wooden railing, her knuckles white and every sinew straining.

'Listen,' Sally said. 'It's not hopeless. Sure, it may be there's plenty of men in Hobart can't read a manifest, and there's bound to be others who won't care. Eliza told me a trick, anyway.'

She looked around cautiously and lowered her voice, for Eliza really had no business talking to her of such things and Nellie might have ripped the hair from her scalp if she knew. Sally squeezed Patsy's hand and prised one of her fingers loose from the rail, rubbing the soft pad of the finger between her own.

'On the first night, Eliza says, which or whatever you've done in the past, maiden or not, you hide a blade by the bed or the pallet and when the deed is done, he'll be snoring and you'll nick your finger, quick as can be.' Sally stopped rubbing and pinched Patsy's finger hard until she finally tore her eyes from the horizon and turned to look at her.

'Then you smear a little blood around, you know, down there, and make sure and get some on yer shift and beneath you. Eliza says there's plenty of girls don't bleed when the maidenhead goes, and it's always better to give him a little extra proof.'

Patsy pulled her hand from Sally's grasp and laughed, hard and low, the bark of a vixen in the night. 'Don't worry. I know all about blood. I seen my own, many's the time in the past years. I seen my blood drip off men and I seen it smeared on their britches and I'll not be seeing it again. I'll live alone. Every woman for herself. And if you take my advice, you'll follow my suggestion about that bitch Gordon, or you'll never again have a moment of peace in your life.'

'I told you once, I'll tell you again. I'm not doing it.'

'Your loss.'

Patsy returned to the shade near the other women, as far from Nellie as could be managed and Sally stayed at the rail sending up prayers and entreaties to the heavens. She prayed harder than she had ever done before. Clinging to the rail, eyes closed, mouth moving with the intensity of the silent words, she begged God to send her a sign, guidance in the path to take. But there was nothing.

Chapter Twenty-nine

Hobart, October 1919, Saoirse

A coal falls in the grate of the sweltering chamber, breaking my grandmother's train of thought. She coughs and sips from the glass I hold to her lips. A bowl of neatsfoot jelly sits disregarded on the bureau. Josie Hendron still insists on sending food up to the room, refusing to believe what Sally Mahon and I know to be true. She has eaten her last meal. And she is close to the end of her tale.

'So that's it? My so-called great-aunt Patsy was a prostitute.' I see her wince, but there is no time for niceties. 'A prostitute who hated men. And to please her, or from whatever hold she may have had on you, you gave up your dream of a normal life.'

'That's not how it was.'

'She and you, pretending to be sisters. Pretending, for the air of decency it gave.'

She nods. The act of speaking is plainly exhausting her.

'And because she hated men so much, you gave up everything for her? You were never married, were you? I won't find Jack Gordon's grave, or any relatives of his who would be kin of mine? There's no hope for that?'

Sally nods again.

'We're alike, so, *Grandmother*.' Sally flinches to hear the sarcasm in my voice and my heart stabs me for a moment, but I do not relent. 'We're alike after all, two wizened old spinsters, withering on our virgin stalks.'

'Not quite.' Her voice is low and weak and I lean in to catch the words better. 'We are not alike. I told you before, try to find love, take it where you find it and run.'

'The love of a friend, however dear, is not what I want. I could have had a husband and a life of my own if things had been different, and you want me to settle for friendship.'

'Patsy and I were more than friends.'

'I know, but that's not enough.'

'We loved each other.'

'It's not enough.'

'We loved each other.'

I look at her in horror and find my hand at my throat.

'You mean. You mean … intimately?'

She cannot mean it. I have heard stories. Stories of men come back from the war, men who in direst extremity had turned to the most vicious of abominations. But not women? Surely not. That cannot be what she means.

'I mean she was everything to me. Mother, sister, brother and husband. Friend and helpmeet. Lover.'

I clap my hand over my mouth and rush to the commode. Everything that is inside me boils out, hot and gushing, until nothing remains within and the pulse pounds in my temples. I sink into the chair beside her bed, and do not even rub at the stains of vomit on the bodice of my dress.

'My mother. You used her. You lied about having a husband so you could find and raise an heir to your business. Where did you find her? In the Queen's asylum? And you raised her here in this unnatural home?'

What chance did I have, raised here? What chance did I have, raised among these sinners? I reach for my rosary and I tell out one decade in silence, to strengthen me for the questions to come.

'I want to know. Why didn't my mother marry my father? Did you forbid her? Could you and Patsy not bear to have a man here to witness your immorality? Did you send her out to conceive an heir and then rob her of a husband as well as me of my father?'

And the heart stands still within me and I think. Did my mother ever have a special friend? Do I remember a woman in my childhood, who might have been more to my mother than a friend? Was my mother one of these people too? Is it catching?

'I welcomed him.' Sally's voice is weak but clear. 'We welcomed him, your father, Patsy and me. We loved your mother, and we wanted to love the man she loved.'

'You did?'

'We welcomed him into our home. He was poor, but so had we been. He was rough, but so were we. Patsy and I were filled with joy to see Margaret so happy, at last. The town was shocked but we didn't care. She was already expecting you. There was no point in pretending to be horrified, when we were delighted. Your parents spent three weeks under this roof, as if man and wife, waiting for the banns to expire. You would have been born in the fifth month of their marriage.'

'If she had married him.'

'If she had married him. There is never any shortage of men who wish to marry a woman with her own income.'

'I knew it. It was about money in the end, and your precious Australasia. You drove him away.'

She shakes her head and sighs.

'It wasn't about protecting my money, or the Australasia. It was about protecting Margaret. She was lucky. He was stupid enough to show his true nature before they married. She came to breakfast one day with a tooth in her hand and a cut below her eye. Spoiled goods, you see. Pregnant out of wedlock. Who else would have her? He thought he was safe enough.'

'But you threw him out.'

She gazes at me. 'Why do think so little of your mother? She threw him out herself. She knew what love was. She wanted what Patsy and I had.'

I shudder. 'She wanted a woman? She was an unnatural freak, like you? An abomination in the eyes of God?'

'She didn't want a woman. She wanted a real man. A man who deserved her. A man who deserved you.'

'And what did you want, Nanna? Didn't you say you missed the children Peggy and Davey? Didn't you always say on the ship you wanted a child of your own?'

'Not always. Not after what I saw on board. And not after what I did.'

Chapter Thirty

Prison Ship Australasia, September 1849

'What the hell is the hold-up up there?' Patsy muttered as the women stood in a bunch, awaiting their chance to climb the steep wooden ladder from the stench of the prison ward to the fresh morning light on deck. To be out under the sky during the early hours of the morning was a blessed relief, drinking in the fresh air before the merciless sun started its work in earnest, shrivelling them and cleaving their tongues to the roofs of their mouths.

'It's Mary Gandon,' answered Liz. 'How the hell is she supposed to do this climb for another four weeks? It's madness making her climb that ladder at her stage, she's fit to split open down the seams.'

'True, let's hope to God that the poor woman hasn't a pair of twins in her. She's big enough.'

With an audible grunt of effort that reached them, twelve feet below, Mary Gandon finally clambered over the top of the ladder and disappeared through the hatch out into the fresh air. The rest of them swarmed up after her, as nimble now as any sailor, but greatly encumbered by the long, swirl of their navy skirts. The dresses were showing signs of hard wear by now, fraying at the hems where the damage from constant friction against the rough planks of the deck, and the damp, piss-wet boards of the prison ward, was working its way through the rough fabric.

'No man could call me vain,' said Sally as she surveyed the damage to her skirt, 'but this blue uniform is by far the finest garment I ever had on my bones. Do you think there'll be another to replace it when we reach Hobart?'

'There better be,' said Patsy, 'or I'll spend the next seven years in rags, as I have spent the greater part of my life.'

An unaccustomed commotion broke out among a group of women several messes along the deck. In general, since the loss of the spare water and the dearth of wind, a strange lassitude had come over the inmates and a fuss of any kind was becoming rare, even among the once-giddy children.

When Sally glanced over at the noise, Mary Gandon was pacing back and forth, a hand pressed into the small of her back and a look of terror on her face.

'Jesus, I'd say she's after starting,' whispered Liz, 'but she reckons her time's not for another month or more.'

'Well, isn't she lucky, then,' said Nellie. 'It'll be nice and small, should come out easy, and with the help of God, die on the way out, if it's too early. Best solution all round.'

There was shaking of heads and muttering, but no one had the energy to tackle Nellie properly, and although Eliza pulled out her rosary and started muttering accusatory Aves, Nellie ignored her and went on stirring the gruel.

Mary Gandon continued her slow, limping progress round their half of the deck, moaning and sniffling until even kind Catherine Colligan was sick of the intrusion and closed her eyes against the pitiful sight.

A sudden shriek caused all nearby to jump in their skins, and a splash of liquid fell out of Mary's skirts and saturated the deck around her, as violent and as startling as if someone had dashed the whole of a pail of water over her. The front of her dress clung to her, soaked through from the knees to the hem and a strange smell, not unlike the chloride of zinc that Sally scrubbed the ward with, arose from the spreading puddle.

'Jesus,' shrieked Nellie as they all scrambled away from the spreading pool of liquid. 'It's like a cow has decided to birth among us.'

Liz and Patsy laughed uneasily, but Catherine Colligan hushed them.

'I don't like the look of that,' she said. 'That's not right at all. When the passage opens, the baby's head should be wedged well down like a cork in a bottle. There shouldn't be enough liquor to dampen a dress, just a trickle down your leg. I never seen a gush like that before that didn't lead to trouble.'

'And do you know a lot about it?' Sally asked, trying unsuccessfully not to gawk over at Mary Gandon, who stood amazed, her thin shoes and stockings soaked, staring at the waters on the deck. Around her, the women of her mess bustled with rags and mops and tried to exhort her to lie down, or to return back down the ladder to her berth. Gandon stood still, blank in the face, too frightened to listen or to think.

'I know enough about it,' said Catherine, 'for my mother was the birthing and laying-out woman in our place and taught me what she knows. And I was always brought along to help her when I was younger, on account of having small hands.'

'Small hands?' Sally asked, until the meaning of the words sank in and she blushed and looked away. Beside her, Patsy was making vomiting noises, but Sally didn't look to see if it was one of her jokes, for fear that she was truly retching and would start Sally off too.

'Well, it's lucky yer here, then, Catherine,' said Eliza, 'for someone will have to help her.'

'Oh, Christ, well it won't be me, that's for sure, for here comes oul' Richardson.' The relief in Catherine's voice was plain and a little colour came back to the cheeks that had been ashen.

Richardson took one look at Gandon — who was now puffing like the bellows in a forge and gripping her stomach — turned on her heel and fled. Silence fell over Gordon's mess and then Eliza said what all were thinking.

'It might be down to you, after all, Kitty.'

Slowly, Mary lowered herself to the deck, with the help of her friends. It seemed that the thought of clambering back down the ladder into the stinking, as yet uncleaned prison ward was beyond her, and the hospital ward was already packed to overflowing, with women as ill as Anne Daly from the mess above Gordon's, and with others just as sick with all manners of fevers, obstipation, palsies and agues.

Mistress Richardson returned, still pale, but composed, with Mr Kilroy in her bustling wake. She gathered up her skirts and tiptoed across the boards that were still wet, though the sun was gaining heat at every moment. A faint shimmer of steam rose up from around Mary Gandon's wet dress and the smell, not unpleasant, grew stronger, then wafted away. Richardson kneeled down beside her, and if her audience had been so foolish as to expect sympathy or compassion, they didn't have to wait long for that hope to be dispelled.

'For heaven's sake, woman. Pull yourself together. You have barely started, the pain can't be that bad. Stand up at once and get yourself down below decks while you still can.'

Richardson turned to Kilroy and pulled a disapproving face. Her eyes nearly disappeared into the dark creases that had recently developed beneath them, and Sally noticed with a shock that the matron's proud, full bosom was definitely less ample than it had been. Maybe the captain wasn't sharing the meat ration with Richardson either.

'Pick her up, for goodness sake,' Richardson snapped, and Patsy and Sally leaned down and offered Mary a hand apiece. She groaned and turned her face from them. Low and long, like a cow labouring in the middle of the ocean, a loud bellow rose from her lips. Richardson tutted and tapped her foot, Nellie sucked in her lips and prodded Mary with the toe of her boot. Mary's messmates set to, to pull and drag her into the vertical but she resisted and hung as a dead weight from their arms, which were greatly weakened with hunger and with the enforced idleness of ten weeks aboard ship.

'Mistress Richardson, I'm afraid you'll have to ask some of the sailors for to help us shift her,' Nellie said.

'Nonsense, she can't be more than half an hour started, all told.'

Kilroy finally stirred himself. Grabbing a nearly dry cloth, he folded it carefully, looking for the cleanest portion, then, taking a careful pinch of each trouser leg, he set the rag between his trousers and the boards of the deck and gingerly knelt down beside her.

'Her pulse is racing, thready and weak, Matron,' he said, gently gripping Mary's wrist and placing three fingers of his other hand in the hollow of her neck. 'If she is so little advanced as you say she is, then there's something seriously amiss.'

'And she's panting far too hard. Don't breathe like that, you silly girl, hold your breath when the pain comes, and it will be easier for you.'

Richardson stood and looked at Kilroy and, for the first time, Sally could see the light of confidence leave the matron's face as she waited for guidance from the man of medicine, the university graduate, member of the Royal College, as she had so often reminded the inmates. He continued to kneel, making no decision, giving no instructions, but vaguely stroking Mary's wrist with the very air of a man holding his friend's hand on a stroll.

'Don't you think it's time we encouraged her to remove herself from the common view, Mr Kilroy, and have her off down below?' Richardson finally asked.

'Indeed, look lively, ladies, and help your friend off those damp boards.'

This time, Patsy and Sally each took a firm grip of a hand, and Mary levered herself on one elbow and tried her best to aid them, although if Kilroy had not suddenly leaped behind her and supported her in the small of her back, she'd have fallen, and wrenched the others down along with her.

'God help us, she's a fearful weight,' groaned Patsy, as between them all they dragged and supported her over to the hatch and to the top of the ladder.

Kilroy and Richardson finally acknowledged what any child on board the ship could have told them; Gandon was not going down that ladder under her own steam, nor with the frail help that could be offered by even the strongest two women, one sent ahead to guide her feet, one above to catch her hand should she fall. The reeking hum of the stale air which blasted up out of the hatch like the brimstone breath of a very hell seemed to decide Kilroy, and, at last, he was all decision and bustle.

'Mistress Richardson. The hospital is full to capacity, and if it were not, the air is full of noxious vapours from the fever patients. Meanwhile, the prison ward remains uncleaned as yet today, and a less suitable birthing space could barely be imagined.'

He scanned the deck and settled on a quiet, private corner formed by a triangle of railing, where a makeshift cover could be rigged, and soon Mary Gandon was out of sight, but, to the woe of her friends and fellow inmates, not out of sound, behind a billowing stretch of sailcloth.

Patsy and Sally at long last took up their pails, wrapped cloths round their faces, as they still did, even though the ship no longer had a supply of vinegar with which to soak them, and set about the long-delayed task of scrubbing Gordon's mess's berth and the floors and walls nearest. Up above them, besides the thumping of feet on deck and the shrieks and laughter of the one or two children who still, against all odds, retained the joy of youth, they could hear the frequent moanings and tormented wails of the labouring woman.

'So,' Patsy said finally, 'that's what you're asking me if I can live without. And I promise you I can. There'll be no children for me. Not if I have the strength in my body to prevent it. And not willingly, one way or the other.'

'You'll feel different when you see the new child,' Sally said, 'sure I seen all of my neighbour's children in the days after their birth, and they would have melted the heart of a stone.'

'Even Nellie's heart?'

'Ah come on, it's not a miracle I'm talking about. Just an ordinary baby, not the second coming of the Lord. It *would* be a genuine miracle if Nellie's not up there now, wheedling her way into Gandon's portion of gruel, or in some wise profiting from the poor woman.'

They laughed and clambered back on deck. Nellie was nowhere to be seen, neither were Eliza nor Catherine, just Liz sitting like a mossy rock beside the ever-dripping filter.

'Come here to me,' she said, as soon as their heads appeared above the hatch. 'Richardson is after taking Catherine and Eliza along with her behind thon sheet.'

'Well, I can understand Kitty, and her knowledgeable and all, but what's Eliza doing?'

'I don't know what she's doing, but I know fine well that she doesn't want to be there and she said you two was to go and release her as soon as you came back up.'

Liz pointed over a few messes down, where Gandon's berth-mates gathered round their own cauldron and fire. 'Richardson won't let Mary's own friends stay with her, on account of it being immoral for them to be seeing the poor woman naked and they having to share a bed later on.'

'For the love of God,' muttered Patsy. 'I have heard every class of stupidity now.'

'Anyway, go on with the pair of you, and let Eliza out of it. Nell'll be back from the stores any minute.'

They groaned and headed off behind the sheet. Eliza nearly knocked Patsy over the rail into the pitching green ocean in her haste to leave the birthing place. Her face was grey-tinged, putting Sally in mind of the ashes Nellie scraped out of the fire-box each morning and gave to Patsy and her to use as scouring powder.

Eliza looked a picture of rude good health though, compared to Mary Gandon, who twisted and turned piteously on a rough bed made of a pile of rags and cloths. Although they were clean, they were rough as sailcloth and built for strength, not comfort.

'Is she supposed to be as white as that?' asked Patsy.

'Don't be bloody stupid,' Catherine snapped. 'How could she be well-looking in her current condition, and sure nothing is right.'

'Could we help to make things right?' Sally asked. 'What could be done for her, Kitty?'

'It's no use,' sighed Catherine, 'everything's totally arse-about-face. Even the simplest things that cost nothing, and that the poorest labouring woman could hope for, aren't available to her.' She cast her eyes towards the horizon. 'She should have the crown of her head facing north, for a start, and if you can tell me which way is north, with the ship swinging and switching like this, you're a better mariner than I am.'

'Anything else?'

'Well there should be a sharp knife under the bed, to cut the pains in half. And a good length of iron blessed by a blacksmith laid across the threshold.'

'For crying out loud,' Patsy interrupted her. 'Sure, we have no threshold and, as has been pointed out a thousand times, fairies can't cross water. If there even is such things, as I am starting to think fairies are as unlikely as the big bogeyman in the sky.'

Catherine jumped to her feet and Sally found herself somehow throwing her small body between them and struggling to keep them more than striking distance apart.

'Patsy, you know nothing about birthing babies. Now Catherine is the wise woman on board, in the absence of any other, and you'll have to mind what she says, or stay silent.' Sally turned to Catherine and placed a calming hand on her dress front.

'A knife, though, Kitty. I'm sure a knife should be possible. For the cook must have at least one, and doubtless has more than one. Will I run and ask Richardson about getting a knife from the galley?'

'You could start by giving me my full and proper title, you young hussy,' boomed Mistress Richardson from behind the sailcloth, and heaven knows how long she had stood there, and what she had heard. Sally swung round and dropped an apologetic curtsey, which did bring a hint of a smile to the matron's lips. Just out of Richardson's eye line, Patsy tossed her head and rolled her eyes heavenward.

'There will be no heathen or superstitious nonsense on board this ship,' Richardson continued. 'Now, Mr Kilroy has kindly offered to spare a few moments from his duties in the hospital ward, and I'll thank you to be silent while he is here, speaking only if spoken to.' She glared at Patsy, but Patsy for once held her tongue and looked meek.

The sailcloth cover flapped upwards, and Kilroy bent his neck and struggled through into the space, which had been small enough and now was bursting.

'Any progress, Mrs Colligan?' Catherine shook her head apologetically.

'I would be able to give her some assistance, if the baby would show any sign of itself, sir. But there is nothing. Even if it were to come rump first, I might have some chance, as I seen the birthing of a few of them sort over the years, at my mother's knee. Feet coming first, I never seen, but I know it's a bad set-up and I'm praying that won't happen.'

Mary Gandon groaned and her eyes rolled in panic. She had lain there, entirely disregarded, during this exchange. Catherine glanced down, a look of pity and shame mixed, and Sally could tell she was angry with herself for speaking so freely in front of the suffering mother.

'Let me have a feel,' said the doctor, placing his hands gently and firmly on Gandon's stomach and chest, then listening with his ear tubes to the sounds in her belly, finally rolling her half over and running his hands down her spine through the fabric of her bodice.

'Well.' He straightened up, the crown of his hair brushing the canvas roof of the shelter. 'Well, the child is alive and vigorous.' Mary Gandon smiled and glanced at the doctor in adoration. 'For the time being, anyway.' He looked down at her, seeing not a pain-wracked woman in mortal fear of losing one or both lives, but a problem to be solved, as quickly, and with as little trouble to himself, as possible.

'The problem is threefold, Mistress Richardson. Firstly, that the child being so high in the abdomen, and the liquor all lost at once, means a dry labour – always painful. Secondly, it's my belief that the child is in the back presentation, its spine driving down along the mother's spine, rather than against her belly skin as God intended.'

Mary groaned again, but all were too busy with the doctor's tale to pay her any mind.

'And thirdly, Mr Kilroy?'

'And thirdly, Mistress Richardson, there isn't a person on board this ship will make the slightest bit of difference to her situation. The queen's own obstetrician couldn't aid this birth.'

'Mother and child are in the hands of God?'

'Matron, I couldn't have put it better myself.'

He placed his hand upon the canvas, to draw back a doorway for himself, and Sally couldn't help herself. Even with Richardson's eyes snapping in her direction as she drew breath, she found the courage to speak.

'Doctor, sir, please. If you would be so kind. Mrs Colligan was hoping to get a knife from the galley, for to place under the bed.'

He swung round to face Catherine, an amused smile on his face.

'A knife, my dear lady, whatever are you planning to do with a knife? We don't want any children entering the world through the stomach, like Macduff from his mother's womb untimely ripped. Eh, Matron?' Mistress Richardson smiled, uneasily.

'Oh no, sir, not anything of malice, sir.' Catherine dropped her eyes from his look of scorn. 'But it has long been known that a well-sharpened steel blade underneath the labouring woman will cut her pains in half.'

'Stuff and nonsense. I've never heard such credulous rubbish. And besides, it's not a doctor's role to reduce a woman's pain in childbirth. Labour is God's punishment for the actions of Eve in the Garden, tempting man and leading to his expulsion from Paradise.'

He turned to Richardson and added, with a wry smile, 'I think you'll agree, Mistress Richardson, that if doctors were to go around relieving the pains of labouring women, the poorhouses and the orphanages would be even fuller than their current status.'

Richardson did not respond. Sally sank a deep curtsey and begged the doctor's pardon while Patsy stared at her with her lip curled, and Catherine sighed for the lack of her knife.

Kilroy swept out and then, as Richardson drew a long breath to berate the women for their insolence and forwardness, he surprised them all by popping his head back through.

'Matron, far be it from me to interfere with the plans of the Almighty but, upon second thoughts, and taking into consideration how close-by the rest of the women are quartered … If the patient appears to be in her final hours, at any point, and the hope of saving mother or child is quite gone, I will spare her a small amount of laudanum.' He nodded, and drew his lower lip through his front teeth. 'To keep the noise and disturbance to a minimum, you understand.'

Richardson swept out in his wake, without a further word. Patsy swept a deep sardonic curtsey in Sally's direction, but Catherine reached over and patted her on the shoulder.

'It was a good thing you done. I'm glad one of us was game to ask him.

For all the good it done her.'

'Well, at least I might get my laudanum before I die, for I can't survive much longer of this.' They all looked guiltily down at Mary – how easy it was to forget that this suffering ball of groaning misery was as sensible as the rest of them.

'Hush, now, Mary, that's daft oul' talk, and all women feels the same way when they're on the first labour.'

'If I die, will you call the child Joseph or Josephine, for my blessed mother, who, thanks be to God, never lived to see her daughter a convict.'

'I won't say it again, I've been at scores of births before, and no one is dying today.'

And Catherine was right, in a way, for Mary Gandon didn't slip out of her agony for two nights and a day more.

As the very last moments drew close, Catherine swore and cried again for the want of a knife.

'Sure, it's too late for the knife, Kitty,' Patsy said. 'The sense is gone from her and though her body shakes from time to time, I do honestly believe that she is past feeling the pain.'

Kilroy had been as good as his word and, during that afternoon, when screams, curses and howls had echoed round the decks, he had doled out three sets of ten drops of laudanum and they had used them all.

'The knife's not for Mary any more, not at all,' Catherine answered. 'I would have a different use for the knife now if I had one.'

'You know what I'd do with a knife, Kitty,' asked Patsy. 'I'd kill the first man who ever lays hands on me, with the intention of getting me the same way as Mary.'

'Christ, you're cracked, Patsy O'Hanlon, whoever heard of such a thing?' Catherine's laugh was high and forced, as she tried to pretend that Patsy's words were made in jest. 'No, the knife is for the baby, to try to save its soul. I never actually seen it done, but I heard of it many's the time in the dark watches of the night, when my mother in her desperation would be joined by other wise women, summoned from parishes further away. They would try with all their combined experience to pull both mother and child through the night. And when it was clear that the woman was a lost cause, they'd talk. They'd think no one was listening, and me, silent as the mouse in the hearth, hearing all and saying nothing.'

'And what would they do, Kitty?' Sally asked.

'I'd have to wait until Mary's last breath — and I heard the death rattle many's the time before now, I'd recognise it for certain.'

Sally nodded, for although she had only heard the death rattle twice, she would never be so lucky as to forget it, or to doubt the immediate certainty that had come upon her, in the instant, that her loving parents had transformed into lumps of cooling, shrinking flesh.

'Then what would you do?'

'Well the old women say that the child in the belly will live a minute, maybe two, after the mother dies. If you can cut it out, in the minute you have then, unless it has died before the mother of course, you can get the holy water on its head in time and say the sign of the cross and mother and child end up in heaven or purgatory together on the one day. Which is the last kind thing you can do for the poor woman, after all your skills have failed her.'

'And if not, of course,' Sally said, 'the baby'll wander in limbo for eternity.'

'Well, only until the judgment day, but isn't that a long enough time for a mother to wait to be reunited with her baby?'

'What a load of shite,' burst out Patsy. 'Isn't it bad enough to be born as women in this world, without believing these tales from the priests, and ruining your minds thinking of innocent babbies languishing in limbo?'

Catherine pulled out her rosary and said, gently enough, 'Patsy, you're free to think what you want, no one can stop the thoughts of your head. But please don't speak your poison into the very ears of a dying woman.'

Sally joined her in a decade of the sorrowful mysteries and Patsy stayed silent throughout. But she laid her hand on the dying woman's cheek and gently stroked it throughout the whole prayer-filled rattling time. Sally kept her eyes fixed on Patsy from behind her lashes, and she reckoned that her friend's touch had more of God about it than the anointing of any poor dying sinner by a priest.

No one had anointed Sally's parents – that much she knew – and if anything had anointed Peggy and Davey, it might have been the slobber of a hungry dog. Patsy was right. The words that Patsy had poured into Sally's brain, words and ideas without number, since the telling of the workhouse story, suddenly crystallised and took a real form.

Against her will and every inclination of her upbringing, Sally finally realised the truth of Patsy's philosophy. It was every woman for herself. And Patsy's crazy, half-cracked criminal scheme might be the only thing standing between Sally and a death like Mary Gandon's. She might die in childbirth, with Nellie in the corner waiting, perhaps, for the sheets to cool beneath her, before suggesting to the grieving widower a way to warm them back up. Sally would not allow that to happen.

For the first time, Sally knew that the prayers she uttered were just words.

The Rosary wound its way to a close at last.

'Will we do a second decade?' asked Catherine, but Sally shook her head. The shackles of the little she had learned in the parish church of Clonsast seemed to loosen around her a little more each moment. Was she doomed? Patsy said her god was nothing more than superstition; a good luck charm or a piseog tied to a fairy tree. Maybe she was right. Why utter any more prayers? Should Sally turn her back on eternal salvation, for the hope of a life *before* death?

Mary Gandon's breathing grew weaker and less regular. Several times they thought her next breath would be the final rattle, but she clung on somehow. Taking her lead now from Patsy, Sally took one of Mary's cold, waxy hands and held it, while Patsy rubbed the other round and round – like a nursing mother who cannot keep her hands from the head of the baby at the breast. Catherine stared at them in silence.

'And would you do it?' Sally finally asked Catherine. 'Would you actually hack open the dead body? And how would you hide your deed from Richardson and the doctor?'

'I don't know, Sally. I don't know what I would do, with a knife I know I don't have, and can't get. Isn't it just as well I haven't got one?'

Mary Gandon was tipped overboard at first light, in a haunted almost-silence, and unborn, unbaptised, Joseph or Josephine went with her, into the darkness of eternal limbo. Or, in Patsy's version, into the bellies of the fishes, and who could say which was the worse ending?

★ ★ ★

Nellie sat up abruptly from where she lay slumped on the parched bleached boards of the deck, and put her hand to her cheek.

'Liz, give over messing will you?' she snapped, 'or I'll hit you a puck in the gob.'

'Oh, that's quare elegant language from Herod's daughter,' laughed Liz. 'Did you learn it in the palace? Anyway, I haven't the first idea what you're talking about.'

'Don't play innocent with me, and stop messing with the water, for Richardson will have something to say to you if you spill it.'

'My hand to God, I don't know what you're talking about.'

Now Sally felt it too. A drop of water plashed on her face. But Sally was staring straight at Liz and knew that she hadn't touched the filter nor the jug.

'It's rain,' Sally cried, leaping to her feet, 'thanks be to God, it's raining.'

All over the deck, women struggled to their feet and scanned the sky anxiously. Although the sky just above them was as blue as ever and the sun beat down still, the wind had picked up and grey-black clouds drifted from the far horizons, not quickly, but surely, towards the ship.

Now the sailors were moving with purpose across the boards of their deck and swarming like nimble fleas up sheets, across rigging, and down into the store rooms and galleys, returning with barrels and pails. Quick as ever, always the first to see the advantage in every situation, Nellie sprang into action.

'Get up outta that, you stupid hallions. Can't you see a rainstorm is coming?' she called over to neighbouring messes, and the other women were too tired and sea-weary even to ask her where she thought her authority came from.

'Run, Eliza,' she said. 'Run quickly to find Richardson and tell her the rain clouds are coming and, with her permission, may we set out our empty barrels, as the sailors are doing.' She paused a moment for thought. 'Tell her it's because of the great desire we have to wash ourselves and to clean the clothing also. And speak politely, as I know you can, when you want to.'

For once Eliza did not object, but nodded and ran off towards the hospital ward ladder.

'Right, you two wastrels, get down into the store room – and all you others – and grab hold of a barrel, they're light enough now they're empty. At the first word of consent, be ready to heave them up onto the deck.'

Patsy and Sally joined girls and younger women from other messes and followed Nellie's instructions.

'You know, we're lucky to have had Nellie,' Sally muttered to Patsy. 'She's always out for her own benefit, but sure doesn't that benefit us too?'

'You say so? Well, I suppose you're right, but that doesn't mean you have to put up with it for ever. You've not changed your mind?'

Sally shook her head and looked away.

Nellie's head appeared in the hatch above them. 'Mistress Richardson agrees with my plan, and says to get the barrels up here at the double. Look smart about it.'

Even empty, it was a trial to hoist and drag the ten-gallon barrels up the ladder and out on deck, where Mistress Richardson stood beside a burly sailor whose strong oakum-blackened fingers flew and knit a complex pattern as he lashed their barrels tight to the ship's rail. The women were astonished to see a man permitted on their deck, but, watching closely, it was plain to them that no woman among them could have tied and threaded and woven that thick rope in the manner needed.

'Jesus, do you smell the hum off him?' whispered Patsy.

'It's fairly strong, all right. He smells worse than my father did after a pig-sticking up at Joly's.'

'I don't mind the smell, not one little bit,' laughed Eliza. 'He's as good to look at as an oil painting in a church, and nearly as naked as most of them.'

'Eliza, for the love of God have a titter of wit. If Richardson hears you …'

'Oh don't be such a baby, Sally. I'm a grown woman and I'm allowed to look at a man. It's not like I plan to leap across Richardson and mount him here in the full view of two hundred oul' biddies and little girls.'

The rain was getting heavier now, still not enough to wet them, but enough that the smaller children were running around the deck, mouths open and tilted heavenwards, tongues out and straining to catch a few drops.

'That's you, look, Eliza,' laughed Patsy, 'mouth open and tongue out for your fine, salty sailor, pig-stinking or not.'

'And why the hell not? Isn't that why the half of us is here, heading across the ocean to God knows where? Sure, if only we could have found a man to protect us and feed us in Ireland, we'd never have done whatever crime we done to get on board this ship. The handful of streetwalkers on board is nearly the most honest among us.'

Sally felt Patsy stiffen beside her, but she didn't react in any other way, and Sally couldn't tell whether Eliza knew the import of what she had said, or not.

'That's not true, Eliza,' Liz Curry said with venom. 'Sure there's plenty of us who wouldn't have our heads turned by a sailor, never, and who remember the lessons we learned kneeling by the hearth at night, calling out the Rosary, and learning about the life of Brigid and Elizabeth and the handmaid of the Lord.'

'All women end up sold sooner or later. You can sell yourself for a coin, at least that's honest,' said Eliza, 'or you can sell yourself for a wedding ring, and keep your wits about you to make sure you leave a little blood on the first night, but it's a sorry business, whichever. If yer going to share a bed, it might as well be with a fine lump of a man, like that sailor, although I'd like mine to have his teeth still in his head.'

'You're a pig yourself, Eliza, as much as the ones my father killed,' Sally said and she strode angrily off to stand alone, away from the ever-vigilant Richardson, from the stench of the sailor and away also from Eliza, who stood with her lips parted slightly, staring at him with a naked look of hunger.

Patsy came over and slipped her arm around Sally's waist.

'It's not true,' Sally snapped. 'My mother didn't sell herself. Before the blight came on the potato patch she was a happy woman at her own hearth.

My father seemed fond enough of her and hardly ever beat her and was often sorry about it afterwards.'

'Why wouldn't he be fond of her, and the two of them with only one child? I tell you, if she'd popped out another hungry mouth every twelve months, like most of us, your father would have been swinging the fist a bit more often. There's nothing like hunger and worry to raise a man's temper.'

'Christ. Well, no man will hit me too often, for I'll up and leave him, if he gets too fond of doing it, and he'll never see me again.'

'Sally, yer an eejit, but sure that's why we love you so much.' Patsy pulled a ridiculous leering face like a simpleton you'd see at the fair, being given a kick by most, and a crust by the charitable. 'I'll up and leave him,' she said in a stupid, thick voice, 'I'll up and leave him! Sure, think about what yer saying. If it was as simple as that, there'd hardly be a woman left married in the whole of Ireland.'

She laughed and spoke in her normal voice again.

'Where will you go if you leave yer husband? Perhaps you'll have a streel of childer walking after you, big and little like a step of stairs, holding their bellies and saying *Ma, what'll we ate?* And the warder of the poorhouse, if they have such a thing in Van Diemen's Land, puffing out his fat stomach at you and asking *Pray, madam, where is your lawful wedded husband? Back you go to him or starve, for the charity of the workhouse is for the deserving — not for wanton, runaway wives.'*

Sally looked over the breadth of the deck at the sailor, at the bulging ripples on his chest and the muscles standing out like hillocks on his arms under his open waistcoat. He had no shirt, as was common among the men, and shiny tracks glistened in the whorls of hair on his chest where the sweat had trickled through. His skin was brown and tanned as leather. Eliza was looking his way still, and so were many of the others.

'And how would a body know, Patsy? How would you choose? For sure, you'd choose a strong man like that, so as he would be well able to work. What else would you be looking for?'

'Well, I won't be looking at all. I've told you before, I will die alone, with neither husband nor child, and now thanks to the bitch Nellie telling my secrets to the world, you have a fair idea why.'

She sighed and her arm dropped from Sally's waist. She pushed the straggles of hair away from her forehead. A few raindrops were caught and sparkling among the strands until she herself looked like a saint in a holy picture, with a big yellow halo around her. 'I'll die an old maid, even if I'm not a maiden.'

'We'll have to go below decks soon, I'd guess.'

Already some of the older women were clambering down into the hatch, and the clouds were scudding towards the ship now at speed. The brawny sailor swung himself up into the rigging, leaping and clambering to join his mates high above in the trimming of the sails. Eliza seemed to shrink as he left their half of the deck behind him with never a backward glance.

'Yes, I suppose we should,' said Patsy, 'although I fancy standing up here in the rain and just letting it sink into me. I feel like a stick, I feel like an old bone that a fox would discard and leave at the side of a ditch. I'm dry and used and I'd like the rain to wash me clean.'

'For God sake, Patsy, you're no older than I am.'

'I'd like the rain to wash me clean. I'd like to close my eyes at night, and never a face or figure to enter my dreams again. I'd like to be able to stand beside that sailor and not feel my heart pounding in my chest, not feel my stomach lurch and my bowels opening.'

'But a husband, Patsy? A husband mightn't do them things? He might be kind?'

'He might, I suppose. A husband might love you like a daughter and cherish you for ever.' She smiled and took Sally's hand in hers and Sally relaxed and felt hope flood back into her veins. Patsy stroked Sally's hand and the warmth and joy returned to the day. 'Or he might rob and kill the old woman of the boarding house, and leave you to swing for it.'

A flash of lightning lit the ship up momentarily, and any answer that might have been found for her was thrust from Sally's mind by a peal of thunder that felt right above their heads and made their ears ring. The skies opened and a deluge of rain, hard as any hail, fell upon their heads and threatened to dash hair from their skulls and eyes from their sockets. Screaming, they plunged down the ladder and, as the last child entered the prison ward, a sailor slammed the hatch down on top.

★ ★ ★

The stalemate that had existed between climate and captain was ended by that storm. The winds returned and they blew in a favourable direction to bring the *Australasia* to Hobart.

The women gave thanks to God, and to Nellie for her quick thinking, as many of the barrels had managed to catch and hold some precious water. Some of the barrels were almost half full, but others had parched and dried during the weeks of the calm, and the collected water had leaked out from between the separated staves and was lost.

When they spoke to Nellie of washing themselves and their clothes, she laughed and replied that even Richardson, having seen how perilous a lack of water could make the future, would not be stupid enough to waste water on washing, and she was right.

Liz continued her vigil beside the dripping filter, but the ration was increased to two gallons for each mess per day, and although it was little enough, to the women it felt like riches.

The allowance for the patients in the hospital ward was increased too, and one by one they started to reappear, emaciated wretches as weak and wizened as any inmate in Naas Gaol, but living and breathing against all the odds.

Things that the women had not noticed stopping, they noticed now, as they restarted. Children laughed and began to run around on deck once more and mothers sang old gentle lullabies to their babies.

Mistress Richardson was no longer needed so desperately in the hospital ward and she began again her duties on deck, supervising her deputies, for among the convicts numbered six who she judged fit to teach the others, three giving their profession as needlewoman, two as dressmaker and another, much sought after for her skills, who was a stocking-maker.

'Christ, I have no luck at this,' Sally sighed, during one of the lessons, looking at the filthy piece of cambric she held, drawing the needle through and making a ragged hem.

'You're as through-other as could be,' agreed Patsy. Sally looked at Patsy's piece of fabric and sighed. Although she had sewn and hemmed and seamed her piece as often as Sally had hers, Patsy's was white still and barely creased.

Around her, thimbles flashed and women sat in silent concentration while Richardson strode between them, encouraging, correcting and chastising. Sally held her breath as the matron stood alongside, sighing theatrically.

'My goodness, girl, you simply get worse and worse.' Richardson snapped the work from her hands and turned it over and over, examining each stitch. Sally flinched as she reached up to take it back, and Richardson slammed a wooden ferrule down on the knuckles of her right hand twice.

'I shall expect that hem ripped out, refolded and finished by this afternoon, properly.'

She sailed off while Sally sucked her knuckles and tried to blow the hurt away. Red welts stood up under the skin and although she tried hard to stop them, tears stood in her eyelashes.

'Give me that, you soft eejit,' whispered Patsy. She reached over and swapped their swatches of cloth. 'Pretend to sew on my piece, but I'm warning you, don't dare put yer needle through my fabric, or smudge it. This piece of yours looks like you used it to clean the fire-boxes.'

Quickly, Patsy ripped out the painstaking work of an hour and set about redoing the hem. 'It's even more difficult when you're using the thread for the second or third time,' she whispered. 'Look at the way you have to wrap the thread round yer fingers, to keep the kinks from tangling.' Sally looked over and sighed, Patsy's right hand was a cobweb of carefully wound thread. 'Now the knots won't form, do you see?' Sally shook her head sadly and the blood boiled under the skin of her neck and cheeks.

'I'm no bloody good, Patsy. I'm useless at sewing,' she muttered, 'for my mother had a needle the size of the pen that Mr Kilroy writes in his journal with, and the only thread she had was ripped from the seam of a corn sack. She stitched me into my clothes at Samhain, and took them apart again at Easter.'

'But you can learn,' Patsy said. 'You can learn anything, and pain is a good teacher. A few more whacks from Richardson and you'll learn to make your fingers fly through the stitches.'

'I don't think so, for each time she hits me, I forget even more of the little I knew.'

Patsy handed back Sally's piece and it was finished.

'It's not the same as yours,' she said, holding the two pieces together and comparing Patsy's pristine work with her more careless approach to Sally's hem.

'Well of course not, you don't think Richardson is blind or stupid, do you? I did it only a little bit better than you would do it yerself, if you would stop crying and just get on with it.'

'The way you just got on with it at the national school, and are such a great scholar, and can read everything Kilroy writes down? Even Nellie can read enough to learn your secrets.'

As the words spilled out, Sally flushed and dropped her head with shame at the uncalled-for cruelty, but Patsy just shrugged.

'A fine lot of good yer book-learning did for you, and wouldn't they have been wiser teaching you to use a needle than to make yer letters. So you can write, can you?'

Sally shrugged. 'I can write a bit. Mistress McNamara at the school in Clonbullogue done her best to teach me, just like she taught my mother before me. It's hard. I can read good and fast if no one is pressing me. If I can find the word I am looking for written down somewhere, I can copy it out on the slate.'

'Well, yer unlikely to be surrounded by books where you're heading, anyway,' Patsy said, 'and even less likely to get yer hands on a piece of paper.'

'Oh, I don't think I could write on paper,' Sally said, 'it looks like flimsy enough stuff and would likely end up black and creased as the cambric I have in my hand.'

She looked down at the material and a plan formed in her head. A plan to undo some of the harm she had done, or at least to assuage her own conscience. Newspapers printed letters, didn't they? She would need paper and ink after all, if she ever got settled somewhere and had a penny of her own with which to buy them.

'Well, what would you write, if you got yer hands on a slate instead of paper?' Patsy persisted. 'Would you write a poem? I done some poems at school. I still remember some the master tried to learn us, on the few days that I did make it to the schoolhouse.' Patsy paused. 'I remember there was one about a boy on a … ' She trailed off.

'The boy stood on the burning deck,' Sally said. 'You know, I think it mightn't be the wisest thing in the world to stand up and say that one out loud.' They laughed.

'Isn't it a strange thing that they learned us a poem about a French boy on a ship in the middle of the burning ocean, and us sitting in Ireland surrounded by potato fields and turf banks? Couldn't they have learned us something about our own place?'

'Ach, Patsy, what difference would it make what they taught us? The history and tales of Ireland won't be much good to us in Van Diemen's Land.'

'Unless you take up with one of Liz Curry's brothers. I'd say at this rate, half of Ireland will end up in Hobart before we're finished.'

'God, Patsy, you hardly think Nellie would marry me off to someone who's not Irish, do you? Who else would be in Van Diemen's Land? Would there be French people there, talking away in their own language and me with no clue what the man was saying at all?'

'I'd say it's mainly Irish and English, sure doesn't it belong to the queen?'

'Well, I'll only marry an Irishman, the English have brought us nothing but trouble.'

'You'll marry whoever Nellie tells you, I'd say.'

Patsy sucked in her cheeks and returned her attention to her clean white cambric, where she was picking out a pattern that, although unfinished, reminded Sally of the flowers that bloomed in the hedgerows of Clonsast. Sally marvelled again at the speed with which Patsy picked up Richardson's new skills, having never held a needle herself until she entered Grangegorman.

'You know,' Patsy said, 'there are people in Van Diemen's Land whose skins are as black as the charcoal in Liz's filter.'

'Ach, don't be acting the maggot.'

'I mean it. Black as yer boot they are. I seen one once, on a ship when I was in Dublin docks.'

'At the docks?' Sally looked down. 'And did you see him like … ' she paused. 'Close up?'

'Not at all, not in *that* way,' laughed Patsy, 'He never came down off the deck of the ship, but I asked one of the older nightwalkers there and she told me about them. There's lands where the sun is so hot, it would burn the skin clean off yer back, and it is in these places that the darkies live.'

'I still don't believe you.'

'It's true, the black skin protects them, for she said that in their own lands, they walk around in the buff like children, and the sun would scorch them if they weren't black-skinned.'

Patsy sighed and then puffed out her cheeks.

'She said them black men and women was savages and wild people. She said it was to learn them the ways of God, and to train them, that the queen was sending over the convicts. And that's how I got the notion to come to Van Diemen's Land.'

'To teach the savages?' Sally gasped.

'Don't be stupid. How could a pack of criminals learn them anything worth knowing? To be *warm*, that's why I came. To be hot, even. I done my fair share of freezing in Ireland. I want to live in a land where the sun would burn the skin off yer back. I want a blue sky.'

'But what about the savages?'

'What about them? I'm not so stupid as to believe what some whore on the dockside in Dublin says. You can't believe all you hear. Do you know what the English newspapers call us Irish people?'

Sally shook her head, but then took a stab at it, for she knew Patsy well enough to know where she was heading.

'Do they call us savages?'

'Of course they do. They call us savages. Then they send over the schoolmaster with the cane and the hard eyes, to learn us about the boy dying in the burning ship. And when they are sending all the food and fine fat cattle out of Dublin dock to England, and the Irish people are wailing and fainting on the quayside, hoping for passage on a coffin-ship to America, the English say *What can you do with these people, sure they're only savages?'*

When Mistress Richardson came back she tutted and clucked over the improved, but still ragged, hem but handed it back without comment. She smoothed out Patsy's cloth and checked the perfect hem, the tiny neat stitches, the straightness of the line. She rubbed her finger gently over the centre of the square where, using only the coarse thread they had been given, that had been used and reused until it twisted and coiled like a sheep's fleece, Patsy had formed in clean, smooth lines the perfect outline of a snowdrop.

Patsy got half a dozen raps over the knuckles of each hand for her snowdrop. 'Nobody is asking you to think,' Richardson said sternly. 'A servant needs only to obey.'

Patsy stuck her knuckles in her mouth to ease them, as Richardson moved on.

'She's a savage, herself,' Sally whispered, and raised Patsy's other hand to her own lips, and sucked out the pain.

★ ★ ★

The ship flew over the ocean now, as she should have done all along, and Mistress Richardson assured the women they would reach Hobart within two weeks. Then, she said, they could say goodbye to the easy, soft life they'd had on board and make themselves ready for work and obedience.

'How will we know what to do, mistress?' asked Eliza. 'Will there be work for all, and what about food and a roof over our heads?'

'The women still in the hospital ward will be taken straight to the hospital in Hobart to regain their strength and become fit once more to pay their restitution to the crown and to society for their crimes.'

Eliza nodded. Anne Daly remained in the hospital ward and by all accounts was a stick-thin, wasted wreck of a woman, bald, without nails, and losing teeth too. Ellen Doyle was still trapped there too, learning how to stagger about on her grievously shortened, limping leg. Kilroy had tried time and again to force the resisting ball of her hip back over the rim of her hip and into its socket.

After three days, the muscles of her thigh were swollen and stiff as boards and he had advised her to learn how to cope with her new infirmity. Unable to clamber up and down the ladder to join her friends and take a taste of the warm sun that would have surely aided her, she haunted the hospital corridor, a few steps at a time, leaning against the swaying walls and weeping.

A dozen other women and children remained below decks, but none had died since old Brid Butler who, all the women agreed, at sixty years of age should never have been on board, and who had had no chance at all after the vomiting illness set in. There had only been six funerals all told, three convicts and three children, and the inmates felt sure that the worst was over for Mr Kilroy and his helpers.

'What will happen to the rest of us, mistress, the ones who are not ill?'

'The prison hulk *Anson* is at anchor in the bay of Hobart, and has rested there for several years now. That will be your home for a week or so, while the manifests are completed and the plans for your employment made. It is during that time that the wheat will be separated from the chaff.'

'Your pardon, mistress,' begged Eliza, as Richardson turned away to another task, 'I'm sure I don't know what that means.'

'Don't you listen to the sermon, when the Good Book is read at your heathen services?' Richardson sniffed and drew her shawl about her, warding off the cloud of sin that hung about their Catholic shoulders. 'On the judgment day, the Lord will separate the wheat from the chaff, bringing the wheat into the heavenly harvest.'

'And the chaff?'

'And the chaff to the furnace.'

'And mistress,' Liz Curry bobbed a respectful curtsey, 'how will we know which way is to be *our* way? I have hopes of meeting my brothers when we reach Hobart, although I don't know whether they are in that city, or on the water, or in Dublin still, perhaps.'

'Your brothers! Those criminals who led you off the paths of righteousness and placed your feet upon the way of sin and crime that brought you here?' Richardson shrugged and rose to her feet, her hand moving to the ferrule that hung from the keychain at her waist. 'Your brothers will most probably be sentenced to hard labour in the countryside, where there is great need of able young men to break the soil and till the land. *You* will be sent to a reformatory factory if Mr Kilroy and I judge you vicious or incorrigible. Otherwise, there will be a hiring fair on the day that you leave the *Anson* and you will go to whichever master or mistress has need of a girl with your skills.'

Richardson rose at last, silenced further enquiries with a fierce glare that brooked no argument, and sailed off, stays crackling and skirts billowing in the stiff breeze that was driving them ever closer to Hobart.

Sally turned to Patsy and pulled her close so no one else could hear.

'A girl with my skills. Jesus, Patsy I'm doomed, for I haven't a skill in the world. I can neither sew nor launder worth a damn and I'm too coarse for nursery maid and too clumsy for piecework in a kitchen, no cook would put up with me.'

'You'll just have to try harder. I see you with yer needle, and you pay no mind to it at all. You don't even look at it when you push it through the stuff. What do you be thinking of? For yer not thinking about the work, that's plain to see. No wonder it's always dirty and crooked.'

'I think about Peggy and Davey. I think about my parents. I think that I murdered the children by taking them from their mother, no matter what her wicked plans were for them.'

'Indeed you didn't. Don't be talking stupid. You stole them away out of fear and to protect them from the soldiers. You never gave any thought to them ending up in the workhouse on account of that bitch Nellie.'

'That's my problem, I never gave much thought to anything I ever done. I never gave much thought to the seven years that is to pass before Nellie gets her hands back on me. Sure in seven years, I'll be a grown woman and free to do as I please.'

'In seven years, we could all be dead.'

'Jesus, Patsy, could you wait until we're on dry land before you start that.' Sally blessed herself, a reflex she found she could not stop, even though the seeds of doubt had sprouted fast in her mind.

'Well it's true. And if you think that Nellie is going to give up her prize now that she's so close, you're wrong.'

'But maybe she'll end up in a factory?'

'She'll never be sent to the factory. Sure haven't you seen her? She's an actress of the highest order, could have been on the stage. Never a word out of place, but always, *Yes mistress, Yes sir,* and chiding us and bidding us do Richardson's will, when Richardson is about the place to see her.'

'But she spoke to Kilroy about the water, without Richardson's knowledge, and that went badly for her.'

'A harsh word and a warning is hardly what I'd call a punishment,' said Patsy, bringing her knuckles up to her mouth.

'Well there's no one on the ship I'd call vicious, if it's not Nellie.'

'That's not what they mean. They mean someone who'll not make a good servant. Someone who might be stealing from the mistress, or making big eyes at the master. They mean a thief. Like me, for isn't that what I was sent out for. They mean a nightwalker. Like me, for hasn't Kilroy wrote it down in his book.'

'No, Patsy, don't say it. If you end up in the factory and I don't, how will we see each other?'

'And do you want to keep seeing me? Maybe in Hobart you'll find another friend, one who hasn't been on the town. A nice fresh girl like yerself, with no secrets to hide and every chance of getting a decent husband, so as the two of you can birth a pack of brats each, and bring them round to show them off and say *Isn't my baby the best you ever seen?* while the other is thinking the exact same thing about hers.'

Patsy was red in the face and the veins stood out on the flatness of her forehead, like the coils of sack-string Sally's mother had used as thread. Sally thought that tears stood in her eyes, the eyes that had remained dry almost for the entire time of their acquaintance, despite the most egregious provocation.

'But Patsy, what are you going on about? Sure, couldn't I bring my baby round to you and show her to you? Why would I need another friend? Since I left my mother's house, and never got a *goodbye* nor a backward glance from

Molly in the cabin beside it, I never had a friend again in the world but you.'

Patsy turned to face Sally and her ugly face shone like sunshine through a grey Irish sky.

'Do you mean it? Do you mean we'll stay friends in the new country, even though you know all about me now — a fallen woman who doesn't even believe in God?'

'Sure can't I believe enough for the both of us?' Sally seized her hand and held it tight until she winced and pulled it away.

'Stop treating me poor paw like a dishcloth,' she laughed, and Sally laughed too.

'Is this what has you so sullen the last few days, since the wind picked up?' Sally flung an arm round Patsy and turned her to face the direction that she imagined Hobart might be. 'Sure look, what's seven years? And *what about* being on the town? Sure aren't you the only person on board this ship that knows that my own darling sister was on the town. You were trying to keep your soul in your body, and stave off the starvation. But Nellie was working hand-in-glove with the ranger, and fleecing the girls who were weak.'

'And you hate and despise her for it.'

'For the love of God, Patsy, I don't hate her for being on the town. Don't be stupid, for the money she had earned from the soldiers fed me and clothed me, and how else was she to get her hands on money? But I do hate her. I hate her for her ice-cold heart and for the way she threw them poor children, Peggy and Davey, to their deaths, without a second thought for them nor for me.'

'So you do hate her?'

'You must be as stupid as you're ugly.' Now both girls were shouting, and starting to draw some attention from the other women. Patsy nudged Sally hard with her elbow and she woke up to the risks she was taking and lowered her voice to a whisper. 'I never, ever said I didn't hate her. How could I not hate her? Sure she's done nothing to you, and you hate her too. In truth, half the ship hates her, and the other half fears her.'

'Well, then, take my advice, follow my plan, live yer own life, marry yer own choice of man, and bring all them screaming youngsters of yours round to see the old maid, and I'll tell you I never seen the like of them before.'

Sally looked round, dropped her voice further and held Patsy's gaze as she whispered. 'You know that thing you said to me a few times?'

'About what?'

'About Nellie, and what she deserves.'

This time it was Patsy's turn to look anxiously around.

'What about it?'

'Were you serious?'

'I'm serious it's what she deserves.'

'We should make a proper plan, Patsy. Every little detail of it.'

'Every detail?'

'Every last one.'

They looked at each other and smiled. Patsy didn't believe Sally, but that was all right, because Sally didn't believe herself either. They lay down in the sunshine and dreamed.

★ ★ ★

'Give me the cloth,' said Mistress Richardson loudly.

'Give me the cloth,' replied a small group of women gathered around her.

'Wash the cloth,' said Richardson, while Lucy Smith made scrubbing gestures with her hands and spoke in Irish.

'Wash the cloth,' repeated the women, some smiling at their cleverness and some sullen and ashamed as the last vestige of dignity was robbed from out of their mouths.

To one side, Patsy and Sally had a small group of children in front of them, no more than five or six, for most of the younger children had picked up English on board the *Australasia* as quickly and as easily as they would have picked a blackberry off a hedge at home.

'Head, eyes, ears, mouth,' they said singsong, pointing to their own features and the children sang it back. Patsy was messing as always.

'Eyes,' she said, rolling her gooseberry-green bulging eyes in her head like a lunatic and drawing the lower lids down till she was a fright to behold.

'Eyes,' chorused the children.

'Tongue.' She stuck her tongue out as far as it would reach, which was almost to touch the sharp point of her chin, then grabbed it with her fingers and flopped it around until the children shrieked and laughed.

It was their job just to teach the words for easy things, for neither of them had any knowledge of Irish to teach the children how to put a sentence together, and could only point, or act out their meanings.

Suddenly Patsy fell to her hands and knees and started sniffing the deck, panting and making the strangest choking sounds.

'My God, is she after swallowing her tongue?' screamed Liz, who had been watching lazily from her habitual spot beside the dripping filter.

Sally dropped to the deck also and put her arms around her friend. She was still panting and shaking her head in the most distressing way. 'Wuuuah, wuuah,' Patsy roared suddenly, giving Sally such a fright that she rocked back on her heels and ended up flat on her back. 'Wuuah, wuuah, bow-wow-wow, DOG.'

'Dog!' screamed the children, and, in a flash, the deck was covered with scampering puppies, sniffing and barking. One little boy went so far as to cock a leg up against the rail of the ship before Mistress Richardson strode over and plucked him from the deck and gave him a shake that rattled the teeth in his skull and made him bite his tongue, so that the joyous barking turned instantly to wailing.

'Dog,' said Patsy quietly, rising from all fours and turning to face Richardson. The woman was shaking with rage, actually trembling with the force it took to keep her hands by her side, when every ounce of power in her frame wanted to slap Patsy across the face, or rip the hair from her head. Richardson never struck any girl while in a rage, she felt that was below her – she administered her ferrule in a calm and slow manner, often many hours after the offence. When Eliza had once plucked up the courage to remind her that Mr Kilroy had promised them no corporal punishment, Richardson strode off to speak with the captain and returned carrying a long leather lash on a wooden handle and had thrown it at her feet. *That's what you might have expected for your insolence, just a few years ago, my fine lady, and make no mistake, you will see plenty of its use in Van Diemen's Land.* They didn't doubt her for, once or twice, early in the morning, the women had heard the awful song of the leather whistling through the air and the sharp crack of it landing on the back of a sailor, four, six, ten times. The man would heave out a tortured groan, or a howl, depending on his nature, and the women would place their hands over their ears and try to drown the sounds. It hadn't happened often, for the captain appeared to be a humane type and used the stockade, or starvation, more often than he deigned to use the lash. But they knew it was there, all the same.

Sally was sure that if Richardson had had her way, she would have lashed Patsy, but she didn't. Instead she handed her a bucket and a scrubbing stone and sent her down to clean the latrine. The latrine was cleaned every day, but never very carefully, for it was too difficult to breathe in the tiny space. All manner of effluent, blood and vomit had soaked into the wooden staves of the barrel so that, even holding your breath, it was as much as a body could manage to swill a few buckets of water around and dash back out.

Patsy returned to deck thirty minutes later, when Richardson sent Sally down to fetch her back up.

'God, Patsy, the hum off you would sicken a pig, or a billy goat.'

She was breathing badly and the red-rimmed eyes streamed and wept in her head.

'I'm sure that can't have been good for her,' said Catherine. 'Maybe we should send her down to Kilroy to be on the safe side.'

'Christ,' wheezed Patsy, 'don't do that, Richardson will never forgive me.'

'But I think Kilroy would be shocked,' Catherine said. 'He'd never put one of us in harm's way, for isn't it his life's mission to get us off this ship as healthy as can be managed?'

'Leave it,' gasped Patsy. 'Sure I brung it on myself.'

'You certainly did, you little fool,' laughed Nellie. 'After all these months, at last you and I can agree on something. One thing you can be sure of, if Richardson had punished the whole mess, instead of having the sense to see it was none of our fault, I'd have given you something to cry about.'

'Christ, Nellie, can you never leave things alone?' asked Catherine. 'Don't you think our position is bad enough without fighting among ourselves?'

'You're just a part of the problem we have here in this mess,' snapped Nellie. 'Here we are, three grown women, and you and Eliza just sit there, letting these girls do as they please and bringing down trouble on us all.'

'I don't see much trouble coming your way. You seem to have everything all fine and dandy. You must be the only convict ever to arrive in Van Diemen's Land better covered than when you left Ireland.'

'If I have kept the flesh on my bones, Catherine, it's only because I am cleaner than you, and didn't go down with a scour that ripped the insides out of me.'

'Cleaner! Cleaner than me!' Catherine hissed under her breath, making sure to make no sound that would draw Richardson back in their direction. 'What's clean got to do with anything? What's clean got to do with my illness? Do you think we're all blind and stupid as well as being dumb?'

She glared around for support, but Patsy was still too weak to back her and Sally, as usual, said nothing aloud against Nellie. Liz busied herself with an unnecessary adjustment to the filter. At length Eliza spoke up, slowly and sullenly, as though the words were being dragged out of her soul against her will.

'It's true, Nellie, we're not blind. We can all see you getting wider in the beam, and the bosom on you. You're nearly as full as Mistress Richardson at this stage, while the five of us are like walking skeletons.'

'What are you saying? It's not my fault that I have a few extra hours up here in the fresh air. I have important work to do, and when we were becalmed and the sun and the lack of breeze would have boiled a body inside in her clothes, I never saw any of you offering to help with the cook-fire.'

'Oh don't take that tone with me,' snapped Catherine. 'As though you would let anyone but Sally come near that cauldron of yours. It's plain to see that you are having more than your share.'

'Indeed, I am not. I take my share and not a mouthful more.'

'Not to mention the water you stole when poor Ellen Doyle broke her leg.'

Nellie jumped to her feet.

'That's a lie and you know it. I no more know what happened to that water than you do. If anything is likely, isn't it that Liz took her chance and swallowed it herself.'

'I never did, and there's no point trying to blacken me, for I was over at the hatch with poor Ellen, like all right-minded women were. And I only recall one person from our mess being absent.' Liz spoke quietly but firmly. 'You know, I put up with too much trouble and violence back at home to be frightened of Herod's daughter.'

Sally looked from face to face, black with anger or pale with rage, eyes flashing and brows knitted. This had never happened before in all the three long weary months of travel. There had been rows and harsh words, but now it looked as though they might finally come to blows.

'Stop, stop, for the love of God,' Sally hissed, 'if Richardson or Kilroy was to come along and see the six of us ripping into each other, they'd write us up as vicious in the manifests and we'll all end up in the factory. Aren't things bad enough as they are?'

'Well, if there's trouble this day, it's all because of your precious óinseach friend. Finally the true spirit showed through in her and she had to act the cur.' Nellie spat on the deck, just a hair's breadth from Patsy, who was still slumped and wheezing. 'She probably learned to bark like that in her days on the docks, with the other nightwalkers and the bitches in heat.'

'That's it.' Catherine was on her feet now too, and the pair of them were so close that they could surely feel the other's breath on their cheeks. 'It's not enough that you steal from us and starve us — that you threw me out of the berth to roll on the floor the night that the fever ripped the baby out of my womb. Now you're throwing up the past in our faces. The past is behind us and never more will we see the face of a single friend or enemy we had then. Why would you take the deeds that were done only to survive, and bring those memories with you to the new life, however hard or harsh it might be?'

'You can't choose yer memories,' said Patsy quietly, with a cough at the end and a dry retch brought on by the exertion of speech.

'Of course you can,' said Catherine. 'You can, you will and you must.

Block it out, close the doors, put the things you can't face in a secret place in your head, and never open them again.' Catherine looked around and flung out her hand to draw in the two hundred women and the children stretched out on the deck, like so many bundles of rags. 'Look at us. We went into Grangegorman weeping. Now look at us. Was there ever a night you spent in gaol, or in Grangegorman, when you weren't woken a dozen times by the crying and the wailing of women trapped in monstrous dreams?'

They nodded.

'And now it almost never happens. People have put the past behind them.'

'You can't choose yer memories,' Patsy said again. 'Leastways, I can't.'

'You'll have to learn, then,' said Catherine. She paused and rubbed her eyes with the back of her hand. 'How do you think I do it? When I close my eyes the oul' face of Margaret Foran – her head stove in and her brains all over the floor – rises up on the back of my eyelids and I just say, *begone*. D'you think I want to recall that sight? D'you think I want to remember Mary-Anne, and her stuck in Ireland with her bastard of a father, and the future that likely awaits her?'

'How do you do it?' Sally asked. 'Kitty, how would I go about forgetting the things I wish had never happened in my sight and hearing?'

'Never speak of them again after you get off this cursed ship.' Catherine curled her lip and looked her straight in the face. 'Let there be no weeping beside the fire. Don't weep for Ireland, for she surely won't weep for you, and she wasted no tears on you when you lived among her rains and her blights.'

'But of course we'll speak of Ireland, sure won't we all be marrying Irishmen, when we get our papers of freedom?'

'There'll be no talk of Ireland, nor her green fields or soft rain at my hearth, if I live long enough for to get one,' said Catherine. 'I'll be a Vandemonian for the rest of my days, and I won't go picking the scabs off of any scars that have healed.'

'You'll be damn lucky to get a hearth of yer own, all right,' said Nellie, 'for what man would climb in naked beside a woman who might take a shovel to the back of his skull while he sleeps, and her after having plenty of practice?'

'I'll sleep alone, if I have to. And if I have to – and me that never done it before – I'll walk the streets, if I must. But one thing I'll not do is cry for a land and a life that is past and over. No one ever came back from Hobart, so we might as well get on with it.'

'I'm going to try to remember the good parts,' Sally said, 'and to forget the bad bits.'

'That's even stupider,' said Catherine. 'Sure that will drive you cracked entirely. If you want to keep hold of your senses, do it the other way about; strike the good bits from yer mind and remember only the pain and the hunger and the soft, damp sound of the clay hitting the skin of yer friends and neighbours, and them without even a box to go into the grave with. That'll make Van Diemen's Land feel like paradise.'

'What came over you anyway, Patsy?' asked Eliza. 'What in the hell did you think you were doing back then?'

'I just wanted to see a child smile and I just wanted to hear a bit of laughter for a change. I was thinking of my father and how he used to chase us around, barking and yelping when we were small, and suddenly I was on my knees.'

'Well, there you go,' snapped Catherine. 'That's where remembering gets you.'

'What's done is done and can't be undone,' Sally whispered, looking Nellie full in the eye.

Catherine smiled. 'That's the right spirit.'

Chapter Thirty-one

Hobart, October 1919, Sally

'What's done is done and can't be undone.' I look my granddaughter in the eye. 'I need you to remember that. Whatever I've done in this life is my own burden, and mine only. I took it upon my shoulders willingly.'

She doesn't understand yet, but she will soon. The end is nigh. The end of my story and the end of my life.

'You were a thief and a kidnapper.'

'A body does what it must to survive, and to make a way for the people it loves. You think you can't forget. You think you'll wake screaming in the night for ever, in fear of your life and your soul and you think you'll never have a day go by when you don't recall the horrors you've seen and the sins you've committed. But like Catherine Colligan said to me, seventy years ago, *you can, you will and you must. Block it out, close the doors, put the things you can't face in a secret place in your head.* The harder you try, the easier it becomes, and a day comes at last when you think of these things for the first time in a week, then in a month. And then you know it's going to be all right.'

'But what have you done? I know you weren't ashamed of your … subsequent behaviour. I know you were proud of Patsy and you, living in sin here, and pulling the wool over the eyes of society.'

'Have you been listening at all? How could you think I could possibly regret the love that sustained me all my life?'

'You need to stop talking in riddles. Every time you close your eyes I think I'm never going to hear the end of this story.'

'I need to take my time. I need you to understand that I don't regret my life. And I need you to promise.'

'Promise what?'

'No priest. Whatever you hear, I don't want a priest in the room when I'm past speech.'

'I can't make that promise. Grandmother or not, you have an immortal soul, unshriven for seven decades. You need extreme unction.'

'If your God is real, I'm past saving.'

'Why did you raise my mother to believe, if you feel this way? Why did you and Patsy watch her teaching me the way, the truth and the life, if you don't believe?'

'I had no right to tell your mother what to believe. If ever a woman had cause to scream in the night, it was Margaret, but she slept soundly under this roof. Her faith kept her sane. The faith I taught her as a tiny child, she believed all her life, as a child believes. No questions. No doubts. Trust me, there were many times I envied her.'

'So you didn't lose your faith till after you raised her? No, you told me you stopped believing on the ship. So you raised her in the faith, although you didn't believe?'

I shake my head. Nothing in this story is as simple as that.

'I didn't raise your mother.' Saoirse shakes her head in confusion and drops her face into her hands, sighing. It's no wonder she is confused. This story needs a conclusion. I wonder if the God I don't believe in believes in me, just enough to give me time to finish.

Chapter Thirty-two

Prison Ship Australasia, October 1849

Shrieking cries of pleasure, shame and fright rose from the deck of the *Australasia*. All of the previous day had been spent watching a team of sailors hoist bucket after bucket of sea water up from the foaming waves before pouring them into four giant vats on the women's half of the deck. Then black cloths had been tied over the mouths of the vats and a rigging of sailcloth strung from one side of the ship to the other, completely hiding the women from view.

When Richardson had ordered the black cloths to be removed that afternoon, the water in the vats was nearly as warm as the bath in Grangegorman.

'Salt water won't clean you the way fresh water would, but it will have to suffice,' said Richardson. Beside each vat there was a thick bar of carbolic soap and lengths of sailcloth, as rough as the stones that Patsy and Sally scrubbed the ward with. More important than anything else, a pile of shifts and dresses lay to one side, brand new, clean and dry. Five huge trunks had been hauled out of the bowels of the ship's hold and opened to reveal this secret treasure.

Mess by mess, the women stepped into the water, which came nearly up to their knees. They scrubbed and rubbed till the skin lifted off along with the dirt. Ladlefuls of warm water poured over their heads as they tried to rinse the soap from each other's hair.

'Quit yer wriggling, Sally,' laughed Patsy as she scooped ladle after ladle of water to drench her.

'I can't quit,' Sally squealed, 'for the soap is in my face and it's cutting the eyes out of me. Go easy, you rough hallion.'

'For the love of God, would you two óinseachs hurry up and finish before Richardson comes over to see what the noise is,' snapped Nellie, who was already out of the tub and drying herself as fast as she could. She had insisted on washing first, and alone, even though, for speed, the six of each mess were supposed to get in together. Gordon's mess was too accustomed to giving Nellie her own way to think about arguing.

'You're some size, Nellie,' said Eliza thoughtfully, 'beef to the heels like a Mullingar heifer.'

'Luckily, I don't know what that means.'

'Don't you, now? And you marked down as a country servant?'

'I'm no servant and I won't be heading off to any farm to live among the pigs. I'm after a decent respectable mistress in Hobart, or another city, if there are any more in Van Diemen's Land.'

'Well, you'll go where you're sent, I'd say.'

'I'm staying in the city, and I'm keeping my sister with me.'

Sally looked over at Patsy, and shrugged. It was the first time in weeks that Nellie had bothered to call her anything other than Sally or óinseach. She was obviously working her way back to the pretence of caring for her sister and her future happiness.

Nellie wriggled and squirmed and tried to hold the small square of sailcloth tight about her as she walked over to the pile of new shifts to gather one for herself.

'Jesus, Nellie. There's no need to be shy. Yer not the Virgin Mary, and we've seen tits before,' laughed Eliza, 'though maybe not ones as big as yours.'

Nellie snorted and turned away in disgust. As she struggled to place her wet head, hair dripping, through the tight neck hole of the new shift, she lost her grip on the sailcloth and it fell to the floor, revealing her in her nakedness.

'Jesus, Nellie,' cried Eliza, 'what in God's name happened to yer back?'

She jumped out of the tub and rushed, naked as a newborn, over to Nellie and grabbed at the hem of the shift, pulling it upwards. Nellie gave her a swift shove and she stumbled backwards, losing her grip on the long white shift which fell to a few inches above Nellie's ankles. Nellie wrapped her arms tight about her chest and gave Eliza a filthy look. 'Keep yer paws off me, Guilfoyle. Dragging at my clothing like that, yer a disgrace to modesty.'

'Modesty? What has modesty to do with anything? What the hell happened to you? Did you fall in a fire?'

But Sally knew, in a moment of clearest inspiration, exactly what had happened to Nellie, and her gut churned as she thought of the calculating way that Nellie had sized up Sally's smooth, flawless skin, in the nest among the furze bushes of the Curragh. One glance at the mass of twisted, whorled scar tissue that covered the whole expanse of Nellie's back was enough for Sally. She never wanted to see it again. Whoever had whipped Nellie had not a merciful bone in their body; that much was clear from the little Sally had seen. Purple, raised and glowing angrily in the sunlight, the scars had rippled and shimmered like a living thing, a serpent or lizard, as she bent and moved.

Sally dried herself and dressed in silence, then held up her hands and moved this way and that as one of the seamstresses pinned and tucked. Finally the baggy, shapeless blue uniform had been fitted some way to her narrow, undeveloped form. Richardson would not permit her to stitch the alterations to her own garment, which was both a surprise and a relief, and she had to stand in the new shift, arms and neck bare to the sun, basking in the joy of it while the seams were sewn and tucks and darts placed.

'Tomorrow, you will wash and repair the clothes that you took off today, and then mark them with your names to be stored away. Soon you will arrive at the *Anson,* and you must be clean and as healthy as is possible.' Richardson supervised a team of sailors as they hoisted the vats on straining shoulders and poured a stream of filthy black water back into the ocean.

The men had been in joyful spirits ever since the crippling work of tacking and coaxing the vessel through the becalming had been lifted from them. They laughed together and chanted a shanty as they set about the laborious task of hauling up clean water and refilling the tubs for tomorrow's laundry. Sally could not remember the last time she had heard the men sing.

She looked at Richardson, and wondered how many days they had left – tomorrow was set aside to wash and dry two hundred odd sets of clothing. In the warmth and the stiff breeze of their travel, it could not take long to dry them all. That meant that Hobart was but a few days away. They would be stepping onto the *Anson* very soon. If she wanted to know about Nellie's back, if she wanted to find some reason to forgive and excuse Nellie's harsh and violent nature, she had only a few days left in which to ask her. But did she want to know?

She had grown out of the habit of speaking to Nellie, answering her when she spoke, which was rare, and avoiding her eyes as much as possible. But now, Sally did want to know. She wanted Nellie to tell the truth. She wanted Nellie to look her in the eye and tell the awful story of her past; what had happened, where her family were, what she had done and what had been done to her. What had turned Nellie into the person she was today? Sally wanted Nellie to give her any excuse, anything, the slightest hint of a reason for Sally to change her mind. Sally wanted nothing more than to change her mind.

Next morning, as she rinsed the breakfast bowls and prepared for the massive labour of the laundry day, Sally begged Nellie to talk. It was Nellie's final chance for redemption, had she but known it.

'Sally,' said Nellie, 'would you give my head peace? Go to the Devil, and don't dawdle along the way.'

'If that's what you want?' said Sally.

'It really, really is.'

★ ★ ★

'Land ho, Flinder's Island to be seen on the starb'd side.'

The cry echoed round the deck, over and over. Every man, woman and child leapt to their feet and a roar of prayer, relief, joy and fear rose above the decks of the *Australasia*. For days they had been sailing down the coast of the great land of Australia, but now they were pulling into sight of the smaller island of Van Diemen's Land.

Overturning pots and abandoning cauldrons on their chains above the cooking fires, women rushed to the side of the ship. Every rule went out of every head and they swarmed over to the rails, swamping the full length of their own half of the deck, and spilling out over onto the crew's deck too. No whistle blew, no voice ordered them back.

Kilroy was as happy as a child, pacing and striding like a bull in springtime and slapping the captain on the back, until it seemed he would be unmanned completely. Mistress Richardson was at the far end of the deck, pressed up to the side, eyes wide, searching for the land which no one but the lookout in the high crow's nest could as yet discern.

Neither Richardson, Kilroy or anyone else paid Sally the slightest iota of attention.

Patsy came swarming up the ladder from the ward, like a monkey, and among the crowd, the mess and the muddle, they found each other's eyes straight away.

'We're here,' she screamed, throwing her arms around Sally. 'We're here, praise be to God.'

'Oh, it's *praise be to God,* now is it?'

'Well if he's up there at all, and it's little enough reason we have to believe that, we've never needed his help the way we need it now.'

They looked into each other's eyes and, in the midst of two hundred shrieking women and fifty hallooing sailors, saw nothing but each other, heard nothing but the pounding of their own hearts.

All around, the women were embracing and laughing and kissing, each seeking her own special friend or her child, and no one noticed Patsy's lips press close to Sally's ear. A thrill of heat rippled down Sally's cheek and the tiny hairs stood up under the touch of her friend's breath, like the brush of an angry cat.

'It's now,' she whispered. 'It's got to be now. Just follow my lead, the way we planned it.'

'Jesus, Patsy, you can't be serious. That was just talk, the way you talk to pass an idle hour. We're not going to do it.' Sally looked up into her eyes and whispered. 'Are we?'

'Aren't we? Well it's not much to me, one way or another. Don't you want to? Don't you want to sleep at night without looking over your shoulder? Don't you want to choose your own husband, and not lie down with whatever dirty oul' boar Nellie will pick for you – and her licking her lips and thrusting herself at your man in your own kitchen, maybe?'

'Jesus Christ almighty, Patsy, it's a sin and a crime.'

'We're criminals already. And she's a murderer. Didn't she tell Teaghan she had killed soldiers from the Curragh Camp?'

'She told me too. And she killed the children … ?' Sally looked to Patsy for support. 'She did, didn't she, she killed Peggy and Davey, that I was trying so hard to save … ?'

'She did. Just think of them two babies.'

Sally closed her eyes for just a second and the screaming and whooping of the women and the sailors became the terror, the howling and sobbing of Davey as the gaoler carried him out of the courthouse, and the shocking, stunned silence of Peggy with blood trickling from her busted lip, holding out her hands to Sally in mute pleading, as their eyes locked together and the men dragged her from the doorway of the chamber. *Don't cry, Peggy. Wait for me, Davey, I'll find you. Wait for me.* But she would never find them, nor lay a posy of bog cotton over their unmarked graves.

'We'll do it,' she said.

She locked her right arm round Patsy's left, and they looked for all the world like two happy, carefree girls, as they scanned the teeming, heaving crowds at the railings.

'Yonder – she's yonder,' Patsy hissed, giving a gentle tug in the right direction, and they moved together towards the ship's starboard edge, where Nellie stood, as always, in her chosen spot. Pushing and shoving and using all the power of their young bodies they inched closer and closer to the front of the mob, until they ended up flanking Nellie Gordon, Sally on her left, Patsy on her right, their arms still entwined.

Sally sank her nails into the hand of a small child beside Nellie, until he whimpered and let go the railing, casting her a bitter glance. He sucked at the four crescent-shaped dents her nails had carved into the back of his little fist, and she dragged her gaze away from his face and concentrated on the job at hand.

They'd been over every move, every detail. Even when Sally had protested that it was only a bit of fun, she'd listened carefully and added her own thoughts upon the matter.

With her left hand, she gripped the ship's rail, in the space she had clawed for herself, and still she clasped Patsy's arm with her right hand as though her life depended on it. In the manner of two men pushing a spooked pony through a gap in a hedge, they wedged their linked arms under the generous curve of Nellie's fine jutting arse.

Patsy and Sally nodded at each other. *Now!*

They heaved their linked arms upwards and forwards and Nellie shot up a few inches into the air, pivoting on her hands locked fast to the rail, as her boots lost contact with the deck. She opened her mouth to let a roar at them and, fast as a mother snatching up a child who has staggered too close to the embers, Patsy loosed her right hand from the railing and shoved a filthy shit-and-urine-soaked ball of wet cloth into Nellie's mouth.

Nellie coughed and gagged and brought her right hand up to claw at her mouth. In Patsy's eyes Sally saw nothing but confidence and trust in her abilities. Sally smashed her left fist down onto Nellie's left hand, the only thing securing her to the safety of the ship. As her hand slipped from the rail, all the weight of that fine, full-grown woman settled onto the linked arms of two desperate, frail half-starved girls. Sally felt her hand, slick with sweat, start to slide along the crook of Patsy's arm. Nellie clawed at Sally's face with her left hand and tried to pull the stinking filth from her mouth with the other.

'I'm losing her, Patsy,' Sally hissed, 'I can't hold on any longer.'

'You can do it, you have to do it. Be strong, Sally. I won't let go.'

All around them women cheered at the land and wept and cried out to God and to his holy mother.

'I can't hold her.'

'You can hold her and you will. Do it for Peggy and Davey.'

Patsy's hand dug into the flesh of Sally's arm and Sally pinched Patsy's thin stick of an arm with her wet, slippery hand.

'Do it for the love of God.'

Nellie slammed her left hand triumphantly back down onto the ship's rail and flashed Sally a look of pure hatred. She opened her mouth to roar for help, but Sally ducked her whole body downwards, and sank her teeth into the back of Nellie's hand, until skin and sinew cracked like gristle between her teeth and she tasted iron. Nellie screamed and pulled away, leaving a tiny scrap of flesh between Sally's front teeth. As Sally straightened up, she poured a year's worth of rage and hatred into every fibre of her being. She heaved upwards with her right shoulder under Nellie's oxter and sent her, cartwheeling, over the side of the ship and down into the water below. The shock of the move nearly sent Patsy overboard too, but Sally grabbed her with her free hand and hugged her close.

'Look, we've been spotted.'

Patsy gasped and pointed to the small boy who was still sucking his sore hand, with a look of terror on his face. Sally bent down and whispered soft and low.

'Do you want to find yourself flying over the side of the ship?' He shook his head. 'Better hold your tongue then. You saw how hard I tried to hang onto my poor sister, but I couldn't save her. And I won't be able to save you neither … if you fall.'

The child, pale and silent, backed away into the forest of legs and skirts.

Sally looked over the side of the ship, leaning as far over the rail as she dared. The ship curved down and away from her, hiding the water just below from her gaze. With straining and leaning, she could glimpse, in the very corner of her vision, a darker blue splash upon the sea-blue water, the billows and folds of Nellie's uniform dress. She held her arms outright at her sides and hung upon the surface of the ocean like Christ crucified. Her head strained up and out of the waves' froth, and she was entirely silent. Not one ounce of power or effort was wasted screaming or crying against the louder noises of the sea; only the stiffness of the woman showed how hard she was working, just to keep her head above the spume. And even at such a distance, thirty feet or more below the deck, she found Sally's pale face as it hung above her, against the bright pale stretch of the sky and the shining sun. Their eyes locked. *Help me.* Sally shook her head, though she knew Nellie wasn't likely to see. A wave slipped over Nellie's head and Sally thought she was gone, but with the great strength she had in her, she came back up again, head rearing against the weight of the coarse, long frock and the tightly buttoned boots. Sally saw her mouth open, just long enough to gulp a mouthful of air. She looked straight at Sally – to Sally's dying day she knew that Nellie saw. *Help me.*

Another wave covered her for a moment, and Sally turned to Patsy and nodded.

'Help! Help, for the love of God!' She screamed and fell to her knees, shrieking high and wild as a she-cat when the tom is on her. 'Help my sister. My sister is in the water.'

She flung her face into her hands and jabbed herself viciously in the corner of her right eye. Sparks flew up in front of the eye and tears and snot gushed forth as she gasped and whooped. Patsy took up the shout.

'Woman overboard, call the captain. Lower the boat.'

Sally leaned over the railing again, screaming. 'Let me down to her, let go of me.'

A crowd of women gathered round her, strong arms gripped her round the middle and Catherine Colligan's words sounded low and soft in her ear, 'Hush, now. Hush, pet.' Sally thrashed and flailed in Catherine's arms, careful not to use her whole strength and break away from her entirely.

'Let me see her, let me see my sister.'

Sally flung herself back to the ship's edge and, four or five women clinging to her dress, she craned over the rail. As she watched, Nellie's hands drifted from shoulder-level to above her head and, to the keening of a hundred women, she slipped under the water.

Sally fell to her knees.

'Oh God of almighty! *Nellie.* The last one belonging to me in all the world.'

She seized Catherine's hands and wrung her fingers like a dishcloth. 'It's my fault she fell, for I clambered too high on the railing, and in reaching out to steady me, she upended and went arse over tit into the water.'

A dozen hands helped Sally to her feet, a dozen arms reached out to embrace her. The voices of women crooned out words of love and consolation.

Above the sounds of the sea, above the creaks of the timbers, above the squeal of ropes as the small boat was lowered towards the pitching waves, bearing three sailors armed with hooks and spikes, Sally heard the voice of the lookout.

Up in his nest, far away from the madness on deck, the lookout stuck to his task.

'Land ho! Flinder's to be seen on the starboard.'

Sally turned her head, and there, floating in the distance, faint and green, a sliver of land, seeming no thicker than a blade of grass laid upon the boundless water. She found Patsy's hand among the melee and they turned their gaze back to starboard. Stretching out, miles away still, was the green-grey glorious promise of Van Diemen's Land.

Chapter Thirty-three

Hobart, October 1919, Saoirse

The fire roars in the grate and the room is sweltering. The murderess, Sarah Mahon, lies shivering beneath a heaping pile of covers and blankets from every room in the house. I force myself today to call her Grandmother, in dutiful acknowledgement of all she did for me in the past, but although she begs me to, I will never say the word Nanna again. I hope that hearing *grandmother* will be enough for this woman I have loved. I try to fool myself that she is too close to the valley of the shadow of death to care about what I call her. I know it isn't true.

When she wakes, for a few minutes every hour or so, she knows me and she tries to speak. Doctor Jenkinson was right, she will die in command of her faculties. If the Spanish flu had truly visited us and swept her away last week in her delirium, I would be none the wiser. I would have buried my grandmother and mourned. Now, I will bury a criminal, and her crimes with her.

Now, I do not know what I will do.

I wait for the final moments of my vigil. Josie Hendron has paid her last respects and she assures me she will lay out the body and bind Sally's jaw and close her eyes. Josie has worked here in this house since I was born. She must know more than she says. I wonder what she could add to my story if I had the courage to ask.

Sarah Mahon stirs in the bed. I move from the easy chair by the fire to the firm upright chair wedged uncomfortably tight between the bed and the window. If there is to be a last conversation it must be now.

She reaches for me and I let my hand rest on hers for just a moment, this hand that in my childhood always, and so gently, held mine; as we walked away from Sister Agatha; as we pored over the books in the fledgling city library; as we walked the harbour wall with breadcrumbs for the gannets; as we shook the carpets and fed the boarders' clean sheets through the mangle. This hand that threw a woman to her death.

'I want to know the rest, Grandmother. I didn't ask to know anything of your life, but you gave me no choice. You have cleared your soul by poisoning mine.'

'I was trying to free you. To show you that you are queen of your own destiny.'

'Instead you have imprisoned me, and taken from me everything I held dear.' I dash a tear from my cheek. 'You have taken my great-aunt, my grandmother, my sainted grandfather in the old country. I no longer know my own mother, even. Why did you ever start to tell me this story?'

Her answering voice is low, so low I bend my head right into the reek of her failing body, the ammonia stink wafting up from her waterlogged lungs and soughing across my cheeks.

'Saoirse, I told you once, a name can tell you a lot about a person. Do you even know what your name means?'

'It's a Gaelic name, an Irish name.'

'And do you know what it means?'

'Names don't mean anything.'

'Of course they do. Everything means something. Sally means a wren, at least it does in Ireland.'

I look out the bedroom window at the nest full of tiny fairy-wren chicks that my grandmother has so delighted in, since taking to her bed, and I smile despite myself.

'My baptismal name, Sarah, means princess.' She stops talking and laughs, which leads to a racking fit of thick, wet coughing. *Don't die,* I think, *don't die yet,* and she recovers and whispers on. 'I read that once in the library while you sat beside me, and I felt like a princess that day, warm and dry and well-fed, and basking in the love of an innocent child.'

'What did my mother's name mean?' I won't fall for her flattery.

'Margaret. Margaret means pearl. That's what she was, *the pearl of great value,* and your father proved he wasn't worthy of her.'

'And me? What does Saoirse mean?'

'Saoirse, did you ever hear me speak the Gaelic language?'

'No.'

'Or your mother, Patsy, or Josie Hendron, or any of the older Irish women you used to know?'

'No, never.'

'I barely had one word of the Irish language, but the one word I had, I gave it to your mother, and she gave it to you.'

'And what is it?'

'The closest thing to your mother's heart. She gifted you the name of the thing she treasured most.'

'Saoirse,' I say. 'But what does it mean?'

I am weeping now, but Sally Mahon is not, she has not the strength to spare. Every ounce of the prodigious strength of her will is focused on her speech.

'Saoirse,' through my tears I see her smile one last time. 'It means freedom. Try to find love. But remember to be free. It was the only wish your mother had for you.'

'My mother could be hard.'

'Yes. She could be hard. She had reason to be much harder than she was.'

'Won't you tell me more, Grandmother? Before it is too late.'

My grandmother fixes her gaze on me, unflinching, and licks her lips. I put a little salve on them to aid her final words.

'When I was young, an Irish girl was a small thing. A tenant farmer didn't take up too much of the landlord's space. Whatever name a child was given, you were lucky even to hold on to that, or someone would take even your name from you, and make it a smaller, meaner thing. Sally, Patsy, Josie, Kitty, Bid. The Irish didn't even have enough strength left in them to spare to fight for their real names, not even a strong man like Patrick O'Loughlin.'

'What are you talking about? What has this got to do with me?'

'What was your mother's name?'

'Margaret. Margaret Gordon, as I thought.'

'Her name was Margaret MacBride, when she was born. And she was so small, and the circumstances of her life so mean, there was no way she was allowed to carry the weight of that big name.'

'Are you telling me I'll find her in the records under a different name?'

'You might, you might, but if you don't, you'll find her in the story I told you. If you've been listening, you'll find your mother. And you might forgive her for being a little bit hard.'

I am fit to scream, I can't take any more of these riddles.

'Talk sense!' And it is almost a shout. A tear flows down Sally's cheek and into the corner of her mouth. I resist the automatic urge to pat it dry. If I touch her I fear I will strike her, or shake her. And I do not know if I will be able to stop. No one would suspect a thing if she died right now, alone with me, but I must keep her alive, and calm, until the story is told.

'What names do you know that mean Margaret?' she asks.

'What? There's too many nearly to list.'

'Try.'

'There's Meg, and Marge, and Moll and Daisy …' I stop. 'No,' I say. 'It's not true. It can't be so? Grandmother …'

Sally Mahon moves her head toward me, nods and smiles. 'Don't cry,' she whispers. 'Don't cry, wait for me, I'll find you.' But she is no longer speaking to me, nor to anyone on this earth.

My grandmother smiles and her face is beautiful again. She closes her eyes. In minutes she will be no more. She is at peace. And perhaps one day I shall be too, even without the answers to all my questions. Perhaps the little bits I know will finally give me freedom enough.

I lean over and press my lips against her pale, sunken cheek. Her lips move silently in her sleep and I hope her dream is a happy one. She may think she has no future left in heaven or on earth. But I have faith enough for both of us. When she opens her eyes in the world to come, my mother and my great-aunt will be there to greet her.

'Goodbye, Nanna.' I say.

Chapter Thirty-four

Hobart, Tasmania, 1862

The gentle rains of spring had ceased at last and tubs of flowers bloomed on the balconies and verandas of Hobart. Sally turned her face up and let the warmth of the sun strike the well-covered bones of her face. She was tanned and healthy looking, a far cry from the sun-scorched spectre who had stepped off the deck of the ship *Australasia* thirteen years previously. She looked in the glass and saw the first hints of a double chin, slackening and stretching the flesh down from her jawline, and smiled.

She had little thought, half her lifetime ago, clambering down the sticky, tarred rope onto the small boat that was to carry her from the *Australasia* to the prison ship *Anson,* that Sally Mahon would ever have enough flesh on her bones to round out her face, or to drop a curve, like a bantam's wattle, down onto the collar of her dress.

Patsy joined her in front of the glass, where now she was pinching the little fold of chin and twisting her head, first one way, then the other.

'You're still a good-looking woman, Sally,' Patsy laughed, placing her hand on Sally's, and turning her head back to look upon her reflection square on. 'Never fear getting old and fat.'

'I don't fear getting old, Patsy, not when it's a privilege denied to so many. I'd be happy to live to a hundred. I thought my mother was an old woman when she died, but now I know she couldn't have seen her fortieth year, and probably was a lot younger still.'

Patsy slapped her on the arse and laughed. 'Who'd ever have thought the pair of us would be fat? Beef to the heels, like Eliza used to say.'

Patsy primped her wispy, dull hair and pulled a ridiculous face in the mirror. She was still the ugliest specimen of womanhood Sally had ever met.

'Get away out of that,' Sally laughed. 'You'll break the looking glass with the ugly oul' face on you, and bring down seven years' bad luck, just when I'm expecting the best days of my life.'

They both moved to the window and stared out at the vast curve of the horizon, straining their eyes for the first sight of a ship's sail, but no new vessel hoved into sight.

'It won't be long, now. The mail boats nowadays is doing in two months what took us the guts of four months on the *Australasia.*'

'I know, Patsy, but I feel sicker with joy, every day that passes. And with fear too, for ships still sink, you know, even the newest ones.'

'You were always one to look for the darkness, Sally. I'm hoping that when the ship lands, ye'll start looking forward to the light.' Patsy laughed and turned to the door. 'You could come down and do a bit of work for a change, take your mind off it. You've scarce done a hand's turn since the day that ship left Dublin.'

The door closed quietly behind her. Sally gripped the flowered curtain and continued to stare out into the dazzling blue of the ocean, willing the first triangle of grey-white sail to appear. Today, it would be today.

She looked down into the teeming port of Hobart. Six great ships lay at anchor and a flurry of small boats scurried between them, sailors calling and merchants crying. Brave young adventurers leaned on the ships' rails and awaited their chance to disembark, into the seething, stinking, prosperous streets of Hobart.

The hulk of the prison ship *Anson*, which used to blight the bay with its presence and with the cries and wails of the women kept on it, was long gone. The good people of Hobart had cried out at last: *No more convicts, we'll have no more the sweepings from the English gaols.* In 1852, one hundred and seventy women stepped off the ship *Midlothian*, and that was the end of the convict trade. Even the very name of the island had gone – Van Diemen's Land no more, it was now Tasmania, as if the country could forget its past as easily as a name change.

Gold fever was sweeping through Australia, even onto Sally's small, distant island, and the streets were thronged with men from every land, their once empty pockets filled with nuggets and with gold dust and quartz, their still empty heads filled with dreams of wealthy old age. The men leaped off the ships and rested a while before they travelled on to Fingal, to The Nook or Nine Mile Springs.

The Australasia was as clean and neat a rooming house as any in the town, and Patsy was so good at figuring, at stretching, at making much from little, at mending and darning, that soon they would have the year's mortgage payment made, and still two months to go till Christmas.

And perhaps there might be another pair of hands to help them soon.

Sally turned from the window, sat down at her bureau and opened the writing table. Her brow furrowed as she focused every energy on the task at hand. She had painstakingly learned to write upon paper, tissue thin and crinkling beneath her nib. Now she sent a letter every six months to the *Leinster Express* and to the *Times* of Dublin too. She had written fifteen times already.

'You know that Davey is dead, don't you?' Patsy had returned to tempt Sally out of the room, and had found her at her forlorn task, sweating and struggling and blotting her letter for the mail boat.

'I don't. I don't know for sure that he is dead.'

Don't cry, Peggy. Wait for me Davey, I'll find you.

Sally signed her name on the end of the page, big careful loops of letters, and tucked it into an envelope.

'Twice a year.' She murmured aloud the answer to Patsy's question, which hung unspoken upon the air. 'Twice every year for the rest of my life I'll write to Ireland, until he comes, or word of his death comes from a person you could trust. My father swore to me that the only way out of the workhouse was in a box, and yet Patsy O'Hanlon is here, as strong as a horse. Why not Davey? This very next mail ship from Dublin might be the one that brings word.'

'Lightning won't strike the same tree twice.'

'Let me write my letters in peace, Patsy, it's little enough to ask.'

Outside the open window the plaintive cries of the port's seabirds rose to a crescendo as a fishing skiff drew into the harbour and tied up by the smallest pier. A shrieking, milling flock tucked their wings against their small bodies and dashed themselves into the waves to catch the discarded guts and heads as the sailors sorted their catch before unloading. It brought to mind the wailing of the crowd on the quay in Kingstown as families and friends called out to the convicts being rowed out to board the *Australasia*.

★ ★ ★

Sally's thoughts strayed back, not years, but a mere twenty weeks in time. There had, by all accounts, been but a little weeping, and no wailing, on the quayside in Dublin as men, women and children had stepped aboard the cutter that was to carry them to Tasmania; free men and women, setting off for adventure and the promise of wealth. The streets of Hobart were paved with gold, and they would prise up some of that gold or die trying. And among that excited, waving crowd had stood a lone young woman, eighteen years old, small but strong, self-contained but not cowed, wearing a new blue woollen coat and a fine-spun shawl over her rich golden curls. The coat and shawl, described in perfect detail in a letter, had been purchased with money eked out from the annual budget of the Australasia boarding house and sent back across the sea and across the years.

'There she is,' cried Sally, clutching Patsy's arm as, their journey over, those same passengers had disembarked in the port of Hobart. 'There she is, blue coat, five gilt buttons and a white shawl with a Claddagh brooch.' Sally's knees had buckled beneath her, she would have fallen had Patsy not reached out to steady her. 'Will she hate me, Patsy? Will she hate me?'

Patsy gave her a gentle shake. 'Whether she does or does not, you have no control over that. You made a promise. You kept the promise. What she feels about you is her own business.'

Sally whimpered. 'It might not even be her, perhaps she's just a stranger who wanted a free passage to the New World. I always knew it was a big risk to take.'

'Be brave, Sally. I'll be here at your side.' Patsy smiled an encouraging smile and, taking Sally's hand in her own, drew her forward – two fish swimming the wrong way through the tide of disembarking passengers.

The young woman had locked eyes with Sally, when she was still many paces distant. She neither smiled nor frowned, but stood still, her small case clutched in one hand, and waited for the two older women to approach.

Sally opened her arms, mute, offering a welcome, with no confidence in her reception. Tears sprang from her eyes, tears of gladness, joy and fear.

The woman spoke in tones of wonder. 'I remember you now. I remember your face and your voice. *Don't cry. Don't cry, Peggy, wait for me, I'll find you.*'

Sally pitched forward and cradled Peggy in her arms, weeping. The younger woman stood still, tolerating, but not returning her embrace.

'I'm so sorry, Peggy, and I'm so happy. I'm so sorry.'

The woman drew back slightly and gently disentangled herself from Sally's arms.

'Thank you for sending me the cost of the passage.' Her voice was formal and calm.

Tears poured unchecked down Sally's cheeks.

'Can you forgive me?'

'I don't know. I don't even know where to start. I'm not sure what I need to forgive, yet. I don't remember much except I had a brother once, and a mother.'

Silently Patsy reached out and took the travelling case from Peggy's hand. 'Won't you come with us,' she asked, 'and see the room we have set aside for you? You can stay as long as you want.'

'For ever,' Sally burst out. 'You will stay with us for ever.'

'For as long as you wish, Peggy,' said Patsy, with a warning glance at Sally.

'Even if that should be just one night to sleep away the tiredness of the journey.'

'I'm free to come and go as I please?'

'Of course.'

'And I'm not a servant?'

Sally rocked back on her heels as though struck.

'Can I have a key?'

'A key?'

'When you've spent as much of your life behind locked doors as I have, all you want is a key to your own door.'

Sally could not muster a word between her sobs, but Patsy replied for them both. 'You will have a key to your own room, so that you can keep the world out, and you will have a key to the front door, so that the world can never again keep you in.'

'Then I will come,' Peggy said. 'I will come for one week.'

'That will be the happiest week of our lives,' said Patsy, tucking her free hand through Sally's arm, while Sally reached out and clutched the sleeve of Peggy's coat in a grip of shocking intensity. The young woman looked at the encircling fingers, as tight as any manacle, but did not protest or try to shrug them off.

Barely a word was spoken between the trio until they turned into the laneway and Patsy pointed out the sign of the boarding house, a brightly painted three-master in full sail, breasting an azure ocean. 'This is the Australasia,' Patsy said, 'and your new home, should you choose to share it with us.'

Peggy stopped in her tracks. 'I will have a key.'

'Yes.'

'There is something else.'

'Anything,' cried Sally, 'if it is in my power. You can have anything.' Patsy tightened her grip on Sally's arm in warning and she fell silent again.

'It is a small thing, but important.' The silence drew out between them for a long fraction more than was comfortable. 'I was … ' she stopped, drew a shallow, shuddering breath and began again. 'I was Peggy. And they told me in the workhouse that I was Peggy MacBride. Perhaps I was. I don't know for sure. But I will never hear that name again. I will not answer to it, I will not recognise it. I will never wear a uniform and I will never answer to the name Peggy again. My name is Margaret.'

'And a surname?' Patsy asked.

'I don't care.'

'Gordon.' The word flew out of Sally's mouth like the crack of a pistol. 'Would you care to be Margaret Gordon?'

The young woman shrugged and they passed in silence down to the gate and then up the steps of the Australasia, where Margaret Gordon lay down in silence in her locked room and fell into an unquiet and terrified sleep.

★ ★ ★

From the hallway below came the joyful sound of young voices raised in laughter. One of these days, Sally believed, Margaret was going to open her bedroom door and look to see the source of the other girls' fun. The first week had stretched into eight, and although she never laughed and rarely smiled, and spent most of her days behind the locked door of her chamber, Margaret showed no sign of leaving.

Sally smiled and turned from the window. *I know Davey is dead. I know he is. And yet, I knew for ten years that Peggy was dead, but Margaret came to me on the spring tide.* She set her letter down on the bureau and turned to the door.

Patsy was right, Sally could not speed the arrival of the mailboat by watching and screwing up her eyes into the white-hot glare of the sea foam. She would go down and help the serving girls – scrub the floors clean and remember once again her days scrubbing with Patsy, on their knees amid the vomit and the blood.

Patsy and Sally had good help in the rooming house, they treated the girls as well as could be managed, and the serving girls were never, ever hungry.

And if the girls noticed that Sally and Patsy shared one bedchamber, that would not have surprised them, coming as they did from their tiny two-roomed cabins. And if they noticed that the chamber had only one bed, deep and soft, that didn't seem to bother them.

If there was a word for women like them, like Patsy and her, women who live as they live, and do as they do, Sally had never heard it.

If there was a word for women like them, that word was *happy*.

Author's note

This book is a work of fiction. For narrative purposes, some facts have been tweaked and rearranged chronologically.

Anne Daly, Eliza Guilfoyle, Ellen Doyle and Elizabeth Curry all travelled to Van Diemen's Land on board the *Australasia* in 1849, together with my fictional characters Sally Mahon, Patsy O'Hanlon and Nellie Gordon. The celebrated case of Catherine Colligan, however, occurred earlier, and she was transported on board the *Waverley* in 1847.

Huge tented temporary encampments of soldiery on the Curragh Plains were frequent events, but the destitute women who followed the soldiers may not have gained their unofficial nickname of the Curragh Wrens until after the establishment in 1855 of a permanent barracks on the site of the present Curragh Army Camp, which provided advanced training for the Crimean War.

Lord Cardigan is known to have occasionally stabled his hussars in Newbridge in the years leading up to the Crimean War, but it is unknown if he himself ever visited Newbridge Barracks.

The Reverend Henry Joly and his family did reside in Hollywood House in King's County, and left behind a wealth of information about life in 'the Big House' during the famine years, from which most of the characters, historical and fictional, who inhabit the King's County chapters have been drawn. Surnames in Ireland at that time were heavily concentrated in distinct regions; where widely different characters share a surname, that is a fact of history rather than a failure of imagination.

Some early readers have asked why my characters do not have 'Irish' names, and they have suggested names such as Siobhán, Sorcha, Beibhín and Niamh. While these are very beautiful names, they are not appropriate to the period of the novel. These ancient names did not come back into common usage until the Celtic revival of the late nineteenth and early twentieth centuries. The names of my characters are mainly drawn from the surgeon's report drawn up by Mr Alex Kilroy on board the *Australasia*.

The description of cooking over long fires of charcoal on deck has been adapted from *Robert Whyte's 1847 Famine Ship Diary. The Journey of an Irish*

Coffin Ship. Details of the cooking arrangements on board the *Australasia* are unknown to me.

The story of the mother who had 'raised nine childer and never a drop of water has touched one of them' is noted in John O'Connor's *The Workhouses of Ireland. The fate of Ireland's poor.*

The Flight of the Wren is a work of fiction, not a biography or a scholarly treatise. Any errors or misjudgements are mine alone. Please get in touch at orlamcalindenauthor@gmail.com if you wish to comment or suggest a correction.

Many of the people, places and events reimagined in the novel can be explored further in the books listed in the bibliography.

Thanks

Thanks are due to so many people who supported the long gestation of *The Flight of the Wren*.

Vanessa Fox O'Loughlin, whose selection of the first draft of the novel in 2015 for the *writing.ie Date with an Agent* at the International Literature Festival Dublin gave me the confidence to pursue the concept and endless help and advice since then.

Martina Devlin, who selected the novel for the Greenbean Novel Fair at the Irish Writers Centre in 2016 and has championed it since.

Liz Nugent, Niamh Boyce and Nicola Barr for practical help and advice.

Averill Buchanan for editorial services.

Fiona Biggs for editing on behalf of my wonderful publishers, Red Stag Mentor.

Kildare County Council Arts Service for awarding me the Cecil Day Lewis emerging writer award to support the research which became *The Flight of the Wren*.

Margaret Scott and Margaret Rowe who listened to my endless doubts and insecurities.

My family, for all their support, and especially my husband, without whose forbearance and patience this novel would have been abandoned.

Alex Reece Abbott, my staunchest literary supporter, for her endless generosity, advice and guidance.

And, finally, Danny McCarthy, founder and director of Mentor Press, who encountered my writing by chance, sought me out, and offered to bring this novel to the world, before he had read even a synopsis. Ar dheis Dé go raibh a anam dílis.

Bibliography

A small sample of books which may interest readers of *The Flight of the Wren* are listed below.

Conlon-McKenna, Marita, *Under the Hawthorn Tree*. Dublin: O'Brien Press, 1990

Conlon, Evelyn, *Not the Same Sky*. Adelaide: Wakefield Press, 2013

Egan, Ann, *The Wren Women*. Ballyclare: The Black Mountain Press, 2003

Fleming, Catherine, *The transportation of women from Kildare to Van Diemen's Land in 1849* (Maynooth Studies in Local History). Dublin: Four Courts Press, 2012

Kraus, Erin, *Wise Woman of Kildare: Moll Anthony and Popular Tradition in the east of Ireland* (Maynooth Studies in Local History), Dublin: Four Courts Press, 2011

Malone, Martin, *The Only Glow of the Day*. Dublin: New Island Books, 2011

McCormac, John, *A Story of Ireland*. Dublin: Mentor, 2002

O'Connor, John, *The Workhouses of Ireland. The fate of Ireland's poor*. Cork: Mercier Press, 1994

O'Flaherty, Liam, *Famine*. Dublin: Merlin Publishing, 1984

Reilly, Ciaran, *John Plunket Joly and the Great Famine in King's County* (Maynooth Studies in Local History). Dublin: Four Courts Press, 2012

Robert Whyte's 1847 Famine Ship Diary – The Journey of an Irish Coffin Ship. Cork: Mercier Press, 1994

An Interview With the Author

Q: Orla, congratulations on the publication of *The Flight of the Wren*.

Orla: Thanks, I'm delighted.

Q: How does it feel to have the 'difficult second book' published?

Orla: I don't really think of *The Flight of the Wren* as 'the difficult second book'. I was lucky in that it was written long before I managed to find a publisher for *The Accidental Wife*. Both were created simultaneously, with no great expectations, just a vague hope that one day they would see the light of day. Unlike many other authors, I didn't have to write my second book with the weight of the success — or otherwise — of the first book on my shoulders. I didn't feel I had to stick to the same genre, or write in the same dialect, because that's what my readers would expect. I didn't have any readers! I had total freedom. *The Flight of the Wren* might easily have been published before *The Accidental Wife,* that's just the way things worked out.

Q: You say 'success or otherwise'. But you have had success with *The Accidental Wife*?

Orla: Yes, in many ways *The Accidental Wife* was a success, far beyond my expectations. It didn't have an enormous print-run or vast, best-selling sales figures. But it has a readership vastly in excess of anything I could have imagined, almost entirely down to the wonderful people at Libraries NI. After Libraries NI chose the book as the inaugural text for the mass public reading initiative, The Armagh Big Read, in 2017, the profile of the book shot up. It was borrowed almost 1,000 times in its first year, which is huge for a debut collection of short stories by an unknown author. Then they recommended it to BBC Radio Ulster's *Nolan Show Book Club,* which brought it to a whole other audience. I'm so grateful to the libraries. I donated five copies to my childhood library in Portadown, County Armagh (where I used to do my homework and study for my exams), and someone read it and loved it. The rest is history.

Q: *The Accidental Wife* **was an award-winner, before Libraries NI ever heard of it, and your new book has won awards also. How do these things come about?**

Orla: *The Flight of the Wren* won the Cecil Day Lewis award from Kildare County Arts Service in 2016. The novel was finished, but I felt it was lacking in adequate detail and was incompletely researched. The CD Lewis award allowed me to buy time to research properly, and also to have a preliminary structural edit carried out by Averill Buchanan, a member of the Society of Editors and Proofreaders. Kildare is an absolute hotbed of great writing, and for me to win that award, out of all the applicants, gave me the confidence that *The Flight of the Wren* was a book worth writing.

Q: **Would you like to tell me something of the process of writing** *The Flight of the Wren?*

Orla: It's strange. I was writing Northern Irish rural stories. Some contemporary, but none set any further back than the Second World War. I was writing in a northern dialect, and nothing was further from my mind than historical fiction set on the Curragh of Kildare. But, one day, I was browsing in Hodges Figgis bookshop in Dublin, one of my favourite places in the world. I idly picked up a tiny book of non-fiction about the penal transportation of women from County Kildare to Van Diemen's Land, and by the time I reached the till, the entire story of *The Flight of the Wren* had fallen into place.

Q: **Instantly, right there in the shop?**

Orla: Yes. Before I started writing fiction, I used to read interviews with writers occasionally, and some would say, 'I spend a year working out my plot, and characters and landscapes before I put a single word down on paper.' And I would nod and think, *that sounds credible.* And others would say 'The story came to me in a dream ... or on a walk ... or in the bath ... fully formed characters, and plot, and all,' and I would laugh and think, *does she think we're stupid?* But that is exactly what happened to me. By the time I had walked back to the car park from the bookshop, I knew almost every vital aspect of my story. It took only fifty days to write the first draft of the book. That was four years ago. The mills of God grind slowly, but they grind exceeding small – in that four years I have taken the book up and abandoned it at least five times, but each time it called me back and the voices of my characters got stronger and clearer each time I rewrote it.

Q: And do you think that historical fiction is your future?

Orla: I don't know if it's my future, but I think reading and studying and thinking about history is vital for the future. Sally and Patsy and the other women in the book are refugees, asylum seekers. By the standards of their time they were also criminals and pariahs. When the book was chosen as one of the twelve winners of the 2016 Greenbean Novel Fair at the Irish Writers Centre, we were in the midst of the absolute worst of the Syrian refugee crisis. I heard a specialist aid worker on the radio saying, 'Don't be fooled into thinking refugees are all poor and destitute people whose current conditions aren't much worse than they were at home – the people who are now killing and eating rats in refugee camps in Lebanon were sipping lattes in Starbucks in Damascus three years ago.' I've never forgotten those words. Our lives hang on such threads over which we exert only the most illusory control. My characters Patsy and Sally and tens of thousands of other Irish people were reduced to eating grass and weeds to keep body and soul together. Of all people, the Irish should understand the drive to escape, to seek a better life elsewhere, when the home country chews you up and spits you out.

Q: And do we?

Orla: I honestly think in the future, we are going to look back at our treatment of asylum seekers and the system of direct provision and it's going to be my generation's Magdalene Laundries. The government will be making public apologies in a few decades' time about direct provision, and we won't be able to say we didn't know.

Q: Okay, I wasn't expecting to go down this route! Can you tell me what is next for you in terms of your writing life?

Orla: I'm very, very lucky because I actually do know what comes next. My publishers, Red Stag/Mentor Books sent readers out into the libraries – see, the libraries again – looking for new Irish writers. When I first met the editorial team at Mentor, they had a battered library copy of *The Accidental Wife* on the table. They asked had I anything else completed and I said yes, I had two books. They offered to take both books, there and then, sight unseen, on the strength of *The Accidental Wife*. That's the kind of vote of confidence no writer could decline. The next book is a companion volume of short stories, following on the lives and intrigues of some of the characters from *The Accidental Wife*, and several new ones. The new collection is called *Full of Grace*, and (if anyone actually reads this far) the title story, 'Full of Grace' is included in the back of *The Flight of the Wren* as a sneak preview.

Q: When will *Full of Grace* be published?

Orla: It is due for publication in January 2019, which, in publishing terms, is the equivalent of tomorrow.

Q: Do you think there'll be a prizewinning story in there, like 'The Visit' from *The Accidental Wife?*

Orla: Who knows? Who can tell? 'The Visit' won the Bord Gáis Energy Irish Book Award (BGEIBA) for Irish Short Story of the Year in 2016, and I was so stunned when my name was called out at the gala awards dinner, that I didn't even have my shoes on! People were clapping and congratulating me and I had my face under the table trying to stuff my feet back into too-tight shoes. I've included 'The Visit' in the new collection as well, to help orient readers who haven't read *The Accidental Wife*. It's a great story to pivot the arc of the book upon. But most of the stories in *Full of Grace* are brand new and unpublished. If a prizewinner comes out of the collection, I'll be thrilled, but the book itself is the prize, as far as I'm concerned.

Q: And then you'll have a well-deserved break?

Orla: Not at all! Then I'll be finishing my fourth book, which is another historical fiction, set in Tipperary at the turn of the twentieth century. I like to ring the changes. I started that book after I won a week's residency at Greywood Arts in Killeagh, County Cork. I sat down in their writing room, looking out over a swinging wooden gate that led to a babbling river. A heron would flit in and out of my eyeline. I was supposed to be editing *The Flight of the Wren,* but I kept looking at the gate, which seemed to open and close of its own volition, every time I took my eyes off it. By the end of the week I had the opening ten thousand words of a novel I had never even contemplated writing before. Magic.

Readers can keep up to date with Orla's progress at www.orlamcalinden.com or on Facebook.

Full of Grace

The following is an exclusive free sample from *Full of Grace* by Orla McAlinden, coming in January 2019 from Red Stag/Mentor Books. *Full of Grace* is the companion volume to the award-winning *The Accidental Wife* by the same author. Follow www.orlamcalinden.com to keep up to date with Full of Grace.

Chapter 1

'Say the Hail Mary.'

'What?'

'Say the Hail Mary, wee lad. We're all ears.'

Shit. How am I going to get out of this one?

There are three of them and only one of you.

The boys have stepped out of the sweet-scented cow-parsley verge and you've had to pull hard on the brakes, wrenching the front wheel around in a dusty arc to avoid crashing into them. They're all wearing shiny new black boots. No one you know can afford boots like that.

Shit.

They are looking for trouble. They haven't even had the wit to cover their faces. You can see them clearly but you've never clapped eyes on them before. You should have pedalled faster and made them decide whether baiting you was worth the pain of getting run over.

A stick hangs casually from each boy's right hand and you look to the sticks for help. They might give you a clue. Hurls would tell you one thing, and you could give them the answer they want and be home and safe in ten minutes. Boys holding hockey sticks or cricket bats would mean something different, more dangerous; still, there's a chance you could get away unbruised. But these boyos are hefting two blackthorns and an ashplant. They haven't nailed their colours to the mast. They're not just looking for trouble, they're looking for sport as well. They're going to make you guess what answer they want.

'Say the Hail Mary, wee lad. We're awful religious, and we just love to hear a wee fella saying his prayers.'

You think hard and fast. You could offer to say the Pater Noster instead. You know it in English, and don't both Prods and Catholics say the Our Father?

But wait. There's something odd about the Proddy Our Father, something different about it. They say 'which art in heaven', not 'who art in heaven', don't they? This makes them godless heathens, according to Father Malachy. It's a strange thing to fight to the death over, but they'll notice if you say the wrong one. The Our Father isn't going to help.

Then you remember your da, ranting and raving last week in the milking parlour. 'Thon hoors over at McGeady's are after selling the six-acre paddock.'

'Our six-acre paddock?' your older brother Alo had asked.

'Well, obviously it's not ours if they're after selling it, ya gom.'

'But we graze it. We always graze it.'

'Well, we'll not be grazing it any more for it's sold. I seen them coming out of McGeady's and spitting on their hands to seal the deal. Why McGeady couldn't have come to me first, or had the bloody thing to auction like an honest man, I'll never know.'

Your da had taken a deep breath and gobbed out a thick wedge of tobacco-phlegm near the toe of your welly.

'Maybe the new owners will let us graze it,' you'd chipped in.

'Not a chance, not a chance in hell. He's as Orange as a Jaffa.'

You've never seen a real orange, or a banana either, even though the war has been over this seven years past. But it wasn't the time to draw attention to irrelevancies.

'How do you know he's a Prod, Daddy? What's his name?'

'I don't need to know a man's name to know his type.' Your father's huge white eyebrows nearly joined in the middle with the scowl. 'I'm living in Tyrone all my life – long enough to know what a man is by looking at his face.'

You study the faces of the three boys in the lane. They are all older than you and have more than a passing resemblance to each other. There's a bigger gap between oldest and youngest than you'd normally find in a group of friends out to start a row. All in new boots. All in waistcoats. They are brothers, surely.

These must be the sons of the new owner of the six-acre paddock. And that means they are Protestants.

Relief floods through you and you give your body a sudden shake as you sense how close your bladder has come to emptying itself. Now you know the answer to their unspoken question.

'I'll not say the Hail Mary.' You smile at the boys and try to look calm, though your heart's fit to burst with your own cleverness. 'What would I be doing, spouting that oul' papish nonsense? Get out of the road now, lads, and I'll be away on home.'

You grip the handlebars and lift your right leg to swing it over the crossbar and away when the middle boy's fist hits you a right puck in the gob. It hurts like hell, but the shock of crashing onto the paved road with the old Triumph keeling over on top of you is worse.

'Bloody Prod,' screams the oldest boy, all bared teeth and flaring nostrils like a nappy pony. 'You dirty Orange bastard. *Oul' papish nonsense?* You'll say a Hail Mary before you leave this place or you'll go home in a box.'

'What?'

'What? I'll tell you what. I'm Joseph Mary Devlin. This here's Francis Xavier Devlin, and babyface over there is Peter. Don't forget us, boy, and do yer best to stay clear of us, for we're here to stay and we're getting our retaliation in first, if you know what I mean.'

Francis Xavier steps forward and says, slow and calm, 'I'll help you. Just listen carefully, make no mistakes and we'll all be on our way. No need for any aggro.' He takes a deep breath and raises his right arm. You flinch, but he laughs and touches his fingers to his forehead. 'In the name of the Father, and of the Son and of the Holy Spirit.'

Joseph Mary gives you a dunt with his shiny new boot. 'Come on, even Prods know how to bless themselves, don't they?'

You haven't lived as long as your father. You didn't see what he said he could see in a man's face. You believed in the lies of the shiny new boots and the fancy waistcoats. See where that's got you! What will you do now? Continue the pretence, say the prayer, cycle home and prepare to explain away your fat lip? But what if Peter Devlin turns up at the schoolhouse on Monday morning with his books under his arm? Then he'll know you were lying, denying the faith. Then what? You make a decision.

'Lads, sure I was only messing with you. I was only acting the oul' cod.'

You pull yourself up off the road and lean the bike into the lee of a whitethorn bush in full flower, drinking in the sweetness and purity of the white blossoms before you turn back to the boys. You rummage in your pocket and pull out your everyday rosary, the brown beads rubbed almost black.

'Sure I was only having the crack, lads.' You hold out your right hand towards Joseph Mary and adopt a stiff and formal manner. 'It's a pleasure to meet you. I'm Anthony O'Donovan, and I've been saying the Hail Mary since before I had teeth. English, Irish or Latin – you choose. Sure I'm a fucken altar boy in Drumaleish church. *Ora pro nobis* and all that.'

'You fucken weasel.'

'Seriously, I was just letting on I was a Prod. It was a joke.'

'Me arse it was a joke. You're a disgrace to the nation, denying your faith. Was it for this that Connolly and Pearse were taken out and shot?'

'Well, you know as well as I do that James Connolly didn't give a tinker's curse about the Catholic Church and –'

All three Devlins jump on you. Joseph Mary and Francis Xavier have decent right hooks on them; Peter is holding you by the legs. You all come crashing down to the road in a hail of fists and boots and hair and nails.

How many mistakes can one fucken eejit make in a day? What the fuck was I doing, trying to give these three oafs a history lesson? His name's Joseph Mary, for God's sake.

'Don't be scrabbing like a wee girl,' Francis Xavier shouts as you rake your nails down his face. 'Jesus, can't you fight like a man?'

'Against three of you yella hallions?' you manage to say between the gasps and the whoops and the punches. One boy is a small enough target for six flying fists. 'You'd know plenty about fighting like men!'

Now Joseph Mary has your left arm up tight behind your back and you can feel your own close-cropped hair bristling against the knuckles of your left hand. You swear the sinews are going to give.

'Stop it. For Christ's sake stop it. You've had your fun.' And then, you say it. The words spill out of your mouth – your brain isn't involved – the words you will spend the rest of your life in atonement for. The words whose undeniable truth you will deny for the rest of your life.

'This is a load of shit. You don't even believe it yourself, no more than I do. There's no Catholic and no Protestant, on earth or in heaven, because every eejit knows there's no such thing as God. Say yer prayers, kneel down for yer ma, fill the holy water font at the front door for fear the priest will find it dry if he visits. But sure youse know as well as I do that it's all a load of shit.'

Peter lets go of your legs and jumps to his feet; Francis Xavier drops his fists and looks at you like you're a bad smell. Joseph Mary lets go of your arm, then hawks up and spits straight in your face.

You try to wipe the slabber away with your left hand, but your shoulder screams with pain and you have to use your right hand, which leaves you totally defenceless. No need to worry, for the Devlin brothers never strike you again as long as they live.

At last Peter speaks.

'We're sorry, all right? We're sorry. We just wanted to be sure the word got around that we're hard fellas and then people would leave us alone.'

Francis Xavier nods. 'It's true. We never meant any real harm. Why didn't you just say the bloody Hail Mary and that would have been the end of it?'

'Come on,' says Joseph Mary, dropping to his knees in the dust of the road and waving to his brothers to do the same. 'Come on, Anthony. We're sorry. We never should have pushed you so hard. We'll all say it together.'

'It's true – it's all true,' you say. You turn to the bike and heave it out of the hedge with your good hand. 'It's true and you know it. It's 1952, for God's sake. We're not peasants in the Dark Ages. We have the wireless and the Pathé News.'

They stare at you, blank as fresh slates.

'Do youse really think there's a god that lets the Germans shovel millions of people into ovens? Do youse think our Blessed Mother in heaven looks down at Russian soldiers chasing wee holy nuns with fixed bayonets and doesn't get her magic, all-powerful son to blast them to kingdom come?'

You straddle the bike and balance on one shaking leg, your other foot on a pedal. 'Because the kingdom's not coming. That's why.'

'Stop it, Anthony. Come on, we said we're sorry. There's no call for this. We're sorry we acted the maggot. We'll say it with you. Hail Mary ... '

'Say the Hail Mary,' echoes Peter.

'Come on. Say it. Say a fucken Hail Mary. We're really sorry. We only wanted to give someone local a few slaps to set the tone, not steal the immortal soul out of your body.'

As you wobble away from them you hear their plaintive cries. 'We'll say it for you. Hail Mary, full of grace, the Lord is with thee ... '

★ ★ ★

'Hail Mary ... Say the Hail Mary.'

'Just the one is it? Say *one* Hail Mary?'

'Hmm?'

'Just the one Hail Mary?'

'What?'

You sit up with a start and come back from miles away and decades ago.

'Just the one Hail Mary is it, Father O'Donovan? I mean, I done my Act of Contrition all right, but I never told you my sins.'

'Oh, sorry.'

You pull at your collar and try to get the top open, but wrestling with a clerical collar in the dark is no easy matter. Thank God — figure of speech — you're in the traditional box with a decent mesh between you and the penitent, not one of those hateful bright 'reconciliation rooms'.

'What age are you, my child?' you ask.

'Will we start again then, Father?'

'Yes, go on.'

'Forgive me, Father, for I have sinned — '

'I doubt that.'

'What?'

'What age did you say you were?'

'I'm nine and a half, Father.'

'You haven't sinned, my child. You're just a little boy who sometimes acts the eejit and puts his poor mother astray in the head. I'd say that's about right, isn't it?'

'Well, I told you the same ones last time and you never said I hadn't sinned.'

'Let me guess – said a bad word, was disrespectful to your mother, didn't clean your room?'

'Yes.'

'Mrs Rafferty always chooses the same list of sins, and by the time her pupils are old enough to actually commit any real ones I'm the last person they'd come to for help.' You sigh. 'Do you understand?'

'No, Father O'Donovan.'

'All right. Let's get on with it. Your sins are forgiven. Go and sin no more.'

'And the Hail Mary?'

'What?'

'Just the one is it, like?'

'Yes. No – wait.'

The child pauses, mid crouch, half risen, hand already on the door. God knows – turn of phrase – what the hell he thinks is going on.

'Say one Hail Mary for your penance.' You hear the child sigh and then you add, 'And say one for me.'

Glossary

Amadán – a stupid or foolish person (male)

Banshee – a wailing spirit who is said to bring tidings of an impending death

Bodhrán – a hand-held drum fashioned by stretching a skin over a round frame

Boke – to vomit

Boreen – a small road, often unmade

Carn – a despicable, worthless person

Cow clap – cow dung

Creepie stool – a low, three-legged stool used for milking or cooking over an open fire

Delph – dishes, china (a reference to the Dutch city of Delft, from where much china originated)

Drouth – drought, thirst

Farl – a quarter of a round soda bread

Fluthered – drunk

Gom – a stupid person

Hallion – a useless, loutish person

Houl' – (hold) your whisht - be quiet/hold your tongue

Iasc – the word for fish in the Irish language. In Ireland the cry of a seagull is tradionally represented by 'isac, iasc'.

Inglenook – a seating area built within a large fireplace

Looderamawn – a dim-witted person

Loy (lái) – a type of Irish spade with a narrow blade and single footrest, used in the cultivation of potatoes

Óinseach – a stupid or foolish person (female)

Oxter – armpit

Piseog – superstition

Pooka – a fairy

Rí-rá – chaos

Samhain – A Celtic festival that marks the end of the harvest and the beginning of winter, traditionally celebrated on the night of 31 October/1 November.

Seanachie – a storyteller

Sheugh – a ditch, usually a boundary marking

Sleán – a type of Irish spade with a right-angled blade, used for cutting turf

Súgán rope – a soft, non-abrasive rope made from twisted straw, commonly
used to make chair seats